FOUR COLOR BLEED

PITHOS

FOUR COLOR BLEED

RYAN MCSWAIN

FOUR COLOR BLEED. Copyright © 2017 Ryan McSwain

First edition.
All rights reserved.

Published by Pithos Publishing

7306 SW 34th #1 #101
Amarillo, Texas 79121
www.pithospublishing.com

Cover design by Rory Harnden, rrry.me
Cover art and Mr. Stiff illustration by Adam Prosser, www.phantasmictales.com

Golden Age Danny Drastic, Jack Spratt, and group illustration by Ben Zmith, twitter.com/delldracula
Ironworks illustration by Chris "Chance!" Brown, cargocollective.com/chance_second
Meta Man illustration by Kevin Kelly, www.kevinartkelly.com
Rika Mizuno illustration by Rian Gonzales, rianbowart.tumblr.com
Titania illustration by Morgan Perry (aka Geauxta), twitter.com/geauxta
Songweaver illustration by Weshoyot Alvitre, www.instagram.com/weshoyot
Danny Drastic illustration by Ben Cohen, www.bencohen.co

Author photo by Dustin Taylor

Edited by Jonathan Baker

Book layout by Phillip Gessert, http://www.gessertbooks.com

ISBN: 0-9904607-4-6
ISBN-13: 978-0-9904607-4-9

For Conley and Carson,
my favorite superheroes

THE MODERN AGE

1

ALPH ROGERS WALKED INTO A LAVISH ROOM FILLED WITH HEROES AND VILLAINS.

The party was in full swing. Dozens of people yelled at one another over the music. Everyone was drinking, and they had a good head start on him. The mix of T-shirts and comic book costumes looked infinitely more surreal in the huge house than in the convention hall. In the living room, a band thrilled a small but enthusiastic crowd. Two men played synthesizers and samplers as a young woman dressed as the 1980s headband-wearing Supergirl sang lead, her red skirt swaying as she danced.

I've fallen into a Justice League frat party, Ralph thought as he passed the line for keg stands. He found a solemn man in a tuxedo tending the bar. "Got any scotch?" Ralph asked. The man nodded. After looking Ralph over, he chose a glass from the shelf and poured in several inches of rich brown liquid. He handed it to Ralph, who found his drink served in a Pepsi glass from 1977. On it, a red and yellow Captain Marvel stood with his hands on his hips, a yellow moon behind him. Beneath the hero was written his catchphrase: "Shazam!"

"Pretty classy," he said, tipping his glass to the bartender. "I'm Ralph Rogers." They shook hands.

"Bartlett, sir. Thank you."

"You don't happen to know Ben Walker, do you?"

"I do, sir. Perhaps you might find him by the pool."

Two men dressed as Wolverine arm-wrestled by the back door, their plastic claws flapping back and forth in the air. Passing them, Ralph walked outside to find what looked like a cross between an X-Men Summer Special and a 1970s swingers movie. Men and women in their underwear filled the pool, their clothes and costumes folded on beach chairs or hanging over the fence. Two topless women, sitting on the shoulders of men standing in the pool, tried to wrestle each other into the water. A man in a Swamp Thing costume carried a laughing, white-haired woman in a bikini over his shoulder. She slapped at his back, leaving handprints in the green makeup. A man in a Spider-Man leotard cannonballed into the water, and Ralph jumped back to avoid the splash. Three Asian women in schoolgirl uniforms giggled at him.

"Rogers!" yelled a man behind him. "You hack fraud!"

Uh-oh, thought Ralph, looking for an escape route. A meaty hand fell on his shoulder and spun him around. Ralph stared up at a man with cartoonish muscles. He wasn't wearing a costume, but Ralph believed the man could pull off a convincing Gorilla Grodd. "You must be Eugene," Ralph said. His pulse thumped in his ears.

"You ruined my life, you piece of shit!" Eugene glared down at him. "Do you have any idea how many copies of *Meta Boy* I bought for my store? Your swindle put me out of business."

Ralph fought the urge to stand on his tiptoes. "Listen, man, I'm sorry to hear about your store. Really. But it was the nineties, comic shops went out of business everywhere. It wasn't my fault."

"Maybe not, but you didn't help, either. So you're going in the pool." He leaned in closely and whispered, "If you're lucky, maybe I won't drown you."

Eugene lifted Ralph off the ground as everyone cheered. The image of Bane breaking the Batman flashed across Ralph's mind. He squirmed and kicked his feet, but it was no use. He calculated the cost of replacing his cell phone as he tried to keep his glass of scotch level.

His thoughts turned to the glorious day that had brought him to this point.

2

ALPH ROGERS, YOU SUCK!" the woman in the Star Trek uniform yelled. Ralph waved to her and went back to his sketchbook.

"I don't know how you put up with that, Rogers," said the artist at the next table. Ralph had no idea who the other artist was, only that he drew popular comic book characters in the nude for an even hundred dollars.

"You get used to it," Ralph shrugged. He'd heard attendance had dropped at these fan events, but there was a decent turnout at the eleventh annual Oklahoma City Comic and Anime Convention. It was nothing like the circus the San Diego con had turned into, but there were plenty of cosplayers, dealer tables, and special guests. Ralph sat at a white plastic table surrounded by the latter, but he did not consider himself all that special. His name was written on a sign at the front of his perch, and few people gave him a second look.

He half-hoped everyone would forget about him, but Frank Reese, his agent, insisted Ralph attend conventions for exposure. Commissions earned Ralph just enough money to justify the trips on paper.

Looking down at his current drawing, Ralph realized he was nearly finished. Doing commissioned art was one thing he enjoyed about comic book conventions. It gave him a chance to prove his talent to a rare fan, and the money was a nice bonus.

This time around, his patron was a shy young woman who wanted Ralph to illustrate a team-up of the Black Canary and Ralph's character, Meta Boy. He had never drawn the Black Canary before, but he was happy with how her fishnets turned out in the pencil sketch. She gave Meta a flirty look as she stood perched beside him on the rooftop.

Despite everything, he still enjoyed drawing Meta Boy. The billowing cape, the high collar, even the buttoned cavalry shirt that looked like an old band uniform. The blue and orange costume would look garish paired with Black Canary's black leather jacket and fishnets, but it looked great in black and white. Meta Boy stared out of the page as if he were about to leap right out into the real world.

Ralph hoped the sketch would end up scanned and posted online, so he could read what strangers thought about his art in the comment section. *Don't be stupid*, he told himself, *none of the comments would be about the art*. He took a sip of water and began darkening in the details.

As he drew, two young men in their mid-twenties paused near his table. One had a scraggly goatee, and the other wore too much black. Ralph could imagine their conversation.

Who's that guy? said the one with the unfortunate facial hair. *I've never heard of him.*

You've never heard of Ralph Rogers? asked his friend. *Surely you jest.*

No, I have not heard of Ralph Rogers.

The friend looked over at Ralph, just missing the chance to catch Ralph spying on them. He probably said, *Then we must go over there and somehow make his sad little day a bit worse.*

"Hi, guys," Ralph said as they approached his table.

The one in black pointed to his friend. "My friend here's never heard of you."

Ralph smiled. "That's hardly surprising." He leaned over and shook their hands. "I'm Ralph Rogers, it's nice to meet you."

"I'm Cal," said Mr. Black. He pointed a thumb at Mr. Goatee. "That's Martin."

Martin looked Ralph over and asked, "Did you really get published when you were thirteen?"

"Fourteen," Ralph said.

Martin nodded in admiration. "Wow, that's impressive."

"See, I told you." Cal pointed at Ralph's sketch. "And this was your guy, right? What was his name?"

"His name is Meta Boy," Ralph said.

"How many issues were there?" asked Martin.

How many times had Ralph answered that question over the years? "Three were finished, two were published," he said.

Martin asked, "Why were only two published?"

Ralph frowned and looked down at his sketch.

Cal grinned. "Because it turned out he copied all the art from other comics."

Martin's jaw dropped. "No way." He turned to Ralph. "Really?"

Ralph felt the other artists around him cease what they were doing. Pencils stopped moving and conversations shushed as everyone leaned in to hear the exchange. Ralph's skin turned cold and clammy. "There's a bit more to it than that," he said, forcing himself to remain calm.

Martin's eyes went wide. "For real?" When Ralph didn't answer, he threw his head back and laughed. "You did! You traced it!"

A stifled laugh drifted from a few tables over. Ralph felt sick. "That's not—"

Before he could get the words out, Cal reached out and tipped over Ralph's cup of water. Ralph moved as quickly as he could, but the Bristol board of his commissioned sketch had soaked through. He looked up, but Cal and Martin had disappeared into the crowd.

"Bastards," said the artist from the next table. "I'll report them to security for you, if you want."

"For all the good it'll do." Ralph watched as his beautiful Black Canary and Meta Boy dissolved into sludge. A good hour's work down the drain.

Ralph stood up. "I'm going to get some air. Watch my stuff for me?"

"Sure, whatever," said the other artist.

Ralph wadded up the soggy drawing and tossed it into a trash can as he waded through the crowd of comic book fans.

3

RALPH THOUGHT ABOUT HIS FIRST BIG BREAK as he walked the rows of comic books, action figures, and bootleg DVDs. Maybe it was nostalgia for that fleeting triumph that kept him accepting invitations, or maybe he hoped to one day encourage a young artist himself. Of course, no kids brought him artwork; his reputation preceded him.

He ducked through a wall of curtains into what qualified as the green room. A few dealers and industry personalities chatted and sampled the snack table. With a cup of sugary coffee in hand, he tried to relax. No one attempted to strike up a conversation, so he sat at one of the round folding tables with a plastic plate of grapes. Beside him, a group of comic dealers were making conversation.

"And that, my friends, is why comic book continuity is like the Bible," said a chubby bald man with a beard. "One story, many authors, knit together over generations."

"That's some impressive bullshit you've created," said a gray-haired woman in a Hawaiian shirt. "Make any good buys while you were thinking that up?"

"No buried treasure here," said the bearded man. "Found a guy with some Mego accessories I bought for myself, but nothing I could make a profit on."

A black man wearing a Legion of Superheroes T-shirt sipped his coffee. "Tell me about it. I got a nice batch of Fawcett stuff, but that's about it."

"Fawcett?" asked the bearded man. "Who needs Fawcett?"

"I have a guy lined up," said the Legion fan. "He can't get enough of it. He puts up the cash for high grades."

"Better hope he lives long enough to pay you," the woman said, and they laughed.

"No, no. He's not that old. He loves Beck's Marvel Family stuff."

The bearded man said, "Me, I love me some Mary Marvel."

The others groaned.

"The new stuff, where she's older! Come on, y'all, give me a break!"

"Are you really making money on that stuff?" the woman asked.

"It's not like they're printing new copies," the Legion fan said, eliciting laughter from the group and an amen from the woman in the Hawaiian shirt. "It all comes down to supply and demand."

"It's not like that nineties crap," said the bearded man. "I could insulate my house with the piles of *Meta Boy* I have in my warehouse."

"Shut up, Johnny," the Legion fan said, glancing at Ralph.

"Ah, shoot," Johnny said. "No offense."

Ralph stood up. "None taken. I'd rather you use them as wallpaper, though."

The dealers laughed, and the woman in the Hawaiian shirt slapped Ralph a good one on the back.

Ralph asked, "You deal with a lot of Golden Age stuff, mister...?"

"Walker. Ben Walker," the black man in the Legion shirt said, and the two shook hands. "These yahoos are Anna May and Johnny." Ralph shook hands with the rest.

"You know, Rogers," Walker said, "me and my buddies, we thought you were the coolest thing in the world when we were kids."

"Thank you," Ralph said. He heard this often.

"I always thought you deserved better after everything went down."

That was something Ralph did *not* hear often.

"Sounds like you deal in some older stuff. You wouldn't happen to have any Fiction House books, would you? I'm trying to get a complete run of *Planet Comics*."

"Those the ones with the good girl pin-up covers?" Ben asked.

"Like a naughty version of *Strange Adventures*," Anna May said, laughing.

"Sorry," Ben said. "But if cheesecake is your thing, I have that issue of *Phantom Lady* with the Matt Baker cover. It's graded at 8.5."

Anna May whistled as Johnny rolled his eyes.

"I *would* be interested in that," Ralph said.

Ben smiled. "Tell you what. There's a party tonight after they lock up the convention. Should be fun. Guy running it collects Golden Age stuff too. Has a copy of *Motion Pictures Funnies Weekly* number one. The son of a bitch even claims to have issues two through four, but he just says that to fuck with me. Meet me there with your checkbook; I bet we can work something out." He scribbled the address on a business card and handed it to Ralph.

"At least somebody's making money this weekend," Anna May said.

Ben looked over his shoulder and said, "Hey, Ralph, you might want to watch out. Some guy named Eugene Sandhurst has been talking about kicking your ass all day. He's always running his mouth, calling you a hack fraud, but he's big as a house. He'll probably crash that party too."

"I'll keep that in mind," Ralph said.

4

FORGOT TO KEEP THAT IN MIND, Ralph thought as Eugene Sandhurst lifted him high in the air.

"Hope you've got yourself some gills, Aquaman," Eugene said.

Ralph looked down at the crisp blue water and wondered how long he could hold his breath.

Everyone froze at the unmistakable sound of a shotgun being cocked.

"Turn around," said a precise voice.

Eugene turned, still holding Ralph horizontally above his head.

Bartlett the bartender faced them, holding a shotgun. Ben Walker stood beside him, looking overwhelmed.

"Please lower the guest slowly to his feet," Bartlett said. He spoke with a level of courtesy that would put Eddie Haskell to shame.

"Are you crazy?" Eugene said.

"Not at all. I have loaded my weapon with alternating rounds of rock salt and bean bags. But the final shell is lethal, I assure you. Place Mr. Rogers gently on the ground."

Eugene put Ralph down on the poolside as gently as a mother would her child. Ralph's glass of scotch never lost a drop.

Bartlett motioned with the shotgun. "Now it would be in your best interest to depart the premises."

The crowd cheered again.

Wishy-washy sons of bitches, Ralph thought.

To his credit, Eugene knew when he was beat. He fled without another word, but as he left he locked eyes with Ralph. Eugene's cold expression made it plain: this only added to Ralph's sins against him.

That can't possibly come back to bite me, Ralph thought.

"Are you all right, sir?" Bartlett asked.

"I'm fine," Ralph said. "Thanks to you two."

Ben Walker laughed. "You're one hell of a bartender, Mr. Bartlett."

"I'm also an excellent butler, sir. If you need further rescuing, I will be making drinks."

As Bartlett walked inside, Ben said, "Sorry about that, Ralph. I ran and got the cavalry as soon as I saw what was going on."

"Thanks for the save. I guess the butler is also the bouncer?"

"He wears many hats."

"Jeez, my heart is pounding."

Ben laughed. "My friends might have something to calm us both down."

Making their way around the pool, they joined two men dressed as the marijuana-themed superheroes, Bluntman and Chronic. Appropriately enough, they were sharing a joint.

"Thanks for the show," Chronic said, offering the joint.

Ralph accepted. "This is the craziest party I've ever been to." He took a long drag.

"You should see what happens in San Diego," Chronic said as Ralph coughed violently.

"We were just discussing which is the best bad movie starring Damon Ripley," said the man in the Bluntman costume.

"Come on," Ralph said. "That guy is great. I love his movies."

"Oh, we do too," Bluntman said. "I bought a motorcycle after seeing *Spit in the Wind*. Changed my damn life. But you have to admit, the man makes some hilariously bad movies."

Ben snapped his fingers. "Oh, it's gotta be *Man Versus Baby*. Did we really need a more violent version of *Three Men and a Baby*?"

Ralph rolled his eyes. "Fine, I'll play. How about *Drive Real Fast*? It had more pointless car explosions than a Ford Pinto convention."

"Dude, I happen to like pointless car explosions," Chronic said. "The best worst Damon Ripley is *Dismember the Alamo*. I mean, come on, you get Ripley as Davy Crockett, fighting off a zombified Mexican Army. That's kick ass. Worth it for the title alone."

"What about *Red Eagle*?" Ralph asked.

"That *Top Gun* rip-off?" Chronic rolled his eyes. "More like *Spread Eagle*."

Bluntman tapped some ash off the joint. "I'd give it to the remake of *The Phantom Empire*. I'll never tire of watching Ripley trying to be a singing cowboy."

Chronic laughed. "Are you kidding? The robots look like cardboard boxes."

"How dare you, sir," Bluntman said, puffing his chest. "That movie is a cinematic treasure. History will vindicate it."

Ben blew out a mouthful of smoke. "You gentlemen are forgetting the greatest jewel in Damon Ripley's crooked crown. A film so full of schlock, so full of chewed scenery, that it hasn't been available to purchase since the Japanese LaserDisc."

The other three thought it over until Ralph took a guess. "*I'm Coming For You, and Hell's Coming With Me.*"

Ben slapped him on the back. "That's right. *I'm Coming For You, and Hell's Coming With Me*. It's his *Plan Nine from Outer Space*, his *Faster, Pussycat! Kill! Kill!* It's so bad it's good, then so bad it's bad, and then it circles back around to being cinematic genius."

Ralph sipped his scotch as they smoked and discussed bad movies and good comic books. The tastes of the liquor and marijuana clashed horribly, but he no longer felt jittery, and his heart stopped pounding

"Bringing back Bucky is my favorite retcon," Ralph said. "Bar none."

"No way," Bluntman said. "The best retcon of all time is what Alan Moore did with *Swamp Thing*. Pure genius."

"What the hell is a retcon?" Chronic asked.

"Retroactive continuity," Bluntman said.

"Doctor Doom and his Doombots are my favorite example," Ben said. "Doom's supposed to be this sophisticated, honorable villain, the most magnificent bastard. But then some asshole writer comes along and makes Doom a megalomaniacal mustache twirler. So the next writer pops up and boom, that last time? That was a Doombot. It wasn't really Victor von Doom, it was just an android pretending to be him."

"Sounds like a bunch of nonsense," Chronic said.

Ben nudged Ralph with an elbow. "I'm guessing you're about ready for that *Phantom Lady*."

The man in the Bluntman costume nodded his approval. "That's one sexy lady. It's not the bondage cover, is it?"

Ralph grinned. "One and the same."

"I'll pay twenty percent over what this guy is paying," the man said to Ben.

"Sorry, buddy, a deal's a deal," Ben called back over his shoulder as he walked with Ralph toward the house. "C'mon, Ralph, our host let me put it in his safe."

As they entered the house, Ralph put his empty Captain Marvel glass on the bar, giving a dramatic salute to Bartlett and feeling oddly jubilant. He followed Ben up the stairs, stepping carefully over a passed-out Captain America.

A ragged high school letter jacket hung in an acrylic case on the hallway wall. It was sewn together from at least a dozen different jackets. Pausing in front of it, Ralph squinted at the strange creation. "Hey, is that the jacket from that eighties movie, *FrankenTeen*? Starring none other than our favorite actor?"

Ben nodded. "Damon Ripley."

"This thing belongs in a museum!"

"Like I said, the host is a collector. He has a ton of these old props."

Ralph stared at his reflection in the glass. "I fell in love with Diane Franklin after seeing her in that movie. That scene where they make out in the graveyard was my *Some Like It Hot*. Did you ever have a crush on her?"

"No, man, sorry," Ben laughed. "I'm more into Cloak than I am into Dagger, if you catch my meaning."

"I read you," Ralph said. His steps no longer felt sure, and the pictures in the hallway hung at odd angles. For the first time in a while, his stomach threatened to expel its contents. "What was in that weed?" he asked.

"Pym particles, by the feel of it," Ben said. "I am royally fucked up."

They walked into a vast, open room. Framed, vintage comics covered the walls. A majestic saltwater tank full of neon tropical fish sat behind the long, beautiful desk in the center of the room. A middle-aged man wearing a loose linen shirt, khaki shorts, and sandals leaned against the desk. He spoke with an attractive, red-headed woman in a green party dress. The two of them stopped their conversation as Ben and Ralph stumbled into the room.

"Ben!" the man said. "So glad you could make it!" He turned to the woman. "This is the guy I was telling you about. Today he helped me complete my 'Mister Mind and the Monster Society of Evil' collection."

Ben bowed as the other three clapped. "Damon, this is my new friend, Ralph Rogers. Ralph, this is—"

"Mr. Ripley," Ralph said, shaking the movie star's hand. "Explains that *FrankenTeen* jacket. I love your films. My favorite movie in junior high was *Free Radicals*."

"Anyone with such good taste can call me Damon," their host said. "I've always said *Free Radicals* is a hidden gem. I loved playing the science geek in that one. Feels like a million years ago."

Ralph waved his hands. "Hey, your new stuff is good too. You should have won an Oscar for that adaptation of *At Swim-Two-Birds*. You always bring it to the table."

"Careful," the woman said. "Damon's ego already threatens every man, woman, and child on this planet."

"That's why I like to remind him that he made *Air Force 666*," Ben said.

"Hey now," Damon said. "I won my fourth Golden Raspberry for that one. Let the man talk. I only wish the critics agreed with him."

Ralph laughed. "If it's all the same to you, I wish the critics would go to hell."

Damon held up a finger. "Wait a minute. You're *the* Ralph Rogers. He is, isn't he? Holy crap. Valerie, do you know who this is?"

"Of course I do," she said. "Hi, Ralph. It's been a long time."

Scrolling through the beat-up Rolodex in his mind, Ralph tried to remember how he knew this beautiful woman. "I'm sorry. Do I know you from somewhere?"

"Don't be an asshole, Ralph," she said.

His eyes widened. "Val? Valerie Hall? Oh my God. You look fantastic."

She smiled. "That's more like it. It's good to see you, Ralph."

"Watch out, Ripley. Looks like you might have some competition," Ben said.

Ralph shook his head. "It's not like that."

Damon turned to Valerie. "You never told me you knew Ralph Rogers."

"It never came up."

"'Never came up!'" he repeated. "Never came up?" He slapped his knuckles into his palm to punctuate the words. "You know that's the kind of thing I would eat up."

"It's nothing," she said. "We just knew each other when we were young."

"Don't be modest," Ralph said. "Valerie is the one who dared me to make the *Meta Boy* book in the first place."

Ben's jaw dropped. "Oh, wow."

Damon Ripley's eyes shined. "This is a story I want to hear."

5

RALPH ROGERS'S LOVE FOR COMICS began in the 1980s, after he stopped wetting the bed and before he started wetting it again. One day his friend Valerie Hall, all freckles and glasses, passed him a comic book under the lunch table. She had three older brothers, and she was always borrowing their comic books. On the cover, a beautiful woman in white underwear stood over a fallen Captain America. Ralph devoured the contraband every time Ms. Clawster turned her back on the class. He recognized Captain America, but the rest of the characters were new to him. He followed the story as best he could until the Clawster confiscated the magazine. It went to live in a locked drawer of her desk until the end of the year.

Ralph talked his dad into taking him to a comic book store that weekend to replace his friend's property. The store was dark and stuffy, but to Ralph it looked like a treasure trove. He blew a month's allowance on back issues from the long rows of cardboard boxes. With no idea what was good and what was schlock, he did his best to get some of everything.

Back home, he took his haul to his bedroom. Pictures Ralph had drawn and copied from books and magazines plastered the walls. Clothes covered the floor, some clean and some dirty. The shelves over his desk were full of toys and interesting things he had picked up in the woods. The only organized spot in his room was the surface of his desk. There, he'd carefully arranged his art supplies beneath the lamp.

He dumped the comics on the bed: *The Mighty Thor*, *Betty and Veronica*, *The Legion of Superheroes*, and a dozen others. There was even a *Vampirella* Ralph had hidden at the bottom of the pile so his father wouldn't notice. A pale woman lounged on the cover, and her red costume was even more revealing than the one from that *Captain America* cover. Ralph hoped Valerie's brothers would consider it an adequate replacement.

But Val would have to wait. That night, Ralph read every issue in the stack by the light of his desk lamp. Afterward, he read them all again. Then he sat down at his desk and started copying his favorite drawings from the comics. He drew every night, sometimes copying from the comics and sometimes doing something on his own with the same characters. He worked until he was exhausted enough to fall into bed. The next week, when he got his allowance, he pestered his father to take him back to the comic book shop. The cycle repeated itself again and again.

In the midst of this growing obsession, his parents went away for a weekend while Ralph stayed at his grandparents' house. Ralph's grandfather was more than willing to listen as his grandson prattled on about mystic hammers and word balloons. "Come to think of it," Grandpa said, "I think I have a few of your dad's old comic books around here somewhere."

Ralph's eyes lit up, and the two of them adventured into the cluttered attic. They reached the layer dating back to the childhood of Ralph's father, and Grandpa pulled down a box full of Aurora plastic monster models. In the bottom of the box were several well-read issues of *Showcase*, *Four Color*, *Whiz Comics*, and *Walt Disney's Comics and Stories*.

One yellowed cover from *World's Finest* featured Batman, Robin, and an astonishing three Supermans. The book had a square cut out of the bottom of the cover. Ralph frowned at this grave injustice and opened the fragile comic.

DRAW INSTANTLY, proclaimed the inside front cover. A boy sat at a desk, drawing a cowboy on a horse. Somehow the cowboy was projected onto the paper from an image on the wall by the Magic Art Reproducer, only $1.98. The order form had been cut out by Ralph's father almost four decades earlier.

"Grandpa, is this thing up here too?" Ralph asked.

They looked through a few more boxes before they found it. Ralph wasn't surprised; his grandfather never threw anything away. His parents said it was because he'd lived through the Great Depression.

The Magic Art Reproducer's box featured the same little boy drawing a cowboy as the ad. Downstairs, they were both surprised when the contraption actually worked, albeit nowhere near as well as advertised. The simple metal box contained a mirror and glass window, all of it suspended over the paper by a thin rod. It reflected a faint image onto the paper that the user could trace. Ralph and Grandpa spent the weekend using the device to copy the simple art of his father's old comic books.

"Your dad used to love to draw," Grandpa said. Ralph looked up from the Magic Art Reproducer, but Grandpa was staring out the window, lost in his memories.

6

RALPH ROGERS WAS THIRTEEN when he took the dare that would ruin his life.

Valerie Hall and Ralph were sitting on the floor of Ralph's bedroom, looking through some of her superhero trading cards. The back of each card had a description of the character and some statistics, as well as a graph rating their various traits.

Ralph dropped the cards in disgust. "There is no way U.S. Agent has more intelligence than Hawkeye."

"What are you talking about?" Valerie asked. "Hawkeye is full of shit."

"Don't be talking about my boy Hawkeye," Ralph said. "At least he can think up his own shtick. U.S. Agent is nothing but Captain America with more boring colors."

"Oh, like there was never a hero with a bow and arrow before. The shield looks cool, though."

"Definitely cool," Ralph said. "Not too many guys have the balls to fight supervillains with just a shield."

"I can't think of any others."

Ralph frowned, racking his brain. "I think it's just those guys, and other people who get a hold of Cap's shield. Like that guy in the future. There's also that Cap rip-off in Youngblood. Oh, and the Guardian."

Valerie rolled her eyes. "Who's the Guardian?"

"The blue and gold guy in Metropolis. He's a clone or something."

"You mean in a DC comic?" Valerie asked. "Lame."

"He's okay. And there's nothing wrong with DC comics."

"Except they're lame."

Ralph crossed his arms over his chest. "Batman."

Valerie slumped back. "Okay. Batman is cool. But DC comics are not cool."

"Yes, they are," Ralph said.

"No, they're not," Valerie said. Ralph saw she was serious, and remembered what happened the previous summer. That argument had been about which movie was better, *Monster Squad* or *The Goonies*. They had not spoken for a month after that one.

"Tell you what," Ralph said. "They're different. Marvel's more popular right now, but there are some cool DC series. And that's okay, right?"

Valerie nodded, and the temperature in the room dropped ten degrees. *But the Monster Squad would still beat the shit out of the Goonies,* Ralph thought.

Valerie started gathering up her cards. "I better get home."

Ralph helped her pick up the cards and the two of them walked outside to Valerie's bicycle.

As Valerie walked the bike down the driveway, Ralph asked, "Can I still go with your family to the movies on Friday?"

Valerie grinned. "Yeah, sure. It'll be fun." She started to pedal away, but squeezed the hand brake and squealed to a stop. "You know, I bet you couldn't do it."

"Do what?" Ralph asked.

"Make a comic book that looked like a Marvel or an Image comic, but felt like a DC comic. I bet you couldn't do that, you're-so-smart."

Ralph thought for a moment while kicking at gravel in the street. He had been drawing almost every day for years now. "I bet I could," he said. "And I bet it would be pretty good."

"I bet you can't. I bet you twenty dollars you can't."

Ralph's jaw dropped. Twenty dollars was easily the most money he had heard of anyone betting on anything in his entire life. "Fine."

"But I get to choose the character," Valerie said.

"Fine," Ralph said again.

Valerie grinned. "Meta Boy."

"Meta Boy?" Ralph asked. "The kid with the cape I used to draw in the fifth grade?"

"That's the one."

"That guy is the worst," Ralph said. "With those stupid buttons on his chest, he looks like he's wearing a high school band uniform. No way."

"I knew you couldn't do it," Valerie said.

Ralph's face burned. "Oh yeah? I can and I will." He put out his hand. "One comic with Meta Boy. Twenty-four pages."

"Plus a cover," Valerie said.

Ralph nodded. "Plus the cover."

Valerie spit in the palm of her hand, Ralph spit in his, and they shook on it.

LATE THAT NIGHT, RALPH SAT with his head on the old drafting desk his parents had bought for him at a garage sale. The black swing-arm desk lamp issued the only light. Ralph gripped his hair, and the threat of a headache loomed inside his skull. Piles of wadded and ripped sketches littered the floor. On the paper beneath his forehead lay a pencil sketch of his character, Meta Boy. Something about the drawing was off.

Everything is wrong, he thought. Ralph had mastered copying the work of other comic artists, at least to the extent that a thirteen-year-old could. He knew how the muscles on a spandex-clad hero should look. A comic panel—that magical frame holding a still-shot of an impossible universe—he could recognize one that had been put together correctly. Yet he had no idea how to create that perfection from scratch.

I should give up, he thought. Then he pictured Valerie giving him a hard time at their cafeteria table, with the kids around them joining in on the fun.

Dammit, he thought. He lifted his head and looked around, as if his sleeping mother in the other room had heard the swear word in his head. Ralph leaned back in his squeaking desk chair and stared at the ceiling. He shared a moment with other aspiring artists across time and space: the realization that recreating an image did not in itself teach you how to create images for yourself.

Look, Val, I know we spit shook on it, but I had my fingers crossed. He sighed. *Val, buddy, I finished it, but I pissed off my dad and he ripped it up. I shit you not. I'm still grounded, even.*

His desk lamp flickered, and he slapped it. The light disappeared completely. But for a sliver of light from beneath the door, Ralph was now in darkness.

Rejected layouts and vetoed character sketches crumpled beneath his feet as he shuffled to his door. He carefully turned the knob and opened the door as quietly as possible.

He felt his way to the hall closet. The light clicked on with the pull of a chain, and he scanned the shelves for the family's supply of light bulbs. They were crammed on the same shelf as his dad's board games: *Shadowlord!*, *Thunder Road*, *Acquire*, *Tales of the Arabian Nights*, and several others Ralph had no interest in ever playing again. There, mixed in with the games, was the black and yellow box of the Magic Art Reproducer. Ralph grinned at the memory of the weekend spent drawing with his grandfather. Grandpa was not an artist at all, but even he was able to do some great sketches with that thing—

Ralph grabbed the Magic Art Reproducer and hurried back to his room, forgetting the light bulb. After a second trip and with the new bulb installed, he opened up a desk drawer overflowing with his comic books. He had read each one at least half-a-dozen times, and he had no problem finding the issue he needed.

He opened up a black-and-white reprint of the old *Spirit* comic strips by Will Eisner. The opening splash page showed a trolley running through a rundown industrial district. Above the image, looking like windswept litter, swam the words, *The Spirit*, and on a discarded handbill danced the name of the story: "The Last Trolley."

Ralph cleared his workspace and propped up the comic on his desk, the spine leaning against the wall. Careful not to damage the corners, he slid a sheet of Bristol board out from under his bed. He clipped the thick white board in place and positioned the Magic Art Reproducer above it. After shining the swing-arm lamp on the Spirit, Ralph looked through the peephole on top of the Reproducer. A faint image of the splash page was there on the paper. With some adjustments, the page filled the board.

His heart beating fast, Ralph lightly sketched over the phantom art, beginning with the panel border. It took a long time to scratch out the image he wanted, but he removed the Reproducer and let out a deep sigh of satisfaction. There, on the paper, was a drawing that felt right.

He spent the rest of the night adding detail to the simple image. He replaced the trolley with a freight train he found in a magazine. As the sun came up, he put the finishing touches on the fragile letters that now spelled out, "Meta Boy!" The playbill remained empty, as he had no idea what to name the story. The finished pencil work was different from the original. It was more detailed, for one. Instead of Will Eisner's organic, flowing lines, Ralph had used his crisp, straightforward style.

Ralph giggled. He was already daydreaming about shoving the finished comic in Valerie's face.

8

VALERIE COMPLETELY LOST HER SHIT.

"Dude," she kept repeating. "*Dude.*"

The two middle schoolers sat alone at the cafeteria table. It was a half-hour until the first bell, and scattered early birds huddled around cafeteria tables. The boys played games of paper football or mercy, while girls put on makeup they had smuggled out of their houses. Unlike lunch, there were no adults in the room to keep kids from getting up to shenanigans. Those in authority correctly assumed that students were too tired first thing in the morning to get into much trouble.

Valerie gripped the photocopies of Ralph's first-ever comic book. In accordance with the bet, the stack contained twenty-four black and white pages plus a cover displaying Meta Boy punching a hoodlum in the face. Blood flew out of the hoodlum's mouth along with a single tooth. The rest of the pages were just as exciting. It had taken all of Ralph's willpower not to show off with an action-packed two-page spread.

Ralph watched his friend's eyes dart from panel to panel, word balloon to word balloon. Valerie's lips pulled into a grin at all the right times, and her eyes went wide on the last page just like they were supposed to. She finished reading and respectfully set the final page down.

"So what do you think?" Ralph asked.

"Bobby Crane is kind of a stupid name for a teenager."

"No, seriously. What do you think?"

"Dude."

Ralph laughed, and Valerie joined in.

"Ralph, you son of a bitch," Valerie said, shaking her head. "It hasn't even been two weeks!"

Ralph shrugged. "I guess that means I win," he said.

"Wipe that grin off your face, you jerk. You'll get your twenty bucks. Christ." Valerie slouched down in her chair, tilted her head back, and sighed. "Truth is, I figured you'd do it. But I thought you'd be working for months. I haven't even started saving."

"Don't worry about it, I had fun making it. It's no big deal."

Valerie snapped forward and stuck her finger in Ralph's face. "You calling me a welcher, Rogers?" Her mouth was smiling, but her eyes were not.

Ralph waved his hands. "Nah, you're no welcher. Seriously. I know you're good for it."

"What I thought."

They sat for a moment, each of them considering the value of twenty bucks.

Valerie's eyes lit up with a flash. "Boy howdy. I got an idea."

"Yeah?" When Valerie was excited about an idea, it was cause for worry.

"Oh, yeah. Come on." Valerie gathered up the pages, careful to put them in the right order. She carried them off like a hostage, and Ralph hurried after her.

"Val!" Ralph hissed as they started down the hallway.

Valerie motioned for him to shut up as she peeked around a tiled corner. With a tilt of her head, she signaled to follow her.

They crept deeper into the school. Anything past the cafeteria was off-limits this early in the morning, and Ralph dreaded the thought of trying to explain his actions to a pre-caffeinated teacher. It didn't help that he honestly had no idea what they were doing.

Valerie found the room she was looking for. With a final look around, she opened the door and the two of them slipped into the darkness. Ralph had never been to a party with the cool kids, but he had heard of Seven Minutes in Heaven. *Oh my gosh,* he thought. *She wants to make out with me.* He licked his lips and gave his armpit a sniff test.

A light clicked on, forcing Ralph to shield his eyes. They stood in a musky storage room. There were cardboard boxes, a copy machine, and a card table with a paper cutter and a stapler.

"What are we doing in here?" Ralph asked.

Valerie said proudly, "Check this out." She patted the lid of the copy machine, then leaned over and clicked a red switch. The machine lit up, humming softly. "Mrs. Jones sent me here to make copies for her once."

"Mrs. Jones the librarian, or Mrs. Jones the drunk theater lady?" Ralph asked.

"Drunk theater lady. She said to use this copier, because all the teachers like the new one. There's never any line. So come on, let's do it!"

"Do what?"

"Make a bunch of your comic books, duh. And we'll sell 'em."

Ralph rolled his eyes. "Are you an idiot? No one wants my comic book."

"Yes, they do. They just don't know it yet."

"No, way. Even if I wanted to make more, I'd make them at the library, like I did with this one."

"How much did it cost at the library?" Valerie asked.

"Like two dollars." But that was a lie. He had wasted another three dollars trying to get the settings right to resize the image and get his pencil art to actually show up.

"We can copy them here for free," Valerie said. "Then we sell them for two dollars—"

"*One* dollar," Ralph said.

"Fine, one dollar. We split it fifty-fifty."

"Wait a minute," Ralph said. "Why fifty-fifty? I made the comic."

"Yeah, but it was my idea to sell it, and I was the one who got us a copier."

Ralph chewed the inside of his cheek, thinking. "Fine," he said. "But just on this one."

"Sounds good to me," Valerie said.

"Then get out of the way. You're on staple duty."

They printed and assembled thirty issues, which didn't look too bad for second-generation copies. Each of them took half, and they sold out before lunch. Once the lunch bell rang, Ralph and Valerie snuck back to the storage room. They printed up another fifty comics as they ate their sandwiches. Those copies were gone by the end of the day, leaving only the copy Ralph had brought to school that day and a particularly nice copy Valerie took home with her.

Somehow they finished out the day without adult intervention. After the last bell rang, they rode their bicycles several blocks before splitting up their loot. Neither of them was all that big, and any number of bullies would have relieved them of their profits with a grin and a threat about snitching.

"Thirty-eight, thirty-nine, forty. Wow." Ralph finished counting the money into his friend's nervous palm.

"Yeah." She looked down at their fistfuls of money.

Ralph shoved his cash into his pocket and climbed on his ten-speed. "Thanks, Val, today was fun. Guess I better get home."

"Waitaminnit," Valerie said. She counted from one hand to another, like a magician doing a card trick, and offered the money to Ralph. "To cover the bet," she said. "Now we're square, right?"

Ralph's jaw dropped. He shook his head.

"C'mon," Valerie said, grinning. "Don't make me stuff it down your throat."

"Like you could," but Ralph was smiling too. He took the money and looked at the crinkled bills in his hand. Sixty dollars. Sixty big ones. Sixty *smackeroonies*.

Valerie jumped on her bike and sped away. "Get started on that second issue, asshole!" she called over her shoulder.

9

RALPH AND VALERIE WERE CAUGHT making copies of *Meta Boy* issue two. A giggling Mrs. Jones opened the door to the storage room and stopped short when she saw the two students making a piss-poor attempt to look like they weren't up to something. The copy machine shot out page after violent page. Through the crack in the door, Ralph watched Mr. Gardener, the boy's gym teacher, slink quietly away.

The discovery led to parent conferences and a promise by the two to split the cost of one toner cartridge and one box of copy paper. The principal also made Ralph and Valerie promise not to sell any more funny books at school.

Ralph's parents, James and Catherine, had no idea their son had created two comic books entirely on his own, and they weren't sure how to proceed. On the one hand, Ralph had stolen supplies from his school and gotten caught. But, as James told his wife in the privacy of their bedroom, "The only thing I accomplished in the eighth grade was learning to smoke. We should give the kid a break."

So, one weekend after Ralph had mowed enough lawns, pruned enough trees, and cleaned enough gutters to pay off his debt, he and James hopped in the family hatchback and drove to Dallas, heading to the biggest comic book convention in Texas. A new art portfolio case leaned against the back of Ralph's seat.

The car reeked of ancient coffee spills, but Ralph didn't mind. It was a smell he would come to associate with his father, and it would have felt strange to ride together in a car that smelled any different.

They cruised along to classic rock, that great middle ground that existed for baby boomers and their offspring. Ralph finished off another strip of beef jerky and washed it down with lukewarm soda. "This is pretty cool, Dad."

"It's always nice to put a few hours between you and your real life," his dad said. They passed a sign for a gas station. "Need to take a leak?"

"Nah, I'm good," Ralph said. He could actually feel those early tingles, but his father took pride in making as few stops as possible. Ralph would rather die than be the first to break.

On the radio, Brian Johnson compared a woman's sexual organs to a car engine.

"You're pretty serious about this comic stuff," his father said.

It wasn't framed as a question, but Ralph replied, "Yeah, I guess."

"That's really neat, son. Really neat," James said. "That's why this weekend is important. It ties into what I always tell you. What do I always tell you?"

Ralph rolled his eyes. "'Don't be a bystander.'"

"That's right. You're getting your stuff out there. You're not drifting along like a bump on a log."

"Say, Dad, did you ever think about doing something other than a normal job?"

"A normal job?" James laughed, and Ralph knew he had said something wrong. "Yeah, I guess I did."

"Really?" Ralph asked. "Like what?"

James shook his head. "It's pretty stupid."

"You can't say something like that and then not tell," Ralph said. "That's cruel!"

"Okay, okay. I wanted to be—" James paused, and waved one hand in flourish. "A *magician*."

Ralph chuckled, but stopped short when he saw James was serious. "That's pretty cool, Dad."

"I thought it was, anyway," James said. "But I'm much better with numbers than I was with the linking rings. I certainly wouldn't have been able to help support the family on one birthday gig every three months!"

"Sorry if Mom and me held you back. Did you ever regret it? Working in an office instead of sawing ladies in half in Vegas?"

"Maybe every now and then, on a Monday morning when no one turns in their reports. But you listen here, buddy." James took his eyes off the road to pat Ralph on the shoulder. "If I'd wanted to do that, it's what I would have done. Simple as that. I decided there was something I wanted more than a hat full of rabbit shit, and that was you and your mom. Get me?"

"I gotcha," Ralph said. "Hey, were you any good? At the magic stuff?"

James laughed again. "Son, I was absolutely terrible."

They laughed as Robert Plant and Sandy Denny sang about the conflicts of Middle Earth.

10

CROWD PACKED THE ENTRANCE to the convention center. There were plenty of kids Ralph's age, but he was surprised how many adults were there without children. Darth Vader—or a close relative—boomed unintelligible instructions over a loudspeaker. Ralph gripped his portfolio tightly against his chest and followed in his father's wake. They checked in at the desk and entered the main floor. Once past the bottleneck, Ralph's jaw dropped. Dealer's tables surrounded them, and everywhere Ralph looked was something he wanted to buy. "Don't forget why we're here," James said. Ralph frowned, but he nodded.

James drug Ralph past more treasure than had been hauled out of King Tut's tomb. Then there were the celebrity guests, most of whom Ralph could not pick out of a police line-up. A gray-haired woman sat next to a framed picture of a sexy alien from *Star Trek*. Ralph recognized the curly-haired star of *The Greatest American Hero*. Though Ralph didn't know who the other guests were, people had already lined up to talk to them, take pictures together, or get something autographed. Ralph let his father walk a few steps ahead before sneaking a peak at a woman who was apparently famous for being naked in a magazine.

According to a vinyl sign hanging from the ceiling, they had finally reached Artist Alley. A number of men and a handful of women sat at wooden folding tables covered in posters, comics, and art supplies.

This was his mom's idea. Catherine's theory was that the only people who could honestly critique Ralph's work were actual comic artists. She had even called the comic shop to find out the best way to go about it. "After all," she said, "this is the first time you've ever shown interest in anything approaching a career. You never even wanted to be a fireman."

So, Ralph repeated his mission to himself: show his portfolio to every professional artist at the convention. He would also be in charge of remembering what was said and writing it down afterward. James would stay out of the way to avoid the deadly Embarrassed Teenager Syndrome.

Ralph had no idea what any of the artists on his list looked like. He scanned nametags, and stopped cold after walking past a half-dozen artists. His shaky hands dug into his shiny portfolio.

The legendary Matt Corrigan sighed and sipped his coffee. He adjusted his thick-framed glasses and dramatically flipped to the next page of his newspaper. He wore a ragged baseball cap and was much older than Ralph had expected. The boy realized how silly he'd been; Corrigan started drawing comics in the 1940s.

No one was standing in front of the old man's table. Ralph squirmed and looked over at his father. James gave his son a smile and two thumbs up, just like he had done five summers earlier when Ralph had been afraid to go off the high dive at the city swimming pool.

Ralph crept up to the table, but the newspaper wall remained in place. He stood there, sweating. "Excuse me, sir?"

The newspaper dropped and Corrigan asked, "What can I do for you, young man?"

Ralph swallowed. "I really like the stuff you did for Timely, Mr. Corrigan."

The old man laughed. "Wasn't that before your time?"

"Back-up story reprints." Ralph felt relief wash over him. Mr. Corrigan looked less scary than he had a moment before.

"What have you got there?" Corrigan pointed to the portfolio case.

"Just some stuff I wanted to show you. Maybe get some pointers?"

"Open 'er up, Mr. I-Read-Timely-Comics," Corrigan said. "Always happy to help another pencil pusher. Especially one with respect for the classics."

Ralph handed over the portfolio, and Corrigan pulled out the thick stack of Bristol board. Flipping through the pages, he asked, "It looks like you have a whole book here."

"Yes, sir. I did another one, but I thought it would be too much if I brought both."

"And you drew this all yourself, did you?"

"Yes, but—"

Corrigan shoved the portfolio and artwork back across the table. "Get out of here, kid. I don't have time for this bullshit."

"But—"

The newspaper wall went back up.

"Mr. Corrigan, please."

"Go away, and tell your buddy he can kiss my ass."

Fighting back tears, Ralph shoved his work back into the portfolio. He slunk away, ignoring his father's questioning eyes.

In an interview years later, Matt Corrigan said, "Yes, that really happened, and I feel terrible for how I treated the poor kid. You should have seen his pencils, though. It's not the first time I've seen a kid that age draw that well, but the composition! Those pages had energy and style that it takes years of professional work to cultivate. There was no way this kid could do that. I thought Kubert set it up as another of his stupid practical jokes."

11

T TOOK FORTY-FIVE MINUTES for James Rogers to convince his son to speak to another artist. Kevin Hunter did the writing and art for his own books, working with independent publishers. Ralph did not own any of Hunter's work, but he'd read some at Valerie's house.

The bald, bearded Hunter examined Ralph's work. "This is good stuff, buddy. I mean, it's really good."

"Thank you, Mr. Hunter," Ralph said. *This is more like it!* he thought.

"Bobby Crane is kind of a silly name for a teenager, but you can always change that. Tell you what. I want to show this to a friend of mine. That okay with you?"

Ralph nodded furiously. Carrying the portfolio, Hunter led Ralph to the booth of ATG Graphics. Ralph recognized the name; it was a company that published creator-owned work. Although only in business a couple of years, ATG had already made a name for itself. It was founded by some of the most popular artists in the business, and their books sold out quickly at the comic shop.

Hunter handed Ralph's work to a man with gray hair and kind eyes. As he looked at the pages, the two men spoke in hushed voices. Ralph waited, too aware of his posture. Finally, Hunter asked him to join them.

"Hi, Ralph," the other man said, holding out his hand. "I'm Paul Simmons with ATG Graphics."

Ralph shook it. "Nice to meet you, Mr. Simmons."

"Call me Paul. Kevin here tells me you did all of this yourself."

"Yes, sir."

Simmons turned to Hunter. "How old did you say this kid is?"

"I'm fourteen," Ralph said.

Looking at the artwork again, Simmons smiled. Hunter said, "You mentioned you were looking for something like this."

"That I did," Simmons said. "Ralph, how long did it take you to do this? Could you do another?"

"I already did the second issue. It took two weeks. It took less time than the first one, since I kind of knew what I was doing."

"Get a load of this kid," Hunter said. "Fourteen-years-old and he's cranking out two pages of pencils a day. When I was fourteen, there was only one thing I was cranking out twice a day." Ralph shrugged, and Simmons and Hunter laughed.

"Jim Shooter," Hunter said.

"Jim Shooter," Simmons agreed.

"Could you get someone to ink and color it?" Hunter asked.

"Without credit? Who do I look like, *Walt Disney's Comics and Stories*?"

"What about Chill?"

Simmons looked thoughtful. "Maybe. Ralph, is that your dad over there, trying to look like he isn't watching us?"

"Yes, sir."

"Get him over here, please. I'm not talking business with you without a guardian present."

Ralph's jaw dropped. "What are you talking about?"

"Kid, how would you like ATG Graphics to publish *Meta Boy*?"

12

Ben, Valerie, Damon, and Ralph sat on the leather couches in Damon's office. The party continued to roar outside. By the end of the flashback, Ralph felt the mixed effects of booze and bud wearing off.

"*Phantom Lady?*" Valerie said, holding up the old comic book. "Seems a little low brow, Ralph."

"My girlfriend, that's Sandra, we collect good girl art," he said. "I guess this is my contribution to the cause."

"Oh," she said. "How long have you two been together?"

"Jeez. Four years now, I guess? A lot of that was off and on. How about you? Seeing anybody?"

"Not right now."

"Only because she won't go to dinner with me," Damon said.

"I've seen how relationships with you end up," she said. "It's enough work just being your friend."

They laughed as Damon topped off their drinks. "Ralph, you have to tell me what it was like. You were the darling boy of the industry. The wunderkind. The comic press raved about your unusual combination of styles. The target audience ate it up, reading a comic by a kid just like them."

"Bobby Crane, stupid name or not, was at the top of all the favorite character polls. You even scored that movie deal with Universal," Ben said. "How long until the hammer dropped?"

"Six months," Ralph said. "You know that story."

Damon nodded, taking a drink from a plastic cup covered with the image of the 1970s superhero team the Champions. "*Wizard* magazine ran that article listing all the panels you swiped. Everyone felt cheated and lied to."

In the back of his mind, Ralph heard the furious phone call from his editor, Paul Simmons. "*You ripped me off, you little shit!*" the man had yelled again and again. Ralph shook his head to clear it.

As if reading his mind, Ben said, "That's too much to put on a kid. When I was fourteen, you'd be crazy to trust me with a lemonade stand. I'd rob the till and throw the lemons at cars."

Valerie and Ralph locked eyes and exchanged a quick smile. They had wasted a weekend together trying to sell lemonade when they were nine years old.

"Enough with the bad vibes," Damon said, standing up and walking over to a cabinet built into the wall. "Since I have you here, I'm not wasting the opportunity." He scanned the contents of several drawers before pulling out a hard plastic case, too big to be a regular comic book. Tossing it into Ralph's lap, Damon asked, "Mind signing this for me?"

Ben laughed. "Son of a bitch!"

Ralph could not believe his eyes. He held one of the original photocopied issues of the first *Meta Boy*. The crooked staples were unmistakable. A few bootlegs had been brought to his attention over the years, but he hadn't seen one of his and Valerie's copies since high school. Teachers had confiscated the majority the week they were made, and most of the surviving copies were thrown away when everyone found out Ralph was "just a tracer."

Ralph pulled out the Sharpie marker he used at conventions and looked the case over, trying to figure out how to open it.

"Sign it on the case, please," Damon said. Valerie stifled a laugh.

"Oh, of course," Ralph said, grinning. "This is surreal, me giving Damon Ripley an autograph. Want me to personalize it?"

"That would be great."

"For my good friend, Damon Ripley," Ralph said as he wrote. "Do you want Val to sign it too? She was the publisher, after all."

"Oh, no, I couldn't," Valerie said.

"Come on," Ben said. "You owe it to history."

"I'm afraid I must insist," Damon said.

"Tell you what," she said. "You put something good in my auction, I'll sign anything you want."

"That I will not do," Damon said. "I gave you everything I could bring myself to part with the last time."

"No deal," Valerie said, putting the cap back on the marker. Ben and Ralph booed.

Damon leaned forward in his chair. "What if I emcee it for you?"

Valerie rolled her eyes. "You wouldn't."

"I would."

She smiled and pulled the cap off the marker with her teeth. Ben and Ralph cheered from the peanut gallery as Valerie signed her name under Ralph's. *Valerie Hall, Publisher.*

Accepting the comic from her, Damon smiled broadly. "This is a momentous occasion for me. It gives this tired old actor hope that one day I'll find everything on my want list."

"Not this again," Ben said. "You're never going to find them, Damon, they don't exist."

Valerie raised an eyebrow.

Damon began to speak, but Ben cut him off with a dramatic groan.

"What?" Ralph asked. "You've got to have one of every comic worth having. I heard you have two copies of *Adventure Comics* number forty, for Christ's sake."

"When it came to the first appearance of the Sandman, I didn't know if I needed that or the 1939 *New York World's Fair Comics*, so I had to have both. Then I found a nicer copy. But I only have one *Adventure* forty now, thanks to Valerie and her damned charity auctions." Damon turned to an annoyed Valerie and said, "I know you did a lot of good with the money. I just can't believe I let you talk me out of the prettier copy."

"Just tell us what the hell you're talking about," she said.

Damon Ripley smiled, his eyes grim. "There are certain comic books out there that are so rare, many claim they do not even exist."

"Because they don't, you egomaniac!" Ben said. "It's an urban legend, like Walt Disney's cryogenically frozen head. It's all nonsense and rumor."

"Hush. Stories differ, but most accounts agree that, in the early 1940s, a minor company called Pithos Publishing tried to jump on the superhero bandwagon. They put out a few issues, but they didn't sell in large numbers."

Ben stopped trying to hold in his words. "Don't listen to him, you guys. I have put hundreds of hours into trying to find these books for him. You'd be better off finding a copy of Jerry Lewis's *The Day the Clown Cried*. Pithos Publishing never published a damn thing because Pithos Publishing never existed."

"Pithos existed," Damon said. "But after putting out only a handful of issues, they closed their doors. Forever."

"Valerie, have you ever heard of them?" Ben asked.

"No, but that doesn't mean much. I deal mostly with making the 78 RPM Comic Book Back Issues and Distribution Company look good on the internet. There are comics I love to read, but I'm not much into the spandex circus."

Damon waved his hand at Ralph. "How about you, Meta Boy? You ever hear of these guys?"

"Sorry, buddy. I have a passing knowledge of most Golden Age publishers, not just National and Timely and the other guys that became Marvel and DC. But Pithos Publishing doesn't ring any bells."

"See?" Ben asked. "I told you, man. You're tilting at four-color windmills."

"They're real. I know it. You're the best buyer I know, but just because you couldn't find them doesn't mean they're not out there somewhere."

"What kind of stuff did they publish?" Valerie asked.

"All heroes," Damon said. "No war comics, no cowboys, no romance. Just adventurers in funny costumes punching bad guys in the face."

Ralph leaned forward from the couch. "But what makes them so great?"

Ben pounded the desk with his fist several times in succession. "Great job, Ripley. Now you've got them doing it. Congrats, you've spread your madness."

"Ignore him," Damon said. "Ralph, these comics are said to be the greatest hidden gems of the Golden Age. The characters, art, and story were decades ahead of their time."

"But it sounds like no one has really seen them," Ralph said. "I don't get it. You could read all day every day for years and not read all the best comics out there. Why get wrapped up in these old books? There's no way they could live up to your crazy expectations."

Damon leaned back in his chair, kicked his feet up on his desk and stared up at his ceiling. "It's hard to explain. When you have enough money, you can buy everything you ever wanted. So you build your dream house, and you buy your dream car. You buy a full run of *Action Comics* and read it like you're twelve years old again. But eventually you run out of things that get your blood pumping."

He sat up. "You need a grail, Ralph. You need a quest, even if it never comes to fruition. I don't care if I'm tilting at windmills like Ben said. Don Quixote was a bad ass." His eyes glazed over. "I want to hold them in my hands one time. Read them—hell, just smell them—just one time. It's something to dream about when all my other rock-and-roll dreams have already come true."

Ralph, who'd once had his dreams come true for a brief time, understood. *The comic industry runs on nostalgia,* he thought. *The buzz from the discovery would be incredible. My old fans might even give me another chance. It's been long enough, hasn't it?*

And the Pithos copyrights are probably expired, so I could pitch a series using all the characters. 'Man Unearths and Resurrects Forgotten Heroes.' The news story writes itself. This could be my opportunity to change everything.

Damon turned to Valerie. "Once I'm done, you could auction them off. How does that strike you?"

"That's great, Damon. Let me add them to my list. I'll add an asterisk, like I did with the mermaid's tears and that piece of the true cross."

"I'll find them," Ralph said. His body felt lighter than air, and his scalp and brain tingled. Ecstasy wiggled down his spine. It felt like a religious epiphany. "I'll find them for you."

I'll find them and become a legend, he thought.

"Attaboy," Damon said, raising his glass.

13

RALPH CURSED HIMSELF for being surprised when he hit a dead end right away.

Leaning back in his chair, he stared at the ceiling. "Fuck a duck."

He sat at the modest computer desk in the room he had converted into a home art studio. Jumbled papers, empty coffee cups, and books covered every surface in the studio, including the old garage sale drafting table which he had never replaced. Torn sticky notes stuck out of the books' pages, marking nothing of real importance. He sipped his coffee and grimaced when he realized it was cold and stale.

As good a sign as any that it's time for a break, Ralph thought. He carried the cup to the kitchen and poured it out in the sink. His stomach churned at the smell.

Unlike Ralph's studio, the rest of his house in Austin was a bright, open place. An original Laurette Patten pastel from the 1920s hung on the wall in the living room. In the picture, a beautiful woman dressed in the tight white-and-red attire of a fox hunter leaned casually on a stone wall, her braided hair curling over her shoulder. The woman's back arched in a way that never failed to draw Ralph's eye.

Ralph's girlfriend, Sandra, walked into the room, wearing her black gym outfit. It was eerie how much Sandra looked like the fox hunter hanging on the wall, but he supposed that's why she bought it. Sandra leaned against the couch, looking even more like the pastel woman than usual. Ralph felt dizzy, and not in a good way.

"You coming with, sweetie?" she asked.

"Not today, sorry. I'm working on that thing. The mystery comics."

She rolled her eyes. "Still?"

"It could be a big deal if I find them. Trust me, it will be worth it when they turn up."

"Whatever you say, sweetie." Sandra kissed him on the cheek. "I can't believe you met Damon Ripley. I had such a crush on him in *Very Important Person*. Just grab a shower, you're stinking up the place."

Ralph lifted his shirt collar and sniffed. "Sound advice. Have fun at the gym." He watched her body move in the snug workout clothes as she walked out of the room. The front door opened and closed behind her.

In the bedroom he put his wallet and other pocket treasures on the dresser and shed his clothes. Turning on the water, he remembered to put everything in the hamper; Sandra was particular about clothes on the floor. As he gathered up his socks, he found a crisp business card. *Must have fallen out of my wallet,* he thought. Valerie Hall's name shined in embossed letters. Beneath her contact information, she had written her personal number in purple ink.

Climbing in the shower, the hot water knocked loose a recent memory.

14

THE SUN SHONE TOO BRIGHTLY the morning after Damon Ripley's party. Ralph, Ben, and Valerie stepped over a stormtrooper sleeping in the doorway. Along with Damon, they had talked the night away. It reminded Ralph of sleepovers when he was a kid, when he and his friends would lie in their sleeping bags and talk about girls and parents and who was faster, Flash or Superman. It was strange to make a connection so quickly with strangers. *Except for Valerie,* he thought. *She's no stranger.* As the four spoke business, life, and everything, he'd caught her looking at him several times. Or she had caught him looking at her; it was impossible to know which. Damon went to bed when the sun came up, and the three of them stood in front of his house, blinking and squinting their eyes at the sun.

"You guys want to grab some breakfast or something?" Ralph asked.

Ben shook his head. "Got to get on the road. I pay someone to take care of my dad when I'm away, and if I don't get back she'll never work for me again. You kids have fun." He turned to leave, and Ralph thought he saw the man wink at him.

Ralph turned to Valerie, "So, how about it?"

She frowned. "I need to get going too. I have a lot to do before Monday. But it was great seeing you again, Ralph. It really was." She pulled a card and pen from her purse and scribbled something. Handing him the card, she said, "Call me if you find Damon's comics. Or for whatever."

While he debated giving her a goodbye hug, she walked away.

15

RALPH HAD A TROUBLED RELATIONSHIP with the internet. If the comic press destroyed him in his teens, the vocal online detractors tore him apart, burned the pieces, and removed his name from the historical record. His mom had cried when she heard about the Usenet newsgroup dedicated to him, alt.ralphrogers.die.die.die.

Wikipedia made no mention of Pithos, and no one was selling any back issues on eBay, Mile High Comics, 78 RPM, or anywhere else. CGC, The Certified Guaranteed Company, had never graded an issue in mint, near mint, or any other condition. Searching Google for Pithos Publishing brought up only rumors.

"Anyone know anything about Pithos Comics?" wrote user KirbyLives in a forum post from five years ago. "I've always heard they're the best books written in the Golden Age of the thirties and forties, but no one knows where to find them. A little help here?" KirbyLives received no answer.

In the archives of an inactive forum, Ralph found his first ray of hope.

"I used to hit garage sales, flea markets, that kind of thing every weekend. I was at one of these swap meets, probably in 1975, and found a box of comics. I wasn't really into comics at the time, so I left them behind. My friend was into old stuff like the Justice Society, so I told him about it. He went to check them out but they were already gone. He asked me what the titles were, I said it was a company that I didn't recognize. When I said Pithos, he about had a stroke. Started swearing at me, the whole bit. We didn't hang out much after that."

Can't go to the DA with that evidence, kid, Ralph thought. *Might be time to call in a consult.*

He sifted through the piles on his desk until he found his cell phone.

"Quarter Ben Comics," a voice answered.

"Ben?" Ralph asked.

"Yes?" The voice sounded doubtful.

Great, he won't remember me, Ralph thought. "Ben, it's Ralph. From Damon's party. We met at the Oklahoma convention?"

"Oh, Ralph," Ben said. "Good to hear from you, man. Catch up on your sleep yet?"

"Trying to. You get back okay? How's your dad?"

"Every day is pretty much the same for him," Ben chuckled. "We're good. What's up?"

"I actually called to ask you about Damon's mystery books. The Pithos comics."

Ben sighed. "Ralph, don't waste your time."

"I'm just having fun looking."

"Fun is all you're going to get out of it, I'm sorry to say. Wasted so much of my damn time looking for those books. You think I have billable hours? In this business, you sell no comics, you make no money."

"Did you ever find anything at all? I found some guy—"

"The swap meet dude? Fuck that guy," Ben said. "You try getting a hold of him?"

"He didn't answer me, but I wasn't surprised. His profile says he hasn't signed on for years."

"That's the whole problem, Ralph. No one really knows anything. I've heard that damn swap meet story at a dozen conventions. People tell it like it happened to them. You get me? It's all bullshit urban legend. Like Bloody Mary or *Polybius*."

"What's *Polybius*?"

Ben laughed. "Supposed to be an arcade game from the eighties. The story is that these machines popped up in Oregon, right? Everyone lined up to play the thing, because it was addictive or something. Then men in black showed up to take all the machines away, and no one's seen it since. People say it was the government testing mind control."

"Crazy," Ralph said.

"No, just an urban legend. Like the Pithos comics. They don't exist. When I tried to find them for Damon, I came up with zip. You won't find anything because there's nothing to find. Damon's a good guy, but he is full of shit on this. Even his movie star money can't buy something that doesn't exist."

"Okay. Understood. Sorry to bug you about this."

Ben's tone lightened again. "You're not bugging me. It's just frustrating when you're used to finding things so easily. It's like the damn cardboard Polaris submarine from that Honor House mail-order company. They advertised that thing in the front cover of every comic book for thirty years. There should be a million of them out there, but I can't find one to buy. I've never even *seen* one except for one faded Polaroid. It's enough to put you in the loony bin."

"I do feel ready for some rest and relaxation in a padded cell."

"Tell you what, email me your con schedule. Maybe we can meet up, talk about some real comics. That cool with you?"

"Definitely. And I'll send you my wish list."

"Pleasant dreams, Ralph. And seriously, get out of the house tomorrow, do something healthy. If those books ever existed, they don't anymore. Some things just disappear, like those stupid cardboard submarines. Good night."

Night? Ralph thought, ending the call. He stood up, his back creaking, and walked to a window. Pulling aside the curtain, he saw it was, sure enough, after dark.

How long was I in that chair today?

He couldn't remember.

I need to give this up. If I don't get some painting done tomorrow, I'm going to have some pissed-off clients.

The next day, he ordered every book he could find that might mention Pithos Publishing.

16

RALPH'S BOXES ARRIVED IN BATCHES each day. He pored over comic book price guides, self-proclaimed "complete" encyclopedias of characters and publishers, and books detailing the history of the Golden Age. There was no mention of Pithos anywhere.

He spent three paintings' worth of money on a huge collection of early comic fanzines. These amateur publications, made using typewriters and mimeographs, were distributed by the first generation of comic fans in the forties and fifties. The art ranged from the crude to the impressive, and there were lists of character appearances, essays, and fan fiction. Ralph nearly forgot his quest as he gently turned the pages of each staple-bound offering. People still made zines, of course, but the internet had taken most of the audience. He felt like a historian, scrutinizing old newspapers and personal journals.

As he neared the bottom of the stack, he read a line that made him drop the zine: "Page 38: Spotlight on Pithos Publishing. Relive the adventures of Danny Drastic and more!"

With a shaking hand, he picked the zine up from the floor. Flipping back and forth through the pages, he grew confused.

The pages were torn out, leaving only scraps of paper jammed under the staples.

The zine's yellowing pages crinkled in his fists.

He took a deep breath and relaxed his hands. Smoothing out the pages, he studied the fanzine. *Gutter Trash,* "Vol. 12 Num. 1," was cover-dated November 1954 and contained only plain text. The zine lacked any author or publisher information, though words such as "colour" and "humour" pointed to it being printed outside the United States.

There was no mention of *Gutter Trash* on the list of zines he bought, so he emailed the seller. He received an answer within a few minutes: "Sorry about the condition. Just an extra book I threw in as a bonus. No idea where it came from."

Resting his head on the cool desk, he thought, *I will not rest until I kill the person who tore up that stupid fanzine.*

His eyes settled on the considerable *World Encyclopedia of Comics*, edited by Maurice Horn. "More disappointment?" he asked the quiet office. "There's always room for more disappointment!"

He lifted the heavy, tattered tome to his lap and flipped through the book, muttering out loud. "Barks, Carl. Captain Midnight. Crepax, Guido. Daredevil. Dan Dare." His jaw dropped. "Danny Drastic. Son of a bitch."

DANNY DRASTIC (U.S.) Written and drawn by Vance Robeson, Danny Drastic was the titular character of the **DANNY DRASTIC** anthology series from Pithos Publishing. The first issue is dated November 1940, and this appears to be the character's first appearance. Drastic rode on the popularity of pulp sci-fi strips like Buck Rogers and Flash Gordon, although he fell more squarely into the superhero style. The time-traveling adventurer journeyed from the distant future to stop Professor Savant, another time traveler, from destroying the present. The goggled hero's arsenal included a rocket pack and the Atomic Disintegrator, a ray gun that made inanimate matter disappear.

Like other comic books of the time, the series contained ten other stories in each issue. Issue 3 had Drastic pop up in another story to help a robot named Potbelly defeat the Ocularist, an absurd villain wearing a giant eyeball helmet. Only four issues were published before Pithos folded, and Danny Drastic is mainly remembered today for inspiring the Hubley Atomic Disintegrator, a metal cap gun sought by collectors and used as a prop in the 1959 film **TEENAGERS FROM OUTER SPACE**.

Ralph's heart hammered in his chest. He was looking for the Pot-belly article when a phone call interrupted him.

"Ralph? It's Reese. Where the hell are you?"

"Hey there, Frank," Ralph said.

"You're late. I'm at the gallery."

"What are you talking about? I'm not supposed to deliver this stuff until Friday."

"It is Friday, kid."

Ralph checked the calendar on his computer. Somehow he had lost a day. *Did I sleep last night?* he asked himself.

"Forget to wind your watch?" Reese asked.

"Everything's already loaded," he lied. "I'll be there in thirty."

17

CCORDING TO THE DASHBOARD CLOCK, he arrived thirty-eight minutes after the call ended. Reese waited for him on the loading dock. He dropped his cigarette and crushed it under his shoe as Ralph pulled up.

"You look like shit, kid," Reese said.

"Give me a break and grab a painting." Ralph handed him a foam-wrapped canvas.

After a few trips back and forth, they unwrapped each of the paintings and leaned them against a wall. With a mixture of satisfaction and anxiety, Ralph looked over his usual styles of pop art and futurist nostalgia.

Frank looked up and down the row. "You were only supposed to bring in twelve pieces. Why'd you bring thirteen?"

Ralph rolled his eyes. "I brought twelve. I've had the lineup for this thing planned for weeks."

"Did they not teach you counting at art school? Wait, sorry, did you go to art school? I can never remember. Hey, what's this one called?"

Frank picked up a portrait. Ralph had never seen it before, but it looked like his style. Staring out from the canvas was a man in an old-fashioned maroon suit and bow tie, standing on what looked like a vaudeville stage. His hands gripped a shiny black cane. Instead of a head, the man wore a helmet that looked like an enormous eyeball. On top of the giant blue-eyed orb was a matching top hat.

"That's not mine," Ralph said. "It must have already been here."

"If it isn't yours, someone is forging for you," Reese said. He pointed to the bottom corner, where the name Ralph Rogers was signed in Ralph's style: garish Rs with the rest of the letters cowering beneath.

Ralph took the painting and examined it. "Huh." Everything about the painting said that he had done it, but he had never seen it before. On the back, someone—apparently Ralph's doppelganger—had written in pencil: *The Ocularist.*

His stomach clenched. "That is really weird."

"What?" Reese asked.

"Nothing," he said, putting the painting back in place. "I just got confused for a minute."

Reese stepped back and looked at the row of paintings. "Striking work, as always. I'll talk to the organizer. I'm sure they can fit in your Optometrist."

"Ocularist."

"Whatever," Frank said, waving his hand. "Kid, I think you're going to make some money. But you really do look terrible." He pulled out his wallet and handed Ralph a crumpled fifty-dollar bill. "Get yourself cleaned up and eat some real food. Try not to sleep through the opening, okay?"

But Ralph didn't hear him. He was staring into the carbon-black pupil of the Ocularist.

18

BACK HOME, RALPH FELT BETTER than he had in weeks. His show held the slimmest chance of being the massive opportunity that Reese claimed it to be. But finding a breakthrough in his search for the mystery comics gave Ralph a buzz like a kid's first cigarette.

I'll be interviewed for sure, he thought. *When I find the comics. All the comic bloggers will want to hear about this, and then the big comic news sites. With all the superhero stuff in the media, I might even end up talking to real journalists.*

Before the tracing scandal, Ralph had been a guest on *Good Morning America,* and they planned to get him on the late-night talk shows after his movie deal. Afterwards, his shame was not even worth a joke in Leno's monologue. The ride from recognition to infamy to anonymity was faster than Professor Zoom.

These thoughts disappeared as he walked into his office. A sterile, chemical smell stung his nostrils, and he stared at the room in shock. Everything was clean. His books and papers were gone.

"Don't be mad," said a voice behind him.

Ralph spun around to face Sandra.

He tried to keep his voice steady. "What did you do?"

"Honey, I'm worried about you. You never leave the house. I'm the only one in the bed most nights."

"You know how I can get," he replied. "I'm trying to be an artist here!"

"Then why aren't you painting? I keep getting calls because you're forgetting to pay the bills. You skipped out on a convention. We haven't had sex in months."

"What did you do?" he repeated. His head felt warm, like his brain was working too hard.

"I cleaned up. If you want to keep playing artist, you need to concentrate on money coming in. What if you'd missed this show, huh? You think Frank is going to keep wasting his time on you, out of the goodness of his heart?" Sandra sighed and brushed the hair out of her face. "Your Meta Boy money is almost gone. So, I cleaned up for you. With the distractions out of the way, you can get back to doing what's best for you. For us."

"Where'd you put the books?" He was burning up now, and the encroaching headache made him squint. "There was a huge book, an encyclopedia. Where is it?"

"I put everything out by the curb with a big 'Free' sign. I finished cleaning, and when I looked outside, it was all gone."

Ralph glared at her, his eyes brimming with the threat of rage or tears. "Do you have any idea—"

"I don't want to hear it," she said. "I did you a favor, and if you can't see that—"

"Get out," he said, defeated.

"What?"

"Pack a bag. Get out of my house. You can come back for your stuff. Just get out."

"Ralph, you're acting crazy."

Behind her, the fox hunter portrait shimmered in Ralph's vision. Again, the sudden similarity between Sandra and the woman in the painting gave him vertigo.

He turned his back on her.

"Fine!" she screamed. "But if you think I'll give a shit when they come to haul you off, you're *already* out of your fucking mind!"

"I'll be back in an hour." He walked out the door. "Please don't be here."

WHEN RALPH RETURNED HOME for the second time that night, he found his front door unlocked. The fox hunter painting was gone, as was the television. *How'd she even fit all that in her car?* he wondered. Sandra's closet was cleared out; even the stacks of empty shoeboxes were gone.

It's like she had someone on call for when she left. How many trucks could she fill with all her stuff?

His studio held another surprise. The smashed computer monitor was scattered across the floor. *Thank God she didn't smash the actual computer. Or drown it in the bathtub.*

But Ralph knew she still cared a little. His art supplies, paintings, and the rest of his studio remained untouched.

He sat in his chair, brushing aside pieces of broken glass with his shoe. Pulling out his cell phone, he called Ben.

"Hello?" said a tired voice in Utah.

"Ben, it's Ralph. Do you have a copy of *The World Encyclopedia of Comics*? I need you to looks something up."

"Ralph? It's two in the morning. What's going on?"

"Sorry. My computer is off, so I forgot to check the clock. So, do you have it?"

"What?"

"*World Encyclopedia of Comics.* Maurice Horn. Huge fucker, like a hardcover big-print phonebook."

"Dammit. Give me a minute, I might have one in the garage. This better be good."

Ralph's forehead pounded. *Where did you go while she moved out, Ralph?* he asked himself. He remembered walking up and down aisles in a store.

Ben picked up his phone. "Okay, got it. I forgot how heavy this thing is. What am I looking up?"

"Danny Drastic."

"Danny Drastic," he said. "Okay. Danny Drastic. Danny. Nope. It goes straight from Danny Dingle to Daredevil. It's not under Drastic, Danny, either."

Ralph tried to swallow, but a lump blocked his throat. "Are you sure?"

"I know my alphabet, Ralph. What's the deal here?"

Ralph rubbed his forehead with his hand. "It was there, in the book. The mystery comics. It talked about Drastic, and this villain, the Ocularist."

"There's nothing here now. Are you sure?"

"I didn't see it the first time. It wasn't until—"

"Wait, wait, wait. It wasn't there?"

"I don't know. I found the name mentioned in some fanzine. *Gutter Trash.*"

"Never heard of it. Who published it?"

"It didn't say. My girlfriend—I mean, my *ex*-girlfriend—she threw out the zine, the book, everything."

The line was silent for several seconds. "Let me get this straight," Ben said. "Everywhere else, you came up empty, right?"

"Right."

"And the only evidence you had, other than that bullshit on the internet, was this book and the magazine. Right?"

"Right."

"And now they're gone."

"Wait a second—"

"Ralph, you know how this sounds, don't you? You said 'ex-girlfriend.' Did she leave you?"

"Tonight. We've been downhill for a while, though."

"All right. Buddy, you need to get a grip on yourself, and I'm not just saying that because you interrupted my beauty sleep. It sounds like you've gone too far in a few places. You're like Doctor Doom raging over Reed Richards. I'm not saying you saw something that wasn't there. I'm not saying you're crazy—"

"Goodbye, Ben."

"Ralph, wait!"

Ralph hung up the phone.

BENTERLUDE

BEN WALKER CLOSED THE HEAVY ENCYCLOPE-
DIA and turned out the light. He stared into the darkness of his house and sighed. "Ralph, buddy," he said to
the empty kitchen, "you're cracking up." He had just reached his
room when the yelling started.

"Ben!" his father yelled from his bedroom. "Ben!"

"Thanks a million, Ralph," Ben grumbled, walking down
the hall.

"Who was that on the phone?" David Walker asked.

"Just a friend, Dad," Ben said. He sat down in the chair beside
the hospital-style bed. "He didn't realize how late it was. I'm sorry."

"It wasn't your mother?" David asked.

"No, it wasn't Mom," Ben said. Monica Walker had been dead
for six years.

"That's too bad," David said. "I've been waiting for her
to call."

"Me too. I promise to let you know if she calls. Tomorrow's
going to be a long day. Mind if I get back to bed?"

"Will you help me first?" David asked. "I made a mess of the bed."

"Sure. Let me grab the sheets and I'll get you cleaned up."

There were no clean sheets in the hall closet. As he dug in the clothes dryer, he felt a pang of annoyance. He pushed it away.

In his late teens, when Ben came out to his parents, it was his father who had never turned his back on him. David had helped Monica through the initial shock. Ben thought of the frustration his friends had gone through, and he always smiled at the thought of David saying, "That was brave of you to tell me," and giving Ben a hug.

Ben took the clean sheets to his father's room and started cleaning up his father and making the bed.

As Ben fought with the clean fitted sheet, his father said, "Son, I want you to know, I appreciate this. And I don't mind if you need to get me out of your house."

"It's no big deal. Let me just—"

"I mean it. You shouldn't have to do this at your age. You deserve a life of your own."

Looking into David's eyes, Ben realized his father was having a lucid moment. It was the first in some time; they were getting few and far between.

Ben smiled. "I don't know about you, old man, but my daddy taught me to never turn my back on someone I love. If you want to move out, go ahead, but you'll be carrying your own bags. Okay?"

But the moment was gone. "Ben, who was that on the phone? Did your mother call?"

"Not yet, Dad." Ben fluffed his father's pillow. "You'll know when she does."

20

'M NOT THINKING RATIONALLY. Ralph sank into his chair, and the cell phone fell from his hand, bouncing off the wood floor.

If I were myself, I would be worried. That means I should be worried, right? Maybe I should call someone Ask for help.

The first face to float into his mind belonged to Valerie.

You've seen Valerie once in, what, fifteen years? You had one admittedly lengthy conversation with her, but now she's replacing your support system?

"What support system?" he asked the dark studio. He considered calling his parents, but that relationship was strained enough. Calling his agent would be as good as begging to be dropped as a client. He'd met all his other friends, acquaintances really, through Sandra. Those bridges were burned now.

Ben was right. He was seeing things that most likely were not there. *And if you can't trust your eyes, what can you trust?*

And who painted the Ocularist?

The question rang out in his consciousness, but there was no clear answer. Ralph painted enough that it was not altogether impossible that he could forget a specific piece. But what about that title written on the back? *The Ocularist.* The same name he'd read in the book.

Or thought you read, Ralph reminded himself. He shook his head. *Sleep will help. I'll go to sleep, wake up in a few days. Call Sandra, apologize. I can still fix this.*

He slid out of his chair and searched the floor for his cell phone, which had slid under the desk. On his hands and knees, he checked the phone to make sure it was undamaged. The light from the little screen lit up pieces of paper beneath the mess of cords and dust bunnies under the desk.

Gutter Trash, read the header on the fanzine.

Ralph smiled.

21

THE CITY OF GREENVALE stretched out beneath a dreary sky, a tiny ocean of older homes, mom-and-pop businesses, and crafter's malls. Ralph fiddled with the radio of his car, settling on a temporary soundtrack of seventies prog rock.

The GPS told him to turn right, but there was no road.

"Par for the course," he said to no one.

The escape from his studio began with an edit.

An online search for defunct comic book publishers had brought up the cache of a deleted wiki article. It mentioned a company that had disappeared in the early forties, whose books deteriorated due to inferior paper used in their printing. Over time, the comics dissolved unless stored in a climate-controlled environment. Collectors would open a box to find nothing but a gooey mess. The user responsible for the article was called "Epimetheus." The name stirred something in Ralph, so he looked it up.

Epimetheus was the brother of Prometheus, the man who stole fire from Olympus. As punishment, Zeus gave Pandora, the first woman, to Epimetheus. The couple were also given a gift, a container eventually known as Pandora's Box. The container was actually a large jar, called a *pithos*.

Holy cannoli, Ralph thought. *This joker knows about Pithos Publishing.*

The dissolving comics explained why he couldn't find any hard evidence. And, if the books were no longer extant in the collectors' sphere, no one would be writing about them.

He sent Epimetheus a private message, but received no reply.

Searching comic forums for users named Epimetheus brought up another hit, this time a profile with an actual name: Elliot Chill.

Contact info for three Elliot Chills showed up on search engines, and one of them was dead. Of the two remaining, one was a dentist. The other sold publishing equipment.

No one at Chill's company answered the phone, so Ralph climbed in his Mini coupe and drove fourteen hours straight to Greenvale. Caffeine pills from the gas station had kept him driving all night, and the GPS told him he neared his prize.

"Your destination is on the left in one hundred feet," said the robotic female voice.

Ralph slowed the car and looked around. On his right was a Crap Cruncher recycling center. The location indicated by the GPS was a vacant lot. He screamed, pounding the steering wheel so that the horn blurted a high staccato.

I went looking for Pandora's Box, he thought, *but it's empty.*

Ralph collapsed in his seat. He cried, hard and loud, appalled at the sound.

"What did you expect to find?" he asked himself.

"Oh, the answer to all my prayers," he answered. "A pile of priceless comics. My ticket to get back in the game. Or something that told me I was on the right track, I hadn't wasted all that time. I needed justification for imploding my life. But there's nothing. Nothing at all."

A man from Crap Cruncher had walked outside and was watching Ralph talk to himself.

Ralph put the Mini into drive and sped away, driving until he found an old diner still serving breakfast. *Saddle Bags,* an old Western buddy comedy starring Damon Ripley, appeared on a wall-mounted television. Ralph had seen it a hundred times, with Ripley and Eddie Murphy playing two cowboys. In the current scene, they argued over who had to be the ass end of a horse costume. With his energy sucked dry from driving and caffeine abuse, Ralph ordered a meal of pancakes, eggs, sausage, and hash browns.

The greasy food rejuvenated him. Ralph thanked his waitress and slid out of the booth. As he paid, he debated what to do next. The urge to paint sat in the back of his mind, but he felt his business in Greenvale was unfinished. "You got a phonebook?" The cashier pulled a coffee-stained yellow book from beneath the counter.

Scanning the white pages, he found a listing for an Elliot Chill, Jr., who still lived in Greenvale. Ralph started to tear the page out like they do in the movies, but pulled out a pen instead. *Let's see if the name disappears when it's in my own writing,* he thought and grinned. The woman behind the counter looked at him oddly and smiled back. Embarrassed, Ralph thanked her and walked to his car.

The GPS led him to a drab house with an overgrown lawn. The picket fence had once been white, but was now a dull gray. Ralph approached the door, his heart beating fast. It reminded him of door-to-door fundraiser sales when he was a kid. Cold calling made him sick to his stomach. He pushed the cracked doorbell button and waited. When no one answered, he knocked. The door creaked open.

"Hello?" he called into the dark house. His feet betrayed him by walking a few steps into the front hallway. "Mr. Chill? Hello? My name is Ralph Rogers. Mr. Chill?"

The inside of the house, furnished like the home of an older gentleman living alone, appeared much tidier than the outside. The living room contained a couch and an easy chair. An open humidor sat next to a marble ashtray on the coffee table. On the table was an open copy of *The Land of Laughs*, turned facedown to save the reader's place. A cigar had been extinguished on the wood floor by the pool of blood.

Next to the cigar was, Ralph assumed, Mr. Elliot Chill, Jr. His body, clothed in a velvet bathrobe and pajama pants, lay face down on the floor. One of his slippers remained on his foot, the other stuck out from beneath the chair.

The back of his head was gone, and blood covered much of the table, chair, and floor. Ralph eyes darted around the room, not for a killer but for a gun. The dried blood and the empty feel of the house convinced Ralph that Chill had been shot in the head some time ago.

Before Ralph realized what he was doing, he was ransacking the house. He flung open every cabinet and closet and dumped the contents of drawers out on the carpet.

He might have given up, but attacking a bookcase revealed a hidden closet. Ralph pulled down the bookcase, sending loose shelves and books crashing to the floor.

The closet contained a metal case, like a safety deposit box. It was locked and refused to slide open. Ralph returned to the living room but hesitated a moment before searching Chill's pockets. As the body rolled to its side, dark ooze dripped from the head onto the floor. The smell of death was overwhelming. Despite himself, Ralph looked into Chill's empty, staring eyes. A key dangled around the corpse's neck by a silver chain. Pushing his nausea aside, Ralph released the clasp.

The key fit the lock and Ralph peeked inside the case. The words *Pithos Publishing* and a bold, ten-cent cover price were all he needed. Leaving the door wide open behind him, he climbed in his car and drove away.

Five minutes later, he called 911. A woman asked, "What is the nature of your emergency?"

Ralph tried to talk, but nothing came out. He looked in the seat next to him at the metal case.

How are you going to explain yourself? a voice asked. *Your fingerprints are on every surface in that house, Ralph. You just robbed a dead man, probably a murder victim. Your name is all over the internet, trying to find this guy. You even touched the body. Who will they think killed him?*

"Hello?" the 911 operator repeated.

"Nothing, sorry," he said. "My mistake."

THE DORK AGE

1

THE TRANCE RALPH EXPERIENCED in Chill's home lingered, even after he checked into the motel. He sat on the papery comforter of the bed, donned the latex gloves he had purchased at the drug store, and slid one of the comics out of the metal case.

His gloved hands shaking, he held the magazine: *Danny Drastic* #1, November, 1940. Cover price, ten cents. The book was in immaculate condition, as perfect as the day it was printed. Unlike modern comics, where a reader is lucky to have twenty pages of story, these Golden Age issues contained fifty to eighty pages, with a variety of comic stories, text pieces, games, and gag cartoons. In the upper right-hand corner was the Pithos Publishing logo, a black vase with a narrow bottom and a wide body. At the top of the vase was a narrow neck and two short handles.

Ralph struggled with the consequences of opening a comic book in such perfect condition; each turn of a page could devalue the book hundreds or even thousands of dollars. It might be a one-of-a-kind, a unicorn. The internet rumor concerning dissolving comic books seemed plausible.

But the desire to *know* took over, and he opened the book to find a grinning Danny Drastic wearing flight goggles, a leather pilot's jacket, and a rocket pack. Holding his Atomic Disintegrator, all knobs and dials and shiny red grips, Danny climbed into the cockpit of an Art Deco space rocket. "Ready to join me in my adventures, chum?" he asked.

"I am ready," Ralph said aloud.

At first he read the funny book like a scholar, studying each panel for its ink, pencils, and composition. But soon the stories took over, and his eyes raced in anticipation of the next electrifying ordeal.

Each story was greater than the sum of its parts; a thousand impossible things happened every ten pages. A friendship could spark, grow, and even end in betrayal; worlds were created and destroyed; true love was ignited and lost, only to be found again.

In the first issue of *Danny Drastic,* not only did Danny battle Professor Savant, but Alan Den and his Genie traveled in time, and Potbelly the Mechanical Man fought Nazis in the Hollow Earth. In *Tales of the Sensational*, the Channeler used his ghosts to stop the Hell Binder, and Oceanus, the alien from beyond Neptune, continued on Earth a centuries-long feud with the bodiless Plutonians.

He found three more issues of *Danny Drastic* in the box. Other comic books were there too, with titles like *Frightful Funnies* and *Red-Blooded American Adventure.* All were filled with heroes and villains, titanic battles and secret civilizations. Ralph could not have been happier if he'd discovered the lost Library of Alexandria—which happened to be the home of Songweaver in *Tales of the Sensational.*

Continuity developed across the stories; Songweaver fought the Channeler's Hell Binder, and Danny Drastic had a cameo in a Potbelly story. The two heroes joined forces against the Ocularist. It wasn't the Human Torch battling the Submariner, but it was noticeable. The series combined to create a vibrant world.

The stories were dated, sexist, and occasionally racist, but the comics were still ahead of their time.

And the Ocularist looked exactly as Ralph had painted him.

Ralph didn't leave the motel for two days, living off vending machines until his momentum with rereading the Pithos comics finally slowed. Still, the thought of using his phone terrified him, and the motel's internet connection was terrible. That night he left the comics in their case and decided to venture out.

A sign in the window of a local coffee shop proclaimed, *We have FREE WI-FI!* Ralph carried in his laptop bag and ordered a venti coffee, plus the two biggest muffins in the display case. Sitting down in a secluded booth, he searched to see if he was wanted for murder and was surprised to find no report of the death in any of the area papers, which meant no mention of the infamous killer Ralph Rogers in connection with any crime. He took a chance and turned on his cell phone. No messages.

Chill's address, he remembered, and reached into his pocket for the slip of paper. Before he could curse himself for holding onto such a damning piece of evidence, he looked down at the crumpled piece of paper. Blank

What's happening?

His phone buzzed. Ralph held his breath and looked at the screen, but it was only Frank Reese.

"Hello?"

"How the hell are ya?" Reese asked.

"Um," Ralph said.

"Okay, then, *where* the hell are ya? You're missing your show!"

Ralph slapped his forehead. "I am *so* sorry. I got caught up in something."

"Kid, I don't care. I just wanted to give you the good news."

"Good news?"

"You know your eyeball guy painting?"

"Ocularist. He's the Ocularist."

"What? Doesn't matter. I've never seen anything like it. Whatever you planned to sell it for, you need to add a zero. Every other painting you had up is already sold. Please tell me the Optometrist is for sale."

"Sure," Ralph said, dazed that he'd sold more paintings tonight than he had in the last two years. "Charge whatever you want, Frank."

"That's the most beautiful thing anyone has ever said to me, kid. I will indeed charge whatever I want. Maybe we'll have a little impromptu auction." Reese laughed. "Have to tell ya, this couldn't have come at a better time. I was afraid I was going to have to drop you from my client list. No offense, but a guy can't live off ten percent of nothing and the occasional nerd convention. Now I have two dozen people wanting a canvas with your signature, and I don't think they care what else is on it. This is a new beginning for us, kid."

"That's great, Frank. That's really great. Hey, you haven't gotten any weird calls about someone needing to talk to me, have you? Like the police?"

"No, nothing like that. You okay, kid?"

Ralph was surprised to hear actual concern in his voice. "It's nothing, never mind. Thanks for calling with the good news."

"Anytime! We'll get together next week to nail down how we make the most of this."

Ralph thanked him again and hung up. The feeling of irreality washed over him again. *At some point I crossed through the looking glass into a world where I sell out a show and my agent loves me.*

The sound of laughter drew his attention. In the booth in front of him, two girls huddled around a laptop screen. He guessed they were about twenty years old. Peering between their shoulders at the screen, Ralph recognized a comic book panel from the night before. The Ocularist stood in a doctor's uniform, with a stethoscope around his neck and a stereotypical head mirror balanced on the giant eyeball. He held a scalpel in his fist and leered at the viewer. Across the bottom of the image three bold white letters proclaimed, *I C U.*

"That one's just bad," said the girl on the left. Her T-shirt showed dozens of robots from television and movies in silhouette.

"Excuse me," Ralph said, and they turned to look him. "Can I ask what you're looking at?"

"Just stupid crap," robot girl said.

"Okay, but where'd you find that?" Ralph said, gesturing to the screen.

"The asshole of the internet."

The other girl rolled her eyes behind her red-framed cat-eye glasses. "It's an image board. People post stuff, mostly pictures, and they do it anonymously. It's fun, if you can get past the racism, surprise gore, and kiddie porn. Last night somebody started dumping scans of all these old comic panels. Now other people are adding text, photoshopping the images, that kind of thing."

"Here's a good one," robot girl said. She clicked on a file, and a photoshopped image appeared. One of Potbelly the Mechanical Man's Nazi foes rode a dinosaur through a photo of Time's Square.

"I like the ones that are funny on their own," cat-eye glasses said. She pulled up a different image of a Pithos hero, the Advocate, silver shield in hand, kneeling over an unconscious thug. Cat-eye glasses gestured at the thug's lap. "Look at the way the hero's cupping this guy's balls." The two girls started laughing again.

"Oh my God, show him the spanking montage!" robot girl said. An animated gif showed a slideshow of still images with various characters spanking villains, sidekicks, and girlfriends. Their speech balloons contained phrases like, "Sometimes a woman needs a reminder!"

"Any idea where those pictures are from?" Ralph asked.

"I'm not into comics," said robot girl.

"I am," said the other girl. "And I've never seen any of these guys before. Someone said they're from some old company. Pisces?"

"Pithos," Ralph said.

"That's right, Pithos."

"Here's a pretty funny one," said robot girl. She clicked on a picture of the Ocularist pointing at the reader. It read, in all lowercase letters, *ocularist saw you mastirbating, ralphie.*

"I guess it's supposed to freak out everyone named Ralph who sees it. Pretty lame." Cat-eye glasses took over the laptop. "This one's not funny or anything, but it's my favorite."

On the screen appeared Wveryn, a heroine with reptilian wings and a claw-like dagger attached to each wrist. Drawn with delicate lines, she held her mask in her hands and looked longingly into the night sky. "Gorgeous, isn't she?" cat-eye girl asked.

But Ralph, unhearing, stared at the other girl's shirt. One of the robot silhouettes looked exactly like Potbelly, the Mechanical Man.

2

ALPH ROGERS CAME TO A CONCLUSION. *If I'm crazy, and none of this is real, then it doesn't matter if they think I killed that guy.*

For all I know, I'm already in a padded cell.

He returned to Greenvale the next day and found the diner again. "Phonebook?" he asked. The heavy book thudded open against the counter. Elliot Chill was no longer listed, but the yellow pages listed a Pithos Publishing.

This time the GPS led him not to a vacant lot, but to an office and warehouse. On the outside was a weathered sign with the black vase logo. Ralph touched the faded paint with a shaking hand. Only days earlier, this building hadn't existed. Now it looked like it had been built before he was born. He winced as the pad of his finger found a sharp splinter. As a drop of blood blossomed, he wondered, *Can an illusion hurt you?*

The interior of the building looked unchanged since the 1970s. A smiling woman in her forties greeted him when he walked inside. "Can I help you?"

Ralph tried to appear calm in a building that had somehow sprung into existence. "I was just driving by, and I wondered if this is the same Pithos that used to print comic books."

"Golly," she said. "You're the first to actually show up here, but people started calling about that a couple of days ago. One of the managers says we did make comics, but that was a lifetime ago."

Lady, you don't know the half of it. "Do you have any information about the comics?" he asked. "Documents, files?"

"I'm sorry, no. Anything like that would have been in the old building, and it burned down before I was born. We rebuilt in the same location, though." Then, as if she could read his mind: "So we don't have a big box of old comics hiding in the back for you." When she saw his shocked expression, she added, "Don't worry, that's what everyone who calls says they're hoping."

Ralph shrugged. "Can't blame a guy for trying, I guess. Sorry to have bothered you."

"Oh, no," she said. "It's made for a fun week. It's like we were sitting on this old secret, and now everyone wants to know about it."

"You wouldn't happen to know Elliot Chill, Junior, would you?" Ralph asked.

"Doesn't ring a bell, sweetie. Want me to ask one of the old timers?"

"That's okay. Thanks."

Next, he drove by the house where he'd discovered Chill's body. Instead of finding a worn down, dead house wrapped in crime scene tape, he encountered a bright and happy home, with a mother and father playing in the front yard with their young children. A three-year-old boy chased his dad around the yard with a plastic ray gun. Ralph thought he heard the dad say, "You'll never catch me, Danny Drastic!"

"I get you, Ocu-ist!" screamed the little boy. "I get you!"

GAME OF VOICEMAIL TAG with Damon Ripley confirmed the actor was at his home in Oklahoma City. The house looked much tamer in daylight hours, but Damon's eyes remained wild.

"Ralphie, Ralphie, Ralphie, so good to hear from you! Get in here, you old son of a bitch. You're lucky you caught me in town. We just finished principal photography on *The Abominable Dr. Phibes*. I said I'd never be in one of Burton's remakes, but you should see the colors in this thing. And the sets! I get to play this crazy organ, you won't believe it. I feel like I've died and gone to heaven."

"That, uh, that sounds great. Can't wait to see it."

Carrying the metal case, Ralph sat down on the leather couch in the bright, open living room. "You sound a little down, buddy," Damon said. "Need a pick me up? McDonald's stopped serving breakfast an hour ago, so we can officially start drinking."

"That would actually be great," Ralph said. *Three days in a padded room might be more appropriate,* he thought, *but for now I'll settle for a drink.*

Damon noticed Ralph's surprise when he was handed his drink in a glass bearing the colorful image of Jack Spratt, the hero's elastic limbs akimbo. Ralph had never heard of the character before. Chuckling, Damon said, "I promise I don't always break out the fine china. But from the sound of your phone call, it seemed appropriate." He took a drink from a glass adorned with the red, white, and blue heroine, Molly Pitcher, from *Red-Blooded American Adventures*. "What have you got for me?"

Ralph opened the metal case and spread out the books on the coffee table. There were seventeen in all: the first four issues of *Danny Drastic*, three *Tales of the Sensational*, three *Red-Blooded American Adventures*, three *Daring Exploits*, and two each of *Buzz* and *Frightful Funnies*.

"Oh, my God," Damon said. "Where did you get these?"

"That's gonna have to be my little secret," Ralph said.

"I hope you didn't have to kill for them."

"Not anyone who'll be missed." They laughed, but Ralph's smiling face was a mask.

"Most of these, I've never even seen them for sale. As far as I knew, there was only one copy of *Buzz* anywhere. And this copy of the first Danny Drastic is in perfect shape, much better than mine."

"Wait, you already have a copy?"

Damon raised his eyebrow. "Come on, Ralph, you know that. I got a little trigger happy at one of Valerie's auctions, paid way more than I should have. They made fun of me for weeks on the late-night shows."

"Oh, yeah, no, of course I knew that. I thought you meant you already had the set of four."

"Gotcha. No, I don't have the rest, just some old reprints of the Drastic stories inside them. So this is fantastic, just fantastic. It almost completes my full run of *Danny Drastic*."

Ralph rubbed his temples, fighting a headache. *A week ago I thought I knew more about these comics than anyone alive. Now it feels like I'm faking my way through a conversation on the finer points of the game of cricket.*

"What are you still missing?" he asked.

"Not much now," Damon said. "I've bought almost every issue as they came out, since I was a kid. Missing a few in the early one-hundreds, and 270-something. I don't have all the *One-Hundred-Page Hall of Fame* issues, since I already have the comics reprinted in them."

"Pretty cool, Damon. That must have taken a lot of trips to the drug store."

"That's what you get when a comic comes out like clockwork every month since 1940."

"Do you have them all here?" Ralph tried not to sound too curious.

"No. They're at my place in L.A." Damon's eyes lit up. "But I got some great news this morning, Ralph. You finding these books for me was an omen."

"Good omen or Antichrist *The Omen*?" Ralph asked.

"The best omen. I got the part, Ralph. For the new Danny Drastic movie. I was worried they were going to go in another direction, but I'm going to be Danny Drastic. *The* Danny Drastic."

"That's incredible," Ralph said, holding back his hysteria.

"So you can see why I'm in such a good mood," Damon said. "I guess the real question is, how much do you want for these comics?"

"I'm not sure," Ralph said.

"Come on, man, don't jerk me around."

"I'm not. I just don't know what would be a fair price. I wanted to bring them by here as soon as I had them."

"Name your price, Ralph."

"Let me make a quick phone call."

"OU DON'T HAVE TO GO THROUGH WITH THIS," Ben said, checking the van's rear-view mirror.

"Yeah, I do," Ralph said. "I was out of my depth. And thanks for picking me up from the airport."

"Least I could do, buddy. Not every day we get a celebrity like Ralph Rogers in Rutland, Vermont."

Ben drove the two of them in the Quarter Ben Comics van. On the dashboard stood a bobblehead of a black superhero named Black Snake, who Ralph had never seen before. The character was dressed for the disco, with snakeskin pants and platform shoes. Seeing Ralph look at the bobblehead, Ben asked, "Remember when they tried just calling him 'The Snake,' for a while?"

"Was that around the time publishers realized how embarrassed they should be for adding the 'Black' prefix to all of their black characters?"

"Yeah. Man, that used to be everywhere. You had Black Lightning, and Black Vulcan on *Superfriends.*"

"Black Goliath," Ralph said.

"Kirby had the Black Racer," Ben said.

"Oh yeah! He was like Silver Surfer but with skis, right?"

"Right. He acts like the grim reaper, helping folks along after they die. And Kirby did the first black hero at DC Comics, Vykin the Black."

"'The Black?' Really?"

Ben put his hand over his heart. "I speak only the truth."

"Damn. Had to be a bit embarrassing for them to look back on those names."

"I don't like to think of it that way," Ben said. "Growing up gay and black, there was a lot of pressure on me to hide who I was, to be ashamed about everything I am. In my personal canon, I like to think those heroes gave themselves those names because they were proud to be black. Like the real-life Black Panthers. They didn't want anyone to miss the fact they weren't white guys underneath their masks."

"That's beautiful, Ben. Pure poetry."

"Shut up. Anyway. I guess they figured if Black Panther could keep his name, so could ol' Black Snake. I know everyone prefers his modern costume, but I loved his old suit. Too bad they never did an inter-company crossover back when Dazzler sang disco and wore roller skates, am I right?" He reached over and gave the figure's head a flick, causing it to bounce.

"You want embarrassing?" Ben asked. "You ever see what they did with Japanese people in Golden Age comics, post-Pearl Harbor? They gave them pointy teeth and ears like demons."

"Yeah. Like those banned Bugs Bunny or Donald Duck cartoons. There's an old Nick Fury story by Steranko that had both Jim Woo, the heroic FBI agent, and Yellow Claw, the evil stereotype. Jim Woo had a normal Asian skin tone, but Yellow Claw had skin the color of a school bus."

"Maybe he called himself 'Yellow Claw' ironically?" Ben asked.

"I don't know if I'm allowed to laugh at that," Ralph said. But they laughed anyway.

They pulled up to Ben's store in an old strip mall. The front window was a wide stone arch, full of signs promising adventure.

"Thanks for getting an early flight," Ben said, climbing out of the van. "I can't think of the last time I had a customer before eleven, but opening late makes my stomach crawl."

"Maybe if I had your work ethic, I wouldn't be such a hack," Ralph said.

"I don't know if I'm allowed to laugh at that." Ben chuckled as he unlocked the store.

Ben flicked on the light switch. Seeing the contents of the comic shop knocked Ralph back a step.

Several of the posters on the walls bore the Pithos logo. Some were new to Ralph, like Urban Decay, the beautiful Titania, and the monstrous Luke the Nuke. A life-size cardboard stand-up of Danny Drastic, holding his Atomic Disintegrator, stood beside the long boxes full of back issues. A detailed resin statue of a woman and her giant robot sat behind the counter. The side of the statue's box had the word *Pithos* in a Kanji style.

Inside an enclosed display shelf stood a row of old Pez candy dispensers with the heads of the Mummy Magician, Ambergris, and other Pithos characters. Beside them sat a blue Karim wrist-watch from the sixties. The face was a lenticular lens, the kind that shows a different image depending on the viewing angle. Ralph stepped side to side, watching it flicker from a clock face to the head of Pithos's ghostly Gentleman.

The next shelf displayed Mego action figures from the late 1970s. Alongside Spider-Man, Batman, and Superman, little plastic stands held up figures of Jack Spratt, the Ocularist, and someone wearing a gas mask and a straitjacket with the arms hanging loose. Ben tapped on the glass. "I love those old Megos. The one-piece cloth costumes make it look like they're all wearing pajamas. Can't believe the Mad Gasser hasn't sold yet. He's the one everyone's missing."

"I always thought the Human Torch looked the silliest," Ralph said. "Do you have that one?"

"Nope. The other characters didn't sell as well as the Pithos guys. There's a market for them, sure, but they're a lot harder to find."

Ralph pulled a stool up to the counter and took out his checkbook.

"You really don't have to do that," Ben said.

"I told you, it's only fair I pay a finder's fee. If it weren't for you, I wouldn't have met Damon and looked for those comics for him. Then you used the pictures I sent to settle on a price Damon jumped at, and got me way more than I would at auction. Between all that, I think forty percent is more than fair."

"It feels like too much. That's a lot of money, Ralph."

Under the glass, Ralph spotted a vintage Darius the Diabolist wallet. In a faintly cracked image, the magician held up a fan of glowing playing cards. It was beautiful, with its synthetic fibers and Velcro. "How much for the wallet?"

Ben slid open the cabinet and handed over the wallet. "Consider it a gift, man. You brought a big payday to my door. I only regret not asking Damon to throw in that cute little robot from his movie *Christmas on Mars*. You just know that narcissistic bastard kept it."

Ralph finished writing the check. "If it makes you feel better, there's one other thing you could do for me."

"Sure, buddy. What?"

"Help me decide if I'm crazy."

5

"So up until Friday, none of this existed." Ben waved his hand across the store.

"No, you don't get it," Ralph said. "Most of it *did* exist. Just nothing related to Pithos Publishing."

"Those comics are some of my best sellers. I don't think I could stay in business if I wasn't selling Pithos."

"But you did. As far as I know, you were fine. Still in business, at least."

"Let's start with you and me, okay? Since we've only known each other a couple of weeks," Ben said. "We met at the show in Oklahoma City, right?"

"Right."

"I sold you a copy of *Nylon Girl*, number six."

"Nope. It was *Phantom Lady*, number seventeen."

"That's wrong, Ralph. Look here." Ben pulled a notebook from under the counter, flipped a couple of pages, and handed it to Ralph. There was Ralph's name, a catalog listing for the Nylon girl, and the price. The entry was in ink.

"We remember it two different ways," Ralph said. "I remember, you helped Damon complete the Monster Society storyline from *Captain Marvel Adventures*."

Ben pointed to the notebook and shook his head. "Nope. I sold him two issues of *Daring Exploits*, to complete the classic Miss Teri versus Vainglorious fourteen-parter."

"How about the times I called you?"

"You called me in the middle of the night. I told you no one was selling those comics right now, and we talked about some of the dead ends. You called me again, and you sounded crazy. You asked me to look up character names in a book. I told you they were there, but it didn't seem to help you."

A headache thudded behind Ralph's right eye. "It's like there's two versions of everything. A world where Pithos was only a rumor, and a world where Danny Drastic is as recognizable as Tarzan, Mickey Mouse, and Superman." Ralph laughed, but the sound came out awkward and high pitched.

"There's something I want to clear up," Ben said. "Every known copy of the first *Danny Drastic* is in a museum or prominent collection. People are going to go crazy when they hear Damon Ripley got his hands on a copy of *Buzz*. Those other books aren't as valuable, but they're at least as rare." He swallowed. "Where did you get them?"

Ralph looked Ben in the eyes. *Maybe it's better for him if I lie*, he thought. "I bought them from the son of the original publisher. That's what I remember. But I went back to his house, and he isn't there. He isn't anywhere. As far as I can tell, he doesn't exist in this version of events."

"Then where'd you get the comics, man? Even if I believe you—and I want to trust you, Ralph, I do—where'd they come from?"

"That's part of the problem. I can only remember things the wrong way. Or the right way, there's no telling." He shuddered. "Ben, have you ever heard of an old movie serial with Captain

America? He's a lawyer instead of a soldier, and he doesn't have his shield."

"Nope," Ben said. "It was the Advocate. Still no shield, but he had a random kid sidekick. Which Golden Age hero punched Hitler?"

"Captain America. And what's-his-name, the blue and red guy." Ralph slapped his forehead with both hands. "Oh, it's going to drive me crazy."

"Daredevil, from Lev Gleason Publications. But the most famous was the Pithos character Keeper of the Peace."

"Not where I'm from," Ralph said. "What started the Silver Age of comics?"

"Debatable. Some say The Fantastic Four. Others go earlier, saying it was the debut of the Barry Allen Flash, but I don't think DC's redesigned heroes would have gained traction on their own. So I fall into the most popular camp. I say the Silver Age began when Danny Drastic came to the modern day to stay, in 1959."

"Did the Silver Age end with the death of Gwen Stacey?"

"Not really. Most agree it ended when Mr. Stiff and The Gentleman ended their friendship. How about stuff of real importance? How did the United States bring an end to World War II?"

"We dropped two atom bombs on Japan." Ralph said, and Ben nodded. Ralph asked, "What happened to John F. Kennedy in 1963?"

"He was shot in Dallas. How many seasons were there of the original Star Trek?"

"I don't know. Two or three?"

"Close enough." Ben turned to a fresh page in his notebook. "I think I know your problem, Ralph."

"I'm certifiable."

"Probably. But if you're not crazy, this is what's happening." Ben handed the notebook and a pencil to Ralph. "Do a quick sketch."

"What do you want me to draw?"

"Anything," Ben said. "Draw a happy clown."

"Okay." Ralph roughed out a smiling clown throwing a pie. "How's that?"

"That's a darn good clown, Ralph. Now I want you to use this red pen, and draw over it. Pretend that the clown's wife left him five years ago for the strong man, and it destroyed the clown's life. The poor bastard never got over it."

Ralph took the red pen and started to draw on top of his pencils. He replaced the pie with a spinning axe and added a noose around the clown's neck, the rope trailing behind him on the ground. The clown's makeup became dark and sinister, and his smile twisted into a horrible frown.

"It's a reality bleed," Ben said. "A real-life retcon. If what you say is true, then the world is changing just like that picture is changing, only a little at a time. Truth is being overwritten. Pithos goes from being nothing to being a company that exists but doesn't do comics anymore. Then it's the biggest comic book publisher in the United States, and has been for decades. Everyone else is being overwritten too—everything from our surroundings to our memories are conforming to a different playbook.

"Your problem is that you're staying the same. You don't remember watching *The Danny Drastic Action Revue* on Saturday morning when you were a kid, because in your old reality it didn't exist."

"So what do I do?" Ralph asked.

"I have no idea," said Ben. "At least it's not something more serious, like Hitler won the war, or you were never born. You can get through this, buddy. If you're not bonkers, I mean. I don't think you are."

"Thanks, man. Really. It means a lot that someone believes me."

"You know that guy who refuses to believe a doll could come to life, and then he gets murdered by Chuckie? I'm not going to be that guy. You can always call me. I'll help you figure out what everyone else remembers, if I can. But you'll have to guess most of the time."

Ralph looked around at the store. "Maybe I should just stay away from anything that has to do with comics."

Ben laughed. "That'll be tough, if you're going to keep putting out *Meta Man* every month."

6

ACCORDING TO HIS DRIVER'S LICENSE Ralph still lived in Austin, but at a different address. The taxi dropped him off and he walked up to a strange house, an impressive structure much larger than the one he'd left the week before. One of his keys fit the front door, so he entered and did his best to take account of his situation.

Meta Man merchandise filled the house: framed posters, statues, animation cels, and action figures. Ralph giggled as he played the *Meta Boy* arcade game in his den. The machine was enormous, with six sets of controls and two CRT screens. Ralph could play as Meta Boy, Ambergris, Jack Spratt, Songweaver, Black Snake, or Danny Drastic. The Pithos vase appeared on the side panels and on the game's opening screen.

In the back of the house he found the art studio of his dreams. Many of the in-progress paintings he remembered were there, but the room was filled with work he had never seen before, like the unfinished pages for the *Meta Man* comic book.

Judging by the empty closets and the dangling wires where a television should be, it still looked like Sandra had left him. A safe sat in one corner of his bedroom closet, containing who knew what, but he didn't know the combination. The shelf by the missing television held a number of impossible DVDs, but the one Ralph pulled out was a clear case containing a burned DVD, the title written in Sharpie: *Cover to Cover 2x21: Ralph Rogers.*

Sandra had left behind a television in his studio, so Ralph turned it on. Damon Ripley appeared on a cable channel, wearing a snakeskin suit and playing poker in his casino movie, *Split the Aces.* Ralph loaded the DVD and sat down in his old leather chair. *I'm glad you're still with me, Old Chair*, he thought, as he popped the top of a beer. In the dark studio, the light from the screen danced on the walls.

The television show detailed Ralph's sudden rise to fame, telling the story of his discovery by Against the Grain Graphics. He recognized some of the photos, like a young Ralph Rogers shaking hands with his old boss, Paul Simmons. Ralph felt sick as he listened to Simmons talk about the scandal that followed.

Simmons's voice echoed in Ralph's memory: *You ripped me off, you little shit!*

"We'd never seen public opinion change so quickly," Simmons said. "Rogers went from being the kid who laid golden eggs to hanging like an albatross around the neck of our entire company. I hated to cut the kid loose, but our reputation was at stake. We needed to act fast. Pithos gave us an opportunity to recoup some of our losses."

Alan Lang, a former editor-in-chief for Pithos, told his side. "We saw an opportunity here. It was like ATG built a railroad, but decided at the last minute not to put the train on the tracks. So we made them an offer."

The series restarted with the first issue, but this time with new art by Ralph and a credit for the inker. Meta Boy became the first creator-owned character at Pithos, although they received half of the money from merchandising, subsequent film rights, and the like.

"We knew the tracing thing would blow over," Lang said. "The public wanted to see the kid succeed. They wanted him to make good, and Pithos gave him the opportunity to do that. Companies like Image and Against the Grain were doing well with creator-owned characters. We saw this as a chance for Pithos to get on board."

Valerie Hall appeared on the screen. "Looking good, Val," Ralph said, as the narrator explained that Valerie worked for 78 RPM and had been Ralph's childhood friend.

"Sales were low the first year," she said. "Some of the issues, like number seven, are valuable for being so rare. That's unusual for something Pithos published in the nineties. I remember Ralph was worried they would cancel him."

Ralph's doppelganger appeared on the screen. *It's like watching a video of something you did while blackout drunk*, he thought. *There I am, but I don't remember any of this.*

"Of course I was worried," said Other Ralph. "How many people get a second chance like that? This was it. My career could have died before I was even out of high school. When we were waiting for those first sales numbers to come in, I couldn't sleep."

It took a moment for Ralph to recognize the next speaker, Eugene Sandhurst, the man who almost threw him into Damon's swimming pool. "I had so many copies of the first issue of *Meta Boy* stockpiled in my backroom," Eugene said. "Looked like I would lose my store because of a bad gamble. But before I used the books to insulate my basement, everything turned around. Those books turned into the smartest investment I ever made." He winked at the camera. "Rogers, if you ever want a ride on my boat, give me a call. You basically paid for the thing."

"Sales picked up," Alan Lang said. "They got high enough that Universal used their rights to make an animated pilot, and the series got picked up. The show lasted four years, for a total of one hundred and four episodes."

"That cartoon was a hit," said Tim Mitchell, a blogger. "There were action figures, T-shirts, bed sheets, an arcade game, the works." The happy man sat in a room filled with Meta Boy memorabilia. In the background, his young daughters played enthusiastically with vintage action figures. "You wouldn't believe the level of nostalgia for that show on the internet. Most importantly, it proved Meta Boy was a moneymaker. Near the end of the cartoon's run, they decided to go for a darker tone in the comic. They changed the character's name and the series title to *M-Forcer*."

"Yeah, M-Forcer was a mistake," said Television Ralph. "What can I say, everyone wanted to go edgy. I had just turned eighteen and it sounded like a good idea. I still get crap for it. We had to fight to keep the original series numbering—first issues are a big deal in the comic book industry. After the backlash we changed it again, this time to *Meta Man*, which is so much better. The whole point was to let Meta Boy grow up—after all, even Invisible Girl got to become Invisible Woman. I'm just glad we got the name right before the movie."

Ralph's eyes widened as clips from the *Meta Man* movie exploded on the screen.

"You have to remember the context of when this movie came out," Tim Mitchell said. "The Danny Drastic and Superman movies came out way back in the seventies. The Batman movies had slid so far downhill they were embarrassing, and the rest of the comic book movies had been stuck in development hell for decades. *Blade* had done well, and that's probably why we got a greenlight. But when *Meta Man* came out in the summer of 2000, everyone bet on it being a huge box office bomb."

Johnny Whitworth, the actor who played Meta Man in the film, said, "It might have looked like a gamble, sure. But the script was solid and they used the budget on good talent and a quality production. I knew it would be a hit from the first day of shooting."

"Most mainstream comic book creators don't make money off movies," said Tim Mitchell. "But the Rogers's contract meant his situation was different."

"It's like I keep winning the lottery," Other Ralph said. "First Pithos rescues me, and then I get to see something from inside my head on the big screen. I bought my parents a new house."

Ralph reached for another beer. "Lucky bastard," he said.

Other Ralph blushed. "I spoiled myself too. I bought a restored Stout Scarab, like the one Danny Drastic drove in the old TV show."

Ralph paused the show and looked for the door to the garage. Opening it, he saw two vehicles: a Lexus and an unusual van he guessed was the Stout Scarab. The vehicle was wide and long, with a winged logo on the hood, two eyeball-like shapes for a windshield, whitewall tires, and beautiful chrome pipes that curved along the rear.

"So, I guess there's that," he said.

Returning to the chair and his beer, Ralph unpaused the video.

"*Meta Man* jumpstarted the comic book movie craze that continues today," Tim Mitchell said. "*First* there was *X-Men*, then *The Advocate* and *Spider-Man*. Moviegoers love comic book films, and that means Hollywood loves comic book properties."

"Meanwhile," the narrator said, "Meta Man's comic book adventures continued to mature."

Damon Ripley appeared on the screen, labeled as *Actor and Fan*. "The story really reached another level with the introduction of the Golden Dawn as a nemesis. And people loved watching Bobby Crane grow up in his civilian identity, especially in his relationship with Cindy."

I introduced Cindy in the issue that was never printed, Ralph thought. *I never even told anyone about Golden Dawn.*

"Meta Man is no longer a series existing solely on the novelty of its teenage creator," Tim Mitchell said. "This is a comic that has grown up with both its audience and creator."

A smiling Other Ralph said, "People keep asking, 'What's next for Meta Man?' Don't worry. I have this thing planned out. What happens with Bobby and Cindy, the true identity of the Golden Dawn, everything. I'm hoping people will be surprised by how it all fits together. But for now, it's all up here." He tapped the side of his forehead.

Ralph looked at the unfinished pages lining the walls of the studio.

"I'm doomed," he said, opening another beer.

7

AFTER THE VIDEO, RALPH FOUND a spiral note-book to keep track of the differences. Carrying it in his pocket reassured him. Fortunately, the findings of the conversation with Ben held true; most of the world remained un-changed, so Ralph could concentrate on keeping up with the many details of his new life. Photos and video of his double haunted Ralph as he explored his altered past. He fought the feeling that the Other Ralph would show up and accuse Ralph of trying to take his place.

The alternatives kept Ralph awake that night, arguing with himself. *You're dreaming,* he thought. *Or worse, you're hallucinating. Redemption? Success? This is pathetic wish fulfillment.*

But it's all so real. And it's been going on for days.

Then maybe you had some kind of psychotic break. This is real, and the memories of your past are bullshit you made up. Explain that idea away, smart guy.

I don't know how. Any physical evidence pooed out of existence. Even the stuff in my pockets.

His body appeared unchanged; he had the same fillings in his teeth, and the scar remained on his shin from when he'd crashed while learning to ride his bike.

Unless maybe I still have the scar, but now it came from a wreck in one of Other Ralph's fancy cars.

The following day, as he rounded the sofa, he nearly tripped over Elliot Chill—the man he had stolen the comics from—lying dead on the rug. He jumped back, but when he looked again, he saw only shapes and shadows.

The growing anxiety of what to do with the comic led Ralph to call his editor. After comparing the contact list on his phone to the names on Pithos's website, he called Charles Caulder first.

"Hey there, Ralph. What have you got for me?"

"Hi, Charles."

"Come on, man. Call me Chuck. You know I think 'Charles' sounds stupid."

Abort, abort! Ralph's mind screamed.

"Of course. Chuck. Okay. I'm trying to get organized over here ..."

"I know how that goes. But you're the only guy under me who has his crap together. You're not going to start freaking out on me, are you?"

I couldn't possibly be more freaked out, Ralph thought.

"No, no. My phone got wet, and I had to replace it. My whole life was on there, and I needed some help patching it together. Like the address I send my pages to, stuff like that."

"Sure, sure," Caulder said. "If I lost my phone, I wouldn't know my parents' number. I'll have Jenny send you a packet with everything."

"You're a lifesaver, Chuck."

"Sure, sure. You need anything else? I got people who need a lot more handholding than you do."

"One other thing. Where am I at on my end? Ahead? Behind?"

"Let me check."

Ralph listened to Caulder rifle through a cluttered desk. "Okay, says here you're two months ahead. You're usually three, but you're still the record holder around here."

Ralph exhaled. "That's good to hear."

"Glad I could help out. Now let me get back to work. Think about backing up your phone, all right?"

A call to Reese assured Ralph he could wait on fulfilling the commissions from the art show, which had still been a success in this iteration of reality. Ralph even possessed a written agreement stipulating he could paint Pithos characters, as long as a chunk of the proceeds went to the company.

So Ralph spent his days relearning the craft of making a comic book. The act of touching up his alternate's layouts felt like a waking dream, but a phantom of muscle memory knew the method. Inking was a scarier experience, but he experimented with Other Ralph's Hunt 102 pen nibs and Michelle 451 brushes. He held his breath as he first put brush to paper, dressing his pencils in dark India ink.

If he wasn't hunched over his desk, he was reading issue after issue of *Meta Man*. A file cabinet held over three hundred comic books: a complete set of the ongoing series and annuals, a few miniseries and specials, as well as appearances in other series. Ralph devoured the pile, by turns loving and hating what Other Ralph had done with Meta Man. Ralph spotted a few rushed pages and forgotten plot threads. The *M-Forcer* issues were garbage. He decided to be forgiving, but the faint jealousy he felt for Other Ralph remained.

When Ralph made the first issues of *Meta Boy* at age fourteen, he had no grand scheme or overarching story in mind. From what Ralph could see, Other Ralph spent the first decade proving himself. Other Ralph took risks to keep his art feeling original, with the story as a serviceable afterthought.

Then, in mid-2005, Other Ralph began raising the plot to the level of the art. Bobby Crane's two-dimensional supporting cast became real, and Meta Man became fallible and interesting.

The series grew up, and the industry took notice, as attested by The Eisner Award in Other Ralph's den. The story was building to something, but Ralph had no idea what. Other Ralph's notes were a jumbled mess, and if there was a master plan hidden somewhere, Ralph couldn't find it.

After finishing the page he was working on, Ralph took a look at his notebook. Big changes were easy to remember, like *More money*, but he made sure to write down details like *Doesn't have a stapler, prefers paperclips*. The minor differences gave him more a sense of unease than the big house. Ralph could imagine a life where he owned a fancy electric car, but he had never thought to keep the nail clippers in the medicine cabinet instead of a drawer.

At least there aren't many calls, Ralph thought. Other Ralph was possibly a bigger introvert than Ralph; aside from his agent and editor, Ben was the only person Ralph spoke to for those first few weeks.

Ben tended to call when business was slow. "How's the next issue coming?"

Ralph balanced the cell phone on his shoulder as he filled in background details in a fight scene. "I think I'm getting the hang of being a renaissance man. Doing my own inking gives me a much-needed sense of control, you know? But I'm grateful I don't have to letter this mess. I'll have to email you later with more questions."

"What's the problem? Still can't log into your bank?"

"No, I got that. Thank goodness for security questions and Social Security numbers." Ralph transferred the phone to his other shoulder. "I'm still figuring out how to write the next issue. This storyline with the Golden Dawn makes no sense to me. And Cindy is supposed to have a surprise for Bobby, but I have no idea what it is."

"Can't help you there."

"Come on, Ben. The internet rumors are useless. You said we met after a Q and A at the Oklahoma convention. Did I say anything?"

"You hinted you might finally reveal Goldie's identity. People have wanted that for years. I had business, so I didn't stay for the whole thing. Maybe somebody uploaded a video."

As he settled into a routine, Ralph's questions grew less frequent. When he reached for a brush, it was where he expected it to be. The clothes in the closet felt like his. He decided Golden Dawn would be an old friend of Meta Man, and it might have been the same decision Other Ralph made. The memory of Elliot Chill's corpse evaporated, like a bad dream. Ralph threw himself into his work, and he felt satisfied at the end of each day.

Ralph stopped paying attention to the news, so he didn't pick up on the more drastic changes until it was too late.

8

ARIUS ROSS ROLLED A COIN across his knuckles as he stared out the window of his shabby apartment. The lights of the city blinked and blurred in the dark. When the silver Walking Liberty half dollar reached his pinkie, it reversed direction, traveling from finger to finger. The coin, worn smooth by decades of circulation, fell to the desk with a dull thud.

Lost in thought, Ross picked up the coin and set it back to dancing along his fingers. *Is it time to give up?* he wondered.

Ross had spent the last three years trying to break into the magician scene in Los Angeles. During the day, he worked as a waiter, and at night he worked in a different restaurant as a magician, walking from table to table doing close-up magic with cards and coins.

He watched as the single coin became two, each held suspended in his outstretched fingers. The coins combined, and the single coin disappeared into his fist only to appear in the other hand.

No one appreciates coin magic, he thought. *They always want card tricks.* Ross loved cards, of course, but his passion was coins.

The level of difficulty was so much higher, as was his excitement when he did his routine in front of his small but happy audiences. But the restaurant gig was not leading to anything with better pay, and he found himself competing for gigs against younger and younger magicians. He looked in the corner at a half-finished cabinet he was building with plans from the internet, which he hoped to use to vanish an underpaid and underdressed assistant on stage. *It's an oldie,* he thought, *but is it a goodie?*

I could go back to Michigan. Go back to school. Meet a nice girl, have a family. Confine my tricks to pulling coins from behind a son's ear. Maybe do birthday parties where there isn't so much competition. It's not like I have any future here. The best thing on my resume makes me look like a fool.

The cold, familiar dread crept into his stomach as he remembered how his local talk show appearance had gone horribly wrong. He had prepared an elaborate routine with his coins, which he performed in front of an eight-year-old child. The producer had hoped the enthusiasm of the child would transfer to the audience.

Halfway through the trick, the child reached over and pulled a coin from under Ross's arm. It didn't matter that Ross had practiced this bit for dozens of hours, or that he performed the trick without error. The studio audience roared, and he could only imagine the damage the video clip had done to his reputation.

No, he told himself. *There's no such thing as bad publicity. I should put a link to that video on my business card. Take possession of it.*

As he reconsidered his future, he again vanished the coin out of habit.

He opened his other hand to show the coin and restart the routine, but his fingers rose to reveal a bare palm. He looked down at his empty hands.

What the hell? Ross looked for the coin on his desk, but it was nowhere to be seen. *Must have landed on the carpet, hiding the sound.* Sliding out of his chair, he searched beneath his desk, cursing himself at the thought of how much it would cost to replace the Walking Liberty coin. He hoped it would turn up in the morning.

But it did not. The coin was gone.

9

THE SECURITY GUARD NEEDED COFFEE.

On a regular night, Janna Clark loved her job at the New York Antiquities Society. After her years in the army, all she needed was low risk, decent pay, and good benefits. The museum also offered what she wanted most of all: quiet.

Her usual responsibilities involved keeping an eye on the exhibition floor and telling patrons where to find the restrooms. Aside from rare incidents, the guests behaved themselves and allowed her to stand silently and observe.

If someone had told her five years ago she would become an art lover, she would have laughed in their face. But after spending day-in and day-out staring at beautiful paintings and sculptures, she had developed a simple but profound appreciation for artists and their creations. She brought her two-year-old daughter to the children's events at the museum, and she secretly hoped it would set off a spark in her soul.

Janna's friend Jim Garrett had convinced her to cover the night shift for him that week, while Garrett and his wife took a second honeymoon. Janna hated to miss tucking in her daughter, but they could use the money. Besides, if she enjoyed the quiet of the museum's daytime hours, the night shift supplied a silence so thick Janna could lose herself in it.

Her supervisor said she was only required to make two indoor sweeps every hour; nothing outside unless she spotted something on the monitors—and no going in the basement. Garrett read during the downtime, but Janna knew she could never sit still. She walked the upstairs route to keep herself awake. Unfortunately, the art collections were difficult to see in the diminished light.

Her watch beeped, reminding Janna it was midnight and time to check the basement archives. She returned to the security kiosk and unlocked a drawer, removing the clipboard from inside. The elevator carried her to the basement, and the doors opened onto a dark hallway. *At least I'm not wandering around outside looking for kids on skateboards,* she thought.

Janna took her flashlight from her belt and searched for the light switch, which was nowhere to be found. *Garrett showed me where the damn thing is. But do I pay attention?* Giving up, she used the flashlight to locate Archive Room E.

"Check it twice a night, at 11:55 and 12:55," her supervisor had said. "It's been a long time since we've had a problem, but be alert. There's some shit in that room people would pay good money for. Stuff people would *kill* for. Make sure everything on the checklist is still there, and for Christ's sake, don't touch any of it."

The key opened the door, and Janna shined her flashlight on the clipboard.

"File 138," she said to herself. "File 138. There you are."

Janna slid out the drawer, which was three feet wide and six inches deep. Shining the light on her clipboard again, she said, "Artifact 817, meerschaum pipe, Uqbar, 1880s." She scanned the plastic labels on the drawer's foam insert. Nestled between object 816 and 817 was an empty space in the foam, in the shape of a smoking pipe. The clipboard clattered to the ground, and Janna's need for coffee vanished.

"Damn it," she said. She shined her flashlight up and down the aisle. She saw no movement, but several of the drawers stuck out a few inches.

She pulled her gun, and steadied it with her left hand, which held the flashlight. A dark form rushed past the end of the aisle.

"Hold it!"

A flash and the tell-tale smell of ozone told her the thief was already gone.

Janna ran to the door of the room. Unlike the basement light switch, she had no trouble finding the trigger for the alarm. She slapped the button and reached for her radio's hand piece. "Emergency situation. We just lost at least one level-twelve artifact at the Antiquities Society. Repeat, missing one level-twelve artifact and likely more. Suspect teleported from the scene before I could make a positive ID, but appeared to be Cicerone, over."

I hope they don't take this out of my pay, Janna thought.

10

NY CALLERS ON THE LINE?" asked Victoria Lehman.

Behind the glass, the studio technician shook his head.

It's always dead by this part of the show, Victoria thought. *We might as well end at two in the morning instead of three.*

The studio technician gave her the signal. She pulled the microphone closer.

"This is Victoria Lehman, and you're up late and listening to *Unusual Fortean Observations*. We're speaking with Jorge Obregon, author of *The Coyame Cover-Up*, about the paranormal history of Mexico. Enjoying your night so far, Jorge?"

"It has been a pleasure."

The studio equipment hummed. Victoria sat across the table from Jorge. She wore comfortable clothes, and her brown hair was pulled back in a messy ponytail. Juan had arrived wearing a bolo and sport jacket, which he had since removed.

Victoria sipped her tea. "Before the break, a caller asked about the seeming rarity of UFO reports south of the border. What do you think, Jorge? Do aliens just not like spicy food?"

"Victoria, I think it all comes down to cultural differences. No matter when or where people live, they see things they can't explain. That's the entire point of your show, isn't it?"

"It's a big part of it, yes."

"So it all comes down to interpretation. When an ancient Roman saw something in the sky he could not explain—"

"Like the phantom ships?"

"Or the siege of Jerusalem, yes. When they saw these things it was interpreted in a religious context. One could argue the same for many of the supernatural events described in the Bible. It wasn't until the dawning of the twentieth century that observers saw the sources of these objects as extraterrestrial. I believe the people of Mexico, as well as Central and South America, have been having these same experiences. Only, instead of seeing them as extraterrestrial in origin, they interpret the events in a religious context. Saints, miracles, *la virgen María.*"

"This is a theory that we've talked about on the show before, Jorge, and something I'm sure many of our more informed listeners will be familiar with."

"I have no doubt about that. Take, for instance, the vision that led to the building of the Basilica of Our Lady of Guadalupe. I'm not here to discourage those of a religious faith, but what Juan Diego saw on Tepeyac Hill fits many of the hallmarks of a close encounter."

"Why don't you explain what happened for our listeners?"

"Of course. Diego was a spiritual man. On December 9, 1531, on his way to church, he heard birds singing and someone calling his name. He ran to the source of the words and saw a young girl, about fourteen years old. She seemed to glow, and they spoke to each other with familiarity. Juan recognized her as the Holy Mother. She asked him to tell the bishop to build her a shrine at that location. The girl told him that she would demonstrate her love for all mankind."

"I bet the Bishop jumped at the chance," Victoria said sarcastically.

"It took Diego delivering fresh, out-of-season roses and an icon of the Virgin."

"So, you're saying what Diego saw was actually an alien."

"I'm simply saying that if one looks at his experience in the context of a close encounter, one sees many parallels. Perhaps Diego saw Mary because he was *prepared* to see Mary."

"Which might explain other theophanies in history, times when humans claim contact with gods," Victoria said. "You could say the same thing about the accounts of people meeting fairies or other intelligent supernatural creatures. But what about the consistency of modern close encounters?"

"Perhaps people see grays and men in black because they expect to see them."

"So you're saying it's self-propagating."

"Exactly. There are even some theories that the mystery airships spotted in the 1880s and 1890s were actually alien in origin."

Victoria chuckled. "I'm going to have to stop you there, Jorge. The history of those airships is well known. One of them is hanging in the Smithsonian, for goodness sake."

"Of course. I simply meant to put forth the theory that some of the airships were actually alien vehicles."

"I understand what you're saying. But when the United States government revealed the existence of Professor Savant in the 1920s, detailed information was uncovered about the airships and his plans for abducting a sizable percentage of the populace. Next you'll be saying that the rediscovery of Atlantis in 1997 was a hoax."

"I'm not an Atlantis denier, Victoria. But it was never truly established why Savant needed to abduct people in the first place. It's not that much of a stretch to think he was planning to hand them over to aliens."

"That's an intriguing take. But our producer is signaling it's time to answer the phones. Please call in with your questions for Jorge Obregon, author of *Coyame Uncovered*."

The phone lines lit up like Christmas. *There are so many cranks calling this time of night,* Victoria thought. *The lines are always too full for the real stories to get through. It can be hard to sort it out when it feels like everything is true.*

She hit the button for the next caller. "You're on the air with *Unusual Fortean Observations.*"

11

RALPH CARRIED HIS DAGWOOD SANDWICH to the couch. He settled down to eat his late dinner and flipped on the television set. A show about ghost hunting appeared on the screen, a program Ralph had seen before called *Astrid Projection*. The beautiful Astrid Rhodes and her team of ghost hunters visited allegedly haunted locations and ran around in the dark with their cameras in an attempt at a documentary style. Ralph had an open mind, especially recently, but Astrid's attempts to find evidence of ghosts wore thin.

"Did you hear that?" Astrid asked one of her co-hosts, a nervous young man.

"No, I didn't. Do you want me to check the EMF meter?"

"No, I want you to get me a sandwich. *Of course* I want you to check the EMF! Get with the program, Jess!"

Jess pulled out a blinking device. "It looks like a big one. Bigger than usual."

Ralph gasped as he watched Astrid and Jess's flashlights go out.

"Any second now," said Astrid calmly.

A luminous shape sped towards the camera. The video flickered and distorted.

"Golly Moses," Ralph said. "It must be sweeps week."

To his surprise, Astrid and her crew seemed unsurprised.

"Can we identify the apparition?" Astrid asked.

Jess shook his head. "No can do, boss. There are no records, and the ghost has no identifiers."

"Maybe we can slow down the film," Astrid said, but Ralph had already run to his computer. He looked up videos of *Astrid Projection*, and was shocked to see the crew nonchalantly filming ghosts in almost every one.

He picked up his phone and called Ben.

"What's going on, Ralph?"

"Are ghosts real?"

"What? I don't—"

"Ghosts, Ben! Are they real!"

"Calm down. You're talking crazier than usual."

Sighing in relief, Ralph fell back down on the couch. "Thank goodness. I thought the world had gone crazy."

"How so?"

"I thought ghosts were suddenly a real thing, and they were on TV."

Ben laughed. "Of course ghosts are real. Everyone knows that."

"Wait, what?"

"What do you mean by ghost? Like the image of a dead person? Immaterial? Glowy?"

Ralph buried his head in his hands. "There is no way that ghosts are commonplace. If anyone could go somewhere and see a ghost, or see one on film, the world would go crazy."

"This isn't a new thing. As far as I know, ghosts have been around as long as people. It doesn't mean anything. At least I don't think so."

"Doesn't mean anything? Ben, if ghosts are real, doesn't that prove the existence of a soul? Of life after death?"

Laughing, Ben said, "No, ghosts don't prove any of that."

"Explain this to me like I have no idea what you're talking about."

"Okay. Uh, what we call ghosts are afterimages. They're extremely rare, but well documented. When an event such as a murder takes place, massive amounts of energy are released, which can imprint on a location."

"Oh my God."

"No, listen, it's not a big deal. Studies show that the activity works on a gradual bell curve. At first there's nothing, but the imprint grows stronger over time. Then it peters out again. It can take years or decades, but I have no idea what makes some last longer. Some last centuries, but it's rare. I guess that's why we don't see caveman ghosts running around everywhere."

"How do you know this? Did you learn it at school?"

"Why would we waste time on ghosts at school? They don't do anything. They can scare you if you're not expecting to see one. I guess there have always been rumors about ghosts that can touch or hurt people, but that's never been proven, I don't think. Only cranks like Astrid Rhodes spend time on them, and I guess enough people want to see a ghost that the show is still on the air. I've heard people call them a quantum echo. Maybe somebody did a study?"

"Have you ever seen a ghost?" Ralph asked. "In person?"

"No, and I don't want to. Ghosts are creepy."

"But they don't have anything to do with the afterlife?"

"Some religious people make a big deal out of them, I guess. But most people just accept that it happens. Ghosts are only images. They don't have anything more to do with Heaven or Hell than a bathroom mirror."

Ralph buried his hands in his hair. "It's finally happened. Either I've gone even crazier, or the world has. This is a bigger difference than comic books. In the world I knew a week ago, people would be flipping out if someone proved the existence of ghosts. And you act like it's common knowledge."

Ben said nothing for several moments as Ralph hyperventilated. Finally, Ralph broke the silence. "I don't know what to do. Is this the only thing that's changed since the last time I called?"

"I don't know," Ben said. "Your calls don't make any sense. I've tried to humor you, but maybe you need to talk to a professional."

"A professional what? I just need someone to help me figure this out! If ghosts are real, what else has changed? We could be in serious trouble."

"Ralph, I'm sorry, I really don't have to time to be your encyclopedia. I'm swamped at the store. My dad is a big help, but he's still adjusting to his new treatment."

"Treatment? Ben, you told me your dad hasn't been able to work in years."

"Are you kidding? He's as strong as ever. The new equipment fits into a headband, so he doesn't have to wear the pack anymore."

"That's not right. You have to take care of him. You told me."

"I don't want to hear about it. I'm glad I got to meet you. I've always loved your work. But you need to get a grip."

"Ben, wait!"

The call disconnected.

"Fine!" Ralph screamed. "The world can fall apart for all I care!" He threw his phone, bouncing it off the couch and onto the floor. His chest heaved and he felt his dinner rising in his throat.

ANOTHER BENTERLUDE

BEN HUNG UP THE CELL PHONE and went back to sorting comic books. Preparing for new comic book day was a big job at Quarter Ben Comics, but having his dad's help made the chore a treat. The treatment was a godsend, and the new headband made it easier for David to move around.

"Who was on the phone?" David asked as he opened another box of comics with a retractable knife.

"Ralph again."

"Poor kid. Has everything a guy could want, but can't be happy. Maybe the pressure of putting that book out every month is getting to him?"

"I don't think so," Ben said. "I've been trying to help him out, but it's confusing. I took him seriously at first, but he's coming unhinged. He has this crazy idea the world is changing around him, but he's staying the same."

David laughed—a heartfelt chuckle. "Sounds an awful lot like getting old. Maybe he's not so crazy, after all. I mean, look at this gizmo." He tapped his translucent plastic headband, full of arcane technology. "I grew up in a world of black and white televisions. Now the stuff they can do is like magic."

Ben looked at the miracle device that had given his father a second lease on life. Ralph's warning echoed in his mind as Ben looked down at the new issue of *Meta Man* in his hands.

"Maybe I should stop taking Ralph's phone calls," Ben said.

He slid the comics into their respective places in the long shelf, alphabetized by title within each company's dedicated section. After this, it wouldn't take long to fill the subscription boxes for his regular customers. If he finished in time, he could update the website—

Behind him, David froze in place. His eyes took on a glazed look. "Son, what have I always told you about turning your back on people?"

David picked up the box knife and extended the blade.

12

O FFICER DUSTIN TAYLOR TURNED ON THE SIREN and put the patrol car in drive.

"Car 66, en route," responded Hossain Ashraf, his partner.

"Been a while since we caught one of these," Taylor said.

"Not long enough. I hate these calls."

"Come on, buddy. Maybe they'll be settled down by the time we get there. Sometimes an argument is just an argument."

"Unless it's one of the rough ones. Domestic disputes are a pain in the ass. Remember when that lady tried to bite my ear off? You'd think she'd appreciate us showing up."

"Before someone does something they regret. Yeah, I agree. I'm just saying this might be an easy one."

"Not with the day I've been having," Ashraf said. "Did I tell you we've got mice?"

"You might've mentioned it."

"We had the exterminator come out last week. Wife texted me earlier, told me it didn't work."

"That's no fun, but come on. Everybody's got mice. I've got mice."

"Not like these mice. They're little thieves."

"What?"

"They took my watch. They keep hiding the mail. The little bastards are driving us crazy. The other day, they stole a twenty. Now I have to lock my wallet in the car at night."

"You're saying mice are stealing from you."

"Little bastards are stealing from me."

"No offense, Ashraf, but couldn't your wife have taken the money out of your wallet?"

"You think she needs to take money from me? She has her own money. And the little bastards got her necklace, the pearl one I bought her last year."

"Oh, she loved that necklace."

"Damn straight. And the little bastards took it."

"Have you seen them?" Taylor asked.

"No, they only come out at night when everyone's asleep."

"Doesn't your cat do any good?"

"Cat's scared of them."

"Cat's scared?"

"Cat's scared. Won't leave her bed unless me or Stephanie go with her."

"Did you try those sticky traps? Last time we had mice, the only thing that would work were those sticky traps. Mice tear themselves apart on them."

"Yeah, we tried those," Ashraf said. "The little bastards just moved them around. I ended up stepping in one, my foot was sticky for a week. You know what's crazy, though? I think they're organizing my stuff. What they don't steal, I mean."

"You're gonna have to clarify."

"Okay. We've got a junk drawer, right?"

Taylor drummed on the steering wheel. "Course you do. Everybody's got a junk drawer."

"You're damn right. Few days ago, I need some batteries. I look in the junk drawer. It's usually a waste of time, can't find anything. I look in there, and it's all organized. Everything is in little bowls or lined up in little rows."

"Mice organized your junk drawer."

"I didn't do it. Stephanie says she didn't do it. The mice are getting into everything else. So yeah, I think they organized my junk drawer."

"I want to tell you all the reasons why that's wrong, but we're coming up on the address. You on shotgun this time?"

"Yeah," Ashraf said. "Think we'll need it?"

"We're just supposed to hold down the fort until backup arrives. We probably won't even see them."

The two men climbed out of the squad car. Ashraf popped the trunk and pulled out the shotgun. While he loaded shells, Taylor called out, "Top of the building!"

Fifteen stories up, Ashraf spotted the silhouettes of two men throwing punches back and forth. "I see them!" he said. "This is great. Knuckle Duster has been my favorite since I was a kid. Who do you think he's fighting?"

"I just hope it isn't the Streak." Taylor grinned as he waved back the gathering crowd. "My kids are gonna be so jealous when they hear I saw the Duster again."

13

RALPH RIPPED A PAGE FROM HIS NOTEBOOK and tore it into long strips.

The host had placed him on the patio, which didn't help. He wondered if he'd been put outside so his appearance wouldn't bother the more important patrons of the upscale restaurant. His eyes darted back and forth at the slightest hint of movement on the street. The pale threat of another panic attack grew in his chest.

The page destroyed, he started on another.

"Ralph?"

He turned to the source of the voice. Valerie Hall's expression told him he must look as horrible as he assumed. Valerie, on the other hand, seemed to glow. Black earrings dangled from her red hair and framed her face. Her simple black and white dress flattered her slender frame.

"Hello, Val. Thanks for meeting me."

"After the way you sounded on the phone, I had to." She sat across from him. Ralph saw her eyeing the pile of torn paper in front of him, so he quickly swept it off the table and into his hand. "I figured you didn't come all the way to Denver just for dinner."

He dropped the confetti in his pocket. "I needed to see someone I can trust, so I took three grand out of the bank and got in the car. I need help. The world's gone wrong, and I don't know what to do."

"Didn't you have someone to talk to in Austin?"

Ralph shook his head. "Sandra isn't answering my calls. I'm scared that if Frank finds out I'm nuts, he'll drop me as a client. I sort of lost contact with everyone else."

"Ben got my number from Damon. He called me before you did," Valerie said.

"What did he tell you?"

She frowned. "He said he's worried about you, that you're not making sense. He thought I might want to know."

"And you know Ben because ... ?" Ralph asked.

"We met at Damon's house, during the party. You know that, Ralph. It's only been a couple of months."

He chuckled. "Time flies. I guess I should be relieved that night still happened. Everything else is different, but at least I still had fun at a party. We'll always have Oklahoma, am I right?"

"Ralph, tell me what's wrong. You don't sound like yourself."

"That's because I'm not myself. I thought I could be the imposter, but it's all too much. *Everything is real.*"

The conversation halted as the waiter brought their drinks. Ralph ordered the first dish listed on the menu.

Valerie waited for the server to leave. "What do you mean everything is real?"

"It's hard to explain."

"Try me."

"Val, the world that I'm used to, it made sense. Sometimes horrible things happened for no reason, but for the most part it made sense. Good or bad, life was at least consistent."

"What changed?"

"It's not any one thing. At first it *was* one thing: the Pithos comics. When the subject came up that night at the party, you said there was no such thing."

"That's silly. Why would I say that? Pithos is one of the big three. You know how much of my job at 78 RPM is dealing with Pithos comics? I said you'd never find those early issues for Damon, but you proved me wrong. I know you had a deal with him, but I can't imagine what those would have sold for at one of my auctions."

"That's how you remember it. But for me, that was the first I'd heard of Pithos."

"But they've been your publisher since you were a kid."

"No, they haven't. I haven't had a publisher since I was fourteen, when Against the Grain dropped me like a bad habit. But don't you think I'd be okay if the only difference was my career didn't die before I was out of high school?"

"I'll play along. What else changed? How are things different than you remember them?"

"Ghosts are real," Ralph said.

"Of course they are. So are buses. And muffins."

"For me, until two days ago, seeing ghosts was something that happened when you were a kid or to your grandmother or to a friend of a friend. They were not on television in high-def. They were not studied under the umbrella of quantum physics. This is all new, all different. There are people who say ghosts should be accepted as witnesses in court!"

"That I don't agree with," Valerie said. "They're too subjective. Like telepaths and psychics."

He put his head in his hands. "You're not joking, are you? Mind stuff must be real too."

"It sounds like you're confused. You don't—"

Ralph cut her off. "You know what else is real, Val? Everything. Everything is real."

"You already said that. What's it mean?"

"I've been on the internet for the last two days, looking up everything I can think of," he said. "The long list of things that weren't real has now been replaced by a list of things that are definitely real and things that are probably real."

"Like what? Start with the definites."

"Atlantis was a real place, now. So was Camelot. You can see Arthur's old crown in a museum. A lot of the old stories are true. The Matter of France. Robin Hood is recognized as a historical figure. Sherlock Holmes too, I think, and Paul Bunyan."

"I don't know about the French thing, but we learned the rest of that in school."

"Not me. And that's only some of the stuff that everyone seems to agree on. The rest is confusing, because not everyone agrees on it, but there's weird evidence everywhere."

"Weird like what?" Valerie asked. "Like tinfoil hat stuff?"

"The tinfoil hat people I remember would have killed for this stuff. Like aliens. That alien autopsy they showed on TV when we were kids? Here, that was never proven to be a hoax. People think it was, but there's no proof. I watched a clip—it's not the same one we laughed at as kids. The Roswell crash is like an open secret. Don't get me started on the Bigfoot clips on YouTube."

"But none of that stuff is proven."

"It's not proven, but I think it might be real. Because the *nature* of it is different. I found a support group for werewolves, and I would have sworn it was the real deal. Big corporations employ people to deal with magic. ESP is a major field of university study. Where I come from, that was just a joke job you saw on *Ghostbusters*. There are amateur photographs of angels that can't be disproven. Back in the real world, a guy named Charles Fort wrote books about Fortean phenomenon. Over here, the guy is recognized as the father of *Fortean science*. Ancient astronauts is a minority opinion, but important folks like Neil deGrasse Tyson have expressed an interest."

"Why wouldn't some people give it a chance?" Valerie said. "The evidence is there."

"Sure! *Now* it is. Then there's the technology. It's mostly the same, but I drove here in a brand new Kamakiri, a car like nothing I've ever seen before. It replaced a Lexus I didn't even own until after I was suddenly working for Pithos. And I've seen news reports about people researching stuff like shrink rays."

"I've heard about that," Valerie said. "It would be great for surgery. The doctor could shrink down and fix up the patient from inside."

"See? That right there. That's like something out of a cartoon. The shrink ray is only one thing, though. Robotics is further along, and so is neuroscience. That thing that keeps Ben's dad up and moving around? That shouldn't exist."

"It's just a wearable neural stimulator," she said. "I'm glad Ben's dad finally qualified for one. They're smaller now, but those things have been around for a couple years."

"They're around now because something about the world is different. The way I figure it, there are people in this world who are so much smarter than anyone in the old world that it's scary. Or maybe the fundamental laws of the universe have changed. There's a serious belief that the earth is hollow, so maybe that's it. How about this? The rumor is people here have access to alien technology, and they've adapted it for things like that neural stimulator. And they're saying there's an ancient city on the moon, with its own little atmosphere."

Valerie nodded. "That all sounds perfectly reasonable to me."

"Reasonable? The supernatural. The paranormal. Pseudoscience. They're all out there on the periphery. People would laugh me out of this restaurant if I started talking about aliens, but they'd all look up at the sky first!"

Ralph stopped talking when the waiter approached with their food. He gave Ralph an uncomfortable look, but left after a reassuring nod from Valerie. She patted Ralph's trembling hand. "You have to look at this from my point of view. The only thing that seems different to me is *you*, Ralph. You're acting crazy. You say the world is totally different. What am I supposed to do with that? Do a system restore?"

"I don't know what I want you to do. I just need someone who can help me work through this. It all started with the comics, but the progression scares the shit out of me. From where I'm sitting, do you know what kind of world this is? The kind of world where magic and super science are the catch of the day? That's a world where—"

Across the street, something exploded.

14

 FIREBALL ERUPTED as windows shattered up and down the block. Car alarms blared. Anyone who could move ran from the source of the blast. Ralph could see several unconscious or dead people on the ground near the smoking building. He heard screams over the ringing in his ears.

"Get down!" he yelled, but when he looked across the table, she was gone. "Valerie!" He searched for her among overturned tables and chairs. There was no trace she had ever been there.

Run, his mind demanded.

In the street, a woman wearing a pantsuit tried to stand up. She paused, and turned her head to the side. Blood poured from her ear, staining her suit and the gravel.

Ralph jumped the fence surrounding the restaurant's patio and ran to the injured woman. "I seem to have misplaced my purse," she said. A purse hung from her shoulder.

"Ma'am, you're hurt pretty bad. How about you come over here and sit down."

"What about my purse?" she asked.

"It's right here," he said, patting her shoulder.

"Oh, that's wonderful. I think I will have a sit down, if that's all right."

What happened? he wondered. *Gas leak? Terrorists?*

A human shape emerged from the gaping hole left behind by the explosion. With mounting terror, Ralph saw that the man was unharmed and wearing metal armor. His arms, legs, and back sported hydraulic cylinders that hissed as he walked. His helmet's face shield raised to reveal a smiling face. The armor was painted red, but it had seen a lot of action; pitting and scarring covered the surface—like a car that had been left out in the hail and then beat with a crowbar.

"Oh God," said someone in the crowd. "It's Red Ned!"

A body, burned beyond recognition, lay in Red Ned's path. The armored man walked over the corpse like it wasn't even there, crushing it with a sickening crack and splattering his leg with remains.

"Sorry for the interruption folks! These things don't always go as planned. Please stay the fuck out of my way and no one will be hurt." He looked around at the bodies on the ground. "No one else, anyway." With one of his gorilla-sized gauntlets, he slapped a parked car, overturning it with the sound of scraping metal.

This is it, Ralph thought as he led the woman with the bloody ear into the entrance of the restaurant. People helped her inside and closed the door after her when they saw that Ralph was staying outside. *This is it. I was right. This is how the world ends.*

Red Ned looked up, and a blur shot down from the sky, hitting him in the chest. The force lifted him off his feet and carried him back into the building. Someone cheered, and soon everyone inside was applauding.

In shock, Ralph heard the sound of metal hitting concrete. The half-demolished building shook as floors gave way. The exterior wall, damaged in the explosion, totally collapsed.

Then, silence.

A heap of metal sailed into the street, skidding to a stop. With chunks of his armor torn away or crushed, the unconscious Red Ned lay still.

Another form emerged from the ruined building, a slender woman clothed in a uniform of green and gold. On her chest was a stylized letter T, and a silk cape hung around her bare shoulders. A golden domino mask covered her eyes. She floated effortlessly a few feet off the ground, like vapor on the wind.

Someone yelled, "Thank you, Titania!" The flying woman raised her hand and waved. A second round of cheering broke out. As she turned, Ralph finally saw her full face.

Valerie saw the recognition in his eyes, and her face blushed nearly as red as her hair. She shot back into the sky and disappeared. Ralph watched as she turned into a speck in the distance. His legs gave out, and he fainted dead away. ⋈

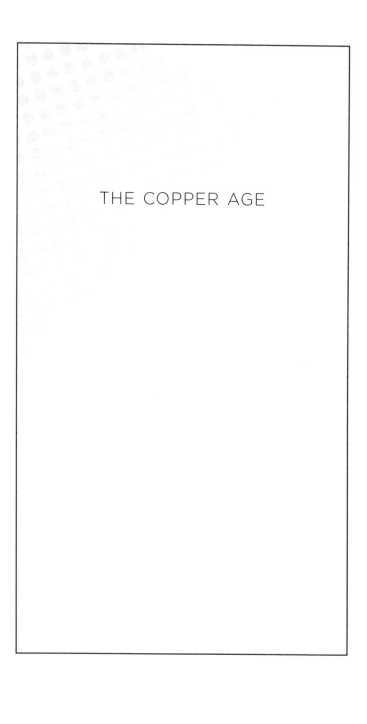

THE COPPER AGE

1

"**W**AKE UP, BUDDY."

Ralph awoke to the face of a paramedic staring down at him.

"Do you know your name, sir?"

"I'm not hurt. Fainted when I saw the—when that lady flew away."

"Titania? This your first time in the city?" He helped Ralph to his feet.

"It's a first for me, yes."

"Wait right here and someone will get you checked out." The paramedic focused on his next patient, a man covering his eye with a cupped hand. Blood seeped through the man's closed fingers.

Someone had already covered several bodies close to the source of the explosion with tablecloths. Ralph watched the woman he'd pulled out of the street being loaded into an ambulance, but Valerie was nowhere to be seen. Men wearing earpieces and black suits locked the still-unconscious Red Ned to a backboard and loaded him into a black van.

Ralph rose to his feet, but his legs threatened to take him back down. Firemen and paramedics had the situation well in hand. He hated to skip out on the dinner check, but it looked like the restaurant had bigger problems. *I'll call them later and sort it out,* he thought. *I can thank them for the floor show.*

Deciding to leave the mopping up to the professionals, Ralph wandered through the gathering crowd in search of a taxi and ended up on a side street. He looked in vain for signposts or landmarks, then went for his cell phone. His pockets were empty; keys, phone, and Darius the Diabolist wallet were gone. *Goddamn it,* he thought. *Someone rolled me.*

He told himself to calm down. *You have to think this through. You're broke and lost in Denver. Worst part is, your last hope to make sense of this was Valerie, and she's neck-deep in the craziness of it.*

Oh, and superheroes and supervillains are now real.

Attempting to find the restaurant again, Ralph wandered into a tall, narrow alley. Realizing his mistake, Ralph turned to find two men blocking the way back to the street. He ran, his lungs burning, but when the alley opened into a dumpster-lined dead end, Ralph understood they'd herded him to this point. A dozen or so people in leather streetwear blocked his escape.

"Sorry to disappoint you," he said, doing his best impression of a not-terrified person. "Someone already beat you to it. I got taken for my wallet, phone, the works. I'm not worth the trouble tonight, trust me."

"Not gonna lie, cash would've been nice," a pale man said. He wore a jacket with the sleeves torn away, revealing arms covered in black and red tattoos. "But money isn't our primary concern."

The men and women, each as thin and pale as the speaker, closed in on him. Ralph saw sharp points in their smiles. "You have got to be fucking *kidding me!*" he yelled, loud enough to stop a few of them in their tracks. "Vampires? Seriously? Vampires are real now?"

"What's with this guy?" snickered a woman with a nose chain.

A thick mist rose up from the ground and flooded the entire alley. Ralph thought it came from his attackers, but they sounded as surprised as he was.

"It's the Gentleman!" yelled the tattooed leader. "Run!"

Forgetting Ralph, the group fled in every direction. The mist thickened until Ralph could only see a bit of brick wall and pavement. The sickening screams and crunches around him kept him glued to the spot.

All became quiet, and a man in a dark gray suit with a long cape appeared in the smoke.

"Thank you, I think," Ralph said.

Beneath the brim of the stranger's hat, swirling mist obscured his face. "There is something wrong about you, Ralph Rogers. Something does not fit. Where do you come from? What are you doing here?"

"I don't know. I'm just trying to make sense of things."

"What do you know of the Ocularist?" the stranger asked.

"Not much. I don't know anything about you, either."

"I am, and ever shall be, a Gentleman," the man said. "It is as good a name as any."

"From the comics, right. Of course you are. Can you help me find a cab?" *Any port in a storm*, he thought.

"That's not of my concern," said the Gentleman. "I simply followed when I felt a disturbance in the aether."

"The vampires?" Ralph asked.

"No, you. Those rats may have been drawn to you for reasons similar to my own. Know this, Ralph Rogers, beware of your effect on reality. It is already under terrible strain without someone pulling at the knots."

"So you won't help me?" asked Ralph.

"That's not my place, nor would I want it to be. At this point, you seem harmless enough. Greater concerns demand my attention." The Gentleman faded from view. "Hopefully we will not meet again."

"Hello?" Ralph wandered out of the alley. "I guess giving a guy cab fare doesn't fall under the definition of chivalry."

A checkered cab drove down the empty street, and Ralph hailed it and climbed inside.

"Before we go anywhere," Ralph said, "You need to know I was robbed, and they took my wallet. If you can get me to my hotel, I'm sure we can work something out."

"I'm sure we can," said the driver, and Ralph relaxed.

The driver reached above the sun visor, and Ralph's momentary relief ended as the car filled with gas.

ALPH REGAINED CONSCIOUSNESS in the manliest room in existence, decorated in brass and polished wood. A classic Irish bar covered one side of the room, while on the other stood a substantial fireplace. Above the mantel hung a coat of arms, flanked by two standing goats. Written on a scroll beneath the coat of arms were the words, "Serve and Obey." Ralph sat up on the oiled leather couch, and the world swam.

"Please proceed with care, Mr. Rogers," said the sophisticated man sitting in an ancient wingback chair. He wore a simple suit, perfectly tailored. Setting down his glass of amber liquid, he said, "The gas is harmless, but its effects may linger. You will find your wallet, cell phone, and car keys on the table in front of you. We tracked them down as a show of goodwill."

"Where am I?" Ralph asked, bending over to put his head between his knees.

"You are in one of our clubs. We hoped to speak with you concerning your recent movements. We would not recommend alcohol, but might we bring you a glass of water?"

"Please don't be offended if I don't trust you not to drug me," Ralph said. "Again."

"Touché, Mr. Rogers. Quite right. Straight to business, then. What brings you to the city?"

"I wanted to see an old friend."

"Yes, Valerie Hall. Our attempts to locate her following the Red Ned incident have proven unsuccessful."

"I'm sure she's fine," Ralph said, pocketing his Darius the Diabolist wallet, keys, and phone. "She knows her way around."

"We're sure she does," said the sophisticated man. "She likely fared better than you, I'm afraid. It seems there was an incident—an attempted mugging?"

"Something like that."

"Fortunately, it appears the Gentleman intervened. That is noteworthy in and of itself, but it also seems he took the time to speak with you. Most unusual. Do you recollect what he said?"

"Nothing special. 'Be more careful,' 'Stay out of alleys,' that sort of thing."

"Ah, of course. The reason we ask why you are here, Mr. Rogers, is because you haven't been acting like yourself."

Ralph stifled a laugh.

"Mr. Rogers? Have we said something humorous?"

"I'm not sure." Ralph collected himself. "You tell me. Why do you care how I spent my summer vacation? How am I not myself?"

"We keep a casual eye on all Pithos employees, especially writers. The company's loose connection to various Anoms is worth keeping tabs on."

"Anoms?" Ralph asked.

"Anomalous humans. It's a fairly common term."

"Sure, sorry," Ralph said. "I misheard you."

This guy knows things, Ralph thought. *I need to get more information out of him than he gets out of me.*

"You're typically a homebody, Mr. Rogers. You travel when work or family obligations require it, or when a significant other drags you somewhere tropical. However, in the last few months you have traveled without any of these reasons. To visit friends, and now to this city."

"I was doing a favor for a friend."

"Yes, a friend. One Damon Ripley, movie star and lead of the upcoming *Danny Drastic* film. We're to understand that you procured for him several rare collectibles."

"Why do you keep saying 'we?'" Ralph asked.

"Because we're speaking on behalf of the Order, Mr. Rogers."

"What order?"

"The Humble Order of Haberdashers," said the sophisticated man.

"Never heard of it," Ralph said. "A name like that, I would remember."

"If you have never heard of it, it is because that is how we prefer it. Now, on the subject of these collectibles, the comic magazines. They are considered valuable?"

"I have no idea what defines *valuable* for you folks. But for us working joes, yeah, they're valuable. Damon paid good money for them."

The sophisticated man smiled. "Of course he did. That isn't our concern. We want to know the origin of the comic magazines. Our reports indicate you performed a fruitless search for them from your home. Then you holed up for several days in a flea-bitten motel before delivering the books to Damon."

"That sounds about right," Ralph said. "A fun way to spend a few days. A mini-vacation. It sounds like you're making a big deal about tiny details."

"We tend to concern ourselves with tiny details. Our question remains: Where did you acquire the comic magazines? You didn't have them when you left Austin, but they were in your possession when you reached Oklahoma City. Your bank account reveals no transactions that could have paid for something so valuable. Where did they come from, Mr. Rogers?"

Ralph thought of the dead man in the bath robe. "I'm afraid that's confidential."

"Nothing is confidential, where we are concerned."

Ralph leaned forward and looked the sophisticated man in the eye. "You don't know where they came from because I covered my tracks. Like you did when you stole my wallet and my phone."

"If that is the case, then we're truly impressed. Allow me to ask you a final question: are you familiar with a man by the name of the Ocularist?"

Before Ralph could answer, the ceiling vanished.

3

"**H**AND HIM OVER, HABERDASHER," said the flying metal man.

Ralph jumped to his feet, his eyes locked on the being who had removed the roof above him. The man—*Robot?* Ralph wondered—had a covering of dark gray, almost black metal. He floated without effort or apparent means of propulsion.

The sophisticated man remained seated. "Please remain calm, Ironworks. We would hate to witness one of your infamous rampages. Mr. Rogers is free to go at any time."

"Sure he is," said Ironworks. "Rogers, would you like me to get you out of here? Just say the word."

Ralph looked back and forth between the well-dressed man and what could be a robot monster. *I'm ill-equipped for this world*, he thought. *I don't know friend or foe here.*

"Rogers, your friend Valerie is worried about you," Ironworks said.

Good enough for me, he thought. "A ride out of here would be great. The last cab I took was more trouble than it was worth."

Ironworks touched down beside Ralph, the floor creaking beneath his weight.

"We'll continue our conversation another time," said the sophisticated man. "It seems you have powerful friends, Mr. Rogers."

"Looks that way, doesn't it?" Ralph said. Ironworks put his arm behind Ralph's back, and the two rose into the air.

"We'll send you a bill for the repairs," said the sophisticated man.

"I doubt that," said Ironworks, and he and Ralph launched into the sky.

The ground fell away. Ralph's stomach sank, like on the first drop of a roller coaster, and he tried to grab onto the cold metal of Ironwork's shoulders.

"Don't worry, Rogers. I've got you. I've been flying with passengers for a long time. We'll level out before you get sick, and I think you'll find it a smoother ride than any airplane."

Ralph held on tight anyway. "Who was that guy?" he asked.

"One of the Haberdashers," Ironworks said. "A higher-up in the organization, judging from the lack of a mask. They're a secret society that's been around for hundreds of years, but in the last century they've delved into super criminal activities. They're bad news, Rogers."

"How can I even hear you?" There was less wind than when Ralph drove with the windows down.

"I cut a precise aeroacoustic path through the air."

Ralph watched the ground glide beneath them. "Are you a robot?"

"Valerie said you might ask that. I'm not quite a robot, no."

"What, then? Are you a man wearing armor? A human brain in a metal body?"

"It's such a long time since I've been asked these questions. I'm a metal golem, created by alchemy in the 1930s."

"Oh my God. You're Potbelly!"

"I have gone by that name, yes."

"But I thought Potbelly was a robot that looked like an old stove."

Ironworks laughed, a surprisingly human sound. "You're working on outdated assumptions. The true method of my creation—that an alchemist created me to fight the Nazis—was revealed in 1942."

"When did you change your appearance?"

"I was ... destroyed. The pieces of my body were re-forged in 1994. Someone else used it for a while, so my current colleagues tracked down what some philosophers call my soul. This allowed me to take back control of my body."

"Take back? Who was controlling it?"

"It wouldn't be hard for you to find out, but I'd rather not talk about it."

Ralph started to speak, but thought better of it.

"Two to dive," the metal golem said.

4

WHAT?"

As the syllable left Ralph's mouth, the world changed around him, though much more abruptly than it had over the past several months.

They flew into a rounded metal hallway like that of a submarine. Copper pipes and bundles of wire snaked along the walls. As they touched down on the grated floor, Ralph felt a sense of antiquity. He heard the clanking of metal on metal as Ironworks walked.

Ralph looked around, trying to keep calm. "How did we get here?"

"Sorry," Ironworks said. "I keep forgetting you won't know things. We're in Atlantis."

"The resort?" Ralph asked.

"No, the sunken city located off the coast of Cuba. The explorer Edgar Ignatius rediscovered it back in the late thirties, not long after his journey into the hollow part of the Earth. He found the place, even hit it off with the Atlanteans. The Freedom Cadre have used it as a headquarters since the forties. Edgar has been gone for a while now, but his great-granddaughter, Helena, is our liaison with the rest of Atlantis."

"This is your secret hideout?"

"You could call it that, I suppose. One dome of it, anyway. It's the only sanctuary we've used that wasn't immediately invaded. You wouldn't believe the trouble that comes your way once the bad guys know your address."

"So what, you meet here once a week?"

"Sometimes," Ironworks said and laughed—an echoing, metallic sound. "The Cadre shows up when they're needed. When a team is too powerful, it threatens the status quo. Governments give us breathing room as long as we aren't perceived as a standing army."

They passed a wide convex window looking out onto the ocean floor. Below them, a branching network of transparent domes, some at least a mile across, stretched into the distance. A vehicle resembling an angler fish—but the size of a bus—zoomed past. A green-skinned child stared back at Ralph from the submarine, and they waved to each other. *It's a Saturday morning cartoon version of Atlantis*, Ralph thought. *This can't possibly be real.*

After the sub was out of view, Ralph saw something enormous drift past, just out of range of the light. He swallowed over the lump in his throat. "Anything out there I should worry about?"

"Relax, the Atlanteans are on good terms with everything living down here." Ironworks stopped at a round hatch. "Here we are."

The domed ceiling of the immense room was completely transparent. Exterior lights revealed a brightly-colored school of fish swimming past. The fear of being crushed overwhelmed Ralph. The vast city of Atlantis stretched out in one direction, making it clear this structure resided on the outskirts of the city proper. The white-marble floor gleamed, and the room smelled simple and clean like an operating room. In the center of it all, men and women sat around a large table, made of the same marble as the floor. Their dress varied from street clothes to fancy suits to brightly colored capes and tights.

Valerie, still dressed as Titania, stood and patted the seat next to her. Her green eyes shined through her golden domino mask. "Have a seat, Ralph," she said, "We're all friends here." The rest of the group looked him over without saying a word.

The table was only half occupied, and Ralph sat down in a surprisingly comfortable chair which felt custom-made for him. The other seats all had some sort of symbol, representing their occupant. Valerie's chair had the same letter T she wore on her chest, and Ironworks's chair had a silver Hebrew symbol.

"What am I doing here, V—?" Ralph caught himself before using her real name. *In this world, that could be a huge mistake.*

Valerie smiled and removed her mask. "That's okay. No one here keeps their secret identities from each other. But don't be surprised if they keep that information from you. You've met Ironworks, so let me introduce you to Songweaver, Rika, and Danny Drastic."

Ralph looked around at the room's impossible occupants. Songweaver was a Native American woman in a fringed leather jacket, just like the comic character from the *Meta Boy* arcade game. A woven orange strip covered her forehead, and short black feathers lined the top and bottom, making her eyes stand out like two pearls. Rika was a young Asian woman in a white tank top with red streaks in her hair. Danny Drastic—*Danny Drastic is real,* Ralph thought—wore body armor and round pilot goggles. His chrome rocket pack, looking like two Art Deco vacuum cleaners, hung by its leather straps from the back of his chair.

Rika cracked her knuckles. "Titania told us your story, but we want to hear it straight from you."

"Are you sure?" Ralph asked. "It will sound—I might just be crazy."

Valerie put her hand on his arm. "Ralph, the members of the Cadre listen to the people they trust."

Danny Drastic said, "You wouldn't believe the trouble you avoid by listening when your friend says the city council has been replaced with reptilian humanoids." The people around the table laughed.

"If you say so," Ralph said.

Then, he told his story.

This time he didn't leave out the corpse or his theft of the comics, but he avoided Valerie's eyes. The group was silent except for a few clarifying questions. Ralph caught the others eyeing each other across the table, but he couldn't read their reaction to his story.

When he finished describing his encounter with the haberdasher, Songweaver said, "Thank you, Mr. Rogers. That's quite a tale. Would you please wait outside?"

Ralph looked to Valerie, who nodded. He walked through what he thought was the same door, but it led him into a beautiful atrium full of fragrant flowers. Sitting down on a stone bench, he listened to the sound of a waterfall. A rainbow floated in splashing droplets of water.

I've lost control of my life, Ralph thought. *Sure, it's been that way since I was fourteen, but now we've reached a point where that lack of control could kill me. That room of imaginary people could decide anything. They might toss me out the airlock. Maybe they'll crush me into a tiny cube and put me on the pile of other suckers they've crushed into tiny cubes.*

Maybe I'll wake up in my bed, and my worst problem will be getting my TV back from Sandra.

After an eternity, Ralph felt the air pressure in the room change. No one asked him to come back inside, to please rise and hear the verdict. The open door was invitation enough.

The round table room appeared much brighter than the atrium. He shielded his eyes, bringing the Freedom Cadre into focus. The other seats at the table were now filled. Some of the occupants, like Ironworks, did not seem entirely human. He recognized several from Pithos comic books.

Beside Songweaver sat a sickly man hooked to an IV, and past him was a Hispanic man in a skeleton body-suit. Further along the table was a woman with a green tint to her skin. Brass buckles and functioning gears adorned her snug leather outfit. Beyond her sat a blonde man in a blue and red uniform, attempting to balance an ink pen on his nose.

Sitting next to Rika was a black man in streamlined riot gear holding a silver shield. Directly to Ralph's right was a muscular woman wearing a uniform that looked like it was made from snake or lizard skin. Two reptilian wings protruded from her back.

It struck him for the first time that this was not a group of co-workers having an afternoon meeting, these were demigods weaving his fate. Ralph wondered for a moment who held his string and who held the scissors.

Valerie stood to greet him. "Let me introduce the rest of the Cadre."

"I might know some of them," Ralph said. He turned to the man in the skeleton suit. "You're Mr. Stiff, right? And the guy in red and blue is Jack Spratt. The man with the shield is the Advocate. And the woman with the wings, you're Wyvern, aren't you?"

Ralph raised his index fingers, pointing at the man with the IV and the woman in brass and leather. "You two, I don't know."

They remained silent.

Valerie put her hand on Ralph's shoulder. "They're Helena Ignatius and Luke. Let's talk." As he took his seat, she said, "Ralph, I'm sorry."

Those words were the starting gun that caused Ralph's heart to race, charging around the track at full speed. His chest tightened and his palms grew clammy.

"We've discussed the results of our tests," Mr. Stiff said in a measured voice.

"Tests?" Ralph asked. "What tests?"

"The first Cadre members you met have dozens of senses beyond the usual twenty-three," said Songweaver.

Ralph didn't know where to begin to not understand that statement.

"We take a close look when someone comes in here acting strange," Jack Spratt said. "You can't be too careful with entities like Red Eye out there. Or when people hire telepaths like Mesmer Eyes just to win at traffic court. Not to mention all the ways you could be an impostor. There's Soubrette. There's Face Swapper, who always leaves a confusing mess. You don't want to get caught up in that game of musical chairs."

"Zip it, Jack," the man in the skeleton costume said.

Valerie spoke up. "While you were in here before, we went over you with a fine-tooth comb. Songweaver? She's the last Dreamer of the Pomo people, and fulfills a unique mystical role in our dimension. On top of the basics like reading your aura, she knows your supernatural inclinations, your precise sympathetic resonance, and the most likely date of your death."

In shock, Ralph looked at Songweaver. "Don't worry, sweetie," she said. "It's almost never today. And even if it is, maybe it'll be quick."

Valerie continued, "Ironworks can see the strength of your life force and if you're in control of your own body. Rika's cybernetics can tell the make and model of the last car you drove. And I can tell if you're lying."

"Is that a magic thing?" Ralph asked.

She nudged him. "No, you big dork. It's because I've known you since we were seven."

"And I can tell if you've recently traveled in time," Drastic said.

X-ray vision is just the start, isn't it? Ralph thought.

"But there's no way to conclusively prove or disprove your story," Jack Spratt said. "Our all-reality-is-bullshit detector ain't all it's cracked up to be."

"Wait a minute," he said. "If you're really Danny Drastic, you have a time machine, right? I can't believe I'm even suggesting this, but you could go back in time and see if I'm telling the truth."

Before Drastic could answer, Rika said, "Wouldn't work. His machine is damaged. It can only travel forward in time. And even if he could go back, there's a good chance it would be along this same timeline. It would be this world's past, not yours."

Valerie, Danny Drastic, and Songweaver nodded in agreement. Ironworks made no movement. *He isn't even breathing,* Ralph realized.

"Okay, fine. What did your tests tell you?" he asked.

"One: you're probably Ralph Rogers," Mr. Stiff said. "Two: you're telling the truth. Or at least you believe what you're telling us is the truth."

"Probably?" Ralph asked. "I'm *probably* Ralph Rogers?"

"Vegas odds are around ninety-nine to one that you're you," Jack Spratt said. "I bet ten dollars against you. Don't take it personal."

Songweaver spoke, her voice crisp and beautiful like a clarinet. "If I saw you on the street, I wouldn't look twice. You look normal in passing. But because of your story, we had to look deeper."

"What about me isn't me?" Ralph asked.

"You're ever-so-slightly out of step with this reality," the skeleton man said. "Just a smidgeon. It's probably what the Gentleman noticed about you. Your story is worth our attention."

"Thank you for that," Ralph said. "But can someone please tell me what this means?"

"It means you're not crazy," Wyvern said, patting his arm. "If you're not lying, and you're not crazy, then this could be a big deal."

Ralph laughed. "I barely understand the power this room contains. What could possibly constitute a big deal for you people? Full-scale alien invasion? Ragnarok?"

The Advocate said, "If you're right, Ralph, and the world is changing, we need to find out if someone is behind it. To find out why they want the world to be different."

The gaunt, robed man with the IV spoke. "But if we're a part of the problem, how do we proceed? At what point did we all show up? If we fix the problem, am I just a guy in a hospital somewhere?"

"Luke, it's okay," Danny Drastic said. "We'll figure this out." He turned to Ralph and said, "We have to focus on you first. So far, you're the center of it all."

"Did you figure out who killed Chill?" Ralph asked.

Songweaver shook her head. "As far as we can tell, the murder never even happened in this reality. But we're confident you're telling the truth that it occurred, and that you weren't responsible."

"What about the comics?" Ralph asked. "The ones I found in Chill's house. This all started with them. Can't you run your tests on the comics?"

Danny Drastic raised his goggles and said, "We already have."

Ralph's eyes widened. "Damon Ripley! You son of a bitch. You're Danny Drastic now, aren't you? The *actual* Danny Drastic."

"As far as I remember, Ralph, I've always been Drastic. Our memories aren't the same, and that's why we need to keep an eye on you." He licked his lips. "It's possible you're the one changing the world around you."

"I'm God now, is that it?" Ralph asked. "I'd love to know how you tested for that. I'm not doing this, Damon, Danny, whatever you want to be called."

"Then why are you the only one who remembers the world the way you say it was before?" the man with the shield asked. "If you're not the cause, Ralph Rogers, what makes you so special?"

"I don't have any answers for you." The possible consequences of this meeting hit him. "How are you going to deal with me? Are you going to kill me?"

"Of course not," Valerie said. "We're the good guys here, I promise."

The Advocate said, "But just in case you're the catalyst, we're going to ask you to stay here in Atlantis until we can get a read on the situation. Helena's given us the okay."

Helena nodded. "Our philosophers are as interested as the Cadre in learning the truth behind the situation."

"So, I'm a prisoner here?" Ralph asked.

Jack Spratt said, "More like a guest who isn't allowed to leave."

"Only until we figure out what's going on," Songweaver said. "We need to find out, if this isn't the way the world should be, how it should work. And if we need to change it back, we need to figure out how to do that. That won't be easy if we cease to exist the moment it happens."

"How do you decide if you should change the world back?" Ralph asked. "Take a vote?"

Ironworks spoke for the first time since he arrived with Ralph. "Sometimes you can be the villain and not even realize it. If you let us, the Cadre can help."

"It's for your own good, kid," Rika said. "Whoever or whatever is capable of altering reality on this level is fucking scary, especially to a guy whose idea of danger is a broken pencil lead."

"There is no safer place in the world than Atlantis," Helena said. "It's a source of pride for my people."

Ralph looked up to the arching, crystal-clear ceiling and sighed. "Fine. I'll stay here. For now. But do you have any idea what could have caused this? Do you know anyone powerful enough?"

Jack Spratt held up his hand, which grew cartoonish and oversized. He counted off on fingers the size of wine bottles. "Periscope Jones could do it. Maybe. Then you've got Alan Den and his genie, but the effects would've only lasted twenty-four hours. And the genie wouldn't have existed in your boring reality, so—"

"That's enough, Jack," Mr. Stiff said. "Ralph, I'm sorry, but we've decided the less you know, the better. Just in case it could prevent reality from shifting further."

"Is there anyone else who knows about this?" Songweaver asked.

"Other than Valerie? Only my friend, Ben Walker."

"We may need to bring them here too," Songweaver replied. "If contact with you is causing the problem, then it's possible the effect could spread exponentially."

"Make sure, when you get him, that his dad will be okay. Ben takes care of him. Or at least he used to." Ralph thought of their argument. "He might not be happy to hear it's about me."

Valerie frowned.

"What is it?" Ralph asked.

"I'm sorry." She bit her lip. "Ben is dead."

5

RALPH EXPLORED THE FREEDOM CADRE'S AT-
LANTEAN BASE.

His favorite area by far was the trophy room, a superhero cliché brought to life. The artifacts preached a false history, each with a plaque providing just enough information to
keep Ralph curious. Glass cases housed many of the items, while
others sat on the ground or hung from the ceiling. Faceless man-
nequins wore uniforms, some made obsolete and others left behind by the dead.

'*Mr. Stiff's First Generation Grappling Hook.*' '*Mummy Magician's Crown.*' '*The Dowser's Pendulum.*' '*The Alchemist's Golden
Nose.*' '*Mad Gasser's Gas Mask.*' '*Nylon's First Uniform.*'

She must have gotten cold fighting crime in that,
Ralph thought.

'*Robot Pteranodon Used by Lizard Men in Attack on San Francisco.*' '*The Bride-Groom's Cake Cannon.*' '*Bastone's Canes.*' '*Molly Pitcher's Ramrod.*' '*The Violition's Violin.*' '*The Mechanic's
Throwing Cards.*' A memorial to Oceanus. A smashed Ocularist mask.

Ralph stood in front of a mannequin wearing Black Snake's old costume: black jeans, a snakeskin vest, and leather platform shoes.

Ben would have loved this place, Ralph thought. He wiped tears from his eyes.

Next to the Black Snake display was a Titania costume, different from the one Valerie wore. Although the color scheme was similar, this uniform showed more ornate details. Valerie's costume was streamlined, but the current model lacked the sophistication of this museum piece. Both costumes had the same *T* emblem, with the crossbar beneath the collarbones and the vertical line terminating in an oval at the navel. Instead of the pants and boots, the older costume possessed a gilded skirt and lace sandals.

The door behind him slid open with a soft hiss. He turned to see Valerie enter the room, wearing the black and white dress from when they met for dinner. Smiling, she looked around at the memorabilia in the room as she approached. "We probably shouldn't let you come in here, but we don't want you feeling like a prisoner. Everything is supposed to be disarmed, but you wouldn't believe the trouble the Mummy Magician's cursed crown can cause. Wearing it would seriously mess up a normal person."

"So I shouldn't have tried it on?" Ralph laughed at Valerie's horrified look. She smacked him on the shoulder. "Don't worry," he said. "I keep my hands inside the car at all times. Is this your old costume?"

"Oh, no." Valerie pursed her lips. "It belonged to my mom, the real Titania. Well, it's a recreation of the one she used. Wyvern made it for me."

"Your mom? Wow. Real Titania? What do you—"

"It's easy to forget how interesting this place can be," she interrupted. "Danny put it all together."

"The Damon Ripley I know loves his kitschy collectibles," Ralph said. He pointed at Nylon's revealing costume. "That looks like something right out of his collection."

Valerie gazed at the costume and frowned. "I was never fair to Nylon," she said.

"What happened to her?"

"Sorry, buddy, you know I can't say anything. I shouldn't have mentioned it."

"Then let's talk about something else. Why so dressed up? Got a hot date?"

She blushed. "Since our dinner was such a mess, I thought maybe we could make up for it."

"This time I won't try to convince you I'm not crazy."

She raised an eyebrow.

"Okay," he said. "That I'm not *completely* crazy."

"I'll get the drinks," she said.

CHINESE FOOD CONTAINERS COVERED a corner of the Freedom Cadre's meeting table.

"There's no way *Text Me Back* is the best Damon Ripley romantic comedy," Ralph said. "That honor goes to *Up Late in Manhattan*. He had so much more chemistry with Janeane Garofalo than Patricia Arquette."

Valerie snorted. "More chemistry? What about the hot tub scene in *Text Me Back*? It felt way more natural and funny than the funeral in *Up Late in Manhattan*."

"I'll give you that." He fumbled with his chopsticks. "At least they're both better than *FBI Love You*."

"I couldn't even finish that one. Damon came across as a jerk, and not in the good way. And I can't stand Kathy Griffin."

"Ah, she's okay. You know what Damon's best romantic movie is? It's not a rom-com."

"*Einstein and Marilyn*," they said together, laughing.

"Katherine Heigl killed it as Monroe," Valerie said. "Damon wasn't bad either. His makeup was so good it was scary. But that accent was terrible."

"So terrible." Ralph adjusted an imaginary pair of glasses and said in his worst German accent, "'Ven a man zits with a pretty girl for an hour, it zeems like a minute. Zat's relativity.'"

"Oh my God. Just stop."

"'Gravitation eez not responsible for people falling in love.'"

Valerie snorted again. "I'm serious. Shut up. You do a worse Einstein than Damon, and that's saying something."

"'God does not play dice with love.'"

Valerie tossed a half-eaten eggroll at him.

Ralph waved his napkin in surrender. "Okay, I give. This food's too delicious for ammo."

"I've loved this place ever since Rika told me about it."

"Did you fly there? Cape, costume, the whole bit?"

Looking sheepish, Valerie shrugged.

"So where did the food come from?" Ralph asked. "Straight from China? New York?"

"Wisconsin."

The two of them laughed.

Ralph dipped an eggroll into a plastic container of sweet-and-sour sauce. "So how are things going out there?"

"You know I can't answer that. The entire point of keeping you here is to stop reality from changing further."

"Is it working?" he asked.

She looked at the floor. "Let's talk about something else. Is there anyone you need me to check on?"

"You already emailed Pithos for me." Ralph sighed. "I hope they don't cancel me. Having my own book is a big highlight in this brave new world."

"I hope it's not the only highlight," Valerie said, grinning. "Don't worry. I spoke with Charles Caulder, and he said they'll handle it. He told me you've turned in more work on time than anyone else at Pithos. If the book goes on hiatus, it might even create some buzz."

"Who spoke to him? Val-you or Titania-you?"

"He knows Valerie Hall, so she dialed the phone number. I told him that you had a personal matter. Don't worry."

Ralph gave up on his chopsticks and reached for a fork. "How long have we known each other, Val?"

"Too damn long," she said, laughing.

"So why didn't we ever give it a shot?"

Valerie pursed her lips. "That sounds an awful lot like outside information, Ralphie. Do I need to write the rules on your hand so you'll remember?"

"Fine. What if I told you why it never happened in the world I remember?"

She finished her glass of wine and slowly poured another. "I suppose that would be all right."

"The way I lived it, during the short-lived success of my comic, I didn't make any time for friends. For you. Then, after the embarrassment of my book getting cancelled, I couldn't stand to be around anyone. That probably went double for you, since you were the driving force behind what felt like an enormous mistake. It wasn't fair to you. I was a selfish, embarrassed kid."

"How'd you end up with Sandra Madison?" Valerie asked.

"Met her at one of my shows. We were great together, at first." He grinned, but his eyes betrayed him. "I felt like a washed-up loser, and she tried to pull me out of that. Not her fault she failed. When she finally left, I was as relieved as she was."

Valerie patted his hand. "I'm sorry."

"I'm the one who needs to apologize. You deserved better. You were too good a friend to let slip away like that."

"Apology accepted." Valerie offered her hand. They shook on it.

"What happened here on the flipside?" he asked.

Valerie waved a finger. "I swear, I'm not going to mess with a marker. I'm tattooing it on you!"

"I'll make an educated guess. I ignored you when Against the Grain first picked up my book, then I acted all pathetic and closed off when I got cancelled. Just like I remember it. But when

Pithos gave me another shot, I went back to ignoring everyone. Then I ended up with Sandra because I was rich and she had excellent taste in artists."

"It's no spoiler that you're a shallow bastard," Valerie said, laughing.

"I really am sorry," Ralph said. "Even if you didn't let me in on your secret, I know you could have used a friend with the whole hero thing."

"I assumed you knew, at least since—" She slapped her hands over her own mouth.

"Now who needs a written reminder about the rules?" Ralph asked.

"Hush. When I saw the look on your face when I fought Red Ned, it told me how serious the problem was. But by the time I got back, you were gone."

"First comic book battle I've witnessed in real life," he said. "It was too much, left me rattled. Did I tell you I passed out?"

"Poor baby!" Valerie said. "We'll have to get you a fainting couch."

Pushing away his plate, Ralph asked, "So how does that work?"

"What, passing out? I think it has something to do with getting the vapors." Valerie fanned herself dramatically.

"Be nice. I mean your powers. I saw you use strength, flight, maybe invulnerability—"

"The classic trifecta," Valerie said. "Invulnerability is pushing it a bit far, I'd go with damage resistant. Sort of a must with super strength. Otherwise I'd break my arm every time I punch some chump. I have a few bonus abilities too. Magical heroes can be a bit complicated."

"Are you super strong all the time?" Ralph asked.

"What did you have in mind?"

"I was wondering if I did this," he said, taking her hand in his, "if you would snap my fingers like twigs."

"Depends on my mood." She lightly squeezed his hand before releasing it. "But yes, I can turn it on and off. Why do you ask?"

"No reason."

They smiled at each other.

"Thanks, Val. I'm glad I have someone I can trust in all this."

"Then it's a good thing I'll be around."

"Promise?"

"You calling me a welcher, Rogers?" She stood. "Come on. I'll show you to your room."

At that moment, in the trophy room, the Ocularist eyeball helmet lit up and red numbers began to scroll across its cornea.

ALERIE AND RALPH WOKE UP on a couch in Ralph's room, as a shrill alarm screamed through the halls. "What's going on?" Ralph blinked the sleep out of his eyes.

"The bubble's been breached," she said. "Put your shoes on. Atlantis is being invaded."

"What? How do you know that?"

Valerie brushed her hair back past her left ear. Ralph could see a faint circular outline. "Communicator disk," she said and went back to searching the couch.

Ralph stumbled out of the way as she tossed aside throw pillows. Finding her clutch handbag, she pulled out what looked like a tattered silk handkerchief.

A bright flash of light forced Ralph to shield his eyes, and the scent of wildflowers overwhelmed him. When he opened his eyes, Valerie was now Titania. He finished pulling on his shoes j before a distant explosion shook the room and knocked him off his feet.

Valerie caught him by the elbow. "Stay here and bolt the door!" She rocketed out the door.

Ralph pulled the door shut, but stopped before bolting it.

Is this who I am now? he asked. *A prisoner who gets shuffled back and forth?*

He steadied himself.

I will not be a bystander. He flung open the door.

Another explosion shook the floor as he sprinted down the hall. The alarm blared and the grating sounds of conflict grew louder, telling him where to go.

Several flights of stairs carried him to the bottom floor and the headquarters' colossal front door, already torn from its hinges. He realized as he dove behind a pile of rubble that he had overestimated his usefulness.

A frenzy of motion filled the open area outside the building. The Haberdashers, armed with energy weapons, had breached the airlocks. Above him, from the second floor, Rika prevented more suited men from exiting the tunnel by firing energy bursts from a mounted weapon.

"Kill my friend and wreck my gear, will you?" Rika yelled. "I'll carve replacement parts from your bones!"

Ralph saw Rika's mech suit, lying on the dry ocean floor with two jagged holes blasted in its chest. He was surprised she had survived.

The Advocate was already dead, his charred corpse lying at the feet of the Ocularist. The villain blasted away with a thick beam emitted from the iris of his helmet. Mr. Stiff, Danny Drastic, Wyvern, Ironworks, and Titania fought against the horde of Haberdashers and traded blows with the Ocularist himself.

Across the chamber, a Haberdasher fired at Danny Drastic. Enraged, Drastic spun and aimed his own blaster. Caught in the beam, the Haberdasher's weapon blinked out of existence. The Haberdasher looked up in shock just as Drastic used the momentum of his rocket pack to slug the man in the jaw, knocking him unconscious.

That's right, Ralph thought. *His ray gun only affects non-living things.*

Songweaver hovered above the crowd, generating crackling, visible energy that intertwined like the reeds of her baskets. At first, Ralph had no idea what she was doing, but he understood when he saw where she focused her efforts. Her magic was all that held together a huge crack in the dome, which threatened to give way and drown them all.

The flying Wyvern dove for an attack, her wings tucked tight behind her. She tore a gash in the Ocularist's back, but he reached out and grabbed her by the wing. He snapped the wing with a sickening crack, and Wyvern cried out in pain as she hit the ground. The Ocularist placed a hand on either side of her face and lifted her off the ground.

"No!" cried Mr. Stiff as the Ocularist snapped Wyvern's neck.

As Wyvern's body fell to the ground, Titania, Danny Drastic, and Jack Spratt lunged at the Ocularist. The three heroes dodged his blasts, but provided little more than a distraction as Mr. Stiff pummeled the villain. Each blow connected, the impacts echoing throughout the dome, but the Ocularist took each strike in stride.

Ralph peered around the edge of the doorway, trying to keep Valerie in view as she attacked, retreated, and attacked again.

Don't die, Valerie, Ralph prayed. A hand fell on his shoulder.

"What are you doing out here?" asked Ironworks. "Trying to get yourself killed?"

"I wanted to help, if I could," Ralph said.

"How are you supposed to do that, kid?" Ironworks asked. "Paint his portrait? You saw what happened to Wyvern and Advocate. Come on, I'm putting you somewhere safe."

Ironworks grabbed Ralph's arm with a cold metal hand and pulled him down a hallway. A few turns later, Ironworks shoved Ralph into the trophy room.

"This room is safe," the golem said. "We'll settle things outside and come for you. No one will reach you while I draw breath, understand?"

But you don't breathe, Ralph thought.

Out loud, he said, "I understand."

"Good. And I have to warn you—if you've lied, if you're the one behind this—you're better off killing yourself before Stiff sees you again."

Before Ralph could reply, Ironworks was gone, locking the door behind him.

8

HE BATTLE CONTINUED as Ralph ran from one cabinet to the next, searching for a weapon he could use to defend himself.

The trophy room is essentially an armory with all the firing pins removed, Ralph thought. *I'm a sitting duck if the Ocularist gets past the Cadre.* Hoping to buy some time by barricading the door, he started with a long cabinet of the original Freedom Cadre's costumes. At first it felt nailed down, but Ralph gave it all he had and edged the cabinet in front of the heavy locked door. Ralph added one display case after another, until the majority of the museum's lower level was pressed against the exit.

Then he heard the crack.

In his early twenties, Ralph wrecked his car, sliding through a stop sign on a rainy night. He was lucky to survive. The sound he heard now, in the Cadre's Atlantis headquarters, was like that car crash, only amplified.

Water began trickling in under the door.

Scrambling for the spiral staircase, he sprinted for the upper level of the room and cursed the lack of a window.

"What the hell's going on out there?" he shouted.

Water filled the room from sources seen and unseen. It no longer came only from under the door, but now seeped around the entire frame. Inside of a minute, the spiral staircase was half submerged.

I'm the rat, Ralph thought, *and this is how rats go out*. He looked around frantically for any sign of hope. His eyes landed on a gold and black shape floating in the water below him.

He jumped over the second level's railing and into water so cold it knocked the wind out of him. He thrashed in the water, sorting through the floating items, until he grasped the Mummy Magician's crown.

What did Valerie say? "*Wearing it would seriously mess up a normal person.*"

Ralph shoved his panic down into his frozen feet and put the crown on his head.

Nothing happened.

"Hope they saved the receipt." He threw the soaked headpiece aside and started up the spiral staircase. It pulled away from the second-level landing with a painful groan and crashed into the steadily rising water level. The heavy staircase sank.

Guess I'll be high enough to reach the second level soon enough, he thought, treading water. *But at this rate it will all be underwater in no time*. He latched onto a floating dummy wearing a 1940s Molly Pitcher outfit and prepared for the worst.

The heavy door exploded inward, sending Ralph's attempt at a barricade out into the room. The water rose faster, but Valerie soon appeared, swimming through the open doorway.

"Take a deep breath!" she yelled. After Ralph filled his lungs, she dragged him under, holding him close to her body as she used her powers to propel herself through the water. She reached the area she was looking for and smashed a hole into the room above.

"Stay with me, Ralph," she said, pulling him out of the water and to his feet. "Sorry it took me so long to get to you, but I had to get Helena and Luke to the control room. If Luke used his powers in the dome, we'd all be toast. Teleporters are offline.

I can get us out of here, but most of the area is warded against magic. We have to find the right exit."

He remembered the endless ocean outside the porthole.

"Please take your time finding the right exit."

Valerie rose into the air as she lifted Ralph off the ground. She planted her foot against the wall and launched her body forward like a sprinter. Ralph clung to her body as they zipped through one wide hallway after another.

"Uh-oh," Valerie said, stopping suddenly.

The vault-like door was blocked by a woman, flanked on each side by suited men carrying machine guns. She wore a red jacket with tails, white pants, the tallest heels Ralph had ever seen, and a rounded black cap. She held a studded riding crop in one hand and a brass bugle in the other. It was Sandra Madison, dressed exactly like the fox hunter painting that once hung in Ralph's living room.

"Slumming it already, Ralph?"

Sandra sneered her candy-red lips at Valerie.

"Get out of the way, Fox Hunter," Valerie said.

"Unlikely," Sandra said. To the Haberdashers, she added, "If she moves, shoot him."

"Just knock them out," Ralph said to Valerie. "I don't think they even have superpowers."

"I can't," she said. "Those guns are loaded with iron bullets."

"So?" Ralph asked.

Sandra laughed and raised the bugle to her lips. The sound it emitted was so loud, it sent both Ralph and Valerie to their knees. His ears ringing, he watched as Sandra struck Valerie across the face with her riding crop.

"Stop it!" He rushed at Sandra, but one of the Haberdashers whipped Ralph in the back of the head with the butt of his gun, knocking him to the ground.

Useless, Ralph thought. *I can't save myself in this world. I can't save anyone.*

He saw a blue snake out of the corner of his eye. By the time he realized it was an arm, the hand at the end of it had grabbed a Haberdasher and smashed him against the wall. The hand grabbed the unconscious man's dropped gun and clubbed the other Haberdasher over the head with it before going limp.

Ralph's eyes traced the arm to its source around a corner. Jack Spratt walked into view, the one arm stretched out and still on the floor. His other hand covered a messy wound in his stomach. Blood trickled from the corner of his mouth.

Sandra lifted her horn for another attack. Jack's extended arm flailed, knocking the trumpet away. The hero took another step forward and collapsed. She scrambled for the trumpet, but Valerie grabbed her by the shoulder, spun the woman around, and gave her what appeared to Ralph to be only a light shove, but Sandra flew back, slammed against the wall, and lay still.

"Is she dead?" Ralph asked.

"If she was, my powers would be gone," Valerie said. She noticed one of the Haberdashers was awake, his hand reaching for a dropped machine gun. Stepping on his outstretched fingers, she said, "Sometimes I really hate the no-kill clause in my contract."

She started toward Jack Spratt, but he shook his head. His arm reeled back in like a tape measure. "Get out of here," he said. "I should be okay."

"You're a mess," Valerie said. "Let me—"

"Go!" he said. "There's more coming. I'll hold them off until the portal disappears."

"See you soon," Valerie said.

Ralph nodded at Jack. "Thank you."

Jack picked up one of the guns with his free hand. "Don't let it hit you in the ass on the way out."

A hole opened in the air. Light exploded around them and Valerie was herself again, wearing her black and white dress. With a final glimpse back at Jack, she grabbed Ralph by the hand, and the two of them stepped through the portal.

9

ITH VALERIE'S POWERFUL ARMS wrapped around him, Ralph fell through a doorway onto soft green grass. She made a wide wave with her hand, and a heavy cushion of air pushed at the open door, slamming it shut. The instant the door reached the frame, the portal disappeared, leaving the two of them in a beautiful and undisturbed woodland glade at dusk.

"Are you okay?" Valerie asked, lifting Ralph to his feet.

"My clothes are dry," he said.

"Don't count on that being the weirdest thing that happens here," she said, surveying the area. Ralph followed her eyes. The woods were overgrown with enormous red mushrooms. Ralph fully expected a caterpillar to crawl onto one and light up a hookah.

He reached out to touch one of the mushroom's jagged white flecks, but Valerie grabbed his wrist. "Please don't touch anything," she said. "If someone tries to give you something, don't take it, and whatever you do, don't eat anything. We don't need that kind of headache today."

"Where are we?"

Valerie dusted herself off. "Tír na nÓg. Just call it the Land of the Young. We're safe here." She tilted her head, reconsidering. "*Relatively* safe. I'm serious about not touching anything. This place has a million tiny traps for mortals."

Ralph looked at the patch of grass where the door had been. A long rectangle of squashed grass was the only evidence it had ever existed. "How the hell did we get here?"

"Emergency exit," she said. "I have permission to come here in special circumstances. Mostly. I'm not sure how they'll feel about me bringing a plus-one, but we should be fine. Ground rules: No touching. Don't mention anything you'd hear someone say in a church."

"What if someone sneezes?"

"Don't even hand them a tissue. Speaking of, don't accept gifts. Don't buy anything. Don't say 'Thank you.' In fact, don't say anything to anyone unless I give you the okay. That includes answering riddles. If you do speak to anyone, don't be a smartass. Don't use the F-word, the one that rhymes with 'Larry,' They hate it." She looked around. "I know you probably wouldn't use my other name, but only call me Valerie while we're here."

"Not Tita—" Ralph began, but Valerie covered his mouth with her hand.

"This is not a time for more screw-ups, Rogers."

"Sorry, Val. What's with all the rules?"

"Remember where I get my power from?"

"From a piece of a magic fair—" He stopped himself before the off-limit word. "From a piece of that magic flag."

"That's right. A banner sewn by the Fair Folk. That's what you can call them when we're here—*here* being their home."

Ralph stared wide-eyed at his surroundings. "Are you telling me we're in another dimension?"

"Maybe."

"What do you mean, 'Maybe?'"

"It could be another dimension. It could be on an island that isn't on any map. Maybe we're somewhere in Scotland or Ireland, underground. I've never been too clear on that. The point is, we're here, wherever 'here' is, and some of the Fair Folk would prefer that you never leave. As in, ever. It's an old game, and they have a lot of experience playing it. I've been doing this since I was a kid, and I'm okay. So be a good Little Red Riding Hood and don't leave the path."

Valerie led the way through the woods. Ralph followed, stepping carefully around the huge mushrooms. Under the blue light of the moon, he had never felt a stronger sense of being watched. Thinking he saw a tiny someone standing on a branch or a fungus, he spun his head but saw nothing but shadows.

Time passed, but the moon remained static in the sky. Nothing seemed out of the ordinary to Valerie, so he kept his concerns to himself. He looked again at the moon. *Is it just me, or is the man in the moon a lot easier to see here?*

He wondered exactly how this sky related to the real-world sky, but he lacked the knowledge to compare. He looked for Orion and the Big Dipper, but nothing seemed to match.

"Val, do you know your constellations?" She didn't answer.

Valerie and the path were nowhere in sight. *Oldest trick in the book*, he thought. *As soon as she told me to stay on the path, I should have run shrieking into the damn woods. Saved us all some time.*

"Valerie?" The only answer came in the form of a howl in the distance.

So much for waiting right here like a good Little Red Riding Hood. Ralph hurried toward what he hoped was the path. The sense of being watched intensified, and although Ralph avoided looking for the source, the creatures seemed less concerned about being seen.

As blind panic threatened to overwhelm him, Ralph spotted a lamp glowing among the trees. Reaching it, he found a parked camper trailer. A blonde man in a flannel shirt sat in a frayed aluminum chair.

"Thought I heard someone creeping around," the flannel man said. "You lost, buddy?"

"I'm with a friend, guess we got separated on the trail."

"I know how that is. These woods act like they're alive sometimes. Don't worry none. I'm sure you'll find her in no time, once the sun comes up. In the meantime, pull up a chair."

"No tha—, I mean, I'm good," Ralph said, looking around. "I won't be staying long."

"Oh, come on. Hospitality requires I at least offer you a beer. It's a little late in the day for me, but we could smoke a bowl if that's your preference."

"That's kind of you, really. But I think I need to keep my wits about me to find my friend."

"What's your hurry?" flannel man asked. "She'll keep. In fact, it's lucky for me you came along when you did. I've got a couple of lady friends inside." He pounded on the side of the camper. "Girls, get out here! We got company."

He leaned toward Ralph and whispered, "I thought I could pull off the dream. You know, both of them at once. But it looks like the only way I'm getting any is if both dancers have a partner, ya' dig me? I'd be thrilled to hook up with either one, so take your pick. You're doing me a big favor here."

A woman appeared at the camper door. She wore cut-off shorts and a T-shirt with such a wide neck that one of her breasts threatened to fall out. Her eyes caught the light of the gas lamp. "What do we have here?" she asked, bending over to retrieve a beer from the cooler.

Behind Ralph came the sounds of clapping hands and laughter. "Robbie, you'd think you'd have learned the long con by now. This is just embarrassing."

"Shut up," the flannel man said. "Hell, most guys don't make it past the beer. I would have gotten the kid eventually."

"Just how is that?" asked the newcomer, an older gentleman in a faded red sports jacket. "The old gag where you toss him something and he catches it on reflex? Dirty pool. The Queen won't even recognize it as binding anymore."

"I'm no amateur, Bill," Robbie said. "I'd appreciate a modicum of respect."

"You're lucky to still be breathing," Bill said, staring straight ahead. Ralph realized the old man was blind, his eyes opaque from bright white cataracts. "This young man is a guest of our friend, Valerie Hall. I've been sent to retrieve him."

"Valerie Hall, no shit? Get him out of here. This I don't need." Turning to Ralph, Robbie said, "No hard feelings, right?" He stuck out his hand.

Ralph shook it and said, "No harm done."

The sound of an animal growling made Ralph turn. It was the older man, his teeth grinding and his blind eyes open wide. "Damn it, Rob!"

Robbie shrugged. "Should have taken him away without mentioning the latest pretender. She and I have a history."

"Wait, what happened?" Ralph asked.

"You *accepted* his *apology*, you damn fool." Bill seethed. "Now you owe him, and you're stuck here until you pay him back."

"I didn't agree to that!"

Robbie winked. "It's implied."

"I might as well deliver you before you get into more trouble," Bill said to Ralph.

"Bye, sweetie," said the woman, one of her long legs dangling over the arm rest of a camping chair.

Don't say thank you don't say thank you, Ralph thought as Bill took him back to the path. Despite Bill's blindness, he never stumbled or lost his footing in the underbrush. The same could not be said for Ralph. "It was fortunate for me that you came along."

"Yes," Bill said, cursing under his breath.

"At the risk of sounding ungrateful, how do I know Valerie sent you?"

"You're finally catching on. She told me to tell you, 'Ms. Jones and Mr. Gardener in the copy room.' Is that sufficient proof?"

"It'll work. Where are you taking me?"

"Queen wants to see you. Got to warn you, she doesn't sound too happy."

10

"YOU LET HIM ACCEPT AN APOLOGY?" Valerie screamed.

"This is Robbie we're talking about here, m'lady," Bill said. "Not some flower-petal pixie. We should be grateful he didn't just eat your servant."

"He's not my servant," Valerie said. "He's—"

Queen Titania raised her hand, and the pair ceased arguing. The wind held its breath.

The queen's court was not what Ralph expected. Instead of a regal castle, the gathered men and women—*They aren't men and women at all*, Ralph thought—stood in a wooded clearing among scattered marble pillars that looked as old as the foundations of the earth and in a similar state of disrepair.

The other beings were dressed like Bill and Robbie, in outdated, battered clothing. He caught an expression like hunger in the eyes of some. Queen Titania, in a silk blouse that hugged her torso, carried herself like an aging silver-screen starlet. Her elegant figure, high cheekbones, and stone eyes lent her a cold beauty.

"Much time has passed since you last set foot in my domain, child," the queen said to Valerie. "You have been missed."

"I doubt that very much," Valerie said. "I've heard at least three of your subjects call me 'the Pretender' since I got here."

"That is inappropriate, and the offenders will be dealt with. Regardless, you are welcome here. We have not spoken since--"

"Since you sent my mother off to die," Valerie said.

For a brief instant, the queen's brow creased, but Ralph couldn't tell if it was in anger or sadness. "I assure you, we still mourn the loss of Marla Hall."

Valerie squared her shoulders. "Please don't say her name."

"I see," the queen said. "Your feelings have not changed." She tilted her chin in Ralph's direction. "Why did you bring him here?"

"Invaders overran our fortress," Valerie said. "Your kingdom was our only chance for sanctuary. I would have asked your permission, but the attack was sudden and the danger immediate."

"This realm is not a waystation for your personal use," the queen said.

"Why not?" Ralph asked. "It's not like you don't have plenty of room."

Valerie frowned at Ralph, shaking her head. The queen glared at him. "You forget your place, both in this society and in this world. There is more here than what you allow yourself to see."

Ralph's heart sped up as the wooded night grew alien and dangerous. Trees transformed into jagged crystal spires, and dark lights danced in the night sky like colossal insects. The people around him changed like the reflections in fun house mirrors, stretching and widening into a gallery of monsters. The queen herself grew until she towered over the assembly, her silk blouse a billowing, engulfing cloak, and her features distorted, revealing a being both beautiful and terrible.

Valerie stepped in front of Ralph. "Fair queen, my companion meant no offense."

Val isn't speaking out of respect, Ralph thought. *That's fear.*

"I'm sorry," he said, trying to sound confident. "I'm only human, and I spoke out of turn. I failed to appreciate your hospitality."

In an instant, the world went back to the way it was before, with Ralph sitting among the marble pillars under a night sky. The creatures once again looked human.

"He doesn't know, does he?" the queen asked Valerie. Valerie said nothing. The queen continued, "Valerie Hall, you are my earthly manifestation, and this grants you certain leeway here. Do not mistake leeway for free rein. Despite what you and your mother have done for me, this man is a disruptive entity. I will not have you endangering my people."

To Ralph, the queen said, "You are not welcome here. Your presence in this plane is troubling, if not outright dangerous. In the unlikely event your situation changes, you are welcome to accompany my emissary here again. Do not return before that time, or I shall crush your soul like an acorn. I will not enjoy it, but my people come first. I trust that I am understood."

Ralph had no idea how to reply, so he nodded gravely. This seemed to satisfy the queen, and she said, "Bill, please escort our guests to the Overlap and make sure they do not dawdle."

"Of course, Your Highness." Reluctantly, he added: "There is still the small matter of Robert."

"I will deal with that maggot," the queen said. "I will give him the apology that this ignorant man gave to me. Such a contradiction must not stay in this world a moment longer than necessary. You are dismissed."

Valerie bowed before the queen, and Ralph imitated her. A smile flashed across the queen's lips. Bill started to lead them away, but the queen called out as they reached the edge of the clearing.

"Valerie Hall, do not mistake my concern for my people as anger toward you. My earthly surrogate is always welcome here. We have not always seen eye to eye, but your mother meant a great deal to me, and you have proven a worthy successor. My kind can feud for centuries without consequence, but time is much more precious for mortals."

"I'll see you when I see you," Valerie said.

She and Ralph left the court behind.

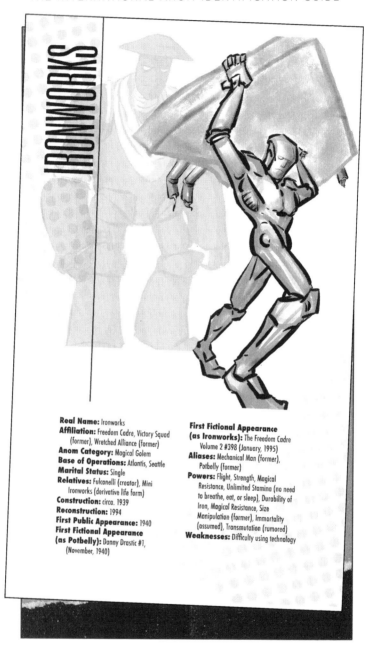

IRONWORKS

Real Name: Ironworks
Affiliation: Freedom Cadre, Victory Squad (former), Wretched Alliance (former)
Anom Category: Magical Golem
Base of Operations: Atlantis, Seattle
Marital Status: Single
Relatives: Fulcanelli (creator), Mini Ironworks (derivative life form)
Construction: circa. 1939
Reconstruction: 1994
First Public Appearance: 1940
First Fictional Appearance (as Potbelly): Danny Drastic #1, (November, 1940)

First Fictional Appearance (as Ironworks): The Freedom Cadre Volume 2 #398 (January, 1995)
Aliases: Mechanical Man (former), Potbelly (former)
Powers: Flight, Strength, Magical Resistance, Unlimited Stamina (no need to breathe, eat, or sleep), Durability of Iron, Magical Resistance, Size Manipulation (former), Immortality (assumed), Transmutation (rumored)
Weaknesses: Difficulty using technology

In 1940, a bulky metal man rose to fame after battling the Victorian villain Radionic in downtown Detroit. Because he resembled a walking potbelly stove, the newspapers gave him the name Potbelly. The slow but powerful Potbelly fought most of the major science villains of the time, including Welteislehre and Danny Drastic's nemesis, Professor Savant.

Most assumed Potbelly to be a highly advanced robot, similar to those used by the Plutonians in their East Coast attacks. The American public was understandably suspicious of such a powerful robot, but when Potbelly's true nature was revealed they took to him immediately. His slow, clumsy walk inspired a short-lived dance craze, and he was one of the earliest real-life Anom heroes to be featured in an American comic book.

Potbelly was the creation of Fulcanelli, a French alchemist whose true identity is still a subject of hot debate. Like the Golem, the Jewish hero of Prague, Potbelly is an inanimate form imbued with a magical life force. His crude construction points to an improvised experiment. Fulcanelli was a major target of the Thule Society, and Anom scholars believe the alchemist created Potbelly during an attack of the occult group.

Rumors circulated that Potbelly fought the Nazis in one of their co-opted subterranean bases under France, which proved to be true when photographic evidence came to light in the sixties. By this time Potbelly had faded from the public eye for unknown reasons.

In 1994, a destructive Anom appeared, allying himself with the occult villains Hell Binder and Orgone the Accumulator. Calling himself Ironworks, he had smooth metal skin, the ability to fly, and the strength to destroy buildings. Oceanus and the Freedom Cadre fought him to a standstill on four occasions, resulting in the tragic loss of dozens of civilian lives. With the help of the immortal alchemist Tycho Brahe, the Cadre discovered that Ironworks was Potbelly, reconstructed and enslaved by Hell Binder. Hell Binder's Wretched Alliance used Ironworks to animate a two-hundred-ton iron monster that attacked Seattle in 1998. It was only through the heroic sacrifice of Oceanus that the Cadre defeated the giant, extricated Ironworks, and freed him from Hell Binder's control.

Ironworks helped the Cadre imprison Hell Binder and his allies. Because of the Mesmer Act, Ironworks was not held legally responsible for crimes committed under Hell Binder's control, but the public called for his destruction. In a controversial move, the Cadre welcomed him into their group. Ironworks was instrumental in saving the world from the Bringer of Blades, but much of the public still distrusts and fears him.

Illustration by Chris "Chance!" Brown

11

N HOUR LATER, Valerie and Ralph stood at the side of a dusty road with their thumbs out.

"Nice of your chums to drop us off somewhere so convenient," Ralph said.

Valerie pulled in her thumb and raised her middle finger. "Nice of my chums not to use your bones to bake their bread, chucklehead." At the sound of an approaching vehicle, she went back to thumbing for a ride. "You shouldn't expect the Overlap to let you out at a pizza buffet." The car passed, the blue-haired woman behind the wheel giving them a dubious look.

Ralph coughed and waved the dirt away. "When are we going to give this up so you can fly us to the nearest day spa?"

"Don't be a dummy, Ralph. Turning into Titania is like firing up a fusion reactor. Our location would be totally obvious to anyone who knows how to look. If the Ocularist has joined forces with the Haberdashers, I guarantee you they're keeping an eye out for us. We are plain-clothes cops until further notice."

They trudged along for several minutes in silence. Ralph pulled out his phone and held it up high, shielding his eyes to see the screen.

"What do you think you're doing?" Valerie asked.

"Trying to get some bars. We can call for a taxi." He looked around at the desolation surrounding them. "Or the equivalent."

She took the phone from him and threw it to the ground, stomping on it.

"What the hell?" Ralph picked up the shattered pieces.

"Did you already forget who tried to stop us from leaving Atlantis? Your pissed off ex-girlfriend. Sandra knows everything about us. You think they aren't waiting for your phone to pop up? We already had to remove the bug the Haberdashers put in there!"

Ralph stared at the jagged pieces of his phone. "All my phone numbers were on there. For all those people I don't really know. Editors, publicist, the works. I'm screwed."

"Don't you back anything up?"

"Back anything up? Until a few weeks ago, this phone didn't exist. It has—I mean, had—more functions than any phone I could afford in my original, boring world. So no, I didn't back it up."

"Cry me a river. Be sure to get the SIM card."

Ralph dug it out of the pile of broken parts and snapped it in two. "Hey, your phone is still un-destroyed. Can't you take the SIM card out and still make emergency calls?"

"Just stick out your thumb, Ralph."

The man in the pickup believed the story of their broken-down car and dead cell phone batteries. Ralph had to sit in the back of the truck, but they soon arrived at the nearest town, which turned out to be El Mirage, Utah. The driver left them at a gas station to call for a tow. As soon as he disappeared around the corner, they started walking.

Ralph patted his pocket. "I've still got my wallet, so we're good on money. You hungry?"

"Always."

As they tore into a pound of cheese fries at the closest restaurant, the Smokehouse in the Sand, Ralph asked, "So the cat's out of the bag, huh? Am I allowed to ask questions?"

Valerie shrugged. "At this point, I can't see the situation being much worse."

Ralph leaned across the table, and she followed suit. "How'd you become Titania?" he whispered.

"You don't have to whisper, ya' big dork. No one's paying any attention. I'm the second Titania. Like I said, my mom was the first. Actually, there were others, kind of, but that was like five hundred years ago."

"Your mom used to make us grilled cheese sandwiches."

"Yep. She also punched a dragon in Kentucky. And did a million other fantastic things."

"That's amazing."

"Amazing is exactly what she was. So, after Mom died, the mantle passed to me." Valerie sighed. "I was nineteen. She left me the scrap of the fairy flag in a safe deposit box. I'll tell you about my first adventure sometime, but you'll have to get me drunk first."

"How did she die?"

"Wish I knew. 'Die' might be the wrong word. 'Disappeared' is better. Titania—Queen Titania, I mean—has been tight-lipped about the whole thing. It's one of the reasons we don't get along like she and Mom did. For Christ's sake, I used to call her *Aunt Titania* when I was little. Dad asked me to give up the search, and I finally had to accept she wasn't coming back."

"Was it tough? Stepping into your mom's shoes?"

"Real tough. It's not like there's a handbook for taking up the mantle for the Queen of the Fairies. I like to think she was planning on training me, but didn't get the chance." Valerie paused, leveling her gaze at Ralph. *Please, God,* he thought. *Please don't let her ask me what I think she's going to ask me.*

"Ralph, was my mom still alive in your world? I've been wanting to ask you for a while, but I couldn't make myself do it."

"I'm sorry." He looked down at his empty plate. "She died from breast cancer when we were in high school."

"Breast cancer? Dian Hall, the first and best hero to hold the title of Titania, dies from cancer. And you think *this* world is crazy?"

Ralph smiled nervously. "I think the queen wants to make up with you."

"Of course she does. I'm her conduit of relevancy. Without me, she's just a character in a Shakespeare comedy."

"It sounded like she really misses your mom. Maybe you should—"

"Maybe I should what? Just forget my mom wouldn't be dead if it wasn't for her? I'll get right on that, Ralph."

They ate silently for a few minutes.

"I can't believe you went to smash town on my phone." He flinched, regretting the words the instant he said them.

Valerie pointed a fry at him. "You're lucky I don't go to smash town on your face. Sandra in Atlantis? That looks bad for you, buddy."

"Hey, wait a minute. You can't put what she did on me. I had no idea she was anything more than a bad habit I was lucky to be rid of. What the hell was she doing there?"

Valerie sucked soda up a straw. "You have to see this from my point of view. The way I remember things, Sandra was active as Fox Hunter for years before you met her. I used to stop her all the time—"

"So she was your nemesis?" Ralph asked.

"Nemesis? More like minor annoyance. That shoplifter has nothing on me. That's why, when she helped me take down a bigger fish, I let her off the hook."

"You two actually teamed up?"

She rolled her eyes. "You're just loving this, aren't you? If you ask if we ever made out, I'll forget about our low profile and throw you into space. Your head will go *pop*!" She made an exploding gesture with her fingers.

"Sorry, forget it. The world I remember, I don't think the two of you ever met."

"We met, all right. Once she stopped pulling jobs in costume, you two started seeing each other. I always felt it was her way of getting back at me."

Ralph sat back in the booth. "So I was dating a reformed—"

Valerie coughed.

"Okay, a *temporarily* reformed supervillain? You didn't think that was something you should tell me?"

"First off, she was hardly super. She barely qualified as an Anom. And you knew about her Fox Hunter thing all along. What we don't know is what you—"

It was Ralph's turn to cough.

"Fine. What the *other you* might have told Sandra."

"What could I have told her?" Ralph asked. "I make funny books! I didn't even know you were a, what do you call it, an Anom." Ralph stopped. His eyes darted back and forth as the wheels turned in his head. "Wait a minute, you said she hooked up with me to get back at you. So, she knew your secret identity." Ralph's jaw dropped. "Does that mean I knew?"

Valerie shrugged awkwardly.

"You told me it was weird I realized you were Titania when we met at the restaurant." Ralph said. "That I'd never seen past it before. But it was because I acted surprised that you knew something was wrong with me!"

"Ralph—"

"That is such bullshit!" he said. People in the restaurant were starting to stare.

Valerie grabbed his arm. "Calm down, Ralph."

"You knew I was going crazy," Ralph said in a coarse whisper. "You knew I had no idea what was real and what wasn't. And you lied to me?"

"It wasn't like that. I called Damon and we both thought—"

"Oh, you and Damon thought, huh? What else did the other me know that I don't? What else are you keeping to yourselves?"

"You're accusing me of holding out? I just lost two of my best friends, maybe more. Mr. Stiff lost the woman he loved. All to protect someone who wasn't even there for me when my mom died." She caught herself. "No, wait, I'm sorry. I didn't mean that."

"It's fine. I should have known better than to throw my lot in with the gods, right?"

"You don't understand. We'll wait until it's safe to contact the Cadre, then we'll find a new place where we can protect you."

"Protect me? Are you for real? Two members of your team are already dead because of me. I'm in the dark, and I'm getting people killed. Maybe it's better for everyone if I go off on my own."

"You don't know what you're talking about."

"Whose fault is that? You and your friends locked me up at the bottom of the ocean, and that wasn't safe enough. Not telling me about Sandra is just part of it."

"You agreed with the lockdown. If there was a chance it could prevent more changes, we had to try."

"Don't you get it? Maybe it was my fault the Ocularist found us. The Ralph from before the change might have done something to sabotage me. Not trusting you is bad enough, but I can't even trust myself." He threw money on the table and started for the door. "Stay away from me, Val. Even if you're keeping things from me, I don't want you getting hurt."

"Damn it, Ralph, wait!"

"Call me, okay? Oh, wait, can't do that. Phone's busted."

Valerie followed him outside. "I know you better than that. You think you're being the martyr here, but you're just being an idiot. Come back inside and we'll talk this out."

"I'm done talking. Searching for answers got me into this mess, maybe it can get us out. And I did that alone."

She grabbed his arm. "There are things I want to tell you, but this isn't the place. Just wait here with me. We'll figure this out!"

Ralph pulled away. "I'm leaving. And I won't let you stop me—unless you want to power up, and we both know you don't want to do that."

She continued to yell after him, but Ralph left without another word. He walked until he found a gas station that let him borrow a phone and a stained phonebook. When the beat-up taxi arrived, he climbed inside.

"Where can I take you, mister?" a woman asked.

"Somewhere I can buy a car."

"What kind of car?"

"The kind you can buy with cash. Cheap."

"I know just the place."

As they drove Ralph fought back tears, trying to take hold of his rage, to confine it.

The cabbie looked back over her shoulder. "You okay, mister?"

"Do you believe in ghosts?" Ralph asked.

"I guess. Why?"

He stared out the window at the setting sun. "Because I need to find one."

12

S THE SUN WAS SETTING, Ralph pulled the old Cadillac Cyclone into the parking lot of Quarter Ben Comics in Rutland, Vermont. The car looked like something from *The Jetsons*, but the steering wheel shook and the smell of burning oil stung his nostrils. The Styrofoam skeletons of his fast food meals littered the floorboard of the passenger's seat. The seat beside him held a stack of magazines, newspapers, and books that Ralph had used to reacquaint himself with the ever-changing world.

You're lucky the other you had plenty of cash on hand, he told himself.

Aside from trade interruptions with Atlantis, the mainstream press only hinted at the undersea battle between the Cadre and the Ocularist and Haberdashers. The assumption appeared to be that there was a natural disaster or a serious technical problem. A few of the magazines dedicated to Anoms mentioned fewer sightings of the involved heroes. The blurb on one cover asked "Where is The Advocate?"

Don't hold your breath, Ralph thought, rubbing his temples.

He reached under a paperback copy of *Our Phantom Friends* by Astrid Rhodes to retrieve a white hardbound book; this one was much thicker than a phonebook. It was a twin of *The World Encyclopedia of Comics,* in which he had first found mention of Danny Drastic and the Ocularist. Only now it was *The World Cyclopedia of Costumed Characters* by Maurice Horn, with the Yellow Kid and other characters replaced by Danny Drastic, Nylon, the classic version of Ironworks, Molly Pitcher, the Mad Gasser, and the like. He flipped it open, and the contents were the same as when he had picked it up in a used bookstore: a catalog of real superheroes, supervillains, costumed vigilantes and criminals, and more. The book contained publicly-available knowledge on Anoms previous to its publication in 1976.

The New York Times read like an issue of *The Weekly World News*. One article discussed the effect of monster appearances on local economies, while another argued which historical invasions were real and which ones faked by terrestrial Anom villains. *Vogue* included lists of best and worst dressed Anoms. Songweaver topped the list of best dressed—"She makes anything look good"—but the writer derided the mecha-controlling Rita for wearing a baseball cap at the Tokyo Sports Film Awards. Picking up one of Sandra's old magazines, Ralph realized Titania had replaced the movie star on the cover.

History is written by the winners, Ralph thought. *But who's in charge of rewriting history?*

The possibilities terrified him. Ralph didn't think about God too often, but this seemed like something only a god could do. The possibilities were terrifying; was it a malevolent cosmic entity that thrived on chaos? Was someone like the Ocularist behind it all?

Is it me? Ralph thought. The Cadre and their tests never ruled that idea out. *Am I responsible for this?*

If that was true, to what degree was he in control of the madness growing around him? Maybe this was the world a man obsessed with comics his whole life would create. And if he was in charge, could he reverse it?

Not if they tear the world apart and kill us all first, Ralph thought. He looked at the closed storefront of Quarter Ben Comics, empty and quiet in the night. *It's not like I don't already have blood on my hands.*

13

HE DOOR FRAME BROKE ON THE FIRST KICK.
Ralph, carrying a black duffel bag over his shoulder,
pulled away pieces of crime scene tape and walked past
a buzzing refrigerator. A sign read, *No Comics in the Bathroom
Unless You Own the Place.*

Someone had cleaned up the mess. The front of the shop
appeared undisturbed, exactly the same as Ralph remembered.
He ran his fingers along the bagged and boarded comics in one
of the alphabetized longboxes. *New Gods. New Guardians. New
Mutants. New Teen Titans. New Warriors.*

Ralph pulled a staple gun and a stack of folded painter's tarps
from his bag. He quickly hung the tarps, blocking the front windows. Confident no one could see inside, he cleared a shelf of
Outliers action figurines and a limited edition Mr. Stiff bust.
Pulling several large scented candles from his bag, he lit the wicks
with a match.

"Are you there, Ben?" he asked the empty room. "It's Ralph.
We need to talk."

The cold room remained silent.

"I'm sorry, buddy, but we don't have time to be nice."

Ralph lifted the ceramic Mr. Stiff head, testing the weight of it in his hand. He raised it over his head and slammed it into the tile floor with a loud crack. Pieces of the bust flew in every direction, clattering as they bounced along the floor.

Ralph looked around. "The book said this would be the best way to get your attention."

He walked behind the glass display counter and grabbed a rolling chair. Beside the front door was the display case full of the Mad Gasser and other dolls from the 1970s, transforming robot toys still in their original boxes, and collectible statuettes. Ralph estimated the value of the lot to be several thousand dollars. With a frown, he lifted the chair and smashed the display case. Glass, broken figures, and torn boxes fell to the ground as he hit it a second, a third, a fourth time.

He dropped the chair and pushed it aside with his foot. "Ben!" he called. Still no answer.

Why's it so damn cold in here? he wondered, rubbing his hands together.

"You're leaving me hanging here," he said. "You're forcing me to up the stakes."

In the glass display counter under the register was a comic book in a plastic case. According to the label, the comic was professionally graded at 9.7 out of 10. It looked as if it had just rolled off the press, as perfect a specimen as one could find of a comic from 1971.

Ralph picked up a piece of the smashed Mr. Stiff bust and shattered the front of the counter. He brushed aside the scarier pieces of glass and reached inside.

"*Black Snake*, number one. July 1971. First appearance of Black Snake and his nemesis, Bone Jack." Ralph whistled. "I don't see a price tag on it, Ben. Was it not for sale? I'm guessing you were pretty proud of this one."

He pulled out a pocket knife and carefully pried open the plastic case.

"I better be careful not to touch it, right? Just touching it would probably lower the value of this beauty." He tilted the opened case, allowing the comic to slide onto the countertop.

"I would say, 'This is going to hurt me more than it's going to hurt you,' but we both know that isn't true." Ralph took out the box of matches he'd used to light the candles. Sliding open the box, he removed a single match.

"Is a grade of 9.7 high for a book this old?" Ralph asked. "It sure seems high. And I read this issue didn't sell in high numbers in the first place. A 9.7 probably makes this the best example of this book in existence." He lit the match and inched it toward the perfect cover of the comic book.

"Wait," whispered a voice behind him.

14

THE TWO MEN STARED AT EACH OTHER across the store. Ben looked normal enough, dressed in a black lightning-bolt T-shirt and khakis. Ralph had worried his friend would be soaked with blood or resemble an EC Comics zombie. But, aside from being somewhat translucent, Ben looked very much alive.

"How's my dad?" the ghost asked.

Ralph blew out the match. "The paper said some government agency called the Grudge took him and the other people who used the neural stimulators. It's too soon to tell, but the others should be okay, maybe even keep the positive effects of the treatment. The rumor online is, the technology came from an alien source, and something dormant took control of the people wearing the devices. The FDA is doing everything they can to cover their ass for approving them in the first place."

"Alien mind control, huh? It's weird, but that makes me feel a little better. How many others died?"

"Not too many. Most of the patients were in hospitals and were restrained before they could hurt anyone. The ones in home care did the most damage. I'm sorry, Ben."

"Sorry I didn't listen to you, buddy. Sorry I doubted you. I was just trying to be a good son, you know? Take care of my old man where he'd be comfortable."

"I know. You were a good son. You did what you thought was best for your dad. You couldn't have known how things would go."

Ben looked around the store, appearing confused.

"Ralph, I think I'm dead. Is this real?"

Ralph nodded, tears filling his eyes. "I'm pretty sure this is real, buddy. But that's what I'm here to talk to you about. I need your help."

"Not sure what kind of help I can be to you, Derrida. I don't really believe in ghosts. Never saw one. This is pretty confusing. I don't know if I'm me or just an echo that thinks it's me. What do you think, Ralph? Am I Alec Holland, or am I the Swamp Thing?"

"Let's pretend we know it's you, okay? Just for the sake of argument, man, because I'm drowning here. I need someone I can trust, and you're all that's left."

"Dude, you're a bestselling writer and artist. You've got to have friends who are easier to get a hold of."

"I finally got around to burning the last of my bridges. Things aren't going too well for the good guys, anyway. I need to keep a low profile—I don't want to get anyone hurt by talking to them."

"That makes me a good choice," Ben said. "Not much anyone could do to me now, aside from sticking me in a containment unit."

Ralph laughed, but his heart wasn't in it. "No one is like I remember them. You're pulling a Patrick Swayze. My ex-girlfriend is a supervillain. My agent answers my damn calls, for Christ's sake. I don't know anything about those people."

"What about Damon and Valerie? They seem like good people."

"Maybe. But they've all been lying to me, maybe this whole time. They're keeping things from me, and I have no idea how much. I remember a world that barely exists. There's no way I can function if I'm working with false *a priori*. It's looking more and more like this is all somehow my fault, and I can't fix it if I can't trust the people around me."

"The world might be mixed up, but I would trust Valerie. Damon, sure, he can be a dick. But Valerie is one of the good ones, and you know it."

"Yeah, I do. Which is one more reason to stay away from her. You're not the only one who's died. I thought if I came to you, at least you couldn't get killed again."

"I hope you're not expecting a lot from me," Ben said. "There's not much of me left here. And I changed along with everyone else, remember? I might not even be the same Ben."

"That's okay. You're still Ben-ish enough to talk me through this. I'm barely holding on here, and I need your advice."

"It's your dime, my friend. I'll do what I can."

"Here's the problem. The world is getting crazier by the minute, and I'm the only one who can see it. If things keep on like this, they have to reach critical mass, right? With a new super-powered slug showing up every five minutes, someone is going to crack the planet wide open. It's inevitable."

"Is it?" Ben asked. "It's been like this for years. Maybe forever, I don't know. The good guys always win eventually. Most of the time, the general populace barely notices it's going on. Did you know there are Anom deniers? They're a fringe group that refuses to believe any of the heroes or villains exist, and that it's all a tricky cover-up by the government. Or a publicity stunt to sell merchandise. Some people go their whole lives without seeing a man fly."

"But people are dying. Yesterday during an Anom battle in New York, a woman was crushed by debris. Last week in Los Angeles, Urban Decay destroyed a packed city bus. If the world was normal, those people would still be alive."

"Maybe," Ben said. "Or maybe that woman would have been hit by something falling off a condemned building. That bus might have gone over a guardrail. There's no way you can know, Ralph!"

"That's right, I can't know! I have to work with the available information, don't I? But that information keeps changing. If I write myself a note to remember something, it could change by the next time I look at it. It's like I can't know the world, only my perception of it. Like watching a TV show. I can't trust it any more than you can trust your eyes when you see an optical illusion or hallucinate. I don't know what's real."

"It doesn't matter what's real," Ben said. "If everything is an illusion, and nothing is real, only one thing matters. The only thing that's always mattered. Doing what's right."

"But how do I know what's right?"

"I guess you have to decide. There are a few ways to make a moral choice. You can do what's best in the moment, or you do what's best in the long run. But there's no way you can know that here, is there? So if everything else is untrustworthy, you have to trust your experience. Have confidence in what you think is right." The ghost paused. "But please remember: My dad was an empty shell in your reality. Here, he has a chance. There's something fantastic about that, isn't there? Maybe this is the better world."

Ralph shook his head. "You're dead because of his treatment."

"What son wouldn't give his life for his dad?" He looked at Ralph, his eyes asking for some kind of approval.

"Dying so that someone else could be saved? That makes you a hero in my book. But it doesn't change the fact you're dead."

"That's not your fault. It's not your job to decide who lives and who dies."

"Maybe it is, maybe it isn't. If I can change things back and don't, then everything that happens is my fault."

"Go with your gut, Ralph. In the end, that's all any of us can do. Just ask yourself, 'What would Meta Man do?'"

"Wish I knew. But thanks, you're a good friend." Ralph offered Ben his hand to shake. Realizing his mistake, he withdrew it.

"I *was* a good friend. Do me a favor, will you? Tell my dad I know he wasn't in control, that I don't blame him."

"Of course."

"Okay. Now, mind clearing out? I'd like to say goodbye to the old place."

Ralph turned off the lamp and carried it and his duffel bag toward the exit. He turned around to say goodbye, but Ben was gone.

15

BEN HAD TOLD RALPH TO GO WITH HIS GUT, SO that's what he did.

This started with finding those comics, Ralph remembered, but he wasn't sure the comic books were the key to returning things to normal. The information inside the books was a part of the world now, and he felt that even if he destroyed them, it would make no difference. This was not a problem to be solved with the destruction of Horcruxes.

If I'm the problem, maybe I can solve things by removing myself from the equation. But if he killed himself and he was wrong, there would be no one left who remembered the way things were. *No,* he decided, *it would never be that simple, anyway.*

So, that leaves only one option: Go to the source of the comics.

It took him three days to reach Greenvale, the largest producer of reality-warping comic books in the known world. Admittedly, his known world was shrinking like an ice cube in a cup of coffee.

After dinner at the diner, Ralph drove by the house where he found Chill. The family was visible through a bay window, eating at the dining room table. The smiling mother served steak and potatoes to the two children as the father joked with them. It looked perfect—more than perfect—and that was the problem. Ralph hadn't noticed the last time, when the little boy played Danny Drastic in the front yard, but the house and its occupants had an unreal quality. The fresh coat of paint on the eaves looked like it had been finished the day before, and the trees and grass looked like they had been trimmed that very morning. The sidewalk had no cracks, and the garage door had no dents from kicked soccer balls. The shingles looked brand new, as did the immaculate patio furniture.

The family inside looked wrong too. The children had factory-fresh haircuts, and the mother might have had a makeup artist hiding around the corner. The father smiled, and his perfect teeth looked capped. Their plates were covered in food right out of a television commercial. While the members of the family all held forks, none of them actually ate or drank anything.

The house held no evidence of being lived in, and the family showed no evidence of living.

Maybe they're actors, Ralph thought. *Hell, maybe they're holograms or robots or shape-changing aliens. There's no way to tell, and there's nothing more for me in that house.*

He drove on to the factory, parking about a hundred yards away and across the street. Ralph pulled a pair of binoculars out of the duffel beside him. Several men in familiar formal attire stood at the entrance to the building. One even patrolled the skylight on the roof, not that Ralph had any way to get up there.

"Motherfucking Haberdashers," Ralph said.

He watched them until long after sundown. They never seemed to notice him. None of them looked armed, but if Ralph understood one thing about his environment, it was that appearances could be deceiving.

I should call Valerie. He touched the burner cell phone in his pocket. But the last time he'd called her for help, it almost got her killed. *No. I'll do it myself.*

But why, oh why didn't I get my hands on a real gun? He examined the contents of the duffel bag in the seat next to him, which he had purchased at a camping outlet. The bag contained a heavy-duty flashlight, a neon orange flare gun, rope, and an assortment of other supplies that would be useless for attacking a guarded building. Reaching deep into the bag, he pulled out a container that looked like a miniature fire extinguisher. The bottle contained bear repellent, a product similar to pepper spray.

"At least I'll be prepared if they use bears as guards." He pocketed the bear repellent along with the flare gun—a decent distraction if nothing else—and grabbed the long metal flashlight.

If the building was worth guarding, it had something inside worth knowing. The Haberdashers appeared to be in on whatever was going on. And since the changes had originated in this town, the warehouse might even hold the means to reverse what was happening to the world. Ralph just needed to slip inside the warehouse long enough to learn what to do next. He was grasping at straws, but it was his only lead.

Ralph turned off the dome light of the Cadillac Cyclone and slowly opened the door. The industrial neighborhood was dark and quiet by this time of night, and it felt good to get out of the car. His legs regained their circulation as he slowly made his way to the back of the old publishing building.

Go back, his mind nagged. *Call Val or Damon. You had a little fight, so what? No big deal. You know they'll be cool about it.*

No, he argued. *I have to start pulling my weight some time. I can't spend the rest of my life getting carried around by people with capes.*

He waited for the guard to pass before approaching the back door, only to find it locked. After a quick look around, he climbed atop a dumpster and tried the window. It was stuck at first, but the latch came free when he gave the frame a gentle pull.

I am one lucky bastard, he thought and pulled himself up and inside. He closed the window with a soft clack and looked around.

The second floor of the factory office was dark and cluttered with empty desks and tables. Making his way through the maze, he thought of super spies and laser grids. He bumped a table, and the legs squealed against the linoleum. Ralph froze and waited for the Haberdashers to rush in, machine guns blazing. When no one appeared, he continued creeping across the room.

Through a window in the door, he could see the open factory floor. Copies of Rika's smaller exoskeletons lined one wall. Dozens of Haberdashers worked at tables, assembling components and passing them to their neighbors on the assembly line. Some worked on bows and arrow, others constructed knockoffs of Danny Drastic's blaster. Each group of workers was putting together a different type of weapon, of which numerous piles already existed. Other Haberdashers entered, boxed up weapons, and exited again.

It's a damn arsenal, Ralph thought. *They're outfitting some crazy army in there. It's definitely time to call Val. Hopefully she'll forgive me for being such an asshole.*

Ralph checked his burner cell phone, but it had no bars. He made his way back to the room where he'd entered. A Haberdasher stood at the window, examining the broken latch and talking into a radio. Ralph tried to sneak away, but the suited man spun around. "Stop right there!"

"No thanks!" Ralph sprayed the can of bear repellant. The stream of offensive fluid shot across the room and splashed in the guard's face. The Haberdasher screamed as he sank to his knees, and Ralph ran the other direction.

In the next room, he came face to pupil with the Ocularist. Ralph froze, mortified.

Up close, the villain's giant eyeball was smooth as a mirror and as bright as a Merrie Melodies cartoon. The tall man's suit seemed to glow red in the darkness. He held his cane like a spiked club. Ralph lifted the bear repellant and hit the center of the giant eye like a bullseye.

The Ocularist laughed. His voice sounded like a smashed walkie-talkie, a warped record, a broken pullstring doll. "You know this isn't a real eye, right?" He tapped the orb with his cane. "You're embarrassing yourself, Ralph."

"Just wait." Ralph pulled out the plastic flare gun and aimed at the man's chest. "I hear this stuff is pretty flammable."

He pulled the trigger. With a flick of his cane, the Ocularist knocked the flare into a corner, where it burned a black smudge into the tile floor, emitting a sulfurous scent like a spent Roman candle. "Don't worry about starting a fire," said the eyeball man. "Through and through, this whole building is grade-A asbestos."

"You really think the Cadre won't find this place?" Ralph asked. "If I found it, there's no way they'll miss it."

"This is but one of a thousand, my boy. You could never collect them all, oh me, oh my. We have the means to copy the most powerful weapons of the most powerful beings on the planet. Even what's left of the Cadre will roll over beneath my army of sharp-dressed men. Oh, Ralphie Boy, don't you just love this brave new world you and I have created?"

Ralph asked, "What are you talking about?" Ralph asked.

"You know exactly what I'm talking about."

He knows about the change, Ralph thought. "Isn't there enough chaos out there without starting a war?"

"It's only chaos for now. Once I'm in charge, it will run like a beautiful Swiss clock. But for now, Mr. Rogers, we need to cut you open. To see what makes you tick."

"I'm not really in a position to argue, am I?" Ralph asked.

"I'm afraid not," said the Ocularist.

Ralph rushed him, hoping to knock him out of the way. The Ocularist took a calm step out of Ralph's path, allowing him to run out onto the catwalk surrounding the factory floor.

"Don't resist," said the Ocularist. "We both know what you were in the old scheme of things: a washed-up little has-been. You don't have the backbone for this."

"You know, for a talking eyeball, you're a huge asshole." Ralph turned his back on the Ocularist and vaulted over the railing.

16

YEBALL? ASSHOLE? *What did that even mean?*
Ralph asked himself as he landed on a long table, cracking it in two. Haberdashers jumped out of their seats
in surprise.

Ralph reached down and picked up one of the many metal
arms sliding to the floor. Wires dangled from the shoulder of the
unfinished device. Gripping it by the wrist, he swung the arm like
a baseball bat and hit the nearest Haberdasher in the side of the
head. The man dropped to the ground.

Sliding off the table, Ralph brandished the arm like a
longsword. A circle of seven Haberdashers closed in on him.
Ralph swung the arm, forcing the men kept their distance. "You
want some of what I gave your buddy?"

"Serve and obey!" chanted one man.

The other Haberdashers joined in. "Serve and obey! Serve
and obey! Serve and obey!"

One of the workers grabbed another arm off the table. Before
Ralph could knock it out of his hands, the Haberdasher gripped
the shoulder under his armpit and pulled back the metal fingers
with his other hand, like he was putting the arm in a submission

hold. The palm of the hand started to glow, and Ralph dove out of the way just as a blue blast of electricity flew past him.

I'm a monkey trying to club them with a rifle, he thought, repositioning the arm and aiming at his opponent. Nothing happened. He must have damaged it when he used it as a caveman club.

He grabbed a Danny Drastic blaster from the next table and fired it. He knew the beam would only affect inorganic matter, but he hoped it would buy him some time.

As he pulled the trigger, the weapon hummed and the armed Haberdasher's flesh blinked out of existence, leaving behind a skeleton in a suit. The costumed skeleton, carried forward by momentum, hit the floor.

I just killed somebody, Ralph thought. He didn't mean to do it, but it was done. *Guess the Ocularist didn't like the non-lethal setting.*

His pursuers turned and ran in every direction. Haberdashers were picking up bows and arrows from another table, so Ralph fired again. The table of arrows exploded like a string of illegal fire crackers, each one a violent fireball.

Oh, Ralph thought. *They're* those *kind of arrows.*

Several of the men died instantly. One caught fire and ran, setting other men ablaze and causing more panic among the remaining Haberdashers. They knocked over chairs and tables in their rush for the doors. The fires set off an alarm, and emergency sprinklers opened up and sprayed a continuous torrent of water.

On the other side of the room, a group of holdouts reached the Danny Drastic blasters. One fired, the beam hitting a Haberdasher approaching Ralph from behind.

Ralph ran. He slipped on the wet concrete, but he reached one of the overturned tables and jumped behind it. The ray guns hummed and their beams hit the table, but nothing happened.

Ralph tried to fire from cover, but the blaster didn't respond. It had broken when he'd slipped. Blue smoke drifted from the exposed circuits. Peeking around the edge of the table, he saw the men slowly approaching.

Far out of reach he saw an intact bow and arrow. *I'll never reach it before I'm disintegrated*, Ralph thought. *How much does it hurt when you get disintegrated?* He decided it would hurt very much.

The droning chant began again, shaking the concrete. "Serve and obey! Serve and obey! Serve and obey!"

Ralph threw the useless blaster at the nearest man and ran for the bow. A beam shot over his shoulder. He rolled, scooping up the bow and one arrow, and hit the ground behind another table.

With his back to the table, he nocked the arrow, gasping for breath, knowing this was it. The Haberdashers were too far apart to hit with one shot, and Ralph was not confident in his ability to hit even one moving person. There was also the chance the sprinklers had ruined the explosive charge.

Way to go, Ralph, he said to himself. *If you're lucky, you might take one of them with you. If he holds still long enough for you to remember what you learned at summer camp.*

He looked around for another option, but nothing presented itself. As he prepared to pull a Butch Cassidy and the Sundance Kid, he looked up and smiled.

Straining to pull back the thick bowstring, he pointed the arrow straight up in the air and released it. It exploded on contact with the factory's skylight. Ralph had already rolled underneath a table as the glass rained down. He watched as an enormous plane of glass sliced one of the men neatly in two. The few Haberdashers to escape injury ran from the room.

Ralph's brain buzzed with adrenaline. As he fought to catch his breath, a fluttering sound drew his attention skyward. The skylight was like a comic book panel, perfectly framing the descent of a god in a billowing cape. Ralph hoped it would be the green and gold costume of Titania, but it was a young man in red and silver. He held a woman wearing a cowgirl outfit, complete with hat and leather chaps. Silver revolvers hung from her hips.

The flying man carefully lowered the woman to the ground. The two of them looked no more than eighteen or nineteen years old. Ralph climbed out from under the table. "I hope you're the good guys."

"We got here as fast as we could," said the cowgirl. "The rest of the Outliers are rounding up as many Haberdashers as they can catch."

"I've never seen so many of them in one place," said Red Cape Guy.

"The Ocularist was with them," Ralph said. "Did any of your people catch him?"

Cowgirl's eyes widened. She touched a finger to her ear and said, "If any of you jerks see the Ocularist, call it in. No more funerals, you got me?"

Red Cape Guy let out a whistle as he looked around the factory floor. "You sure did a number on this place. What were they doing in here?"

"Making weapons," Ralph said. "I tried to use some of them to fight my way through the Haberdashers."

"Nice shootin', Tex," the cowgirl said, smiling.

Red Cape Guy nodded. "Yeah, you wailed on those overdressed sons of bitches. But why didn't you just use your powers?"

"My what?" Ralph asked. ◣◤

THE BRONZE AGE

1

RALPH MUNCHED ON A PLATE OF FRIED SUSHI and flipped through page after page in an updated version of *The World Cyclopedia of Costumed Characters,* retitled *The International Anom Identification Guide.* It was his third time through the book. A TV in the corner played a Damon Ripley court drama, *Tell It to the Judge.* On the screen, Damon comforted a young boy whose parents had been killed by a mugger.

Those kids knew me, he thought. *They knew the other me who lived in this world.*

Red Cape Guy, whom Ralph now knew was named Baron, had flown Ralph back to the Lincoln as sirens approached. Baron had flown off before Ralph could question him further, and Ralph had no intention of talking to the police or, worse, to the Grudge. He drove until he arrived back in Austin.

Now he sat in Nyotaimori, a favorite sushi restaurant from times past. Sandra had introduced him to the place, and she always gave him a hard time for ordering the fried monkey balls. The *Identification Guide* was less helpful than he'd hoped; it only included information that was publicly available, of course, and many of the entries were artists' renditions derived from a variety of sources. Not all Anoms stopped to pose for photographs.

"Why didn't you just use your powers?" Baron had asked.

What powers? Ralph wondered. He felt the same as he always had; he'd spent an hour standing in an Oklahoma field, trying to figure it out. He jumped as hard as he could, but his body refused to stay in the air. The large rock he tried to lift did not budge. If he had heat vision, it was not powerful enough to start a grass fire. His body would not stretch, transform, or move at super speed.

He picked up a piece of spicy tuna with his chopsticks and popped it in his mouth, chewing it thoughtfully. *If Bruce Banner forgot he was the Hulk, would he still transform if he got mad?* Looking at the handful of other customers in the restaurant, he wondered if they were safe with him there.

His only clue was coming through the factory fight without any injury. The odds of that felt astronomical. Yet when he poked his thumb with the tip of a knife, a dot of blood oozed out. *Invulnerable? Not so much.*

Maybe I was *a heavy hitter, but I've been depowered. It's not unusual for fictional heroes to lose their powers. It could be a common occurrence in this world too. Or maybe the Ralph Rogers who lived in this timeline had superpowers, but I took his place, and I don't have powers. That fits what I've been assuming, that the world changed around me. Maybe my body didn't change.*

"Do you need anything else, sir?" the waiter asked.

"Another sake, please."

Maybe my past has changed to that of an Anom, he thought. *It would make sense. Everyone else seems to have a cape in their closet now. My backstory changed, but since I'm the only one that doesn't change, I don't have the abilities to match my new past.*

The waiter returned with a bottle of cold sake. "Haven't seen you in here for a while," he said.

"Sorry, Scott, it's been a bit crazy lately. I'm just glad you guys are still here."

"We're not going anywhere anytime soon. How's Sandra doing?"

"We broke up."

"Sorry to hear that, but I'm sure you'll be all right. She could be a bit mean, couldn't she?" He tapped the cover of Ralph's book. "Seen an Anom recently? Trying to identify who it was?"

"No, it wasn't anything recent. I'm actually trying to figure out the name of a hero that might not even be around anymore."

"Oh, an oldie? Those books only cover the folks active in the last year."

Ralph sighed. "Great. I wish the guy at the bookstore had told me that."

The waiter said, "I think we have last year's copy behind the counter, if you want to give it a look."

"That would be great, thank you."

Scott returned with the book and Ralph leafed through it. When he reached the halfway point, he laughed out loud. "Thanks, Scottie, you're a lifesaver! Mind if I keep this? I'll leave you the new one."

"No problem. Just promise that when you get yourself a new girl, you bring her in here."

Ralph left a generous tip. Outside, he opened the book to make sure his face was still inside staring back at him.

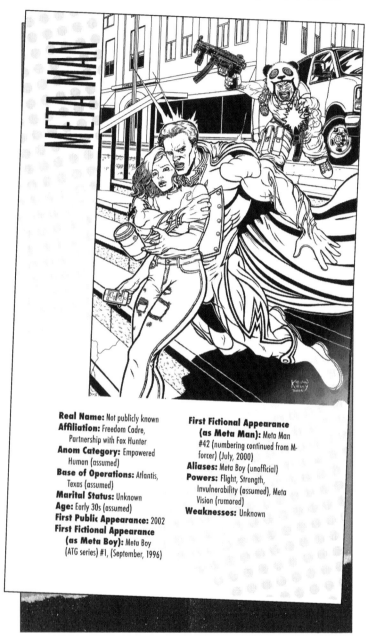

META MAN

Real Name: Not publicly known
Affiliation: Freedom Cadre, Partnership with Fox Hunter
Anom Category: Empowered Human (assumed)
Base of Operations: Atlantis, Texas (assumed)
Marital Status: Unknown
Age: Early 30s (assumed)
First Public Appearance: 2002
First Fictional Appearance (as Meta Boy): Meta Boy (ATG series) #1, (September, 1996)

First Fictional Appearance (as Meta Man): Meta Man #42 (numbering continued from M-forcer) (July, 2000)
Aliases: Meta Boy (unofficial)
Powers: Flight, Strength, Invulnerability (assumed), Meta Vision (rumored)
Weaknesses: Unknown

The real-life Meta Man remains a mystery. The source of his powers is unknown, though some speculate he is connected to the alien Oceanus, who died two years before Meta Man first appeared. This is a minority opinion, since Meta Man apparently lacks Oceanus's more obscure powers, such as wave vision, and he seems to lack the world-mover strength of the fallen hero.

Meta Man is a rare example of a hero emerging after his comic-book likeness, leading many to believe he was a publicity stunt for the **META MAN** feature film. It wasn't until Meta Man's involvement in the Cadre's millennial battle with Overmorrow that the public took him seriously. At this point he became an active member of the Cadre, helping them take down the Monster of Crackowa and free Galatea from Pygmalion.

The Golden Dawn serves as Meta Man's comic book nemesis, but that villain has yet to make the leap to the real world. Meta Man's earliest known conflicts involved low-level gimmick villains like the Shutter, the Philatelist, and the Fish Peddler. Following the Overmorrow incident, he again found widespread acclaim by rescuing a family from the murderous Joisey Devil.

In an unexpected turn of events, Meta Man developed a partnership with the reformed thief Fox Hunter. The two teamed up on a number of occasions, generally to assist in hostage situations and natural disasters. The unlikely duo has recently dropped from the public eye, creating widespread speculation and concern. The Freedom Cadre has been silent concerning his absence, but insiders report his reserved seat remains at their table.

Illustration by Kevin Kelly

2

ALPH PARKED THE CAR on the street in front of his Austin home. Sitting in the car, he surveyed the dark windows of the house. No one in a suit or an eyeball helmet leaped out of the bushes to grab him. *At least not yet,* he thought.

He looked down at his hand. Opening and closing his fist, he again wondered what he might be capable of. He reached into the car's cup holder and retrieved a coin. Pinching it with his forefingers and thumbs, he tried to bend the quarter in half. Nothing happened.

But why wasn't he hurt? Aside from a few judo classes as a kid, Ralph had no training in how to fight. He had no idea how to fire a gun, either—robot arm or traditional.

Yet he'd survived the warehouse and killed maybe a dozen people.

He frowned at the thought. It bothered him that people had died, but not as much as he thought it should. Each time he had pulled the car over for a cat nap, he'd slept peacefully and without the burden of guilt or bad dreams.

It's like it didn't matter. Like people in a video game, or extras getting shot and flying over a handrail in a bad movie. Everything around me is so far removed from what I'm used to, maybe I can't connect with it anymore. Maybe this is what it feels like to be a sociopath.

"Or maybe you know it was them or you, and you can live with that," he told himself out loud.

The quarter made a clattering sound when he tossed it back in the cup holder. He climbed out of the car and reached his front door unmolested. His keys were at the bottom of the ocean, but the spare was still in the fake rock he'd purchased in a different reality. With the door unlocked, he entered the house.

"Hello?" he called out, not expecting an answer. The air smelled stale. He walked to his bedroom and slid open the closet door, feeling around the edge of the door frame, but he found no concealed switch. Taking armloads of hanging clothes, he soon removed the closet's contents. He poked and prodded at every corner, but located no hidden panels. Standing in the empty closet, he made a frustrated grunt and kicked a hole in the drywall. There was nothing inside but pink cotton-candy insulation.

In the living room, he turned on his new television to kill the silence. The set of a late-night talk show appeared on the screen as the band played upbeat intro music. A handsome man strutted onto the stage. He wore a double-breasted brown suit made to look like a door, complete with a shiny knob where a button should be.

The music stopped, and the man called out, "Knock knock!"

"Who's there?" yelled the crowd.

"You know who!" the man said. The audience roared. His catch phrase delivered, he continued, "I'm Knock Knock, the a-door-able Anom villain so likable they gave me my own show! I'm legally obligated to tell you that. Sure, I'm officially reformed—but you never know, am I right?"

The television audience ate it up. While he listened, Ralph pulled books from the shelves, spilling everything onto the floor. He grabbed a light sconce and ripped it out of the wall.

In the background, Knock Knock continued his monologue. "And so the guy said, 'Ma'am, before you do that again, you might want to move your cat.'" The audience nearly drowned out the rimshot with laughter. "Our next guest is Damon Ripley, star of the upcoming *Danny Drastic* movie—"

"Where is it!" Ralph yelled into the empty house.

After tearing apart every room in the house, he went to the garage. He checked the attic and felt around under the Stout Scarab. Finally, he decided he was wrong. The house was just a house.

He went into his studio and grabbed a bottle of beer from the old monitor-top refrigerator. Popping off the cap, he took a long drink. "I've totally lost it," he said. "I honestly thought I'd come in here and find a hidden compartment with a Meta Man costume inside. They should lock me up in Arkham."

He stood up, knocking over a bottle of black India ink. It shattered on the white tile, creating an oversized Rorschach test.

"God damn it!" He chugged the rest of his beer and chunked the largest pieces of glass into the bin. While wiping up the ink, he heard a hollow dripping sound. The puddle of ink revealed an indented line in the tile.

Jumping to his feet, he grabbed his drafting desk and threw it aside. Pencils, pens, inks and brushes flew in every direction. A wooden T-square snapped under the weight of the desk. On his hands and knees, Ralph touched the tiles on the floor until one of them glowed blue under his fingers. He fumbled backwards in an awkward crab walk as a section of the floor lowered and slid out of sight, revealing a staircase.

Grinning, he walked down the staircase and found a basement room with smooth white walls. In the center of the room stood a transparent column holding a blue costume, exactly as he had pictured it, as he had drawn it a thousand times. There was no mannequin; the cape, mask, and suit hung in the air as if worn by an invisible man. As he approached the column, it slid into the floor, leaving behind the floating costume.

Ralph stripped down, leaving his clothes in a pile on the cold floor. The costume lost its shape as he took it from its place. He slid it on. The cavalry-style jacket felt like smooth leather. He carefully threaded the buttons on the chest; the suit fit better than anything he'd ever worn.

Below the floating mask, he saw a thin clear disk about the size of a dime. Remembering Titania's communicator, he took the disk and placed it behind his left ear. It comfortably clung to his skin and made a soft beep as it came online.

"Titania," he said, "I need to talk to you."

The air next to him came alive, and he jumped aside. Titania stepped out of a green and gold fire.

"I was hoping you'd call," she said.

"Val, why didn't you tell me Meta Man was real?" he asked. "Oh, and that he happens to be *me*?"

"Sweetie, you weren't yourself. Put yourself in my goofy cuffed boots. Do you have any idea how many times one of our friends has been replaced or mind controlled? Maybe we're on a sliding timeline or something, because I've lost count. I had to treat you like you were a different person than the Ralph I knew, because you *were* different. You have to see that. I hoped seeing the Cadre all together in Atlantis would jog your memory, but when it didn't, we decided not to tell you."

"You could have trusted me," he said.

"I know that now. But even if I wanted to trust you, it wasn't just about me. You have inside info on the Cadre, and that's only for starters. If you still had your powers but didn't have the same—I don't know, experience? Conscience? Morals? I know you've never seen what it's like if someone with the powers of Meta Man goes bad, but I have. It happened in London in the eighties, and we can't afford a repeat of that."

"You know I'm not like that," Ralph said. "Maybe I'm not the same Ralph you remember, but he and I should be enough alike that you know I'll be one of the good guys."

"I want to believe that," she said. "But how do you think the Ocularist broke into Atlantis? Do you think maybe—just maybe—Meta Man's reformed ex-girlfriend might've had something to do with it? The Ralph I knew brought her down there a couple of times. Supervised, obviously, but maybe she's more clever than we gave her credit for. So maybe it was Meta Man who sold us out."

Ralph looked down at his fists. "It doesn't matter now, does it? Whatever powers you remember me having, they're gone now. I'm just a guy in a costume."

"Maybe," Titania said, lifting a revolver from under her cape.

She pointed the barrel at Ralph's chest and pulled the trigger.

3

"**V**AL, WHAT THE HELL!" Ralph yelled.

Titania lowered the smoking gun. "Ralph, look."

He looked at his chest, and felt the location of the impact with his hand. It felt warm, but he was unharmed. "Nothing happened."

She pointed at the floor with the gun. Ralph looked down and saw a shiny rock. Picking it up, he realized it was the metal slug of a bullet, squashed like a gum drop.

"Your powers are dormant unless you're using them," Titania said.

Ralph looked back and forth between the slug and Titania. "You could have killed me!"

Titania rolled her eyes. "Stop being such a baby. Grab your mask and let's get out of here." She kicked at his discarded clothes with her foot. "Are those your underwear? Are you seriously free-balling it in there?"

"Hey, I don't know how Other Ralph did things, but it feels good like this. Unconfined but supportive." Ralph held back his hair as he pressed the fitted mask to his face. He reached for the cape.

"Oh, come on," she said as a shimmering portal appeared. "You haven't worn that silly cape in years!"

"Don't ruin this for me," he said, attaching the cape to his shoulders. "Let's go."

"Fine. But bring your change of clothes. Don't know when we'll be back."

They stepped through the portal into a restaurant. An enormous window held a breathtaking view of the New York skyline. The floor was filled with round tables with white tablecloths and red vinyl chairs. Art Deco murals and light fixtures lined the walls. Three framed posters from Damon Ripley's spy trilogy—*Spy on the Wall*, *Spy Me Away*, and *Spyswatter*—were prominently displayed. Damon himself, wearing jeans and a hooded sweatshirt labeled *Superman Lives Film Crew*, stood behind the extravagant bar, mixing a cocktail.

"Looks like you finally brought Meta Boy up to speed." Damon tasted his drink and grimaced.

"Don't be an asshole, Damon." Titania left the revolver on a table.

"Where the hell are we?" Ralph asked.

Damon vaulted over the wooden bar, somehow managing not to spill a drop from his highball glass. "Welcome to the Cloud Club, way up on floors sixty-six, sixty-seven, and sixty-eight of the Chrysler Building. I bought it when I needed a crash pad in New York. You do *not* want to know how many shitty roles it took to buy the place and restore it to its former glory. Can I get you a drink? My usual bartender isn't here, so expect strong but terrible."

"I'm good," Ralph said.

Titania shook her head. "After what happened last time, future boy, you're never mixing me another drink. Are the others upstairs?"

"Just waiting on you," Damon grabbed the bottle off the bar and led the way up the spiral staircase.

"Is Stiff here?" Ralph asked.

Damon laughed. "He must have given you the whole you're-better-off-killing-yourself speech. Don't worry, kid, he knows the Fall of Atlantis wasn't your fault. Turns out it was an old Ocularist mask I added to the collection that led them to us."

A woman wearing a Victorian explorer outfit walked up behind them. "Stop calling it 'the Fall of Atlantis.' That's like me calling the Alamo 'the Fall of the United States.'"

"Fair enough," Damon said. "Ralph, you remember Helena Ignatius, Ambassador of Atlantis and my favorite ex-girlfriend."

"Um," Ralph said.

"Don't let him throw you off," Helena said. "Weird to be introduced to someone I've known for years, but I guess you're getting used to that, aren't you, Meta Man?"

Upstairs, members of the Cadre were scattered around the room: Ironworks, Mr. Stiff, Luke, and Rika. Ralph was surprised to see Songweaver, who looked exhausted but otherwise unharmed. There were also Baron and the cowgirl from the warehouse. According to the *Identification Guide*, her name was Buscadera, leader of the Outliers.

Rika leaned against the edge of a table. "Oh my God, he's wearing the cape."

"Told you so," Titania said.

"I think it's great," Baron said.

Ralph smiled. "Thank you."

"He's being sarcastic," Rika said. "We all know he only wears a cape to be ironic."

"Don't listen to her," Baron said. "Capes are making a comeback."

"Shut up about the damn capes." Mr. Stiff's hood was pulled back to reveal his face. He was an older Hispanic man, with the sides of his hair graying. "We need to sort this out."

"I contacted the Cadre after the Outliers cleaned up your Haberdasher mess," Buscadera said. "You didn't seem like yourself, and it looked like something huge was going on."

"Not to mention the Ocularist showing up," Baron said.

Ironworks spoke up. "We apologize that you had to handle that situation on your own. It's impressive you survived at all, considering your confused state. By the time we recovered from the Atlantis attack, we'd lost all track of you."

"It's my fault for running off," Ralph said.

"Damn right it is!" Damon said. "But we're all prima donnas around here, so we forgive you. Just fill us in on what happened before Songweaver has to read your mind."

Ralph told them about the Haberdasher armory and the Ocularist's claim there were a thousand more just like it. When he had finished, Luke was the first to speak.

"It should have never gotten this far. It's time to take down the Haberdasher organization."

"There's more to it than the weapons," Ralph said. "I think the Ocularist is aware of the reality bleed transforming the world. He might even be behind it."

"Again with this shit!" Rika said. "Ralph, the world is fucked up, but it's *always* been fucked up."

"Watch it," Titania said. "If Meta Man says the world is changing, I believe him. And if the Ocularist backs him up, that scares me even more. Once we round up all the Haberdashers, we'll figure out what to do about the reality bleed."

"How exactly are you going to track down all the button men?" Buscadera asked. "You guys look like crap. Even with my team helping out, there's no way we can track down that many installations."

"First of all," Damon said, "fuck you, I look fantastic. Second, we'll have plenty of help. We'll call in the reservists."

"Reservists?" Ralph asked. "Like your kid sidekicks?"

"Kid sidekicks?" Rika asked. "What are you, crazy? No one does that anymore. That's child endangerment."

"Reservists are former Cadre members in good standing," Titania said. "And the folks we call in on special occasions. Friends of friends, folks like that. There are other teams we can contact in a pinch."

"Wait a minute," Ralph said. "Just how many Anoms are there?"

Luke laughed. "That's a bit of a German tank problem. But our best estimate is around six thousand. That's including unpowered folks that function at the loosely defined Anom level."

Songweaver said, "We'll put the word out so all the freelancers know what's going on. If we can track down these weapon factories and coordinate things from here, the job's not impossible. There's a lot of respect in the hero community for Wyvern and the Advocate. They'll want to pitch in."

"It sounds like Ocularist is using tech stolen from some of the major players from the other side," Ironworks said. "There's a good chance that, if worse comes to worst, they might pitch in. Even if it's only to eliminate the competition."

Damon finished his drink. "Excellent. Rika, you're in charge of setting up communications. Mr. Stiff, get our spy satellites looking for Haberdasher facilities. I'll send out the alarm to the reservists, bring them up to speed, and then let the Grudge know what's going on and how they can help. The rest of you, contact every Anom you know, good or bad. Take plenty of communication discs so you can get everyone on our network. Good meeting, everybody. Try not to get killed."

JACK SPRATT

Real Name: Not publicly known
Affiliation: Freedom Cadre
Anom Category: Empowered Human, Voluntary Shapeshifter (Type 1)
Base of Operations: Atlantis, St. Louis
Marital Status: Unknown

Age: Perpetually 27 (Born 1937)
First Public Appearance: 1964
First Fictional Appearance: The Freedom Cadre Volume 2 #37 (August, 1964)
Aliases: The Human Rubber Band, Stretch Armstrong (unofficial)

In 1958, the anomalous hero PneuMan discovered a rash of kidnappings, which served as the initial phase of an interdimensional invasion. PneuMan followed the methane-based lifeforms back to their home dimension through a portal, defeated them with his wind powers, and rescued their prisoners. Unfortunately, one abductee was brought back to Earth in a liquid state and presumed dead. His family allowed the Grudge government agency to study the remains at one of their facilities. It wasn't until 1963 that Jack Spratt managed to reconstitute himself into human form. The Grudge has since apologized for holding Spratt against his will and for their attempts to recapture him after his 1964 escape.

Jack Spratt's body is highly elastic and resilient, allowing him to assume any shape. The extent of Jack Spratt's powers are not currently known. Most famously, he saved the town of Dayton, Ohio, during the Falling Sky event by stretching his body into a rubber band several miles wide. Oceanus and Titania used Spratt's body to bounce the asteroid back into space. This is believed to be at the upper limit of Spratt's abilities, because he required months of rehabilitation.

After Spratt defeated Mantra Ray and rescued a stadium full of people from the Mummy Magician, the Cadre recruited the stretching hero. Jack Spratt, Spacenik, Danny Drastic, and Milly Meter formed the second wave of heroes to join the team since its return in 1961. Together with Oceanus, the second Advocate, N-Ray, and Molly Pitcher, the team enjoyed one of its most popular periods. They held back the so-called Venusian Invasion, saved the American heartland from Deluge, and stopped the Living Planetoid from destroying the Earth. This era ended with the public outing of the Advocate's secret identity, resulting in the murder of the civil rights icon and his family, as well as the reporter and publisher responsible for the story. Jack Spratt tracked down the invisible murderer Gyges and brought him to justice. The terrible event strongly affected how journalists view secret identities. The press now reveals the identities of Anom heroes only in extreme circumstances.

Jack Spratt's quick wit and charitable activities have made him a favorite of the press and the public. His heroic presence at every major Anom event provides continuity for generations of do-gooders, and he will hopefully inspire heroes until we reach Danny Drastic's distant future.

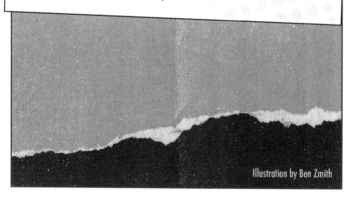

Illustration by Ben Zmith

4

ITANIA GRABBED RALPH BY THE ARM and dragged him aside. "I want you to stay here," she said.

Ralph did a double take. "Are you kidding me?" he asked. "I just found out I'm a superhero. This is literally my dream come true. I'm going with you, where the action is. I'm going to punch a bad guy into space."

"You are not punching anyone into space. That is not what Meta Man does. You're noble. You punch people to the police station, so they'll receive a fair trial. You're supposed to inspire people."

"I can do that. I can inspire. I'm like the most inspiring guy ever."

Titania put her hands on his shoulders and looked into his eyes. "Ralph, what are your powers?"

He stared at her.

"Exactly," she said. "You don't even know."

"Wait just a minute. I know. In the comic, Meta Man has super strength, invulnerability, and—this is so amazing—he can fly. That means I can do those things, because I am Meta Man. Transient property."

"Being bulletproof one time does not make you Meta Man. All your knowledge comes from a book that was purposely written to give everyone the wrong idea about your abilities and how they worked. How strong are you, Ralph? How much punishment can you take before you get crushed? Do you have any idea how to fly?"

"No, but it can't be—"

Titania interrupted. "If you say, 'It can't be that hard,' I am going to twist your nose off. I can do it too, because I have super nose-twisting powers. Your Meta powers only activate when you want them to work."

"Like Ultra Boy from the Legion of Super-Heroes."

"Stop assuming I'll get your stupid nerd references. But no, not like Ultra Boy. He can only use one at a time, which makes no sense to begin with. Wouldn't his bones break if he used his super strength, or he'd explode if he switched to super strength in the vacuum of space?" She shook her head, as if to clear it. "Speaking of, can you breathe in space?"

"I don't know. Probably."

"Probably? Probably?" She smacked him on the forehead. "You idiot, no one can breathe up there. There's no fucking air. *That's what makes it outer space.*"

"Val, don't be like this. Take me with you, you can tell me what I need to know as we go. Like a coach."

"That right there is symptomatic. 'Like a coach.' It's like you're writing a checklist for how to get me killed. That's not all of it, either. Those kids in there told me what you did at the warehouse, Ralph. They found bits of Haberdasher everywhere. That's not how our Ralph would handle things. He'd find a better way."

"I didn't know." Ralph tried to blink away tears. "I'm not the bad guy here."

She hugged him, wrapping her fingers in his hair. "Sweetie, shh, I know that. And we'll fight all the bad guys together that you want, I promise. Your heart's in the right place. It's tough to get all that power at once, I understand that better than anyone. You just have to, I don't know, develop the discipline to use your powers."

"Don't leave me behind," he said. "It's emasculating."

"I wouldn't be talking about emasculating, you big crybaby. They'll need a heavy hitter to back them up here. If nothing else, Rika will need someone to do the heavy lifting. And if you're here, I know I'll come back. Okay?"

Rika walked by the hallway carrying a box of cables. "I'm not babysitting your idiot boyfriend, Valerie."

"Don't be a bitch, Rika," Titania yelled over her shoulder. She turned to Ralph and whispered in his ear, "If the eyeball guy shows up, don't let them get killed. And don't you dare get killed, either. And for Christ's sake, by the time I get back, lose the cape. You look ridiculous."

RIKA MIZUNO

Real Name: Publicly Known
Anom Categories: Augmented Human, Technology User
Base of Operations: Atlantis, Tokyo
Marital Status: Single
Date of Birth: June 27, 1990
First Anom Activity: 2005
First Fictional Appearance: The Freedom Cadre Volume 2 #581 (March, 2010)

Powers: Genius-level Intellect, Augmented Intelligence and Reflexes, Skilled Hand-to-Hand Combatant
Equipment: Projectile and Energy Weapons, Explosives, Drones, Mary (the name for various mechas designed and piloted by Mizuno)

Rika Mizuno first gained international attention when her science fair exhibit leveled a Japanese high school auditorium. Because her quick thinking prevented any loss of life, and because she was still a minor, she was not charged with any crime. The publicity allowed Mizuno to work as a prominent tech consultant before striking off on her own.

It's unknown when Mizuno began experimenting with nootropics, but a combination of secret chemical and neural experiments allows her to double and redouble her intelligence for short periods. Under the influence of these treatments, she created Mary, her mecha robot. Mizuno used Mary to defend Japan from numerous Anom attacks, most notably against the Final End.

Rika joined the Freedom Cadre in her early twenties. The Anom team is generally seen as an American organization, and this decision drew controversy. Because she had become such a powerful role model for the youth of Japan, her use of chemical augmentations was also a source of debate. Health professionals went on record, questioning the long-term effects of her nootropics. But when the Cadre saved Japan and the rest of the world from the Bringer of the Blades, she silenced even her most vocal critics.

Illustration by Rian Gonzales

5

ALPH CALLED DOWN THE NARROW HALLWAY, "Rika! Where do you want the relay?"

"Anywhere it fits!" she yelled back. "I suggest checking your ass first!"

He set the metal casing down on the ground. It was the size of a washing machine and looked like it weighed at least two hundred pounds, but it felt like lifting an empty cardboard box.

After hooking the relay into the system, he climbed out of the spire and made his way back to the Cloud Club. Thick cables covered the floor, tying into the nerve center Rika and Jack Spratt had assembled. Ralph suspected the computers wouldn't work with the physics he was used to, so he did as he was told and stayed out of the way.

Jack Spratt operated the control panel, dressed in a white T-shirt and a pair of gym shorts. A plastic band encased his midsection, treating his injuries with a turquoise gel. He was uniquely suited for the job at hand, his fingers stretching several feet long as they pushed buttons and swiped touch-sensitive monitors. A piece of skin from his elbow reached over and grabbed a bottle of water from a cooler. Ralph approached, careful not to trip on any cables or Jack's snaking body parts.

"I thought this would be a job for Ironworks," Ralph said.

"What? Oh, right, the amnesia thing." One of Jack's fingers took a break from its duties to draw circles around his ear.

"I don't have amne—"

"Ironworks isn't an android, he's a magical golem. Like Mr. Peanut or the Kool-Aid Man. It's an easy mistake to make. It's not like we can plug something into the guy's head—the magic would fry the computers. I personally think Mr. Stiff is better at this kind of thing, but Drastic said something about me being used to coordinating a lot of things at once. Whatever that means." He shrugged as he spoke, his shoulders rising high above his ears.

"Thanks for saving our asses in Atlantis," Ralph said. "I thought we were toast."

"No problem, kid. You don't remember, but Meta Man had my back more than a few times." Jack puffed out his chest to comical proportions and patted his stomach. "And I heal real quick-like. Comes from having rubber skin and gummi organs."

"Oh, okay. Is there anything I can do to help? I've moved all the equipment Rika ported in. I think she's getting tired of having to explain everything to me."

"Don't mind Rika. That girl would take a bullet for any of us. She's just frustrated she lost her mecha and hasn't had time to build a new one." He checked to make sure Rika was within earshot before saying loudly, "Between you and me, I think she was a little in love with that thing."

"What can I say?" she called back. "Not everyone wants a boy made of silly putty."

"Ouch!" Jack pretended to be shot in the chest. "See? I told you she loved us."

"Shut up and flip the switch," Rika said. "We should be online."

"We're up and running. Thank you, Rika, you're a genius." Jack's head twisted like a corkscrew to face Ralph." Meta, I hear you survived the Ocularist without using your powers. That's impressive."

"I got lucky—"

"Did they really have Danny Drastic disintegrator guns modded to destroy soft living tissue? Leave the skeletons behind?"

"Yeah—"

"That's amazing. I've been wondering what would happen if I got hit with one of those things while I'm stretching. Are my bones still similar enough to count, or would they get vaporized? Would it be a pile of bones that were all stretched out? Would they be hard like bones are supposed to be, or would they be all flimsy?"

Ralph changed the subject. "Are you really the original Jack Spratt?"

"Sure am."

"You've been around for decades, but you don't look older than thirty."

"Twenty-seven, actually, but thanks. I haven't aged since the origin story. Figure I'll stay young as long as I stay relevant. You want to ask about my sex life, right? People always wanna know about the sex life."

"I wonder who you were before everything changed."

"Before what?"

"Nothing," Ralph said. "There were bows and arrows at the warehouse too. Any idea who they belonged to?"

"Probably Eros and his buddy, the Cupid Kid. Maybe Thunderstroke. Oh, or Upshot. She's hot right now. Were the arrows just kill-you pointy or did some have boxing gloves and handcuffs?" As Jack talked, Rika placed a black shiny cube on the floor, about the size of a tissue box. A hologram appeared, filling the room with a slowly revolving Earth. As she and Jack entered the input coming in from the satellites and over the communication network, red flags appeared on the globe. A green flag showed the location of the factory that Ralph destroyed in Greenvale. Within the hour, red flags dotted the globe. One even popped up in Antarctica before quickly turning green.

"Good ol' Cryotic put the kibosh on that one." Jack tapped a monitor with a six-foot pinky finger. "They should have worn warmer socks."

Many of the factories were in developing countries. "You see this a lot when the bad guys are manufacturing," Jack explained. "The locals turn a blind eye and there's zero oversight. The Cadre once busted a factory making chocolate-covered people for Easter. Talk about your health code violations."

With Rika and Jack busy on monitor duty, Ralph experimented with his powers.

Or lack thereof, he thought as he stood in his jeans and faded Pithos Publishing T-shirt among the tables and chairs of the Cloud Club.

He balled his hands into fists and willed himself into the air, an angry yogi incapable of levitation. Climbing onto a chair and jumping off yielded no results. For a moment he considered jumping over the railing of the upper area. *With my luck I'd just break my leg*, he thought.

Or would I? Looking down at his left fist, he thought about Meta Man's invulnerability. Super strength was weird enough. Walking to the mini refrigerator behind the bar, Ralph took out one of the eggs Damon kept handy for Round Robins. He held it in his fingers, and it did not explode. With his other hand, he easily lifted the refrigerator off the floor, careful to keep it level.

That's how I got into the Ocularist's warehouse. The window wasn't unlocked—I broke the latch. And this is why I didn't get hurt when I jumped down to the warehouse floor, or when I fought the Haberdashers with those crazy weapons. Not because I'm lucky or clever or a badass.

He pulled an olive fork out of a drawer and examined the dagger-like prongs. With a swift motion, he stabbed it into his hand.

The tines sunk into his skin.

"Son of a bitch!" he yelled, trying to catch his own blood in a cupped hand. The wiggling fork remained embedded in his flesh. *Stick a fork in me,* he thought. *I'm done.*

As he washed his aching hand in the bar sink, he heard Rika's voice. "What kind of cocktail are you making down here? Expecting vampires?"

"No, thankfully. Met some vampires in Oklahoma. Seemed like real tool factories."

"Oh, right. With the Gentleman. Just be glad they weren't like the ones we have back in Japan. Those bastards hop. They hop *everywhere*. Annoying as hell. Let me get you the first aid kit."

As Rika wrapped his hand, Ralph asked, "How did that happen? I feel like an idiot, but isn't Meta Man bulletproof? Or are cocktail forks my kryptonite?"

Rika laughed. "I get the feeling you make your own kryptonite, kid. But let me ask you this: Do you know why you can't tickle yourself?"

"No idea."

"Your brain knows it's coming and prepares itself. Same thing with most Anom invulnerability. That's why you can shave and trim your fingernails. Some of the tanks and you flying bricks out there can even control it enough to get an injection at the doctor's office, but I don't know if that applies to you or not. Maybe you can ask Mr. Stiff. That sneak knows the limits and intricacies of everyone's powers."

Ralph examined his bandaged hand. "So I'm still tough?"

Moving faster than Ralph could react, Rika grabbed a bottle by the neck and smashed it against the bar. Green glass and expensive alcohol showered the carpet. She slashed Ralph across the chest, cutting the vase of the Pithos logo in two.

Ralph's hands went to his chest, but nothing was ruined except his double's old shirt.

Rika tossed him the broken bottle and laughed all the way up the stairs.

As the Cadre's work progressed, more and more of the Anom community pitched in to help. Word came in over the network that criminal Anoms were showing up to help with the operation.

"That's something you don't see every day," Rika said.

"Hasn't happened like this since that meteor storm on the East Coast in the eighties," Jack said. "The Falling Fire event. I'll tell you what, it was weird seeing the Made Man pulling people out of the rubble. We live in strange times."

Ralph said, "You have no idea."

He looked out the window at the jagged New York skyline. Below, streams of yellow cabs flowed. In the distance, someone in a bright costume swung from one building to another.

"Speaking of things you don't see every day," he said.

"What's that?" Jack asked.

"Just saw a guy in neon underwear doing a high-rise trapeze act."

"That's not unusual on its own," Rika said. "It's a bit rarer to see the same person do it twice."

Ralph looked to Jack, who laughed. "It's even more dangerous than you think it is. Most swingers don't survive the first attempt. It's one reason New York requires Anoms operating in the city to have medallions, like the cabbies."

"And to cut down on Anom overcrowding on the island," Rika said. "The logistics were crazy. Before the medallions, every morning there were dozens of tied-up people left in front of police departments. No evidence, usually not even a note. Took all day to sort out who was actually a bad guy."

"Do I—did Meta Man have a medallion?" Ralph asked.

"You're in the Cadre, kid," Jack said. "You don't have to worry about that stuff."

Rika went back to tinkering with the communication hub, pausing only to make a component with the fabricator or to swear at Ralph for being in the way. "She gets that way when she replaces sleep with nootropics," Jack said. As for Jack, it seemed that his unusual biology could function without rest, so Ralph tried to nap in short stints as the hours stretched into days.

He woke on one of the restaurant tables on the first floor of the Cloud Club. He'd fallen asleep in his costume, mask and all. Sitting up, he blinked the sleep from his eyes to see Rika at the bar, hunched over a steaming cup. Without turning, she said, "Hey there, hero. Come have some of this terrible coffee with me."

Ralph raised his arms and stretched as he walked to the bar. "You okay?" He sat on the stool next to her and poured himself a cup.

"I'll need to crash soon. I make sure my special mix of stimulants and cognitive enhancers is safe, but I get diminishing returns when I have to up the dose for a marathon like this. Drastic is sending some relief our way now that the array is finished."

Ralph took a sip of the coffee and grimaced. "It can't be healthy to push yourself like this. You've been up for, what, three days?"

"Four. I was in the middle of something else when we got pulled into this crisis you uncovered."

"You should have had more help before now."

"They'd only be in the way," she said. "There aren't many of us who can create a communication system that can adapt to this many Anoms but is secure enough to keep the button men and Mr. Eyeball in the dark. We had the best possible set-up back in Atlantis, but nothing is that water proof."

Ralph gave up on drinking the coffee and just held the cup, letting it warm his hands. "Rika, I know you're good in a fight, but do you have powers?"

"People are worried about another computer coming along that can make a better computer. Then that computer can make a better computer, and so on. The last time it happened was a mess. But I'm like that. I'm smart enough that I can make myself smarter. And I've done that 137 times. I'm at the end of the curve, where I can only hit the absolute top of my game for short periods. It's like fucking *Flowers for Algernon* over and over. The process isn't fun, but it lets me play the game on the same level as the rest of the Cadre, so it's worth it."

"So, not all Anoms are created equal."

"It's all relative," she said. "At a school for the blind, anyone who can see is an Anom. Look at our Mr. Stiff, the fourth one to use the identity. The guy trained his whole life for the honor of putting on the duds. Aside from a few prosthetic implants, he's as human as—well, not you or me, but as human as the average Joe. But he can strategize and scheme better than anyone I've ever met, including me—and I once beat a fourth-dimensional computer at Go. Are his talents an anomaly? Certainly. But are they enough to count as super powers? That's up for debate.

"That's probably why I've been giving you a hard time. People like me and Mr. Stiff bust our asses to be a part of this world, but you fall right into it with the powers everyone wishes they had. And it's always one of you that ends up mind-controlled or gets amnesia. For Anoms who are supposed to be invulnerable, you toughies end up the weak link an awful lot."

Ralph considered this as he sipped his coffee. "I've been wondering about Anom technology. You seem like the person to ask."

"You're making me blush. Ask away and I'll try to dumb it down for you."

He smiled. "You have a mech suit. Teleportation. And that's the tip of the iceberg. Why are people still driving cars and flying around in airplanes? Why do they still use phones if they could use something like these communicator discs?"

Rika laughed. "You're catching on quicker than I thought. Anom tech is about as dangerous as a grenade with the pin out. Sometimes it's tied to a specific Anom's powers. Most super science can't be recreated in lab conditions at all. It's called the Wardenclyffe Principle."

"Wardenclyffe?"

"After Tesla's one-of-a-kind wireless electrical tower. No one else could make it work. You don't see mechas down on Broadway because it takes a badass to pilot one. Some people use unobtrusive tech, but you wouldn't notice it, would you? That's kind of the point. It will get more widespread once the cost goes down and it's more reliable. As is, most people don't want surgery for implants that are obsolete in a year. The communication discs we use are only useful if you have an operator on the other end directing your calls. Great for people like us who can't carry a phone into a punch-up, but useless for the masses needing to send a text message."

"And the teleporter?"

"That's proprietary Atlantean tech, and they keep it close to the vest. After all the underwater nuclear tests, Atlantis doesn't trust most of us barbaric surface dwellers."

Ralph pushed aside the thought of a teleport gone wrong. "Do you think, in general, Anoms are a good thing for the world? Do the benefits outweigh the risks?"

"That's a question people have been trying to answer for a long time, Rogers. By helping—and, let's face it, sometimes hurting—humanity, do Anoms prevent the human race from moving forward?" Rika's cell phone beeped, and she took several pill capsules from her pocket and tossed them down her throat. "But look at me. I've transformed myself. Are we holding the world back? I don't think so. I think Anoms are the part of humanity moving forward."

Rika knocked back the last of her coffee. "But as far as I'm concerned, you earned your stripes on this one. If you hadn't turned us onto the Ocularist's plan when you did, we'd be facing an end-of-the-world scenario." She slapped him on the back. "Good work, kid."

The two of them turned as the viewing window exploded inward.

6

HREE HABERDASHERS SWUNG IN through the window, unclipping themselves from black ropes as they landed. Outside and sixty-six floors above the ground, Ralph saw what looked like the gondola attached to the bottom of a blimp.

"Shit!" Rika yelled. "Not this again."

Ralph stepped in front of Rika as a Haberdasher lifted a machine gun. The bullets bounced off Ralph's costume-clad skin. The impacts felt like paintballs shot at close range. One of the ricocheting bullets hit a Haberdasher in the ankle, sending him sprawling.

"Why aren't they using the Anom weapons?" Ralph yelled as they ran for the stairs.

"At the top of a skyscraper? If they hit something structural, the whole building would come down. And not all of us are bulletproof, you stupid ass! Check your five o'clock."

Ralph stepped in front of another rain of bullets. The window behind the Cloud Club's bar shattered. "Damon's going to be pissed."

"How the fuck did they find us?" Rika yelled as they reached the second-floor landing. "Even the Grudge couldn't trace us with my setup, and they record what everyone sings in the shower."

"Did they beat one of the teams out there? Get the location that way?"

"More likely one of the bad guys Stiff recruited did a double heel-face turn. But why'd they send only three? They must want the communication hub in one piece, but they have to know any of us could deal with three dorks in suits."

"Rika!" a voice yelled from downstairs.

Ralph and Rika poked their heads around the banister and saw a woman in a pink dress, torn open at the chest to reveal her breasts. She had no arms, and instead of a head, she had a strange fleshy opening. Flies poured from the empty hole where her face should be.

Ralph's head swam at the sight. "What is that? How is she even talking?"

"Venus de Flytrap. She's one of the stranger baddies. If you're feeling sick, it should pass. The Haberdashers are waiting for her to take the lead, so we have a few seconds." Rika pulled out a tablet computer and started tapping Japanese characters. "Ralph, you've got a job to do here: You have to keep them from getting upstairs. Jack is keeping our people safe out there, and I'm in no shape to fight. I'll put together some automated defenses, but you have to keep them out."

"Are you kidding? I can't fight whatever that thing is. I don't understand how my powers work. I don't even know how I stopped those bullets."

"Don't overthink it, you'll be fine. But watch out; just because you can't see her arms doesn't mean she can't hit you. Whatever you do, don't punch her in the face—it's gross. If you handle her, I'll make sure those Haberdashers need a seamstress. Now go get 'er!"

Ralph vaulted the banister and crouched as he landed on the floor, his cape floating behind him.

I bet that looked amazing, he thought. *I'll have to show Val, so she'll understand why capes are so awesome.*

Venus approached him, silent except for the buzz of flies emanating from her horrible throat. Ralph held his fists in front of him, wondering what to do. Venus twisted her body, and flies erupted from inside her. The flies merged into a giant fist connected to her smooth shoulders.

"What the hell?" Ralph asked as the shimmering fist slammed into him, knocking his body backwards. The back of his knees buckled against the broken viewing window, and he tumbled out.

There was an instant where Ralph wondered if he could survive a fall from that height. He reached out and grabbed one of the Haberdashers' ropes dangling in the sky over Madison Avenue. Venus floated out the broken window toward him, standing on a cloud of flickering flies.

He gripped the rope for dear life. As Venus approached, the flies formed an enormous pair of scissors. He lunged toward her and jumped, grabbing her around the waist as he crashed through a window several floors below the Cloud Club.

They landed in a crowded area of cubicles, desks, and office workers. People screamed and ran for the emergency exits. Venus's flies lifted a man, his coffee cup falling from his hand and shattering with a brown splash. The woman flung him towards Ralph, who caught the man like a dodge ball and set him running toward the stairs. A bell sounded, and red, yellow, and blue emergency lights flashed. An Anom fight was apparently worth pulling the alarm.

"Please stop this!" Ralph yelled over the clanging bell.

"*Bzzzzzz*," was the only reply.

He picked up a desk and threw it at the vaguely feminine thing, but a wave of flies swatted it aside. Drawers and pencils flew in the air as the desk crashed into a wall.

I wish Rika had told me how the hell to stop it, he thought. *Is it okay to kill this Venus thing? I can't knock it out, she doesn't have a head to hold a brain. Is it even thinking?*

"Ralph are you there?" a voice asked.

"What?" Ralph looked around for the source of the voice.

"It's Jack. I'm talking to you through your communicator disc. You really don't have any idea what you're doing, do you?"

"What do you think?" Ralph yelled, dodging flying chairs and cubicle walls.

"Listen to me. Venus de Flytrap has only rudimentary intelligence, but you can't kill it. It's an extra-dimensional entity that possesses women with double amputations."

"That's fucking weird, Jack." Ralph picked up a cubicle wall and waved it like a giant fan, dispersing the flies.

"It's an eight out of ten, I'll give you that."

Venus raised her fly-formed arms in a graceful motion. The light bulbs closest to her shattered, followed by more exploding in waves. Ralph covered his eyes with his cape.

"Talk quick, Jack, I'm getting my ass handed to me!"

"Okay, you have to neutralize the flies. They regenerate, so you need to take as many of them out as you can. Water doesn't work, they just get wet. You need smoke. Fire won't kill them, but the smoke makes them sleepy. Like bees. Rika already shut down the sprinklers on that floor, so set something on fire."

"Do I have heat vision?"

"I'm not going to dignify that with a response."

As Venus swatted office furniture aside with her fly constructs, Ralph ran from one cubicle to another. He grabbed a purse off the floor and dumped out the contents, but there was no lighter. The second purse had cigarettes but nothing to light them with. He hit pay dirt with the third purse, and he quickly lit a box full of tissues on fire. Dropping the box in a trash can full of paper, he picked up another cubicle wall and waved the flames and smoke toward Venus.

The air grew thick with dark smoke, forcing Ralph to cough. He pulled the collar of his uniform up over his mouth and kept waving. The flies grew sluggish until, one after the other, they dropped from the air. Venus ran toward him, the black dots of her arms evaporating. She fell as she reached him, and Ralph caught her. He watched as the strange folds of her head rejoined like a self-repairing cleft palate, and a face emerged. The pink dress melted like wax and transformed into normal clothes.

"You got her?" Jack asked.

Ralph said, "I got her."

The alarm stopped blaring, and the colored lights ceased flashing. The sprinklers lowered from the ceiling, extinguishing the fiery wastebasket and drowning piles of immobile flies.

"Not bad for a bumbler with only a childlike understanding of the world," Jack said. "Now get your ass up here, we've got real problems."

7

RALPH EXITED THE ELEVATOR on the sixty-sixth floor, dripping wet and cradling the unconscious woman in his arms. The three Haberdashers, wearing only silk boxer shorts, slumped against the bar, their hands zip-tied to the brass foot rail.

"You guys okay?" Ralph called.

"We're good!" Rika yelled. "Get up here so I can turn on the defenses."

Ralph hurried up the two flights of stairs and laid the woman down on the cot he'd been using for catnaps. He was heading for the communication room when Rika planted her hand in his chest. "Where the hell do you think you're going?" she asked. "You're soaking wet. You trying to fry the equipment we just saved?"

Ralph stammered.

"Don't listen to her, buddy," Jack said. "You done good. Most heroes have a harder time against Venus, she's just so icky. First I've heard of her used as a weapon, though. No idea how the Haberdashers figured out how to do that."

"Where's the girl?" Rika asked.

"In the next room," Ralph said. "Is that all right? I didn't know what to do with her."

"Yeah, she'll be out for days," Jack said. "We'll have Song-weaver give her a look-see. But you need to get the lead out. Titania radioed in, said she needs you to back them up."

"Are you sure?" Ralph asked. "What if another blimp shows up?"

"Gah, fucking blimps," Rika said. "We'll be fine. More backup is en route."

"She left me here because I don't know what I'm doing," Ralph said. "Why does she need me now?"

Jack laughed. "Don't hold a grudge, Romeo. Go punch some bad guys with your girlfriend."

Rika led Ralph through the access corridors up to the roof. "Can't you teleport me there?" he asked.

"With the amount of information going through that hub, your feet would end up in France and your head would wind up in Brazil—and that's if you're lucky. No, your fastest bet is to go sub-orbital." She handed him what looked like two plastic pebbles. "Stick these up your nostrils. Your body won't need any special protection up there, but you'll need some air. Breathe through your nose and these will create a pocket of air in your lungs. Lasts a little less than an hour, nice piece of Atlantean tech. I always have Mary carry a few spare sets."

"Who's Mary?"

"My mecha, currently busted. Titania's team is in California. Just go straight up. Jack will track your altitude and guide your re-entry. Any questions?"

"How do I fly?" Ralph asked.

"Are you familiar with fight or flight, little baby bird?" Rika shoved him over the edge, shouting as he fell: "For starters, don't be such a pussy!"

8

INDOWS SHOT PAST RALPH as he plummeted toward the ground. He turned in the air, and the ground raced toward him. Pedestrians looked up at him in shock.

He jerked his body and experienced a sensation like the first time he did a back flip on a trampoline as a kid. Gravity released its grip on him, and he shot up into the sky. His hands cut through the air like a knife. It felt like falling, but in the wrong direction. The island of Manhattan shrank beneath him. The view ahead changed from blue to black, and stars appeared.

"That's high enough, Ralph."

Ralph floated at the edge of the atmosphere, his heart pounding. *Oh my God, I'm in space*, he thought.

His planet floated beneath him, blue and serene. The moisture trapped in his indestructible cape turned to ice. Particles flaked off, looking like fireflies dancing in the starlight.

"I can't believe this," Ralph said, unable to hear the words with his ears.

"Ralph, I show you've stopped going up," Jack said over the communicator. "The communicator produces vibrations inside your skull, so you can hear me. Don't worry about trying to talk. Or physics. I just want you to take deep breaths. When you feel ready, find California and aim for it."

Feel ready? Ralph thought, looking incredulous.

Jack continued. "You'll be going fast, so I need you to pay close attention. I'll give you course corrections so you'll reach the target, but there will be a communications blackout. Shouldn't be more than a couple of minutes."

Ralph took a final deep breath and set his eyes on California. His will drove him toward the Earth. As he reentered the atmosphere, his skin felt hot, like he'd forgotten to use a potholder and picked up a hot pan with his whole body.

Just when he thought he wouldn't hear from Jack, there he was again: "Go left," he said inside Ralph's skull. "A little more. Now down. Crap, something's going on. Be right back."

Ralph's dry eyes blinked in disbelief as California grew larger.

Jack's voice returned. "Oh, you're way off. Up a bit, go way to your right. A little more. Perfect. Now keep going straight, you're heading right for them. It's Titania and most of the Counted. They also have the villains Matadora and Absolute with them, so keep an eye on those two. Oh, and get this. According to the GPS, Titania's signal is coming from the Danny Drastic museum. Grab me a snow globe from the gift shop when you're done, m'kay?"

The ground filled Ralph's vision and he crash-landed in a parking lot.

He climbed out of his crater to face Damon Ripley's giant, goggled face. The sign welcomed Ralph to *The Danny Drastic Destination, the Official Danny Drastic Museum.*

"Jack, I've landed," he said. "Please tell Titania I'm here."

Jack didn't answer, so Ralph approached the building. Signs of battle filled the scene—other craters, knocked down trees, scorch marks. He walked through a huge hole in the wall of the building, finding himself in the gift shop. Danny Drastic T-shirts, action figures, comic books, spark-firing laser rifles, child-sized rocket packs, and other memorabilia lined the ruined walls and littered the floor. A shelf of snow globes, each previously housing Drastic posing with his blaster, was overturned, every globe shattered, their glycerin contents pooled on the floor.

"Sorry, Jack," Ralph said to the silent communicator. "Looks like you'll have to settle for a mug."

The museum proper was the camp equivalent of the Freedom Cadre's trophy room. With the refined taste of a roadside attraction, Danny Drastic's beaming face covered every surface. A mannequin wore what a placard proclaimed to be an "Original 1960s Danny Drastic Outfit" and a reproduction of the iconic rocket pack. A pillar was plastered with artist renditions of Drastic's distant future home, all floating cities and flying cars. Beside it, a diorama inside a glass case showed Danny and the hero Oceanus zooming over a skyline, battling a humanoid rock monster as tall as a skyscraper: *Drastic and Oceanus fight Konkor, 1963*.

"Titania?" he called out. "Guys? It's Ral—It's Meta Man."

It was quiet. *Why did she ask me to come?* he asked himself. It looked like the team had finished and moved on, or—

Let's not worry until we know we have something to worry about.

He walked into an area full of display cabinets. Titania sat in a chair, her back to him.

"Titania!" he said. "What's going on?"

She still didn't answer. He walked up and touched her on the shoulder, and her body slid out of the chair and onto the floor. In shock, he bent down to help her, but found only a blank-faced mannequin wearing a wig and dressed in a Titania costume.

"Help me, Ralph," said a voice behind him that sounded like Titania. He turned to find himself looking into the enormous blank stare of the Ocularist.

"Help me, Ralph," the Ocularist said again in Titania's voice. "Help me, Ralph."

9

"WHERE'S TITANIA?" Ralph demanded, rising to his feet.

"Bagged and boarded," the Ocularist said. No longer using Titania's voice, he again sounded like someone speaking through a broken walkie-talkie.

"If you've hurt her—" Ralph began, but a magenta beam shot from the pupil of the Ocularist's helmet and hit Ralph square in the chest, knocking him backwards. His body slammed through a glass case containing a full-size recreation of Ribauldequin's organ gun, a siege weapon fitted with a dozen brass pipes. Glass and brass clattered to the ground like an upended percussion section, filling the air with a deafening cacophony.

Ralph stood, gasping for breath. He was in one piece, but his chest ached and his guts felt wobbly. He saw double; two Ocularists advanced on him, knocking a table aside with a casual wave of his hand. The air smelled like an overheating car engine. *A few more hits like that,* Ralph thought, *and it won't matter how tough my skin is. My guts will be soup.*

The eyeball helmet began to glow, and Ralph jumped to the side as another beam sliced through the air behind him.

He picked up a bundle of organ pipes and swung them in a horizontal arc at the doubled Ocularist. The clanging strike knocked the villain into the wax figures of the original Freedom Cadre. Ralph took a moment to shake his head and blink his vision back to normal. He dropped the pipes and walked toward the mess of limbs, torn fabric, and distorted wax faces.

Ralph threw aside the red curtain, expecting to find an injured man in a velvet suit and eyeball helmet. Instead, he walked into another room, this one housing the largest exhibit, a Corona typewriter as big as a tour bus. The walls were lined with shadowboxes of costumes and weapons, but the Ocularist was nowhere to be seen. *How does he move so fast?* Ralph thought.

"Jack, can you hear me? We fell for a trap. It's the Ocularist. Titania's team isn't here." Still no answer. "Jack!"

No reply. Ralph figured the bastard must be blocking the transmission somehow. *Face it, Ralphie,* he thought, *you're in over your head. This is the guy who killed Wyvern and Advocate: experienced heroes with full control of their abilities. You don't even know if you're bulletproof. Come down to it, you don't know much of anything.*

The beam slammed into his back, lifting him off his feet. He tucked his head at the last moment, his right shoulder taking the full impact as he slammed into typewriter keys the size of manhole covers. Pain exploded across his back, shoulder, and arm. He tried to push himself up off the jumbled mess of keys and levers, but his arm wouldn't support him. The muscles spasmed, shooting waves of pain down his arm and up his neck.

"To my untrained eye," the Ocularist said in his garbled voice, "it looks dislocated. You'll want to get that looked at—or save yourself the trouble and just hold still." His eye glowed red, and an electric hum floated in the air.

Ralph rolled, gripping his limp arm against his body with his other hand. Numbers and letters disintegrated behind him. With his good hand, Ralph pulled himself to his feet, only to find the Ocularist standing a few feet away.

"A failure in every reality, eh, Mr. Rogers?" the crackling radio voice said.

They both looked up as the skylight shattered above them, raining down glass.

Titania slammed into the Ocularist like a linebacker making a tackle. They crashed into a display of purple light bulbs the size of beach balls. The bulbs exploded like soap bubbles.

An energy beam incinerated the sign over an exhibit entitled *Weapons of the Black Light*.

Titania and Ocularist spilled out. Each time the Ocularist paused to charge his beam, Titania punched the helmet. Beams flew wildly toward the ceiling, the floor, and the walls.

Two more members of Titania's squad arrived on foot. "Meta Man!" Buscadera called. "Get over here!"

"Remember you can fly, Forgetful Jones!" Titania yelled.

"Shit," Ralph said, rising into the air and streaking toward the other costumed heroes.

"Jack realized something was wrong when you didn't answer your com," Buscadera said, shoving her revolvers back into their holsters. "Grail!" she yelled. "Get over here and have a look at this shoulder."

A raven-haired woman in a white tank top stepped up and cradled Ralph's injured arm. She had a tattoo of a golden cup on her sternum, ending in her cleavage. "Severe dislocation, nothing broken," she said, placing Ralph's hand on her shoulder. "You invulnerable folks always find a way to still get hurt, don't you? Listen, your powers are blocking my ability to numb your pain, and I don't have time to be nice. This will hurt like a son of a bitch. Now shrug your shoulders."

"What—" Ralph asked as she twisted his arm. Fireworks exploded across his vision, and then the edges began to go gray. Something struck him hard on the cheek.

"No time to be a pussy," Grail said, slapping him again. It was surprising how much it hurt when she hit him, but the second slap cleared his mind.

"You don't know my friend Rika, do you?" he asked. "I think you two would get along." His shoulder ached, but he could move it normally, and the nauseating pain was gone.

"Don't worry, you'll get a bill," she said, shoving him toward Titania and the Ocularist. "Now stop lollygagging and get back in there, you're in the middle of a team-up. We'll help the others check the building."

Ralph's feet left the ground and his fist collided with the Ocularist's helmet, evoking a satisfying thud. The man in the helmet staggered backward.

"About time, buddy," Titania said, grinning. "Getting pretty tired of saving your ass."

"I only got in this mess because I thought I was saving yours," Ralph said.

The Ocularist shot straight up, bringing down the ceiling and skylights. Ralph and Titania dodged the falling rubble.

"Please don't tell me he got you with the old costumed dummy bit," Titania said. Seeing Ralph's expression, she laughed. "Oh my God, I don't believe it. He's really got your number, doesn't he?"

"Just tell me how I can help."

"The current plan is to hit him in the head until his laser eye thing stops working. The rest of my team is making sure the mall is empty—and getting word back to Jack and Rika." She chunked a chair at the Ocularist, and he blasted it out of the air.

Ralph picked up a metal bar from the typewriter and rushed the Ocularist, landing one hit before the Ocularist knocked it out of Ralph's hands. The indention of an M marred the Ocularist's helmet. Titania took advantage of the distraction, flying up behind the villain. Her fists rained down quick blows on the helmet, a blur of green and gold.

Why does it seem to be going so much better than the last time, in Atlantis? Ralph wondered as he flew to the side of the Ocularist and punched the helmet as hard as he could.

The Ocularist stopped fighting back, and the eyeball helmet cracked, half falling off and revealing a man's face. His head was shaved, and wires snaked from his scarred scalp into the circuitry of the helmet. He fell to his knees.

"Help, please," the man said in a regular voice.

It isn't him, Ralph realized.

He started toward the man, but Titania held him back. "How do you know this isn't another trap?" she asked.

The part of the helmet still attached to the man's head began to blink. Then came an unbearable squeal, quickly rising in pitch.

"We've got a bomb here, everyone get down!" Titania screamed into her communicator as she grabbed Ralph's hand and pulled him toward the ceiling. She flew so quickly, Ralph barely had time to look back and watch the man pull off the broken eyeball. The bald man threw himself over the helmet as it exploded.

10

"EVERYBODY STILL GOT THEIR FINGERS AND TOES?" Titania asked.

Ralph hovered beside her. *I'm flying,* he thought. *I'm actually flying in the sky again. Last time wasn't a fluke.*

"We're all here," said Buscadera over the radio. "Greaser and the others had already checked the building. Except for the Ocularist, the museum was empty when the bomb went off. Drastic is going to be pissed we blew up his typewriter. You guys okay?"

"I've got Meta with me. We'll count fingers and toes after the mission. Anyone got a visual on eyeball?"

"Nope," said a voice Ralph didn't recognize. "Is it too much to hope the blast got him?"

"He was a regular guy under the helmet," Ralph said. "I think he might have been an inno—"

Titania hushed him and held her finger up to her lips. She said to the others, "There's a chance we're done with that guy. Jack will send a clean-up crew to put out the fire. We'll know more later. Meta and I will check out the next target and meet you at the rendezvous point."

"You got it, boss," said Buscadera, and Ralph felt the line go dead.

"What the hell were you trying to do there?" Titania asked Ralph.

"I saw him cover the bomb with his body. Like a soldier on a grenade."

"You can't be sure that's what he was doing."

"I'm pretty sure, Val. I think—I think he was just a normal guy, and someone stuck a helmet on him."

"Look, I know you feel bad about how it played out. I do too. But we've got some green Anoms on the team—not as green as you are, obviously, but they don't know that—and right now they don't need to worry about what may or may not have been an innocent victim. We're facing the best bid for world domination since Mussolini got the Helmet of Constantine, and we need everyone on point. I don't know if that blast could have killed us, but it might have. It definitely would have come close. We got the bad guy, Ralph."

"But why was he so much easier to fight this time? He beat the whole Cadre in Atlantis. Two of you died."

"He didn't have an army with him, and I wasn't protecting you this time. Plus, we weren't fighting in a dome that could collapse under the weight of the ocean. We weren't even able to keep Advocate and Wyvern's bodies from getting lost in the flood."

"It just feels like it was too easy," Ralph said.

"Easy, sure. If I hadn't shown up when I did, you'd be a Jackson Pollock painting. That doesn't sound like a frolic in the park to me.

Ralph sighed. Below, a flock of birds chirped happily to one another. "Maybe you're right."

Titania floated closer and gave Ralph a punch in the arm. "Jack said you went sub-orbital so you could help us out. That must have been crazy for you."

"It wasn't as scary as thinking something might happen to you."

"Oh, shut up," she said, blushing. "Want to see how fast you can go?"

"What?"

"Try not to get any airplanes in your teeth," she said, and took off like a shot, leaving behind a surprised Ralph.

When Rika shoved him off the Chrysler Building, he'd flown so he wouldn't die. Same thing in the mall. But he'd never considered how to control the speed. *Maybe if I lean into it?* he wondered, but his course only dipped toward the ground.

Maybe if I push myself the direction I want to go. Like falling, only faster.

He stared in the direction Titania had flown and felt the wind in his hair. He pictured the ground moving faster below him, and reality soon matched the image in his mind. The ground and sky stretched into streaks of color. He was in a rainbow corridor, sensation rushing past. The sun moved in its arc above him.

Someone gripped his collar, and he turned to see Titania mouthing the word, "Stop!"

The two of them slowed down. His heart pounded away.

"I didn't expect to see you shoot past me," she said. "Oh, shit, cover your ears."

A thunderclap sounded.

"What was that?" Ralph asked.

"Our sonic boom, you big dork. You really lit a fire under it. Sorry, I forget you don't know what you're doing."

"If I think too much, I can't do it, period. This is all impossible."

"Good thing you're not much of a thinker then, huh? We're going to arrive soon. We'll scope things out, but when the rest of the team shows up, you need to be aware. We have Matadora and the Absolute with us. They're both criminal Anoms, helping us stop the Haberdasher plan. Once word gets out that the Ocularist is dead, there's a chance they might turn on us. Be careful."

"Is Matadora the sexy bullfighter lady?" Ralph asked.

"Yeah, you can't miss her. But she's not that sexy. Absolute is the guy in a white costume covered with math symbols. Plus signs, numbers, stuff like that. It's even stupider looking than it sounds. He has a factorial exclamation point right over his junk. But keep an eye on him, anyway, it wouldn't be the first time a D-lister took out a heavy hitter."

Ralph's communicator tingled as it came back online. From the Cloud Club, Jack said, "Guys, you're coming up on your next target. Satellites suggest it's your classic volcano secret base. No other intel available, so be careful going in."

"I see it," Titania said, eyeing a mountain on the horizon.

"Been awhile since we've done one of these," Jack said. "Have fun, roast me some marshmallows."

"Doesn't look like a volcano to me," Ralph said. "Looks like a mountain."

Titania laughed. "That's just what we call them. There was a time where every dormant and active volcano had an Anom mastermind hiding under it. That went out of style, but every now and then someone uses a mountain. It'll be a while before the rest of our team shows up, so let's scope it out."

"Got any binoculars in your pocket?" Ralph asked, pointing at her waist.

"Hardee har har," Titania said. "Maybe you could tuck your goofball cape into your belt so it doesn't draw their attention. I'd hate for them to laugh themselves to death before I get to punch anybody."

"What is it with you and capes?" Ralph asked. "My cape looks fantastic. You have a cape."

"It's not a cape, it's a chlamys. And it's a manifestation of the fairy flag that gives me my powers. Even if it was a cape, I'm a girl. Ladies wearing capes isn't as played out. See how my chlamys is short? That's cute. A big cape that goes down to your ankles is ridiculous. Wait a second, do you see that?"

"What?"

Titania pointed. "Right there, on that cliff. What's going on?"

Squinting, Ralph tried to see what Titania was talking about. He spotted a flat area midway up the mountain. They were far enough away it looked like ants, but as they got closer, Ralph could make out people. It looked like a group of Haberdashers, but some seemed half the size of the others.

"I think they have kids with them," Titania said.

"What are they doing?" Ralph asked, just as the shorter figures walked over the edge of the cliff.

"Slow down before the catch or you'll explode them!" Titania screamed and shot toward the falling children.

11

ALPH FOLLOWED HER, pushing himself as hard as he could. Air roared past his ears as he watched seven tiny bodies fall ever closer to the ground. Titania was going for the ones furthest down, so Ralph aimed for the three highest up. Once he was close enough, he saw that two, a boy and a girl dressed in rags, were holding hands. He remembered at the last second to slow his speed and plucked the two screaming children from the air.

He spotted the third child, a girl, and his momentum changed in a stomach-lurching instant. The child looked at him with horror as Ralph caught her.

The adrenaline pulsed in his temples as he looked for Titania. She had caught two of the other kids before they hit the ground, and now she was going after a third. Ralph realized she couldn't reach the last boy in time.

Hugging the three children close to his body, he yelled "Hold on!" and threw himself toward the ground like a crashing rocket. He heard the screams of the children he already carried, but he told himself that screaming children were breathing children.

Ralph reached the small boy and matched his speed. At the last moment, Ralph swooped and lightly caught the unconscious boy, as the bottom edge of Ralph's blue cape cut a line in the dirt. He locked eyes with Titania, who nodded and headed up toward the cliff.

Ralph let his feet touch the ground, and he set the children down. The last one he had caught was already stirring. "Wait here," Ralph told them, not knowing if they understood. "I'll be right back."

The cliff raced toward him as he willed himself upward. He rose over the edge and saw Titania yelling at the Haberdashers. Handguns littered the ground, wadded up like discarded paper. The suited men held their hands above their heads in surrender. A crowd of children cowered behind them.

"You animals!" Titania screamed at the men. "What the hell are you doing?"

One of the Haberdashers seemed surprised at the question. "Someone killed the Ocularist. Game over. We were getting rid of the evidence before getting the fuck out of here."

"By killing little kids?" Ralph landed beside Titania. "Why are they even here?"

"We're making delicate items," the Haberdasher said. "Little hands are good for the work. But word came over the wire to shut it down, and we were stuck with more brats than bullets. We figured this way we could just roll some dirt over them."

"I saw something down on the ground." Titania said. "How many have you already killed?"

"That was the first batch, so none," said a Haberdasher. "Unless you dropped some?"

"Shut the fuck up, Cole," said another of the Haberdashers.

"You shut up, Todd. You think pleading the fifth is going to help us now? We'll be lucky if they don't throw us into space, just for fun."

"You're not getting off that easy." Titania lifted Cole the Haberdasher off the ground by the collar of his shirt. Ralph noticed the man had already wet his pants.

He walked up to Titania and put his hand on her shoulder. "Titania, stop. We've got them. Don't let them off the hook that way. Let them rot in jail—it will feel so much better."

"I'm not sure about that." Titania reached up and took the man's chin in her hand. With a flick of her fingers, she broke his jaw with a sickening crunch.

"Titania," Ralph said again, "I left some kids down on the ground. Can you go check on them?" She waited a moment, seeming to debate with herself, and dropped the man in a sobbing, drooling heap.

"Time to call the rest of the team and fill them in." She took off into the air. "I'll start clearing out the base. Don't let anyone get past you."

Once she was out of sight, Todd the Haberdasher said, "Thanks. I thought she was going to slaughter us."

"She still might," Ralph said. "And I'm on the fence, so you might want to keep your mouth shut before you end up like your friend."

Ralph was trying to comfort the Spanish-speaking children when Baron showed up, carrying Buscadera and Matadora. They had plastic riot cuffs for the Haberdashers, and they continued Titania's sweep of the mountain base.

The interior rooms were carved out of the rock, each one with skinny children cuffed to workstations where they assembled different Anom weapons. It didn't take Ralph long to figure out how to use his strength to release the kids from their bonds without injuring them. Matadora, who spoke Spanish, was surprisingly good with the children, convincing them to reveal the hideout's floorplan, including their secret hiding places. One by one, the heroes gathered the children together while Greaser, an Outlier member with a rockabilly outfit and a killer pompadour, played his electric guitar to calm them until they cleared the factory hideout.

Satisfied every child was free, they rejoined Titania, Grail, and the rest of the team, who had their own collection of Haberdashers and rescued child laborers. They took the crowd of prisoners and children outside as the Mexican authorities arrived.

"This is all very Temple of Doom, isn't it?" Ralph asked Titania.

"No time for love, Dr. Jones." Titania smiled before growing somber. "Thank you for stopping me back there. I can't believe what I was about to do, especially in front of those poor kids."

"Don't worry about it. That creep would've deserved it."

"I'm just glad you were there." She took his hands in hers.

Their communicators clicked on. "Titania and team, come in," Jack said.

"Titania here," she said.

"We've got teams rounding up the last of the Haberdashers. Stiff says it's time to send everyone home."

"You heard the man," Titania said to her team. "Follow me to the extraction point. We'll fly ahead with Matadora and Absolute and send them on their way first. Ralph, you up for piggybacking some non-flyers? It isn't far."

"I'll give it a shot."

Baron carried Absolute and Greaser, while Ralph took off with Grail and Matadora. After catching falling children, it was much easier to fly with two adults. They each put an arm around his neck and held on tight. Titania took Buscadera and led the way over the rocky landscape.

"Greaser's pretty good with that guitar," Ralph said. "Does he use it for magic like Songweaver? Maybe an energy attack?"

Matadora laughed. "He just hits people with it."

"How very El Kabong," Ralph said.

"It has a titanium frame," Grail said. "I think his real superpower is keeping it in tune. How's the shoulder?"

"Feels great, thanks. And you too, Matadora. Those kids really took to you."

"You'd think they'd know better," she said. "Guess you never lose the knack. Growing up, I raised four little brothers."

"I didn't know that," Grail said. "That's a lot for a kid to take on. Where are they now?"

"I'd rather not talk about that." Matadora stiffened. "Careful, fly boy. I know this setup is every hero's dream, but concentrate on keeping us in the air, okay?"

Titania led them over a canyon, rich with colorful strata. The group approached a wide mesa, jutting out of the red dirt and reaching high into the sky. Ralph dreaded the landing, but their feet touched the ground like a soft kiss.

"The location of a Cadre drop point." Absolute whistled. "This would fetch some real money on the open market."

"You know we'll be changing it," Titania said. "But thank you for your help. The deal remains the same. Safe passage home, and we won't come after you unless you commit a crime."

"Then I guess I'll see you tomorrow." Matadora winked at Ralph. "Thanks for the lift, sailor."

Titania tapped her communicator disc. "Okay, Jack, they're ready."

Matadora smiled as Grail and Greaser winked out of existence.

"Son of a bitch," Titania said. "The baddies ditched their discs."

"Guys?" Jack sounded confused over the communicator. "Everything okay up there? They just got two unexpected guests in Atlantis."

"Atlantis?" Ralph asked.

"I fucking knew it!" Matadora screamed.

Baron turned to Matadora and held up a pair of the riot cuffs. "You've done a great job helping out. Make this easier and don't try to resist."

"That wasn't the deal!" Matadora said.

"Stop being nice and do it," Titania said.

Matadora took off running. Buscadera took the lasso from her belt and swung it over her head. Before Matadora made it more than a few steps, the rope was around her waist. In an instant, Buscadera was on top of the bullfighter and cuffing her.

Absolute stepped backwards. "I have acquired additional powers that you don't suspect!" Wild-eyed, he pressed his palm against a black X on his chest. Suddenly, instead of one gangly middle-aged man in a white costume, there were at least a dozen.

"You thought I was just a square!" the identical men echoed. "Now you can all suck on my long division!"

As Ralph blinked his eyes at the dizzying sight of so many math-themed body suits, Grail reappeared behind them. She quietly approached one of the men and brought the butt of a pistol down on his head. The other Absolutes blinked out of existence.

"How'd you know which one was the original?" Baron asked as he bent down and restrained the unconscious Absolute.

"Magic," Grail said, returning the pistol to the concealed holster in the back of her jeans. "Or maybe he was the only one with dirt on his costume. It's hard to know sometimes. Let's just get these yahoos back to base."

Ralph looked at their former allies, an unconscious man in a ridiculous costume and a furious woman who missed her brothers. "What the hell is going on?" he asked.

"This is Mr. Stiff's plan to save that boring world you keep talking about." Buscadera coiled up her lasso. "What, didn't he tell you?"

12

HE REST OF THEIR SQUAD OFFERED to deal with the prisoners, so Ralph and Titania left together. The clouds drifted beneath them as they soared side by side. "I was worried Rika might throw you off the building," Titania said. "I should've warned you. She has a history of solving problems that way."

Ralph laughed. "Can't argue with the results." He spun in the air like a corkscrew; his clumsiness only revealing itself when he stopped. She grasped his hand, steadying him. Her hand felt warm in his, despite the altitude.

"I didn't mean to blow that guy up at the warehouse," Ralph said.

"I know. Danny told me about the difference in the guns. The thought of it scared him to death." She pulled Ralph toward her. They slowed to a stop and straightened up, floating high over the earth. He wrapped his arms around her waist.

Don't screw this up, Ralph thought.

She laid her head on his shoulder and said, "It's not that I thought you were a murderer. I just didn't want you getting killed because you didn't know what you were doing. Should've known better."

"No, you were right, I have no idea what I'm doing. If I stopped to think right now, I'd fall like a stone. Maybe if I had someone to show me the finer points of living with powers?"

She pulled back from his embrace.

I screwed it up, Ralph thought.

Valerie reached into a pocket on her belt. Floating back to Ralph, she shoved something into his nose. He recognized the feeling of the breathing apparatus.

She pulled him in tight. "First lesson," she said. "Staying in the air despite distraction."

Together, they shot higher and higher, escaping the Earth for a bed of stars.

TITANIA II

Real Name: Not publicly known
Affiliation: Freedom Cadre
Partnerships: Siegfried (former),
   The Lost Arcader (former)
Anom Category: Magically
   Empowered Human
Base of Operations: Atlantis,
   Denver
Marital Status: Unknown
Age: Early 30s (assumed)
First Public Appearance: 2001
**First Fictional Appearance
   (Titania I):** The Terrific Titania
   #1 (February, 1978)

**First Fictional Appearance
   (Titania II):** Titania #1
   (December, 2001)
Aliases: Flag Bearer
Powers: Flight, Strength,
   Invulnerability, Teleportation
   (rumored), Magic (rumored)
Weaknesses: Lead, Fairy Flag (if
   used to tie her up), Lunar Eclipse
   (rumored)

The first recorded appearance of Titania was in 1977, when an unnamed masked woman in a cape and skirt fought a runaway Leopardon robot at the Dallas-Fort Worth Auto Show. The robot, from a Japanese television show, was an immobile prop magically brought to life by Pygmalion to steal the ticket money. Titania became one of the most prominent heroes of the seventies and eighties, battling villains like Batty Fang, Mummy Magician, and the Emperor of Ice Cream. She rose to the status of cultural icon, with her pin-up poster second only to Farrah Fawcett's in popularity.

The Anom hero allegedly acted as an avatar for the real Queen Titania, although many scientists argue against the existence of the Land of Faerie. Titania's popular cry of "For the glory of the Queen!" lead many to speculate she believed in the mythological source of her powers. It is widely assumed that her powers come from her cape, which resembles the Fairy Flag of Scottish legend.

Titania became a member of the Freedom Cadre during their revitalization period, when they moved their base from Cleveland back to Atlantis. She fought alongside the Cadre during the Falling Sky event, the Red Eye plague, and against the Bringer of Blades. After the Cadre's battle with Overmorrow in 2000, she disappeared from the public eye. It is unknown if she retired or passed away.

Titania II appeared nearly two years later. The original Titania is known to have been pregnant at least twice, and once fought off a horde of headless Blemmyes while holding an infant. Due to the strong resemblance, including the trademark red hair, most Anom scholars believe the new Titania to be the daughter of the original, although some who believe Mr. Stiff undergoes a de-aging process every generation argue Titania did the same. The new Titania wears a streamlined uniform and the degree of her connection, if any, to the Queen Titania of legend is unknown.

After a disastrous first outing, Titania II found her footing through teaming up with heroes like Ambergris, Siegfried, the Lost Arcader, and Molly Pitcher. The Cadre took notice and recruited the young Anom, who brought some much-needed muscle to the team after the loss of Oceanus and the original Titania. Although some hold out hope the original will return, most agree that Titania II is a worthy successor.

Illustration by Morgan Perry

ALPH TRACED A LINE on Valerie's back with his fingernail. The fan spun above them in the darkness of his bedroom back in Austin, Texas.

"I'm sorry for flipping out on you after you saved me in Atlantis," he said.

"Thanks, but it's okay. A lot was happening to you that you couldn't understand. If I can't forgive an outburst every now and then, I'm in the wrong business."

"So, when I met the Cadre in Atlantis, everyone had to pretend not to know me?"

"You're the one with a multiple-choice reality, buddy. There was no way to know if you were already an Anom or not. But that's how I remember it. If you'd been a little less overwhelmed, you'd have seen right through us. Jack has a terrible poker face—everything keeps wiggling around."

"So what was the real reason for wanting me in a media blackout quarantine? I'm not mad, I promise, I'm just trying to wrap my head around it."

Valerie laid her head on his chest. "Do you remember when Superman first met Supergirl in the comics? His cousin Kara hops out of this crashed ship, smiling even though everyone she's ever loved is dead out in space. She asks, 'Can I come live with you?' and Superman says, 'Nope.' Then he sticks her in an orphanage."

"Always thought that was a dick move."

"But think about it. Clark Kent was such a good guy because he happened to be found by two good people. And he had his whole life to get used to his powers with the help of his adoptive parents. Kara is fully grown. He can't raise her, she's already an adult. If they had a conflict, it would be apocalyptic. And she has no reason to care about humans. So, he sticks her in an orphanage, where she can see firsthand what it's like to be weak and vulnerable. He doesn't have to worry about her getting hurt or molested—she's freaking Kryptonian. Clark eased her into humanity as he eased her into the role of Supergirl."

He stroked her red hair. "That actually makes a lot of sense."

"Ralph, suddenly finding out you're an Anom is a major test of character. There's a reason most Anoms go dark. When you came to me for help, you were afraid, paranoid even. If you'd known, you could smash your way out of Atlantis—"

"I would have. So you weren't keeping me in Atlantis to stop the world from changing—"

"Right. It was to keep an eye on you, keep you under control. To ease you into the role of Meta Man."

"And you definitely weren't planning on hooking up with me."

She punched his arm. "How dare you! It never entered my mind."

They held each other and laughed in the dark.

When it was quiet again, he asked, "And you don't have any idea where my powers came from?"

"Nope," Valerie said. "As far as I know, you never told anyone."

"Don't you mean the me who was a member of the Cadre?"

Valerie rolled her eyes as she propped herself up on her arm. "I think it's silly to keep qualifying it. You don't seem any different to me. Yeah, your memories are different than mine, but you're still the same guy. Super powers or no, you were still dumb enough to move in with Sandra."

"You're so *cute* when you're jealous. To tell the truth, I keep expecting the other shoe to drop. I got back the career I lost, I'm with the girl of my dreams. As if that wasn't enough, I've got superpowers. It's like I got three wishes with a monkey's paw, and now I'm waiting for it to blow up in my face."

"Stick with me long enough, sweetie, and you'll rethink that dream girl stuff. I'm not wish fulfillment. You'll drive yourself crazy thinking like that."

"But you have to admit it's intimidating for me to compete with a guy who succeeded in the same career I failed in. Oh, and he fought crime and probably saved the world a few times. I keep looking over my shoulder, wondering when he's going to show up to take his rightful place."

She put her hand on his chest and said, "You know one thing you've done that the other you never did?"

"What?" Ralph asked, smiling.

"Take me to bed."

Ralph rolled over on top of her. "Then I declare myself the winner," he said and kissed her.

A cell phone buzzed on the dresser.

"It's yours," Valerie said.

"Let it ring."

Handing the phone to him, she said, "Could be important."

Ralph glanced at the screen. "You're right, it's my folks. I'll be right back."

"Be sure to tell them what they're interrupting." She swatted at him with a pillow.

Sliding into his jeans, Ralph thought about how he had avoided talking to his parents since the reboot. He was worried they wouldn't be the people he remembered. His folks were sharp too. They would know right away he was pretending to remember things. Once he had discovered his powers, he was unsure he could keep that secret from them.

"Hello?"

"Hey, son," James Rogers said.

"Dad, hi. What's going on? Everything okay?"

"We just hadn't heard from you in a while. Your mom saw on the internet you missed a convention appearance. You know how she worries."

"Tell mom everything's fine. I had some personal stuff come up, but nothing for you two to worry about."

"Personal?" James asked. "This wouldn't have to do with the, you know, the *long underwear* thing?"

He knows.

"You could say that," Ralph said, sitting down at the drafting table in his art studio.

Neither of them spoke for several beats. James broke the silence: "Well, you be careful."

"Dad," Ralph said, "Do you ever think, 'What if the world was different?'"

"What do you mean, son?"

"What if there weren't any Anoms or anything like that. If everything was more, I don't know, more normal. And what if things hadn't worked out with me and the comic book."

"Ralph, those parts of your life—the long underwear, the success—you didn't have control over that. Not saying you didn't work for that comic, but a lot of people work hard and don't find the success you have. The powers thing, lots of folks want that but never get it. It's like winning the lottery. Winning is just luck, it's how you use the money that says something about you. And you've done well with your opportunities. I know if those things hadn't happened for you, you'd still be a good person, and we'd be proud of you regardless. I mean, you're not disappointed in me, just because I never became a famous magician."

"Of course not. You're totally right."

"What's this about, Ralph?"

"I was just thinking. Wondering if you'd be disappointed if the world wasn't like it was. If it was less exciting, less amazing. If fewer things were real."

"I'm not sure I understand. But it wouldn't matter if the world was boring. It doesn't matter what's real. The most important thing is doing what's right. Don't be a bystander."

"That's the same advice I got from a good friend. You've been a big help, Dad. Just like always. Tell Mom I love her, okay?"

"Will do. Don't make us wait so long for a call next time, all right?"

Ralph hung up the phone. He thought back to that first meeting with the Cadre in Atlantis, when he asked how they would decide whether to change the world back.

"I wish they had just taken a vote," he said to the empty studio.

14

WEEK LATER BACK AT THE CLOUD CLUB, the
Freedom Cadre and a sampling of their allies gathered
on the first floor. Bartlett, the butler Ralph first met at
Damon Ripley's comic book party in another reality, tended bar.
The tuxedoed man handed Ralph a scotch in a crystal tum-
bler—no Captain Marvel glass this time—and gave him a quick
wink of recognition.

Ralph nodded a thanks and examined the room. Along with
the surviving members of the Cadre were Buscadera, Baron, and
the rest of the Outliers. He recognized a few other faces from
his Anom guides: the Ancient Astronaut, Nylon, the Gentleman's emissary, Cryotic, and Zambo. On behalf of the Otherkin
team was Jinnalaluo, a man with the head of a bird. Gideon
spoke for the Judges, and Endless Nine represented the Counted.
The crowd contained international heroes, like Siegfried of Ger-
many, Shamir of Israel, Atman of India, and Krama of Cambo-
dia, with her magic scarf. Sitting at a table and nursing a beer
was Ben Walker's hero Black Snake. He had on a modern, tactical
uniform, and his black hair had a touch of gray, but he looked
like he could still fight with the best of them.

By the bar, Siegfried conversed with the Lost Arcader, a former Outlier. Ralph recognized Siegfried from the tabloids, but Lost Arcader was popular with the internet crowd. His Anom ability—creating solid constructs composed of three-dimensional cubes—resembled the pixel graphics of classic video games. To Siegfried's great amusement, Lost Arcader was using his powers to form a small, sixteen-bit replay of his recent battle against the Queen of Swords and Fata Morgana on a flying, upside-down Spanish galleon. As Ralph and Valerie walked past them, the two men made momentary eye contact with her before returning to their joking around.

Valerie groaned quietly and whispered, "Don't you love when your ex-boyfriends get together?"

"I don't know about boyfriends," Ralph whispered back, "but the thought of you and Sandra in the same room gives me a chill down my spine."

The murmuring voices silenced as Mr. Stiff stood and pulled back his hood to reveal his face. "The plan is progressing exactly as we'd hoped," he said. "I know many of you were against capturing the criminal Anoms that helped with the Haberdasher problem, but it gave us the head start we needed. Of the villains that were helping us out, Jack Spratt was able to teleport the high-risk individuals directly to Atlantis, and the rest were captured with little incident. By pooling our resources, we have since been able to track down and capture the majority of our at-large problems and get them out of the public eye. The rest of them are lying low or have gone into hiding, which should still serve our purposes."

Nylon spoke up. Her voice sounded crisp and intentional, like a stage actress. "What's the legality of us putting all these people in deep freeze?"

"As most of you know," Stiff said, "the Grudge granted our team the ability to put Anoms in emergency detention. We know we're stretching the definition of probable cause, but if the plan works, it will be a moot point soon enough."

Black Snake tipped back the last of his beer and wiped his lips. "Don't get me wrong, I'm glad we finally got proactive on these assholes. But I don't see how this is going to solve the weirdo problem you keep telling us about."

There were murmurs of agreement from the other heroes.

"Ralph," Mr. Stiff said, "please come over here."

Ralph returned his glass back to Bartlett and walked to where Mr. Stiff waited.

"You all know and respect Meta Man as a hero and a friend. But he doesn't remember meeting anyone in this room until only two months ago. His memories are of a world without Anoms or aliens or magic. We have determined it is not a case of mind control, false memories, or the amnesia that seems to plague all of us at one time or another. We also know, without a shadow of a doubt, that this is truly Meta Man. Although he now has no reason to trust me, I have trusted this man with my life and never regretted it."

Several of the heroes in the room looked shocked as the Gentleman's emissary spoke. "Please explain to us why this other world is any concern of ours."

"That's exactly the problem," Mr. Stiff said. "The Cadre doesn't think it's another world. It's this one. Something has changed, and Rogers is the only one of us who can see it. From what he's told us and what we've seen for ourselves, the situation is getting progressively worse. The Cadre's base was overrun. The goddamn Haberdashers nearly took over the world. Advocate and Wyvern are dead. What if this isn't what the world is meant to be? What if the best thing we can do to protect people is disappear?"

"But what about the problems only we can handle?" the Ancient Astronaut asked.

"The working theory is that if we're out of sight, Anoms will not only be out of mind but out of existence. The battles only we can fight simply won't happen."

"What happens to us in this plan?" Baron asked. "Do we just disappear?"

"Meta Man knew at least a couple of us before reality changed. We should all revert to normal people and forget any of this ever happened. That's our hope, anyway."

Black Snake scoffed. "Who wants to be normal?"

"What about those of us who aren't human?" Ironworks asked. "What about me, or the ivory Galatea? What about those who should be dead, like the Gentleman or the Executed Man? Do we all disappear? Will I turn into a pile of scrap? Will the Gentleman be a decades-old corpse?"

Stiff's eyes narrowed. "We'll cross that bridge when we get to it. How many of you have lost someone you love to this insanity? Black Snake, Bone Jack killed your wife. The Gentleman died along with his entire family. I lost my father, my mentor, and my son. Now I've lost Wyvern. If we can stop that from happening to anyone else, we have to try. There's even a chance those people will come back to us if the world reverts back to baseline."

The room was silent. Bartlett wiped the bar with a rag.

Stiff continued. "You have three days to spread the word to every Anom out there, good and bad. We're talking to all of you, the big players, because this is worldwide. Everyone is out of the game, or they have the Cadre to answer to. I know some of you dislike working with government agencies, but the Grudge is on board with the plan. They'll help us police each other until the change takes effect. You live your lives as civilians, and under no circumstances do you do anything anomalous, even if a life is at stake. If you go out of bounds, the entire world is at risk. You want to help people, you do it like a normal person. Join the fire department, be a cop, be a paramedic. Join the army, join the Red Cross, join the Girl Scouts."

Luke used his IV pole to pull himself up and said, "Those who don't have secret identities, can't control their powers, or are otherwise unable to blend in with the regular population will join me and Helena in Atlantis. We'll keep an eye on the situation from down there and find a way to reintegrate if the plan starts working."

Mr. Stiff nodded. "If Meta Man is right, it should be a gradual transformation that you won't even realize is happening. One day you'll wake up and live your life as if you never put on the costume. The important thing is that no one breaks the silence. There will be a covert team standing by to stop anyone from interfering in everyday disasters and to stop any leftover Anom villains without the public even noticing."

Valerie said, "I know it will be difficult to ignore what you see as your responsibilities, but this is for the good of the entire world, maybe all of reality. There's a good chance the Ocularist was behind this, and we all know what he was capable of. If we don't stop this now, everything could end in chaos and destruction."

"This will only work if you all take part," Mr. Stiff said. "This is not a debate or a democracy. Anyone that breaks the ceasefire, no matter how noble your reasons, will be locked up with the bad guys. The Cadre and the Grudge will come for them. Is that understood?"

There was grumbling from the other Anoms, but most nodded in agreement.

"So get out there and spread the word. Three days until the stage goes dark."

The heroes left the Cloud Club by the roof or the elevator. The Gentleman's emissary disappeared in a smoky haze. In the end, only Mr. Stiff, Songweaver, Damon, Valerie, and Ralph remained.

"Jack and Rika will maintain our communication network to keep an eye on things," Damon said.

"What about the Ocularist?" Ralph said. "I know the rule about not finding a body. That guy didn't even seem in control of himself. What if the one behind everything is still out there?"

Songweaver put her hand on Ralph's shoulder. "Stiff, Ironworks, and I will keep working in the shadows for emergencies. You'll go back to your life and live as normally as possible."

"Guess I'm stuck with the boring life of a rich movie star," Damon said. "Try not to cry too much for me."

The group laughed as Rika appeared on the upper landing. "Hey, guys, Ironworks just picked up Fox Hunter! She says she knows who was really behind the Ocularist's plan, but she'll only talk to Ralph and Valerie."

15

ALPH AND VALERIE MATERIALIZED IN AT-
LANTIS. This area looked different than the Cadre's
headquarters, more smooth with white plastic, like the
inside of a spaceship in a nineties movie. Helena Ignatius and
Luke the Nuke greeted them.

"We have someone down here who wants to talk to you,"
Luke said, leaning on his IV pole. "We've got the rest of the prisoners in suspension here in the Panopticon, but this sounded important enough to wait before putting her in the blue."

"She's a bit of a bitch, Meta Man." Helena elbowed Ralph in
the ribs. "Did you two really used to date?"

Ralph sighed. "That was a reality ago. Give me a break."

The others had a good laugh at his expense as they took a
pneumatic tube to the prisoner holding area. A school of colorful fish swam outside the transparent material.

"She was one of the last Anoms unaccounted for," Luke said.
"We've scanned her for hidden weapons, and she's clean. I don't
think she really has anything useful to tell you, but we thought it
was worth you making the trip."

"Where'd you even find her?" Valerie asked.

"She triggered the alarm in Ralph's house," Luke said. "On purpose, I think. When Ironworks showed up, she was waiting out front."

They approached a window in the wall, the interior obscured by shifting, opaque mists. Ralph recognized the woman's silhouette.

"The prisoner has control over the cloudy setting for privacy reasons," Helena said, tapping on the glass. "You can override it with this panel here. It will also let her hear when you're ready to talk."

"We'll be right outside, but there shouldn't be any trouble," Luke said.

"Try not to ask her too much about your boyfriend's sex life, Titania," Helena said.

"Hardee har har," Valerie said as Luke and Helena left. They could hear Helena laughing at her joke in the hallway.

"So I'm your boyfriend now, am I?" Ralph asked, wiggling his eyebrows.

"If you're lucky. But what happens after the ceasefire?"

"If the plan works, you'll forget being Titania."

"But we still knew each other before. You said we reconnected at that party. I gave you my card and everything. Can't drop a bigger hint than that."

"How about I wait until after things go back to normal and then call you?" Ralph asked.

Valerie grinned. "Don't expect me to fall into bed with you again."

Sandra pounded on the glass from inside her cell. "You know I can hear you in here."

Valerie slapped the control panel and the cloudiness disappeared. Inside stood Sandra in her ruined Fox Hunter uniform, her arms crossed over her chest. "I know we broke up, Ralph. But you're still listed as my emergency contact. Haven't got around to changing that yet."

"What do you want, Sandra?" he asked.

"I just wanted to see you with your rebound girl," Sandra said.

"We're done here." Valerie reached for the control panel. "You're ready for the blue."

"Wait!" Sandra said. "I have information you need. I know who put the Ocularist helmet on that poor sucker, the whole thing. But I want a deal."

"You helped kill my friends," Valerie said. "We aren't making any deals. Tell us what you know."

"I'll tell you everything," Sandra said. "Come here, Ralph."

He walked up to the glass. "Before you say anything, I don't know what your Ralph did, but before the reboot I wasn't fair to you. I was miserable, and you tried to help me. For whatever it's worth, I'm sorry."

She stared through him.

"Please tell us about the guy in the helmet," he said. "Was that really the Ocularist?"

"I didn't mean for any of this to happen, Ralph. I was mad after I left you. The Ocularist found me, and he said I'd have a chance to pay you back. For hurting me. The Ocularist has always been a classy bad guy. He played by our rules. I had no idea anyone was going to die. They did something to my head. But he promised that, if I could just talk to you, face to face, you wouldn't have to suffer like the rest of them."

She pressed up against the glass, her eyes glowing red.

Valerie shoved Ralph out of the way.

"Val—" Ralph said, but it was too late.

Time slowed. Valerie turned to face him, a look of resignation in her eyes.

He reached for her arm as the twin beams hit her.

I can save her, he thought. *Like when I caught that little boy. I can save her*.

Her body became an empty collection of sparks which dispersed as his hand passed through them. They swirled in the air like fireflies and disappeared.

Nothing was left behind but the smell of scorched hair.

Sandra had already collapsed. Her eyes were burned away, the sockets empty, smoking pits. ⋈

THE SILVER AGE

1

ALPH SAT IN HIS DARK STUDIO, bent over his drafting desk. A bright desk lamp shined on the page in front of him, the lamp's large magnifier distorting the image.

She didn't die. She was teleported. Or she was shrunk down, or sent back in time. It wasn't her, it was a double. It wasn't her, it was a robot. It couldn't be her, she can't be dead, she just can't. Hologram. Shapeshifter. She's not dead, she's just not.

It was her, Mr. Stiff had said. *And she's really dead. Just like the Advocate. Just like ... They're gone.*

You have to help me bring her back.

He picked up a craft blade and sharpened his soft pencil to a point.

Can't do that, Ralph. I told you the plan. No exceptions.

I know the rules, Stiff. There's no body. Anoms come back from the dead all the time, right? We can save her somehow.

No we can't, kid. Just trying could destroy everything. Live your life. Maybe she'll come back when the world turns back to normal.

The tip of the pencil snapped under the pressure, tearing a ragged streak in the Bristol board.

You can't know that. You have mystics and magicians and time travelers. Help me save her.

We can't do that, Ralph. Go home.

He put his face in his hands and sobbed.

2

ALPH TRIED TO LIVE this version of his life. Freshly purchased cell phone in hand, he called his editor.

"Glad to hear you're back on the job," Caulder said. "Everything work out all right?"

"What's done is done," Ralph said.

"You've got two weeks before your head start runs out. If you don't get me something by then, Meta Man will have its first late ship since your high school graduation."

Franklin Reese was also glad to hear from him.

"Ralph, buddy, you can't leave your agent in the dark like that. My favorite client goes off the grid for weeks, what am I supposed to do? You had a sold-out show. Never seen anything like it. Lots of commissions on the hook too."

Ralph spent his days working on the comic book and driving around in the Stout Scarab. The bizarre vehicle drew plenty of stares as he went nowhere in particular, listening to the radio and thinking about nothing.

The music ended, and a call-in show started. "It's been three days now without recorded Anom activity," a woman said. Her voice sounded friendly and welcoming, like cookies and cream.

"Everyone is wondering what's going on. Jason, what do you think?"

Jason's voice was snarky and judgmental, the kind one would hear in a horrible job interview. "We've seen this kind of thing before, Janet. A big flare up, like with this Haberdasher situation, and then a lull. The big players are home celebrating or licking their wounds."

"If that were the case," Janet said, "I agree, it wouldn't be unusual. But we're seeing a complete absence of costumed heroes and villains, even on the street level. When was the last time Knuckle Duster took a week off? Or Black Snake?"

"I'll entertain the idea something weird is going on. But what would be the reason? Why would the entire Anom community, hero and villain alike, take a break?"

Janet said, "Let's take a look at the last newsworthy events. There was that bank robbery with the Mechanic."

"Is that the card guy?" Jason asked.

"That's the one. Lots of card gimmicks. He hits the bank in a daylight robbery, and it looks like he's going to get away with it. Hostages, demands, the whole bit. Then the building goes dark. When the lights come back on, the Mechanic is just gone."

"Not a bad exit," Jason said.

"Not bad, except he left the money behind," Janet laughed.

Stiff's shadow team, Ralph thought. He parked the van on the side of a quiet road on the edge of town and unbuckled his seatbelt. Climbing between the front seats, he edged around the table and laid down on the bench seat.

"Then the last one, which was a bigger deal," Jason said. "The Outliers, along with alumni member the Lost Arcader, were fighting Tunguska in St. Louis. The fight hit an easy seven on the Drastic Scale, maybe even an eight. Then the heroes and the villain all just disappeared."

"With no explanation," Janet said.

"With no explanation," Jason agreed.

"We're going to the phones to see what you think is behind the absence of Anom activity. First caller is Edward from New Mexico."

"Hi, Jason, Janet. Long-time listener, first-time caller. Politicians have said for a long time they want to get a handle on the Anoms, and I think that may be what happened."

"You think this is some kind of government censor?" Jason asked.

"I think they're rounding up the Anoms and putting them all somewhere."

"I'm going to politely disagree with you, Edward," Jason said. "I still don't think this is anything to worry about, just an unusually calm period. But even if something weird was going on, I don't see how the United States government could be behind it. I'm not sure we have the facilities to hold something like the Bringer of Blades even if we wanted. What is that thing, anyway?"

"Cosmic entity," Edward said.

"Don't be too quick to dismiss this," Janet said. "Don't forget the tech we saw when the Grudge tried to take down Ironworks back in the nineties. No one had even *heard* of those weapons. I'm thinking that the government has access to things we still don't know about. My problem with your theory, Ed, is that this isn't isolated to the United States. Tokyo, Moscow, Brazil, all the other hotspots for Anom activity are quiet."

"All I'm saying is that the Grudge knows what's going on, whatever it is," Edward said.

"I'd tend to agree with you, Edward from New Mexico," Janet said. "Next caller is Jennifer from Kansas City. How you doin' today, Jennifer?"

"Doing fine, Janet." Jennifer sounded like a spirited older woman. "My theory is the Anom community is policing itself somehow."

"What do you mean by that, Jen?" Jason asked. "Policing itself? In what way?"

"The way I see it, there must be something going on behind the scenes. If there's no activity going on, good guys or bad guys, somebody big must be keeping things quiet on purpose. I'm guessing the Cadre or one of the other major groups. We're definitely looking at some kind of ceasefire."

"That's an interesting theory," Janet said. "But why? What would be the motive?"

"That, I'm not sure about," Jennifer said. "There are hundreds of known Anoms that should be out there, but they're all silent."

Some more silent than others, Ralph thought. *Some as silent as the grave.*

Ralph listened to a few more callers. None of them got closer than Jennifer from Kansas City to figuring out where all their heroes had gone. When music started playing again, Ralph got back behind the wheel and started up the engine.

Back home, he sat down at his desk and went back to work on the comic book. He stared at the page, which he had started breaking down that morning. The penciled panels, which he had been proud of an hour before, now looked amateurish and out of place. He spent the afternoon trying to fix it, but ended up throwing the page away and pouring himself two fingers of scotch instead.

His cell phone buzzed, and he retrieved it from the drafting table. The display read, *Number Blocked.*

Answering it, he said, "Hi there, Mr. Stiff."

"Ralph, you know you can call me Javier. We're all friends here."

"I know, sorry. What can I do for you, Javier?"

"Just calling in for the daily update."

Ralph sighed. "No change, far as I can tell. The world seems to be the same as yesterday. Everyone remembers the Anoms and wonders what happened to them. Everybody okay on your end?"

"We're still dealing with some of the more hot-tempered heroes. The street-level vigilantes are all driven individuals, as I'm sure you can imagine. None of them are happy about being benched. You may have heard about the Outliers."

"I don't blame them," Ralph said. "I know you're doing this because you believe me, and you want to do what's best for everyone. I appreciate that, I really do, but I wish you didn't need to call every day. I'm still mad you won't let me try to save Valerie."

"I've told you a thousand times, Ralph. You saw her die, turn to dust. I've seen the video. That's not the same as when one of the good guys gets caught in an explosion, or when a bad guy falls off a cliff but no body is recovered. It's hard, I know, but you need to accept it."

"You don't understand."

"Trust me, kid. I understand."

Ralph cursed himself for forgetting. "I never did say how sorry I am about Wyvern."

"You don't remember because your memory has been swiss-cheesed, but her real name was Courtney. Losing her in that fight with the Ocularist nearly killed me. But I'm still here. We all hated losing Valerie, but you're still alive, and we're going to save the world. You know she'd be on board. It *will* get easier, Ralph. Just give it time, and give the plan a chance to work."

Ralph decided to change the subject. "So, I guess you'll be calling tomorrow?"

"Every day until the world is boring," Javier said. "Or until Mr. Stiff stops existing. Or until he never existed."

Several weeks later, after Ralph had sent in the completed pages to his editor, he stopped hearing anyone mention Anoms. Up until that point, all anyone talked about was "What happened to them all?" Then, there was nothing. Ralph didn't notice the change right away.

His phone buzzed for his daily call from Mr. Stiff.

"Hello, Javier."

"Hello?" It was Mr. Stiff, but he sounded confused.

"Everything okay?" Ralph asked.

"I'm not sure," said the voice. "I have this extra cell phone at my house, and it only has this number in the contacts. I know I'm supposed to call it once a day, but to be honest I'm not completely sure why."

"Then you may not need to call it anymore," Ralph said.

"Maybe you're right," said the voice, still dazed. The call ended.

Ralph went to his bookshelf and retrieved the old *Cyclopedia of Costumed Characters*. He placed it on the coffee table and stared at it. There was a bizarre doubling effect. Depending on how he looked at the book—the tilt of his head, the squint of his eyes—it looked like something else.

"*The World Encyclopedia of Comics*," Ralph said, watching the cover image switch back and forth.

Stiff's plan is working, he thought. *We're reverting to a more mundane reality.*

He rushed to the shelf and grabbed the burned DVD with his episode of *Panel 2 Panel*. It was still there, the clumsy label unchanged. He pulled out the cardboard longbox with the full run of *Meta Man* that he had found in the studio. Every issue was still there, although it remained to be seen if the contents had changed.

It looks like we're holding at the version of events where Pithos kept publishing and picked me up after the tracing scandal. Not totally back to normal, but a lot closer than where we were.

But what about me?

He tried to find the tile on the floor that activated the door to the basement hiding his costume, but he touched every panel he thought it could be and nothing happened. Out in the garage, he tried to lift the front end of the Scarab. It moved a fraction of an inch but stayed on the ground.

Whatever powers you had are gone now, he told himself. *Hope this is what you wanted, because you're stuck with it now. Even Mr. Stiff forgot you, and I didn't think he was capable of forgetting anything.*

Ralph's phone buzzed in his pocket. Relieved, he saw that it was "Number Blocked."

"Javier, you had me worried," he said into the cell phone.

"This isn't Javier," said the voice of Danny Drastic.

3

T's Damon Ripley. Did I catch you at a bad time?"

"No, no. What's going on?"

"I'm calling with bad news. Valerie is dead."

Of course she is, you idiot.

"Oh, God. What happened?" Ralph asked.

"No one's really sure. I mean, after she went missing we were all hoping ... But they finally found her car. Looks like an accident, probably died instantly. The whole thing is so weird."

Ralph stopped listening. *A body. There's a body. They found a body. If they found a body she's really dead.*

"You still there, Ralph?"

"Sorry. It's a shock. We'd just reconnected after such a long time."

"It's hitting me hard too. She had a lot of nice things to say about you after that night at the party. Her parents are having the funeral back where you guys grew up in Flatland. I just wanted you to hear it from a friend."

"Thanks, Damon. I know you're a busy guy. It means a lot you'd take the time to call."

"No problem. First Ben and now Valerie. If I didn't know better, I'd say that party was cursed. You keep safe, Ralph."

"You too, man. Good luck on that Danny Drastic movie."

"Don't hold your breath on that one. It got stuck in development hell. At this point, it looks like I'll never get to be Danny Drastic."

"That's a shame," Ralph said. "You were perfect for the part."

4

H E KNEW IT WAS A TERRIBLE IDEA to take the old
Scarab on such a long trip, but Ralph drove it to Flatland for the funeral anyway. He slowly made his way up
the map on back roads, daydreaming about flying in the clouds
with Valerie.

In the current threeboot timeline, his parents still lived in a
condo in Florida, so he didn't have to negotiate that confusing
relationship while he was in town. He arrived in Flatland with
just enough time to get to the funeral, so he changed into his suit
at a gas station and went to the funeral parlor where the service
was held. He sat in the back row of the sparsely attended service.
Valerie lived in Colorado, and a wake had already been thrown
for her there. This service was mostly for family and old friends
before they buried Valerie in the family plot next to her mother.
He recognized her father and three brothers in the front row.

Ralph didn't comprehend a word during the funeral; he just
stared at the closed box that supposedly held Valerie. *If she's really
in there, then she's gone. She's not coming back. But only if she's
in there.*

The room emptied so mourners could prepare for the grave-side service. Ralph waited for his chance when everyone was occupied with the family. He found the casket in a hallway, waiting to be loaded. The lid was locked tight. As he looked around for some way to open it, a voice said, "You don't want to do that."

Turning, Ralph found himself face to face with one of the funeral directors, a gaunt, older man. "You don't want to do that," the man repeated. "Trust me. She was missing for some time before they found her."

"I have to know that she's really in there," Ralph said. "I have to know it's her."

"I'm sorry. I understand, I do. But I can't help you," the funeral director said.

Ralph looked up and down the hallway to make sure they were alone. He pulled out a hundred-dollar bill and handed it to the man. "Please. Just a peek."

The old man frowned, but he produced an Allen wrench from his pocket and slid it into an inconspicuous opening on the casket, opening the lid wide enough for Ralph to look inside.

The mortician had done his best, but as the funeral director said, Valerie had been missing for a while. An antiseptic smell covered something darker and rotten. Ralph failed to stifle a gasp as he saw the distorted face of the woman he loved.

But it's her, he thought. *That's definitely her.*

"Thank you." He left without looking back.

CLICK.

"Ralph, it's Chuck. Remember me, your editor? We have to talk about these pages you sent me. You can't kill off Titania without talking to me about it, kid, she's not your character. She's got her own book, she's appearing in the Cadre monthly book. We pay several charities good money for the rights to use her likeness, and we're going to keep using it. I don't get it, man, you've never been a hassle before, but first your little sabbatical and now this. We can make this work, but you've got to call me, all right?"

Click.

"Hey, buddy, it's Frank. I've been getting calls from a couple of folks that paid half in advance for those commissions. It sounds like you still haven't called any of them back about the work. Dealing with your disgruntled customers isn't part of my job description, so please just call them okay?"

Click.

"Mr. Rogers, this is Mike at the body shop. Whatever happened in Denver did a real number on your Kamakiri. Hope you paid your premium, because this car is totaled. Give us a call and tell us what you want to do with it."

Click.

"Ralph? It's Damon. Got your drunk texts. Sounds like you're going through a rough patch, but please don't buzz me so late. I've got some early call times on this film, and I need my beauty sleep. If you want to talk, call me anytime the sun's up."

Click.

"Mr. Ralph Rogers, this is Detective Simon with the Austin Police Department. I'm calling in regards to a missing person, one Sandra Madison. Please call me back immediately."

Click.

"This is Songweaver. If you want to bring Valerie back, answer your damn phone."

6

"So why are you still a superhero?" Ralph asked.

It was the middle of the night, and Songweaver sat on the couch in Ralph's living room, still dressed in her leather jacket and jeans. Her acoustic guitar leaned against her legs. Behind her was the blank wall where the fox hunter painting had hung.

"The reversion is a lie," she said. "At least for now. We're faking it till we make it. The major players are all on board, and everyone else is playing along. If there's one thing Mr. Stiff can do, it's organize. The government, especially that damned Grudge agency, has always wanted to get Anoms under control, so they've solidified the lockdown. The Outliers were the only ones with enough guts to go rogue, but Stiff and the Grudge tracked them down. Now they're on ice with the villains in Atlantis."

"But what about my *World Encyclopedia of Comics*? It changed back."

She reached for her guitar and gripped the neck like it was a security blanket. "I'm sorry. That was all me. I'm no Doctor Fell mind-controller, but I can read minds a bit. I can do glamours. That book is still the *Cyclopedia of Costumed Characters*. What you saw was simply a dream object made real. Nothing has changed. The world is still full of Anoms."

Ralph's hands shook. "The hidden room with my costume is gone! My powers stopped working. I went out in the backyard a couple of days ago, and I couldn't fly."

"Mr. Stiff hacked into the door controls. Rika refused to help, but Stiff is no slouch. As for your powers—if they're gone, it's probably all in your head, just like before."

"Why? Why did you and Stiff do all this?"

"You're powerful, Ralph. Or at least Meta Man can be. We couldn't count on you to toe the line, especially after what happened to Val. You were too much of a wild card. Maybe we could have put you in blue stasis down in Atlantis. But the reversion, if it works at all, might need you to believe it. There's no way to know. So Stiff wanted you as free as possible."

Songweaver picked up the guitar and began tuning the strings. "I didn't speak up before. I'm a team player. I don't mind singing backup vocals if that's what's best for the band. But I don't want to give up who I am. I spent years training to be a hero. Do you have any idea who I'd be if I wasn't Songweaver, 'The Mistress of Musical Magic?' Pretty sure I'd be a cat lady in California. But here and now, I'm the Dreamer of the Pomo people. I'm not giving that up." She locked eyes with Ralph. "And you won't give up on saving Valerie."

"I told you, I've lost my powers. I don't think being able to lift a car can raise the dead, anyway."

"No. But I know how you can get to the afterlife and get Valerie back."

Ralph laughed. "The afterlife? I thought you knew some kind of spell to reanimate her."

"I have a song that could make a body alive, but it wouldn't be Valerie. Not without her soul. Besides, you know there was no body."

Ralph slid his hands down his face. "Before all this, I wasn't sure people even had souls."

"Says the man who spoke to his friend's ghost," she said. "But I know that people have souls, and that soul lives on. So you're going to Pennsylvania."

"Wait. Why Pennsylvania?"

"In a forest in Hellam Township, there's an old gate. Local legends say that it used to lead to an insane asylum that burned down. During the day, it's just a gate, but at night it's the first of seven gates that lead to Hell. I'll take us to the first gate, and the two of us will bring Valerie back."

Ralph jumped to his feet. "There's no way Val is in Hell!"

Songweaver laid the guitar on the couch. "Of course not. The same gates lead to both. Heaven's not known for having back doors. Hell doesn't mind trespassers, that's the whole point!"

"This is all impossible. If you can do this, why didn't you do it for the Advocate and Wyvern? Why don't you do it for everyone?"

"We usually take a hands-off approach with this. Sometimes folks come back, sometimes they don't. But my sources tell me that Valerie didn't die—she was physically taken to the afterlife."

"But I went to her funeral. I saw her body."

"You also saw her turned to dust. Whoever you saw at that funeral, it wasn't Val. Just another of Stiff's manipulations. The dust left behind when she was zapped, that was all done by the Ocularist."

Ralph rubbed his forehead with his hands. "I want to believe you, so I will. But what about Mr. Stiff?"

There was a loud snap as a man materialized beside them. He wore his skeleton suit, and the skull mask covered his face.

"That's a good question," he said. "What about Mr. Stiff?"

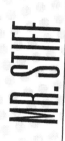

MR. STIFF

Real Name: Not Publicly Known
Affiliation: Freedom Cadre
Anom Category: Augmented
Human (Rumor)
Base of Operations: Atlantis
Marital Status: Unknown
Age: Unknown (currently assumed to
be in his 40s or 50s)
**First Recorded Public
Appearance:** 1919
**First Fictional Appearance
(Original):** Mr. Stiff newspaper
strip (Sunday, August 17, 1919)

**First Fictional Appearance
(Current Incarnation):**
Falling Sky: Rebuilding Special
(August, 1988)
Aliases: La Muerte Que Recorre
("The Death Who Walks")
Abilities: Superior Intellect,
Reflexes, and Athletic Ability;
Master of Hand-to-Hand and Armed
Combat; Physical Augmentation
(rumor)
Equipment: Handguns, Bolas,
Smoke Bombs, Grappling Gun,
Crossbow, Navaja folding blade

The legacy of Mr. Stiff stretches back generations. The first man to assume the name grew famous in Spain during the 1920s, wearing a simple skull mask as he battled criminals and corrupt noblemen. At some point in the forties, the mantle passed to a new Mr. Stiff, who battled Nazis, crooks, and Anom villains. The second Mr. Stiff traveled outside Spain, eventually settling in the United States. He fought against Anoms on the Axis side, like Loose Lips and the tragic German hero, Eupraxis.

The Bones of Judgment fell from the public eye in the fifties, until another man calling himself Mr. Stiff emerged a decade later. He joined the Freedom Cadre in the era of Jack Spratt, Nylon, and Danny Drastic, fighting alongside them against the inaccurately named Venusian Invasion.

In the eighties, Mr. Stiff died in the well-known Falling Sky disaster. Two men competed for the right to wear the skull mask until one revealed the other was Overmorrow in disguise. The current Mr. Stiff took over leadership of the Cadre after the death of Oceanus, leading them to victory against the Bringer of Blades and Overmorrow.

The majority of Anom scholars believe the Mr. Stiff title to be an inherited one. A minority rejects this idea, claiming instead that the Spanish hero somehow regains his youth once a generation. Regardless, Mr. Stiff is an inspiration to many, as he appears to be an ordinary human leading the world's greatest heroes against our gravest threats.

Illustration by Adam Prosser

7

SONGWEAVER DOVE FOR HER GUITAR.

"Not so fast." In a smooth motion, Mr. Stiff grabbed her by the jacket and, using her momentum against her, threw her into the wall. As Ralph backed away, Stiff grabbed the guitar from the couch and smashed it against the ground. He held the instrument's snapped neck as its shattered body swung below on two unbroken strings. Songweaver, on the floor with a bloody lip, screamed in anger as the skeleton man dropped the useless pieces to the ground.

Ralph stepped between them. "Don't do this, Stiff."

"You think I don't have a bug in your cell phone?" Mr. Stiff said. "Songweaver blocked all the bugs she knew about, but I have this house wired for sound. Rogers, you're currently the most dangerous man on the planet. You're the source of the crazy."

"When you called, you'd reverted back to being a regular guy."

"That was just an act to help you on the road to recovery. Progress had stalled out, and I thought it might help us get things all the way back to normal."

Songweaver shoved him. "Who are you to decide what's normal?"

"We're the good guys, 'Weaver," Mr. Stiff said. "Our job is to keep people safe. And this time, that means we give up being special. This could bring back Courtney. Are you really so selfish?"

"Damn right," she said and pulled a wooden flute from inside her jacket. Before Stiff reached her, she put her bloody lips to the mouthpiece. Her slender fingers danced. Beautiful notes reached Ralph's ears and continued to resonate. Mr. Stiff grabbed the flute from Songweaver, crushing it in his hands, but the sound continued to get louder and louder until Ralph put his hands over his ears. The last thing Ralph saw before his house disappeared was Mr. Stiff throwing back his head and screaming in rage.

The music dwindled as leafless trees replaced Ralph's living room walls. It was still the middle of the night, but the three-quarter moon was bright enough to light the scene.

Ralph stood at the end of an overgrown dirt road. Disoriented, he jumped as his cell phone buzzed in his pocket. He pulled out the phone to read a text message from a blocked number. "Don't move. I'll be there soon to collect you." It was signed with a skull emoticon.

Ralph threw the phone into the trees. "Damn it, Songweaver. I don't know what the hell I'm supposed to do here. You didn't exactly give me a map."

Past the end of the forgotten road was an abrupt gap in the wall of trees. Walking toward it, he realized the nightscape was quiet, lacking the sound of cicadas, birds, or wind. He shivered and wished he had a jacket.

Two posts framed the gap in the trees. The wood was splintered. A lone bolt, red-brown with rust, stuck out of one of the posts.

Could be the remains of a gate, Ralph thought. *Maybe. But what do I do?*

He looked around again, hoping Songweaver had escaped Mr. Stiff and followed him.

She's not coming. She risked it all to get me here, and now I'm on my own. And if I don't get going, Stiff will find a way to catch up. He can't use the teleport to jump straight here unless the site was prepped, but there's no way to know how close he can get. Better get a move on, Ralphie.

He took a deep breath, closed his eyes, and walked between the posts.

Opening his eyes, he didn't see flames or demons. He kept walking. The trees grew younger and sparser until they opened into a clearing.

The foundation was all that remained of a building, which he assumed was the burned-down institution from Songweaver's urban legend. The crumbling concrete hinted at the building's layout. Intent on finding another gate, Ralph nearly fell down the uncovered basement stairs. Bad graffiti and beer cans spoke of the teenagers who had tripped their way to the fabled Seven Gates of Hell and partied to cover their disappointment at the Devil not showing up. Ralph peered into the darkness of the basement.

Not unless I have to, he thought and kept walking.

After stepping off the far end of the foundation, Ralph walked until he came to a fenced-in area, the remains of a garden. It looked to only have one entrance, but the metal gate was the only one in sight. He opened it, listening as the old hinges squealed.

Tripping over a rock, he painfully scraped his shin as he went down into the tall grass. His head narrowly missed a piece of marble. Lifting himself out of the dirt, he saw writing on the stone, barely legible: *Elizabeth O'Neil. 1871-1891. May the next life be kinder to her.*

Ralph scrambled to his feet. The garden was a graveyard. Many of the plots were unmarked, but some had headstones, the most recent being over eighty years old. The earliest still legible commemorated a life cut short in 1878.

One grave had been kept clear of weeds. Except for a cross enclosed in a circle, the stone was worn smooth by a century of weather. A bundle of fresh wildflowers lay propped against the marker. A red glass jar contained a flickering candle.

"Because that's not creepy at all," Ralph said to any unseen ghosts.

Past the graves stood a gate he knew had not been there before he entered the graveyard. Unlike the rusted iron of the cemetery entrance, the twisted black iron of the waist-high gate looked new. The latch lifted, but the heavy gate wouldn't budge. On the third push, the gate swung freely, as if saying, *Fine, buddy, it's your funeral.*

Leaving the graveyard, the forest closed back in and the sliver of a moon barely gave enough light for him to find his way. *Would have sworn the moon was fuller before,* Ralph thought as he carefully followed the hint of a path through the trees. At the end of the path was a fence and a gate like the last, but the iron-work was more intricate, and the spiked fence was at least eight feet tall. Ralph opened it without hesitation or hindrance.

"Four down." Ralph stepped through. The path disappeared, and brush gripped and stabbed at his jeans. Several times he came to deadfalls, which he clumsily climbed over, the decaying wood shifting under him. A wolf howled, the first living sound he had heard since his arrival. Ralph doubled his speed.

On the other side of the last deadfall was an unexpected wooden door, like might be found in any ordinary house, standing in the air without visible support. The brass doorknob turned freely and Ralph stepped through the frame.

The background changed in an instant, and he found himself standing in a black space. It wasn't dark, as he could see the door and his own body without difficulty. But the ground he stood on and the area around him was empty. In the distance he saw a structure, so he walked toward it.

As he approached, he realized the next gate was made completely of bone. The skulls along its high arch suggested they were human, intricately arranged to create an archway. Spines, fingers, hipbones; everywhere he looked were the dried remains of human beings. The handle was the polished joint of a thigh bone, and turning it caused the bones to vibrate as the door opened. The jaws of the skull above him jittered, clattering like a row of broken castanets.

He walked into further darkness, but this time the door appeared right in front of him. Like the last gate, this one was made of people, but instead of bone it consisted of dead bodies, lashed together into a bound horror. The nude corpses stank of rot, and his dinner threatened to escape. Every instinct urged him to turn and run—to forget about playing hero. To forget about Valerie.

Ralph forced his body toward the obscenity. No latch or knob was visible, so he reached out and pushed. His hands sank into the rotten flesh, but the gate opened easily. Holding his breath, he entered.

SONGWEAVER

Real Name: Nancy Hansen
Affiliation: Freedom Cadre,
Sisterhood of Secrets (Rumored)
Anom Categories: Magically
Empowered Human, Magically
Inclined Human
Base of Operations: Atlantis,
San Francisco
Marital Status: Single
Date of Birth: January 12, 1971
First Public Appearance: 1988
**First Fictional Appearance
(Leslie Andrews):** Tales of
the Sensational (December, 1939)

**First Fictional Appearance
(Nancy Hansen):** The
Freedom Cadre Volume 2 #300
(July, 1988)
Aliases: Dreamer, Smoke Moon
Powers: Magic, Flight, Dimensional
Travel
Equipment: Wooden Flute, Bone
Whistle, Bullroarer, Acoustic Guitar
(Martin D-76 Dreadnought)

Songweavers are female protectors, using the primal power of music to defend humanity from threats both natural and occult. Each "Mistress of Mystical Magic" uses instruments or her voice to influence reality. A nameless Russian Songweaver saved the world from the first Tunguska event, and a German bearing the title defended the world from interdimensional invasion in Nuremberg, 1561.

The role of Songweaver goes back to the dawn of civilization. Myths detailing their exploits are found in every culture, but it wasn't until World War II that a Songweaver became a visible and vocal presence on the world stage. It was through Leslie Andrews, USO performer and Songweaver, that most details of the strange role are now known.

Andrews battled the Axis on every front, defeating Anom threats and encouraging sol-diers. It's assumed the title passed from Andrews at the time of her death, although another Songweaver wasn't publicly known until the late eighties. A Native American named Nancy Hansen, basket-weaving prodigy and Dreamer of the Pomo people, took on the mantle and saved San Francisco from the revived Vainglorious.

The Freedom Cadre recruited Hansen, who filled the position of magical expert after Darśana's retirement. She provides invaluable insight and support, although she can hold her own against the strongest Anom threats. Her role was instrumental in rescuing Ironworks from the influence of Hell Binder, preventing the Bringer of Blades from entering our reality, and stopping Overmorrow from destroying the world. She has also become a valuable voice for the Pomo people and other Native American communities.

Illustration by Weshoyot Alvitre

8

THE RIVER SMELLED OF DEAD FISH AND GRAVE DIRT. Ralph avoided the mud as he walked to the shore. A dense fog hung over the ground and water, reminding him of a childhood lake trip in the early spring. He reached out and his fingers ran along a cluster of cattails, plucking their thin stems like the strings of Songweaver's guitar.

An aluminum fishing boat hugged the shore, beat to hell but seaworthy. It had no motor. A fisherman had set up camp, and he sat huddled by the fire. The hood of his sweatshirt hid his face.

Can't wait for the chuckles at my expense, when I see what's under that hoodie, Ralph thought. *Smart money is on a skeleton, folks, but we're also taking bets on zombie, claymation monster, and absolutely nothing. For those feeling a bit more adventurous, you can take one-hundred-to-one odds on Ralph Rogers seeing his own face staring back at him.*

"Hello, stranger," said the fisherman as Ralph stepped into the light of the fire. "Sit down and rest for a while. I'm guessing you've come a ways."

"Thank you."

The fisherman pulled back his hood and Ralph was relieved to see the normal face of an older man. He looked to be sixty years old or so, with gray hair and a beard that was not so much by design but the natural result of not using a razor for a few weeks.

Ralph reached out to the fire and warmed his stiff hands.

The fisherman tapped a faded red cooler with his boot. "I can cook up some fish if you're hungry. Caught more than my lazy ass wants to haul back."

Ralph thought of the land of the fairies and their tricks. "No, thanks. I'm good."

"Are you?" the fisherman asked. "Don't worry, buddy. Eating some of my fish ain't going to trap you here. Folks that show up here are trapped already—at least, that's usually the case. You're an odd one, aren't you?"

"That about sums me up. I'm thinking I need to get across that river."

"Only way out is through," the ferryman said, nodding and rubbing his bony fingers. "I'd be happy to take you across, but times are tough. Afraid I'd need you to pay me for the service."

Ralph breathed out through his clenched teeth. *Damn it, Songweaver. This is the kind of detail you would have handled.*

"How much?" he asked.

The ferryman chuckled. "You got me all wrong. I'm not trying to cheat you." He pointed a thumb at the aluminum fishing boat. "It's not exactly first class. I'd take you over for a buck. Hell, I'd do it for a quarter."

Ralph pulled out his plastic Darius the Diabolist wallet. "All I've got is a fifty."

"That'll do, but I got no change," the ferryman grinned.

"Fine."

The ferryman picked up a metal bucket with a lid full of holes and filled it up in the river. He dumped the water on the fire, which he stirred with a stick. Ralph saw something in the charred remains of the fire that looked like bone.

"Help me with this, will you?" the ferryman asked. After they pushed the boat toward the water, he said, "Better hop in before you get your feet wet. You don't want to be touching that water."

Climbing into the boat, Ralph sat down and gripped the seat as the ferryman grunted and gave the boat a final shove into the river. Ralph helped the old man into the boat. With a push of the oar, they were in deeper water.

"That wasn't really a campfire back there, was it?" Ralph asked.

"Not in so many words, no." The ferryman carefully removed a pair of galoshes and put them under the stern of the modest vessel. He handed Ralph one of the oars.

Ralph slid the oar into the water, careful not to splash, and threaded the handle into the oar lock. "Then why go to the trouble of putting it out?"

"What you're doing, kid, you don't want anyone seeing it. I was doing you a favor."

The ferryman set a slow pace with his rowing, and Ralph followed his lead. Once the shore was out of view, they rowed on in empty twilight. Ralph squinted, trying to see the other side of the river. "Should we be wearing life jackets or something?"

"Ain't got any. Not like we're going to get hit by a sudden storm. That were to happen, we'd be good and fucked. You'd be better off drowning, trust me."

Ralph thought again of Songweaver.

"Something worrying you, pal?" the ferryman asked.

"I was supposed to have a friend with me, but she, uh, she got held up. I'm hoping she's okay."

"If she weren't, we'd know. She's the one ought to be worrying about you."

Ralph missed a beat in his rowing, jerking the boat to one side. He shifted uncomfortably on the metal bench and put the oar back in the water.

"You get many celebrities?" Ralph asked.

The ferryman laughed. "I've seen all kinds. What would really surprise you is who I haven't seen yet. But I'm not one to kiss and tell."

The other side of the river came into view. As their momentum carried them closer, Ralph spotted movement on the shore. "What the hell is that?"

"No idea. Maybe your guide skipped ahead of us."

Ralph leaned forward. The lack of light and the fog on the riverbank prevented him from making out the person he was seeing. "Did she make it to the other side without you seeing her? Could that happen?"

The ferryman was silent. Ralph wondered if he could fight his way onto shore without falling in the dangerous water. Finally, a voice reached them.

"Ralph Rogers, you old son of a bitch!" Ben Walker waved his arms above his head. "About time you got here!"

HE FERRYMAN TOSSED BEN THE ROPE. Ralph noted Ben was solid enough to catch the rope as his friend pulled their boat onto the muddy beach.

"Buddy, am I glad to see you," Ralph said.

"Bet your ass you are," Ben said, grinning. He was wearing the same lightning bolt T-shirt he had on when Ralph conversed with his ghost. "I had this feeling that if I waited here long enough, you'd show up."

"That'd be true of anybody." The ferryman pulled on his galoshes and dragged the boat further onto shore.

"You know what I mean." Ben offered his hand to Ralph and helped him out of the boat. "I hope this guy hasn't given you too much trouble, Ralph."

"No, he's been a real sweetheart." Ralph reached into his pocket. "Gave me the discount rate."

Ralph started to hand the worn fifty to the ferryman, who was smiling broadly.

Ben grabbed Ralph's wrist. "Is that all the money you've got?"

The old man's smile disappeared.

"I wasn't planning on a vacation," Ralph said.

"That's the way it works. I've talked to plenty of his passengers. The cost to get across is whatever you've got on you. The bastard took my number one dime. I've had it since the first sale I ever made at my shop."

"So he overcharges the rubes, big deal." Ralph asked. "What, am I going shopping for souvenirs?"

Ben rubbed his face in frustration. "Ralph, give it some thought. I know you're not here for keeps, you're too solid. How are you going to pay him when you try to go back? Wash dishes? No one over here is loaning you anything, everyone's flat broke."

Ralph looked at the ferryman and raised his eyebrows.

The old man shrugged. "Can't blame a guy for trying. Tell you what. Fifty bucks, that'll cover the return trip too."

Ben coughed into his hand. "And passengers."

The ferryman rolled his eyes and threw his hands in the air. "For fuck's sake, why not? Fifty bucks round-trip, plus passengers. I silenced the beacon, I kept the kid out of the water. Look what it gets me. Kee-rist!"

"Better shake on it," Ben said.

Ralph put out his hand, and the ferryman shook it. His skin was smooth and cold.

"See you when we get back," Ben said.

"Nice doing business with you," the old man said sarcastically. As Ralph and Ben walked away, he added, "But seriously, be safe out there."

Once they were out of earshot, Ralph said, "Thanks for saving my bacon. So which way do we go?"

"Uphill," Ben said. "Trust me, we want to go uphill."

10

RALPH AND BEN WALKED AWAY from the river and found a highway. The four lanes were smooth and dark, with fresh blacktop and vibrant white and yellow paint. Ralph strolled out to the median and stood in the grass, looking down one way, then the other, but saw nothing but an endless road stabbing the horizon.

"I thought you said we needed to go uphill?" Ralph asked.

Ben sighed. "You just had to be from the panhandle of Texas, didn't you? Just had to be from the flattest place in the universe, and now this place is a reflection of that. Don't worry about the uphill thing, it's not meant to trick you. If we just go, we'll get where we're supposed to go. Choose a direction."

"I don't have a coin to flip. I hate eeny, meeny, miny, moe. So all things being equal—"

"Just choose, Ralph."

The two of them started walking left.

"So the boring scenery is my fault?" Ralph asked.

Ben nodded. "Landmarks are tricky business, but this is more or less where I arrived. One minute I was talking to you in the comic shop. You know, a ghost. The next thing I knew, I was here on the road. Only, it wasn't this one. There were trees and hills, like outside of town back in Vermont. It was beautiful, Ralph. Your road looks like something from freshman geometry."

"'Freshman Geometry' would make a great band name," Ralph said.

"Damn right, it would," Ben laughed.

"You didn't walk down your road?" Ralph asked.

Ben shook his head. "Almost did. Took a few steps, but then I made a right turn and walked until I reached the shore."

"How long were you waiting there?" Ralph asked.

"That's the kind of question you want to avoid here," Ben said. "It doesn't mean anything. It feels like I just got here. Or I've been here forever. Doesn't matter."

"Okay, then how about: What have you been doing while you were at the shore?"

"Ralph, I'm getting the idea you don't trust me."

Maybe because I'm not sure you're Ben, Ralph thought. *Or if you are Ben, how you just happened to be waiting for me. I was almost tricked here once already.*

"Just curious," Ralph said.

"I watched the boat come to shore, watched people pay the ferryman. Sometimes I'd follow them down their road a while, sometimes I would catch up and chat a while. Everyone was pretty friendly."

"What'd you talk about? How they died?"

"That'd be rude, wouldn't it? Mostly about good movies, people they were hoping to see, stuff like that."

"Were they all going uphill?"

"I didn't follow anyone that I didn't have a good feeling about," Ben said. "I'd hate to end up somewhere I don't want to go."

They walked on a while. Ralph noticed he was no longer wearing his regular clothes. "How long have I been wearing my Meta Man costume?"

Ben chuckled. "What'd I tell you about questions like that?"

"I know, I know. But I had my wallet in those pants."

"Maybe you compressed your clothes into a tiny ball and put them in a pocket in your cape. Did you check the pocket in your cape?"

Ralph rolled his eyes. "Doesn't matter."

"It's weird that your clothes changed. Why Meta Man, anyway? Is that some kind of psychological symbolism, becoming the guy from your comic books?"

Ralph laughed. "I forgot, you've been out of the loop. It turns out Meta Man is really Ralph Rogers, mild-mannered scribbler for a great metropolitan comic book publisher."

"Holy shit. Why didn't you tell me?"

"Last time we talked, I didn't know. Or I wasn't Meta Man yet. Who knows? Before that, superheroes didn't exist in the real world."

"Oh, right, sure. The reality bleed thing only you can notice."

"Yeah, the reality bleed thing only I can notice. That's actually pretty confusing right at the moment. So—humor me, here—I have to ask you if Anoms are real."

"Sure. They've been around in one form or another forever. Why would you ask that?"

"Since you died ... Never mind, it doesn't matter."

Ralph sighed. *It means the afterlife is just as changed as everything else, Ben. I was hoping this place might have some answers. But if you died before Anoms were real—yet you remember them—it means there's nowhere left unchanged.*

Ben put a hand on Ralph's caped shoulder, and they stopped walking.

"Ralph, it's okay you don't trust me."

"Hey, no, I trust you."

"No, you don't. I know you don't, because you haven't told me why you're here when you're still alive. You think I've been compromised or something. Or you don't believe I'm me at all. Maybe you think I'm someone else trying to trick you, like our friend the ferryman."

It's not helping that you're able to read my mind, Ralph thought.

Ralph started walking. "Let's go, man."

Ben grabbed Ralph's cape and pulled just hard enough that Ralph stopped walking.

"Don't do that," Ralph said without turning around.

"Right, sure, I won't spit in the wind, either. Talk to me, dude."

Ralph spun and pulled his cape out of Ben's hand. "Fine. You're right. I don't know if I can trust you."

Ben crossed his arms. "Even after I saved your ass from the ferryman."

"*Because* you saved my ass from the ferryman." Ralph threw his hands in the air. "I'm out of my depth here. Songweaver was supposed to come with me—"

"You know her?" He paused. "Of course you do, you're Meta Man now. I love Songweaver. I have the album she put out on vinyl, with an extra copy still in the shrink."

"She was supposed to come with me, and she would know what to do. Then good ol' dead Ben Walker just happens to show up when I need help. What am I supposed to think?"

"I said it's okay, Ralph. These are the kind of questions you should be asking. How about we do the old tell-me-something-only-the-real-Ben-would-know test."

Ralph looked at Ben and reluctantly nodded. "Okay. The wallet I was talking about, that disappeared with my pants. Which wallet was it?"

Ben grimaced. "How the hell am I supposed to know that? You think I—wait, no, it wasn't the Darius the Diabolist wallet I gave you, was it?"

"That's the one."

"Damn it. That thing is a collectible, you shouldn't be carrying it around!"

"You gave it to me!"

"After you gave me a fat wad of cash! It was a thank you! If you'd pointed to the cash register, I'd have given you that!"

"Excuse me, but my friend died and the wallet reminded me of him."

"That's touching, really, but you should have known putting it in a nice display would have honored me better," Ben said, but he was smiling.

"I'm still sorry you died, man."

"Oh, I might as well have been dead for years. I started taking care of my dad, and I forgot how to take care of me. That night with you, Val, and Damon, that was the first real conversation I'd had in years."

"It happens to the best of us. Even though we'd just met, you were the one I kept calling when all this craziness started."

"I'll tell you this for free. If I could do it over again, I'd find some happiness for myself. Outside of my business, I mean. Find the right guy, settle down. The worst part about what happened, my dad was getting better. I could have turned things around."

"You were a good son. And you're a good friend."

"Oh, look at you. But you didn't have to come all the way here just to tell me that."

Ralph took a deep breath. "I came because Val was killed."

"Valerie? That's terrible. Who killed her?"

"Sandra, my ex. After everything changed, she turned into Fox Hunter."

"See, that right there is why I make sure the guys I date don't know one another. I'll try not to be too hurt you didn't come here just for me. So, you think you can get Valerie back?"

"That's what I'm hoping. Songweaver sounded pretty confident we could do it, but Mr. Stiff showed up before she could explain why."

"Mr. Stiff? Why wouldn't he want you to bring Valerie back?"

Ralph explained the plan to change the world back to the way Ralph remembered it and how Mr. Stiff tried to stop Songweaver.

"So, will it work?" Ben asked. "Will things change back?"

"No idea."

"Will your powers come back?"

"Again, no idea. If the world hasn't really reverted, then I should still have them."

"Why don't you give it a shot? Humor me."

Ralph stopped walking again, crouching and balling up a fist. Taking a deep breath, he punched the ground as hard as he could.

"Well?" Ben asked. "Expecting the ground to split open?"

Ralph examined his knuckles as he opened and closed his fist. "Didn't hurt."

"Did you expect it to? What's supposed to happen when you punch the yellow brick road? That's not really the ground, dummy. That's probably not even your fist. Doesn't prove anything one way or the other." Ben continued along the highway.

Pushing himself up and down on the balls of his feet, Ralph tried to lift himself off the ground. When nothing happened, he hurried after Ben.

The highway narrowed and gave way to a county road. A town came into sight, and the next moment they were on the outskirts. Ralph caught the smell of an apple pie cooling on a windowsill.

The first building they came to was a gas station with an attached garage. The square, white building was freshly painted. Under the canopy out front were two bright red gas pumps, the kind with a glass globe on top. The words *Sky Chief* were written on the glass in crisp red letters, and the gas cost twenty-seven cents a gallon.

"It's like a Norman Rockwell time machine," Ben said. "Middle America as the baby boomers think they remember it. This is fucking great."

A man walked out of the garage, wiping his hands with a rag. He looked to be in his late fifties, and he wore a dirty coverall and a blue baseball cap. According to the nametag, his name was Doug.

"Afternoon. Excuse me if I don't shake hands." He grinned and held up his greasy mitts.

"No problem at all," Ralph said. He could see the hood of a car poking out of the garage, all chrome and cherry-red paint.

"That's just my old Commodore." Doug beamed at the interest. "She runs great, but there's always something to fix. I don't mind, though."

"How long have you been working on her?" Ralph asked.

Doug laughed and said to Ben, "Get a load of this guy, with his 'How long have you been working on her.'" He nodded to Ralph. "I thought you looked unusual, and not just because of the cape and long underwear."

"You're right. I'm here to find a friend of mine, a woman named Valerie Hall. Would you be able to point us in the right direction?"

"Afraid I wouldn't know what to tell you, but I'll give you a ride into town."

"We'd appreciate it," Ben said. "We'd love to pay for the gas, but we're broke."

"Everybody's broke, don't worry about it. The prices are there to comfort new arrivals. Tell the truth, I don't remember the last time I filled up the old girl. Just give me a minute to wash up and change."

While they waited, Ben asked, "What do you wanna bet, if we went in that garage, there'd be two more pairs of coveralls, labeled 'Ben' and 'Ralph?'"

The interior of the Commodore was luxurious but lived-in. Ben called shotgun so he could look at the dashboard. In the back, Ralph reached for his seatbelt, and grinned when he realized the vehicle had none.

"Nice of you to give two strangers a ride," Ralph said as they rolled into town.

"Think nothing of it. Not exactly risky up here, is it? And you're not strangers. You're Meta Man, ain't ya'? And you, you're Ben Walker, the guy who's been helping people out on the road."

"I was just waiting for my buddy here to show up," Ben said.

"Well, the ones who ended up passing through town, they sure appreciated it."

The town looked like the older towns Ralph had seen all over the United States. The difference was, this one wasn't run down; everything looked freshly painted and the brickwork and signs weren't weathered. The people they passed on the street all waved to Doug; the Commodore seemed to be a welcome sight. Doug dropped them off at the drugstore, waving as he drove away.

The sign's raised red letters called it the Central Drugstore, and the air conditioning that greeted them inside felt wonderful. A pharmacist gave them a wave as he helped a customer. On the right side of the room, there was a glass counter where smiling children drooled over penny candies. A soda fountain and a counter with stools filled the left side of the room. Ben went straight to a stool and sat down beside a freckled, redheaded boy sharing a soda with a pretty blonde girl. Ralph hopped onto a stool between Ben and a man in a brown suit.

"We need to hurry up and find Valerie," Ralph whispered to Ben.

"Nothing says we can't enjoy a little refreshment while we ask around."

Behind the counter, a young Asian woman wore a white apron with a nametag reading *Myra*. "Do you fellas need anything to drink?"

"I would love a root beer float," Ben said. "Toss in a little vanilla, if you don't mind."

"Don't mind at all. And you?"

"I'll have the same, thank you," Ralph said.

As she started scooping ice cream, Ralph asked, "Have you seen a redheaded woman? She might be wearing a cape."

"Mister, you're the only one I've seen brave enough to wear one of those."

"Is this your job?" Ben asked.

The woman giggled. Several eavesdroppers seated at the counter laughed.

"When I was a little girl, we visited my grandmother and she took me to see the soda fountain. It's one of my favorite memories; my dolls used to sit at a soda counter instead of a tea party. So when I got here, I thought I'd give it a try. I don't have to hurry, my feet don't get tired, and I get to meet so many friendly people. So, sure, today this is my job. And let me tell you, it's a nice break after teaching high school for thirty years."

As Myra went back to making drinks, Ralph considered mentioning that she didn't even look thirty years old, but realized how unnecessary it would be. *She's like Doug, working on his beautiful car for kicks,* he thought. *If she tires of this, she'll move on to something else.*

Ralph looked down at his costume, shining in orange and blue. *If you could do anything you want, would it always look spectacular to other people? If you were just an artist, with plenty of funds, working for your own pleasure, would it matter that you blew an opportunity when you were fourteen years old? Aren't there plenty of people who would do anything to have what I had?*

"No crying at Disneyland, Ralph," Ben said. "Hold my spot while I go get some candy? I'm a sucker for good licorice."

"Sure, buddy." Ralph wiped his eye with a gloved hand as Ben made his way to the candy counter.

The man in the brown suit seated beside him asked, "Are you *the* Meta Man?"

"Seems that way. It's a bit confusing, tell the truth."

The man shook his hand. "You saved my wife from a burning building once. Tried to save me too, but it didn't work out. Do you remember that?"

Good to know even the other me could fail, Ralph thought. "Something happened, and I can't remember anything I've done as Meta Man. I'm sorry."

"That's all right. I'll remember it for the both of us."

"I meant I'm sorry I couldn't save you too," Ralph said.

"Don't be. You can't save them all, Meta Man. You're not God. I ought to know, I just met the guy."

Ralph didn't know if he should be surprised. "Where was that?"

"He's got a farm on the edge of town. You guys should check it out. If anyone knows where your friend is, it'll be him."

"What'd I miss?" Ben sat down with a long piece of red licorice sticking out of his mouth.

"Here are your floats, boys," Myra said. "Enjoy."

"Thanks," they said in unison.

Ralph took a sip of the most delicious beverage he'd ever had, and wondered if it might spoil his enjoyment of normal food. But somehow he knew that wasn't the case; anything he had here would only help him appreciate the same thing more back on Earth.

"I can't believe that tastes as good as the licorice," Ben said. "You gotta try one of these, it's unbelievable."

Ralph wiped foam from his mouth with a napkin. "You want unbelievable, wait until you hear our next stop."

HE FARM WAS IDYLLIC, as expected. Fields of golden wheat danced in the breeze, and a red barn rose in the distance, with a shiny green tractor sitting inside. The farmhouse looked comfortable, like a favorite sweater. Out front, there was a well-tended garden.

As they walked up the road to the farmhouse, Ralph said, "You're sure having a good time here."

Ben shrugged. "I think it's like my love for toys and comics from the decades before I was born. I've always enjoyed the nostalgia of other people's childhoods."

"I can see that. But I don't know why this is my heaven—it isn't what I thought it would be at all."

"Maybe it's not your heaven," Ben said. "Maybe it's Meta Man's."

Before Ralph could reply, a woman waved to them from the porch swing. "Good afternoon! Hope you didn't have any trouble finding the place!"

"Not at all," Ben said. "Seems like we just took a step, and this is where we ended up."

"Then get on up here," she said. "I made some fresh pink lemonade."

She was an attractive woman in her fifties wearing a simple summer dress. The contrast of her gray hair magnified the youthfulness found in her face. Her smile lines looked like they'd been earned through great effort.

"I would love some lemonade," Ben said.

"I was actually hoping to talk to God," Ralph said. "Would that be you?"

"Oh, no, sweetie. I'm his wife. The one you're looking for is in the house." Seeing Ralph's perplexed expression, she said, "Don't overthink it, honey."

"Is it all right if I go inside?" Ralph asked.

"He has a long-standing open-door policy," she said. "Go right on in."

"You coming?" Ralph asked Ben.

Ben, lemonade in hand, sat on a chair of twisted metal, painted white. "I'd love to, Ralph, but I'm agnostic. Going in there would ruin all my fun."

God's wife laughed. "Aren't you a peach!"

"I surely am, ma'am," Ben said. Ralph opened the door and stepped inside.

The interior of the farmhouse was pleasant and dim. There was no television, and the furniture was arranged for conversation. A cabinet held a collection of delicate china dishes and a line of fishing lures hung on a pine plaque.

Across from the living room, a man sat at the kitchen table, drinking a cup of coffee from a World's Greatest Dad mug and reading the Sunday funny pages. Ralph recognized several of his old favorite comic strips, many he hadn't seen in years.

The man lowered the paper. He looked a little older than his wife. He was mostly bald, with a ruffled plaid shirt and round eyeglasses that covered bright, energetic eyes.

Hello, Ralph, God said. Would you like a cup of coffee?

"That would be great," Ralph said. "And I'd like to talk with you, if that's okay."

Of course. Ask away, while I get you a cup.

As God went to the cabinet, Ralph noticed that, out of the corner of his eye, God looked different: an enormous man with fiery eyes, flowing white hair, and a golden cape.

But when Ralph turned to look, God looked like an old farmer again. He poured coffee into a mug and handed it to Ralph. On the side of the mug, Popeye the Sailor Man held a can of spinach and proclaimed, "I yam what I yam!"

Ralph took a sip. "Thank you. I'm guessing you already know this, but we came here looking for my friend, Valerie Hall."

I'm afraid she isn't here. Your enemy arranged to send her directly downstairs. It's a new trick, and from me that's saying something.

"You're telling me Val is in Hell?"

Don't worry, no harm has come to her.

"But she doesn't deserve that! Why didn't you get her out of there?"

I'm doing something now. I'll phone ahead, make sure they don't give you any trouble. If you died in hell, you would be trapped in the endless cycle of death experienced by the people there. Once in the bowels of hell, it could take you centuries to find your way out. Hell is as much a journey as Heaven.

"This is crazy," Ralph said. "You're all buddy-buddy with the other team?"

The other team still has to do what I tell them.

Ralph sighed. "I don't understand. If you can fix it, why didn't you already do it? Why did I even make this trip?"

You made this trip because I wanted to talk to you, Ralph. I needed you to come to me so we could have this conversation. It's important that you were the one who came to see me, and not the other way around.

"Why? It makes no sense."

It makes sense because I'm fair, Ralph. I'm forgiving, but first I have to be even-handed. That means I don't meddle in people's lives. It's not fair to meddle when you know how everyone will respond. It would be like tricking a dog into going to the vet by promising him a car ride. You had to come to me so I can give you a hint.

"All this for a hint?"

A hint is playing fair. You came all this way, you walked in the door. That gets you a hint, and it is this: Trace it back. You forgot about someone, and you need to figure out who it is.

Ralph sipped his coffee. "Val's in hell, and I forgot something. That's all I get, because you don't meddle."

Oh, I've done my share of meddling, but only so I don't have to be fair all the time. Everything else will work out in its own time.

"If I'm talking to you, does that mean the other gods and stuff are false? But that guy that got us across the river is a Greek myth, right? And what about all the Anoms running around that claim to get their powers from Zeus or Vishnu or Ahura Mazda?"

I don't change, Ralph. But your perception of me can change.

Ralph swallowed hard, trying to wrap his head around it. "I have to ask something else before I pay hell a visit. Can you tell me if Heaven—if you—were always like this? Did you exist before everything changed? If everything goes back to normal, will you disappear?"

That's an interesting question. My perception of reality is all-encompassing. Yet, is it possible for that perception to be clouded? I know that I have always existed, but did I actually spring into existence because Ralph Rogers became obsessed with finding a comic book? Will I disappear if such a situation were reversed? It's certainly fun to ponder.

"You didn't answer the question."

Walking Ralph to the door, God replied: Learn to be comfortable in ambiguity, It's time for you to go and get your friend. Tell Ben he's welcome here any time.

"He says he's agnostic."

All the more reason to have a chat. I love those folks, they keep us honest around here. See you when you get back, Ralph. Remember, everything will work out, one way or another.

"Does that mean I'll survive it? That the people I love come out of this unharmed?"

You know it doesn't. See you soon, Ralph.

As God closed the door, Ralph caught another glimpse of that golden cape.

12

OD'S WIFE AND BEN had two bicycles waiting when Ralph came outside, black cruisers with red and chrome accents. Ralph noted with a grin that they had stylized wing-shaped chain guards, a single cyclopean headlight, and even a faux gas tank. "Can you believe this, man?" Ben asked. "Black Phantoms! The coolest bicycle to ever get a playing card stuck between its spokes! And just our size."

"Don't worry about returning them," the smiling woman said. "I've got loads."

"Hear that, Ralph?" Ben grinned ear to ear. "Loads! Loads of Schwinn Black Phantom bicycles!"

"You were born too late, buddy," Ralph said, laughing.

Ben shrugged. "I guess it works out, seeing as how I died too early." To God's wife, he said, "Thank you for the lemonade, ma'am, I had a lovely time. I don't know whether or not your husband exists, but please give him my best."

"Of course. You kids have fun."

As they rode down the road side by side, Ralph told Ben about the conversation in the farmhouse.

"Sounds to me like God was fucking with you," Ben said as he peddled the bicycle. "Theophanies, man, what a bitch. He didn't say, 'Seek and ye shall find,' did he?"

"No."

"That shows remarkable restraint."

By the time Ralph finished his story, they were back at the highway.

"That makes a hell of a lot of sense," Ben said sarcastically. "How'd we get here? I'd love to see a map of this place."

"I'm sure it's way beyond our comprehension," Ralph said. "Like Narnia. Or Fraggle Rock."

Ben put up his hand. "Wait a second, put on the brakes." Their bicycles skidded to a stop on the blacktop.

In the middle of the highway they saw a dazed, bald man walking in the direction they were riding. His red suit was scorched and torn.

"Holy crap," Ralph said. "It's the Ocularist."

They put down their kickstands and approached the man with caution. *No eyeball helmet,* Ralph thought, *but that doesn't mean he isn't dangerous.*

"Hello?" Ben said.

The man blinked his wild eyes, looking at Ben and then to Ralph.

"Hi, Mr. Meta Man," the unmasked Ocularist said. Then, to no one in particular, he said, "I'm dreaming about Meta Man again. I thought this was a new dream, but I guess it's the same one."

"A new dream?" Ben asked.

The man tilted his head, his forehead furrowed. "I dreamed I was a supervillain. Isn't that silly? Then everything blew up, and now I'm dreaming about this road."

Ben asked, "What's your name, buddy?"

"I don't remember. You don't always remember real life when you're dreaming, do you?"

Ben whispered to Ralph. "I don't think this guy is dangerous."

"Did you tell Sandra to kill Valerie?" Ralph asked.

"Sandra? Oh, the fox girl," the Ocularist said. "I didn't tell anyone to do anything. The Eye did a lot of talking, but it usually didn't let me hear it. Maybe it told the fox girl to do that? In my dream, I was inside the Eye, and it took me where it wanted me to go. It was like a carnival ride, wasn't it?"

"The eye?" Ben asked. "Was that the helmet?"

"The Eye was everything. But the helmet, I thought it was the helmet making me dream. But you broke the helmet, Mr. Meta Man, and I haven't woken up yet."

"I am totally lost," Ben said.

"I'll explain later," Ralph said, then he asked the Ocularist: "Why did you throw yourself on the helmet last time we fought?"

"The Eye didn't talk to me much," the Ocularist said. "But it made one thing clear: if I tried to take off the helmet, it would explode. It didn't seem to matter, since it was only a dream. But when you broke the helmet and I was still dreaming, I remembered all those old war movies I watched with my dad. I remembered what a good guy did if a grenade landed in his foxhole. I thought it would be nice to dream about being a good guy for a change. Did it help?"

"Sure, man, it was a very heroic thing to do," Ralph said. "So, you don't remember who you are, or who put the helmet on you?"

"Put the helmet on me? But the Eye is just part of my dream."

Ben pulled Ralph aside, and whispered, "I've seen some people show up on the road like this. Confused, amnestic. But not this bad. It's like he's in shock. If we were on Earth, I'd take this guy to a hospital."

"When I fought him, I felt like it was the helmet controlling him. But there was no way to be sure. I mean, this guy tried to kill me. And the way he talked, he was the only one other than me who remembered baseline reality."

"This guy doesn't remember his own name," Ben said. "I think your instincts were right, that he was Mad Hattered. I be the Ocularist's voice didn't even come from this guy. And now he's not telling us anything useful."

"Then what do we do?" Ralph asked.

Ben caught up to the dazed man, who had started back down the road. "You're going the wrong way."

"I am?"

"You sure are, buddy," Ralph said. "Think you could ride a bicycle? It'll get you there faster."

The man brightened. "I think I could ride a bicycle. That's the one thing you never forget, right?"

"That's right." Ralph handed over the bicycle. The man rang the bell on the handlebars with his thumb and grinned, slowly climbing onto the leather seat.

"Thank you. I'll do my best to remember you when I finally wake up."

They watched as the false Ocularist rode away, finally disappearing over the horizon.

Ben patted Ralph on the shoulder. "You old softie, giving away your bike. Have fun walking to Hell."

"You ever give someone a pump?" Ralph asked.

Ben sighed. "Just keep your damn cape out of my face."

"No promises."

Ralph climbed onto the handlebars of the bicycle.

S THEY APPROACHED THE MODERN SKYLINE of the island city that was Hell, they saw an enormous red suspension bridge before them. The sounds of police sirens and scattered gunfire echoed across the black water, and the air smelled of burning garbage.

Ben pedaled the bicycle, peering over Ralph's shoulder as Ralph sat balanced on the handlebars.

"On a scale of one to ten, how different is this than you expected?" Ben asked.

"After Heaven turned out to be Podunk, Kansas, I didn't know what to expect. How about you?"

"This is *exactly* what I expected."

There wasn't a soul on the bridge, but they climbed off the bike and walked anyway. There were no boats in sight, but in the distance, out in what could not possibly be the ocean, was a monument resembling the Statue of Liberty. Instead of aged copper she wore polished bronze, and in her raised hand she held not a torch, but a sword.

"Give me your tired, your poor, your huddled masses," Ben said, walking the bicycle along. "Methinks it be time for a plan."

"Seems insane to make plans when the world keeps changing around me."

"It's been pretty consistent here, hasn't it? All things considered, I mean."

Ralph checked back over his shoulder. "I guess so. God said he'd call ahead, so we shouldn't have any trouble."

Ben laughed as they reached the end of the bridge and entered the city. "What trouble could we possibly run into? Oh, that's right, we're in Hell."

The sound of a roaring engine froze them in their tracks. A woman in a convertible roadster painted with bright yellow and black stripes spun around the corner. An old-fashioned police van followed in close pursuit, complete with officers in blue uniforms and helmets hanging from the side, blowing their whistles and waving their nightsticks.

"Good gravy!" Ben yelled. "Is that a paddy wagon?"

The yellow roadster crashed into a fire hydrant, and a geyser of water shot into the air. The woman leaped out of the car. She wore a form-fitting bumblebee costume. The paddy wagon screeched to a halt and the policemen piled out.

"You'll never take me alive, coppers!" The woman threw a beehive grenade at the police. It shattered when it hit the ground, and thick honey erupted. There was far more of the fluid than the beehive could possibly contain, and it created an enormous puddle that tripped up the policemen. The ones who lost their footing found themselves stuck to the ground, unable to move. The bee woman ran off, cackling wildly and carrying a canvas bag with a dollar sign on it. The remaining police officers ran after her.

Ralph started toward the policemen stuck to the ground. Ben put his hand on his shoulder to stop him. "Are you sure you want to do that?"

"I don't think they're dangerous right now, do you?" Ralph asked. Ben reluctantly followed him.

"Meta Man!" said the first policeman they reached. "Come to join the fight? We can barely handle all these Anom bastards!"

"What happened, officer?" Ben asked.

"The Honey Bee robbed the jewelry exchange. Nailed us with one of her honey bombs—*again*. I'll bust her fucking head open for this, not that it'll do any good. She'll just be back again tomorrow. This is so much more fun than the law firm I worked in, you know, back when I was alive. Hey, can you guys help me out of this?"

"There's no time!" Ralph said in his closest approximation of a superhero voice. "I need to find the Devil immediately."

The man eyed him suspiciously. "His office is at 666 Fifth Avenue. Everybody knows that. You guys new or something?"

"Just arrived," Ralph said. "Stay strong. I'm sure backup will be here for you soon." Ralph and Ben hurried away without looking back.

The further they moved into the city, the more the pandemonium escalated. A window shattered above them, and a man in a strange helmet jumped out. He appeared to have his own field of gravity, as he ran along the side of the building, jumping over each window and landing on the wall again.

"I don't recognize any of these Anoms," Ralph said.

"I remember reading about Honey Bee," Ben replied. "Before your time. But it's like that lawyer playing cops and robbers. Some of these folks may not have been Anoms until they showed up here."

A six-story mountain emerged from a nearby street, its skin the cold gray of cracking stone. With each step, it shook the ground and left footprints in the pavement. Its eye sockets and gaping mouth were empty black pits. The monster roared as it smashed its fists into the buildings around it. Ben and Ralph ran into an alley as brick, metal, and glass rained down onto the asphalt.

Jeeps and tanks flooded the streets. Bullets struck the monster; in its rage, it shrugged them off. When an exploding shell struck it in the shoulder, leaving a smoking crater, the monster finally turned on the army, kicking vehicles aside like aluminum cans.

Following the street signs, Ben and Ralph worked their way to Fifth Avenue. Ten blocks from their destination, aliens invaded.

"This place sucks," Ben said as several silver flying saucers descended from the sky, halting several meters over the street. Floating stair steps appeared and little purple men, wearing golden uniforms and bearing rifles, walked down to the ground. Ben and Ralph crouched behind a newspaper vending machine. The headline read, *Meta Boy Dies in Fire*.

One of the aliens spotted Ralph and Ben and shot at them. A yellow burst of energy hit the wall beside them, pulverizing the building's decorative tiles.

Ben grabbed Ralph by the cape and dragged him around the corner onto an empty street. Ralph breathed a sigh of relief. *Almost there*, he thought as they reached another bend.

Around the corner stood a mob of maniacs in primary-color costumes. Many carried flaming torches. Registering the presence of Ralph and Ben, the crowd halted. At the front, leading them, strode a brown-haired woman in a red cigarette girl uniform. She carried no torch, but her eyes burned with rage. "Smoke 'em if you got 'em!" she screeched.

The mob charged at them, screaming battle cries and curses.

"Run!" Ralph shouted.

"No shit!" Ben called back over his shoulder.

They ran back the way they had come, only to see the alien army advancing. Ducking down an alley and behind a dumpster, they watched the villains pass by and collide with the invaders. Ray gun blasts and bad one-liners filled the air.

Ben shielded his eyes and looked up. "These buildings are pretty close together. Maybe we can get off the street and Batman it from roof to roof."

Exiting the other end of the alley, they found the front entrance into one of the taller buildings. Finding the doors unlocked, they ran inside. Ralph looked for something to try and blockade the doors, but the lobby was empty.

"Elevator or stairs?" Ralph asked.

"Elevator," Ben said, fighting to catch his breath. "Definitely the elevator."

"Recognize anyone in the mob?"

"I think the cigarette girl might have been Coffin Nails. Used to tangle with Danny Drastic back in the forties. She's only been dead for, what, like fifty years? Not sure about the others, but I'd rather not get to know them."

They reached the bland elevator with its mirror ceiling, and Ralph pushed the button for the top floor.

As the elevator doors slid shut, Ralph took stock of Ben. "Why are you worn out, anyway, ghost guy?"

"Dunno. It's more tiring getting around here than on the road. How about you—are you invulnerable? I mean currently?"

"No idea." Ralph said. "I'm not that invulnerable, anyway. Fighting the Ocularist, I dislocated my shoulder. Maybe I'm only nigh-invulnerable."

"How long did God say you'd be stuck here if you died? Am I killable here, since I'm already dead?"

"Not sure."

"What about those aliens? Are they really here, or are they a creation of Hell? If they're really here with the humans, is it because they died on Earth?"

"Maybe we should table this debate for another time."

"I really should have talked to God," Ben sighed. "You didn't ask any good questions. Next time, I'm making you a god damn list."

The elevator opened at the top floor. The hallway was splattered with blood and punctuated with bullet holes. No bodies could be seen, but the smell and the buzzing flies made it clear they weren't far away.

Ben pulled his shirt over his mouth and nose, and Ralph did the same. They followed the signs and found the door leading to the roof.

Ben tried the handle. "Locked." He stepped back and gave the door a kick. It didn't budge, leaving Ben hopping on one foot and swearing.

"Let me." Ralph tried the handle, but it remained stuck.

He closed his eyes.

You're a pretender, said a voice in his mind. *You failed before most people bothered to start, and you've been a failure ever since. Even if this other Ralph Rogers is real—and you know deep down he isn't—you are not him.*

Ralph squeezed the warm door handle.

That's not true, he thought. *I didn't earn any of this, sure. But from what I've seen, I'm just as good at making comics as that other Ralph. And I fought the Ocularist and lived.*

The Ocularist was a nobody in a mask, the voice said.

Tell that to Wyvern, Ralph thought. *I destroyed the Haberdasher factory. That was before I even knew I had powers in this reality. And I saved those kids. That was me, no one else.*

But this world isn't real, the voice said.

It doesn't matter if this world is real or not. It doesn't matter if I'm a raving lunatic in a rubber room. If I'm living in a dream world, I'm going to be a hero in that world.

The knob made a painful crunching sound, but it turned smoothly. The door swung open.

"What's that mean?" Ben asked as they ran up the stairs.

"We might have a hope in Hell, after all."

They stepped out onto the loose, crunching gravel of the roof. The nearest rooftop was much further away than it seemed on the ground. Walking up to the edge, they peered over the side. Purple aliens flooded the streets below. In the distance, the monster smashed through buildings.

"Watch out for that first step, it's a doozy!" Ben said. "There is no way I could make that jump."

Ralph peered over the edge. "My powers might be back. Maybe I could throw you across."

"'*Might* be?'" Ben asked. "'*Maybe?*' Not exactly inspiring confidence there, buddy. I'm no physics major, but I think if you threw me hard enough to carry me over, *maybe* I'd break some bones when I landed."

"Can you break your bones in the afterlife?" Ralph asked.

"Probably not where the streets are paved with black licorice. But where there are bloody hallways and rock monsters? Yeah, I'd bet it's pretty easy to get hurt here, maybe permanently. Could you jump across with me on your back?"

"I don't understand how the powers work," Ralph said. "What if they cut out before the jump? Maybe we could rig up a bridge."

"I'm not the Road Runner, and you're sure as shit no Wile E. Coyo—" Ben froze in mid-sentence.

"What is it?" Ralph asked.

"Shut up!" Ben said, holding up his hand. There was a crunching sound, like a foot walking in gravel.

The two of them spun around to face a man in a green costume. On his head he wore a giant hand grenade with a hole where his face poked through. His eyes were wide and unblinking, and froth had collected at the corners of this mouth. He wore numerous bandoliers of hand grenades. Ralph recognized the Mk 2 model from World War II; his grandfather kept a defused example in his office when Ralph was young.

"Has it come down to this, Meta Man?" the madman asked. "A final rooftop confrontation?"

"Let me guess," Ben said. "Captain Hand Grenade?"

"So you've heard of me." Captain Hand Grenade smiled broadly.

Looking to Ralph, Ben asked, "Can you survive a hand grenade? Like if you blocked for me, would we make it?"

They each took a step backward, bringing them to the edge of the roof. "I wouldn't bet the farm on it," Ralph said.

"Then what's the plan?"

Captain Hand Grenade beamed as he reached up to his shoulders, hooking a cord with each thumb. As he pulled it, dozens of grenade pins sprung loose with soft pinging sounds. Screaming, the human bomb ran full-tilt toward Ben and Ralph.

"Do you trust me?" Ralph yelled.

"Sixty-forty!" Ben yelled back.

"Close enough."

Ralph grabbed Ben in a bear hug and fell backwards off the roof.

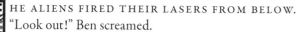

14

THE ALIENS FIRED THEIR LASERS FROM BELOW.
"Look out!" Ben screamed.

Ralph flew quickly, one arm around Ben's waist and the other stretched out in front to steer. Leaning into the turn, Ralph took them between two buildings. Clotheslines stretched between the buildings. Long johns slapped their faces as they passed.

More set dressing, Ralph thought.

Having outpaced the aliens, Ralph slowed down to gather their bearings.

Behind them, a violent crash erupted. The stone monster stormed into the intersection, his legs wrapped in electric lines and traffic lights. Seeing Ralph and his passenger, the monster roared.

"Take us up!" Ben yelled. "Up, up, you idiot!"

Ralph flew out of the monster's range. He looked back over his shoulder at the raving beast and wondered if he was any match for such a creature.

Ben read Ralph's mind. "Don't even think about it. Even if he didn't flatten you like a pancake, I'd be nothing but raspberry jelly. Just get us to Fifth Avenue."

"Where is it?"

"I've been counting the blocks." Ben pointed. "It should be that way."

This high up in the air, they had a better view of the city. The skyline stretched on forever, but they could see the aliens clashing with Coffin Nail's army, and several Anom battles were wreaking havoc throughout the area. Cracks had split the street several blocks away, and red lava melted everything in its path. Other flyers and one helicopter ignored Ben and Ralph for now, but that could change at any moment.

"This should be Fifth," Ben said, adding sarcastically, "Which building do you think it is?"

"No idea," Ralph said.

The skyscraper, towering over the others, shined in the sky like a broadsword. The ebony glass and blasphemous stonework loomed over the serrated skyline.

"Top floor?" Ralph asked.

"Definitely top floor," Ben said.

Ralph looked at the sloping roof, hoping for an easy place to land. They would slide right off the violent architecture. "Should I just crash through the glass?"

"This isn't a movie, Ralph, and that won't be sugar glass that explodes when you touch it. You've watched *Die Hard* too many times. Windows like that would slice me to ribbons. Maybe you too, Mr. Nigh-Invulnerable."

"Then what—"

One of the windows slid out of view, revealing an opening in the sharply-angled roof. Ralph hesitated, scrutinizing the hole.

"Don't be a wimp, Ralph. This is where we've been trying to go. Let's save Val."

"Anything could be in there. Can't we just duke it out with the rock monster?"

Ben rolled his eyes. "Do not pull that 'the devil you know' bullshit. Not here, man, it's too silly."

Ralph lowered them through the opening into an enormous office. The miles of marble floor consisted of black and cherry chevron, and behind the desk gushed a waterfall of what had to be blood.

The desk was as long as a truck and looked twice as heavy. Its surface was clear, except for a red rotary telephone and a bronze bust. The burgundy leather chair behind it faced away from them. As they approached, the chair slowly turned around.

"Welcome."

The thing in the chair looked like a normal man with black hair and a goatee. He wore a costume-party devil suit: red tights and a cape with black lining. A crimson domino mask covered his eyes. Out of his hair poked two horns. They looked to be artificial, but it was difficult to tell.

"Not exactly Tim Curry in *Legend*, is he?" Ben asked.

"Are you kidding?" Ralph said. "He's not even Jack Nicholson in *The Witches of Eastwick*. You know, Ben, until right now, I thought you might be the Devil in disguise."

Ben bowed. "I'm flattered."

The Devil smiled. "You should take this act to vaudeville. What can I do for you fine gentlemen?"

"God told us he would call ahead," Ralph said. "That there wouldn't be any trouble. We barely made it here in one piece."

"Really?" The Devil pulled a cell phone out of his pocket and glanced at the screen before tossing it on the desk. "Oh, badness me. I sent someone to help you, can't see how you missed him. Terribly sorry. He's a giant rock monster. But you made it here anyway, so no harm done, right?"

"Cut the shit, Old Nick," Ben said. "Where's Valerie?"

The lights in the room went black. The fountain emanated a strange glow, and the Devil's form shifted and swam between countless horrendous, rotting creatures.

"Do not make the mistake of equating my appearance with my power. I can crush you, dear children," it said.

The lights came back on, and once again a smiling man in a tacky Halloween costume sat in front of them. "Now, then. What do you require?"

"The Fair Folk did that trick with more style," Ralph said. "We came for Valerie. For your sake, she'd better be okay."

"The lady is perfectly fine, Mr. Big Boy Pants. Watch this, I just had it installed."

A circle appeared on the marble floor in front of the desk, then lowered and slid out of sight. Valerie rose out of the shaft in the floor, wearing her Titania uniform, gagged with a piece of green and gold silk, her hands tied behind her. She looked unhurt and relieved to see Ralph and Ben.

The two men started toward her, but found their feet stuck to the floor.

The Devil held up a hand. "Not so fast."

"You didn't tell me Valerie was Titania!" Ben said, punching Ralph in the arm.

"Sorry. I didn't think it was important."

"Not important?" Ben said. "Damn it. Is she tied up with her own cape?"

"Cha meh!" Valerie grunted around the gag in her mouth.

"What?" Ben asked.

Ralph sighed. "She's saying 'chlamys.' It's not a cape, it's a chlamys."

Valerie nodded.

"Shut the fuck up, all of you!" the Devil yelled. "Judas H. Iscariot, how do you people get anything done? Look, I don't even want her here, she ruins the tone. She wasn't the intended recipient of that spell, Ralph, it was supposed to be you. But I made a deal to imprison whoever got sent to me, so here we are. You're welcome to her. The deal didn't cover fighting off a rescue from Meta Man."

"'But?'" Ben asked. "Isn't there always a 'but' in this kind of thing?"

The Devil smiled. "That's right. You're welcome to her, but first you have to listen to my case."

"Here we go," Ben sighed.

His elbows on the desk, the Devil rested his chin on his thumbs. "I know what you've been trying to do. You have this idea the world used to be different. I don't remember the world being different, but that doesn't matter."

He lifted his hands, as if making a tiny cheer.

"I love coming into work. Every day is a beautiful disaster, and, oh, it's so exciting. I have agents sneaking around the mortal plane, causing trouble, and every day I have more subjects showing up to fight forever in my own private Valhalla. This is the sweetest gig you can imagine, kids, and I don't want to give it up."

"So you don't want us to change it back," Ralph said.

"This may surprise you," the Devil said, "but I'm not like God. I am not entirely confident I didn't spring into existence the instant Meta Boy over here got his crazy on. So, I want you to consider letting things stay this way. Stop mucking about, trying to change everything back."

"That's it?" Ralph asked.

"That's it."

Ralph stared at him, doubtful. "I'd have thought you'd want to make a deal."

"Deals don't mean squat when you can't trust the parties involved. And you'd be a fool to trust me. You're not a fool, are you Ralph?"

"No, I—"

"I'm not a fool, either. But I think I can trust you to, at the very least, consider my words."

"What happens if I refuse?" Ralph asked.

The Devil started to say something, but Ben cut him off. "Nothing happens. God told you to stay out of it, didn't he?"

The Devil's smile leveled out.

"We'll take your request under heavy advisement," Ben said. "Will that be enough?"

"I guess it'll have to be," said the Devil. "But I don't just hand out advice, so you'd best remember this: you're dealing with someone I don't want to tangle with. That's your takeaway here. Ask yourselves, 'Who damned Valerie? Who made the deal?'"

With an annoyed wave of the Devil's hand, Ben and Ralph could move again. Ben undid Valerie's hands while Ralph untied the gag. Once the gag was off, she said to the Devil, "Thank you. You have been a perfectly terrible host."

"Oh, come on. We had a great time. You've only been tied up for what, twenty minutes? Just for the effect."

"Sure," Valerie said, "but the food was almost as bad as the company. Just tell us the fastest way out of here."

The Devil smiled and clapped his hands in two deafening strikes. One wall caved in; bricks, glass, and splintered wood showered the room. A stone hand the size of a school bus filled the penthouse. The fingers laid flat and heavy on the marble tile like the pillars of a ruined temple.

"Consider this the express train," the Devil said.

"There's no way that's safer than just flying out," Ralph said.

The Devil laughed. "Leaving Hell is not the same as entering. If you think getting to me was tough, wait until our denizens realize you're trying to reach the bridge. Do you have any idea how long it's been since some of them have killed anyone *alive*, Mr. Nigh-Invulnerable?" He mimed firing a rifle into the sky. "I'd hate for you to catch a stray bullet and be stuck here for the duration. Konkor will ferry you to the border."

"You have got to be kidding," Valerie said. But Ben was already climbing the cracked, rocky joints of the stone monster's index finger.

Ralph looked from Valerie to the hand and back to Valerie. "Do you think it's safe?" he asked.

Valerie nodded. "Nope." She grabbed Ralph's hand. The two of them floated up to Ben.

"This is so awesome!" Ben tapped the stone palm. "Do you think Konkor has lava for blood?"

Valerie grunted. "I know he has three idiots for passengers."

The fingers closed over them. There was a painful grinding sound as the hand was pulled out through the hole in the wall. Valerie, Ralph, and Ben shielded their eyes as dust and crumbled rock fell through the gaps in the fingers and rained down on them.

Ralph's stomach lurched as the hand moved through the air. The fingers opened again, and they were level with the monster's shoulder. Without hesitation, Ben leaped to the monster's shoulder. Ralph and Valerie followed.

"Remember," the Devil said. "The stakes here go well beyond the mere distinction between life and death."

"We'll remember." Ralph looked over the edge of his perch on the monster's shoulder. Vertigo threatened as he saw Konkor's feet far below. "He's bigger than before. He's gone from King Kong size to Godzilla size."

"1954 Godzilla or 2014 Godzilla?" Ben asked. "Please don't say Matthew Broderick Godzilla."

Before Ralph could answer, Konkor spoke. The monster's voice sounded like a rock crusher set at low speed, and the three humans on his shoulder felt the words like the ebbing shockwave of an explosion.

"Hold. On. To. Your. Asses."

15

THE ALIENS ATTACKED FIRST.

The purple humanoids fired lasers from the ground, but the green light had no visible effect on Konkor's geologic skin. Try as they might, the ground-troop aliens couldn't find an angle to hit the shielded humans.

The hubcap flying saucers posed a greater threat. The body of each ship spun around its center. The central hubs opened like the apertures of mechanical cameras, and mounted weapon emerged. They fired the same green lasers in rapid, machine gun bursts. Konkor swatted at the ships with an open palm, knocking them from the sky like wasps. The crumpled saucers crashed into the buildings below, exploding in colorful bursts.

Hell's army rolled in for the second wave. Their weapons were still ineffective on the monster, but a near miss from a tank's exploding shell sent Valerie, Ben, and Ralph scrambling closer to Konkor's neck.

Tanks exploded under the monster's slow footsteps. Their heavier artillery destroyed, the soldiers below scrambled for cover.

Remember, Ralph told himself, *these people are already dead. The only ones at risk here are the three of us.* This did little to ease his conscience.

Dozens of supervillains emerged onto the rooftops. A furious Coffin Nails led them in an organized assault. Captain Hand Grenade's explosive barrage made Konkor pause in his tracks. Explosions of electricity, ice, fire, and shadows filled the air around them.

"Give me a break," Valerie said.

A cloud of bees attacked them, directed from below by Honey Bee. They tried to stay calm, but the buzzing swarm could probably kill as effectively as an explosion. Ralph pulled his cape over his face.

Konkor turned his massive head to the side and blew a gust strong enough to send the bees flying without losing his passengers. He then shielded them with his hand as his steady trek continued. With his free hand, he knocked villains from their perches on the buildings, killing them instantly or sending them screaming to the street below.

"This guy's good," Valerie said. "Can't see him joining the Cadre, but he's very good."

When they reached the bridge, Ralph expected them to stop. Instead, Konkor walked into the water, which barely slowed him down. At its deepest, the water nearly reached Konkor's shoulders.

They reached the other side, and Konkor emerged from the sea, his charges still dry and safe. Waterfalls streamed from areas of his body where pools had collected. The monster raised his wet palm. The group hopped to his open hand, and Konkor bent, lowering them gently to the ground.

"Thanks, big guy!" Ben yelled, shaping a megaphone with his hands. "If you want to get to Heaven, just keep walking down this road!"

Konkor paused. "Heaven?" he rumbled. "Thought. I. Was. Already. There."

As he walked back into the water, Konkor's laughter and footsteps felt like an earthquake colliding with an avalanche.

"Your rescue had style, I'll give you that," Valerie said as they watched Konkor disappear into the distance.

Ralph shrugged. "Yeah, well, everyone looks like they know what they're doing when they're riding around on a rock monster."

"What about you, Ben?" Valerie asked. "Are you coming with us?"

"I don't think so," Ben said as they walked. "But I'll get you to the boat."

"Come on, man," Ralph said. "We need all the help we can get."

"From a non-Anom? I might be genre savvy, but that's hardly a super power. I'd just drag you guys down. Besides, Heaven's calling me."

"Is it really that great?" Valerie asked.

"They got Black Phantom bikes!" Ben yelled. "Loads of them!"

"What about your dad?" Ralph asked.

"Low blow, Ralph. Dirty pool. My dad had no control over what he did. My coming back won't change what already happened."

Ben led them off the road and into the brush, which soon opened out onto the shore. The ferryman waited for them with his boat. He checked his watch. "Took you kids long enough."

Valerie looked at Ben with tears in her eyes and climbed into the boat. The ferryman offered her his hand for balance, but she refused it.

"Come on, buddy," Ralph said. "Think about the fun we could have saving the world."

Ben put his hands on Ralph's shoulders. "Ralph, you're like the brother I never had, but you've got to try and understand. I'm just fucking with you."

"But we—" Ralph began. "Wait a minute, what?"

Ben climbed in the boat. Valerie, laughing, gave him a hug while the ferryman rolled his eyes. With everyone aboard, the old man pushed away from shore. Ralph volunteered to help row. As he matched his strokes with the ferryman's, he explained the current situation to Valerie.

"So what's the master plan when we get back?" Valerie asked. "Stick with Stiff's idea? Or do we try and find this person both God and the Devil saw fit to warn you about?"

"Whatever we do, I want to help," said Ben. "Not just sit in my shop and wait for another of Ralph's loony phone calls."

"Of course you'll help," Valerie said.

"No, you don't get it. I don't have to be a sideliner anymore. I didn't want to show you until we got back, but look what I got."

Ben held out his hand. Inky smoke swirled, and a familiar shape appeared. But instead of looking like a plastic prop, the long, three-pronged fork was made of black, barbed bone.

"Oh, fuck me," the ferryman said.

"You didn't," Valerie said.

"I did!" Ben said. "The Devil gave me his fork! He handed it to me when the monster's hand busted in through the wall. It disappeared and now it's like a part of me. I'm thinking I'll call myself Black Trident. What do you guys think?"

"I think you're crazy," Ralph said, laughing and shaking his head.

"Crazy like a fox. Now it's a team-up. And I want Black Snake's phone number. These are my demands." The fork disappeared, and Ben turned to Ralph. "So, who do you think God was hinting to you about? Who did you forget?"

"Think about it," Ralph said. "This little adventure started with four of us. Who's supposedly been around the longest? Who sent me after the Pithos comics in the first place?"

"No way," Valerie said. "It couldn't be him."

"I think it is," Ralph said. "We're going after Danny Drastic."

M

THE GOLDEN AGE

Real Name: Danny Drastic, Publicly Known

Affiliation: Freedom Cadre

Anom Categories: Time-Displaced Human, Technology User

Base of Operations: Atlantis, New York, Los Angeles

Marital Status: Single

Relatives: Professor Savant (father, rumor), Coffin Nails II (granddaughter, rumor)

Birth: circa. 3010 (unconfirmed)

First Public Appearance: 1939

First Modern Fictional: Freedom Cadre vol. 2, #275 (June, 1986)

Aliases: The Anachronistic Man

Abilities: Assisted Flight, Excellent Reflexes, Skilled Marksman, Slow Aging

Equipment: Rocket Pack, Disintegrator Ray Gun, Retrofitted Stout Scarab (destroyed), Time Machine (damaged)

Danny Drastic hails from the distant future. He has claimed different origin points, most commonly 1,000 years from the present. With his trademark flight goggles, rocket pack, and Atomic Disintegrator—a humane weapon that only damages inanimate matter—he has haunted the twentieth and twenty-first centuries.

His stated mission was to stop Professor Savant from destroying the past. The evil scientist arrived before him, famously using airships to kidnap entire towns in the 1920s. Drastic appeared in his time machine in 1939, publicly battling Savant over the skies of New York. Although he did not totally defeat Savant at this time, he continued to fight for the people of his adopted time, teaming with Freedom Cadre against the Axis and all manner of Anom threats. His ongoing feud with the popular female villain Coffin Nails was widely covered in the press. Although a weak seller during the stints Drastic was missing, the **DANNY DRASTIC** comic book was the first comic book published by Pithos Publishing, and is the only Pithos comic to remain in monthly circulation since the 1930s.

Savant damaged Drastic's time machine in their initial confrontation, rendering the machine incapable of traveling backward in time. It could still go forward, so when Savant escaped to the 1960s, Drastic followed. Drastic emerged in 1963, finding a world that had moved on since his disappearance. Tragical-ly, he failed to prevent the assassination of President Kennedy. He regained his prominent status, teaming with Oceanus and the Cadre against Konkor. On his own, he defeated Honey Bee and other colorful Anoms of the time.

As the sixties drew to a close, Drastic decided to return to the future. Following a tearful farewell with Nylon, Jack Spratt, and his other teammates, he departed in his time machine. Assuming Drastic had returned to his own time, the world again moved on.

From Drastic's perspective, in the next moment he found himself, not in the distant future, but in 1986. It turned out that the villain Overmorrow had blocked Drastic's journey, stranding him again. Drastic joined the Cadre, a different group than the one he remembered. He witnessed one of his old friends, Potbelly, return as the murderous Ironworks. Saving Ironworks was only the beginning of a graver threat, including the near destruction of reality by the Bringer of Blades. Following this victory, it was revealed Overmorrow was none other than Professor Savant, who was attempting to recreate the future of Drastic's birth. Sacrificing any chance of returning home, Danny Drastic defeated Savant once and for all. Drastic regained his ability to go forward in time, but decided to stay in the present. "What can I say," he explained in a press conference. "It's grown on me. It's like the Wild West, but you can order stuff on the internet."

Illustration by Ben Cohen

HE Seven Gates led back to Ralph's living room, still in shambles from Mr. Stiff and Songweaver's battle.

Ben surveyed the damage. "I hope you have Anom insurance. Aw, man, they broke your *Meta Man* arcade. I've always wanted one of these."

"What the heck?" Ralph asked. "Why aren't we in Pennsylvania?"

Valerie looked around. "Songweaver must have prepared the teleportation spell to be round trip."

Ben kicked at the rubble. "I'm not sure I buy that."

"Just be glad we aren't riding a Greyhound in full costume," Valerie said. "I'm grabbing a shower."

"What if Stiff shows up?" Ralph asked.

"Tell him I'll try not to use all the hot water." Valerie disappeared into the bedroom.

"Stiff wouldn't risk a fight with Titania, even if you aren't working at full capacity," Ben said. "It goes against his whole plan."

"But he's the planner, right? He could still be listening in. There could be an alarm to tell him we came back."

"Good point. Perhaps we should mum's-the-word on our next step."

They discussed the biological implications of the rock monster until Valerie finished her shower. She appeared wearing Ralph's old Flatland high school sweatshirt and a pair of jeans.

"Aren't those—" Ralph nearly said *Sandra's jeans*, but thought better of it.

"I can't switch back to my own clothes without making a power spike that the Cadre satellites will pick up," Valerie said. "Hope you don't mind."

"No problem. At least I'm not the only one being paranoid." Ralph raised an eyebrow to Ben.

"Just don't make that damn fork pop up," Valerie said. "There's no telling what kind of reading that damned thing would give off."

"Heh," Ben laughed. "'Damned thing.'"

He took the next shower as Ralph and Valerie checked over Ralph's Stout Scarab van in the garage for any of Stiff's surveillance.

"Too bad about the Kamakiri," Valerie said. "At least the van is roomy."

"This is pointless." Ralph closed the hood with its winged air vents. "Stiff has access to teleportation technology, and that's just for starters. If he wanted to bug my van, he could do it with something the size of a grain of sand."

"Due diligence, Ralph." Valerie shined a flashlight into the air-conditioning vents. "Wouldn't you feel stupid if we could have found it but didn't?"

"I guess. But shouldn't we take another vehicle? A car this rare will stand out, making it easy to track."

"Are you kidding? No, I guess you're not. Sorry. You're stuck thinking in a different iteration. People went crazy for these things because of the Danny Drastic show, so they put the Scarab back into production in the fifties. They made the same model for decades."

"Like the Volkswagen Beetle?"

Valerie peered under the seats. "Maybe it's an insect thing. Anyway, the Scarab was huge in the sixties. Hippies painted flowers all over 'em. These days they make an updated version, and it's safe as houses. Only modern vehicle where you don't have to wear your seatbelt." She clicked off her flashlight. "Find anything?"

"Don't think so," Ralph said.

"Then let's load up!" Ben said, walking into the garage. He carried a shopping bag, bulging with cash.

"Where'd you get that?" Valerie asked.

"The safe in Ralph's closet," Ben said. "Plenty of funds for our road trip."

"How'd you open the safe?" Ralph asked. "I have no idea what the combination is."

"You used your birthday." Ben handed him the bag. "Not too bright."

"How do you know my birthday, ya creep?" Ralph asked.

"Because it's written on a sticky note on the back of your safe, you big dummy." Ben took the green sticky note from his pocket and stuck it to Ralph's chest, patting it in place. Valerie giggled.

"At least that version of me isn't any smarter than this version of me," Ralph said.

He took a quick shower—Ben and Valerie had hardly left him any hot water. His Meta Man costume packed away, he piled into the van with the others.

"You sure you know where to find Damon?" Ralph asked, taking the driver's seat.

Valerie, sitting in the front passenger seat, nodded. "This time of year, he should be at his place in California."

"Sounds like a road trip." Ben stretched out on the booth seat in the back.

"Sounds like." Ralph started the engine.

2

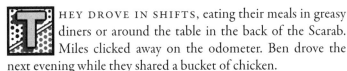HEY DROVE IN SHIFTS, eating their meals in greasy diners or around the table in the back of the Scarab. Miles clicked away on the odometer. Ben drove the next evening while they shared a bucket of chicken.

The AM radio crackled as Ben found a talk show. "Still no word on our missing heroes," the host said. "Even those Anoms whose true identities are public are nowhere to be found. The mainstream media stopped reporting on the situation days ago, but—" The station went silent. Ben spun the dial, but could not find it again.

"Because that isn't creepy," Valerie said. "Pass that chicken over here."

"Looks like Stiff is still keeping things quiet," Ralph said.

"Or the folks at the Cloud Club are still active and following his orders," Ben said. "They might even have something automated that shuts down anyone talking about Anoms on the air, online, stuff like that."

Ralph reached for some fries. "Across the whole world?"

Valerie pointed upward. "Cadre satellites. But don't worry, he shouldn't notice us once we're at Damon's house. The satellites are reverse engineered from his future technology. He made all his homes permanent dead zones."

"I still can't believe Damon could be behind all this," Ben said. "Not the man who starred in the heartwarming family classic, *Robot Babysitter*."

"I'd rather think it was him than someone currently in the car," Ralph said.

They were silent for a few moments, each evaluating how paranoid they should be.

Ben broke the silence by loudly sucking the straw in his drained soda cup. He shook the cup of crushed ice. "Can't wait to try out my kickass trident."

"What do you think it does?" Ralph asked. "Other than offend sweet old ladies?"

Ben shrugged. "I don't know. Shoot out a devil laser? Block out the sun?"

"Can't believe you accepted a gift from that guy," Valerie said. "Would you have eaten candy if he gave it to you?"

"Devil candy?" Ben asked. "You bet I would. Unless it was those pink circus peanuts. Had a bad experience with a whole bag of those as a kid. Can't even look at the things."

"Trust me," Valerie said. "I've seen this kind of bullshit in the Twilight Lands. The son of a bitch thinks on a higher level than you, so he had a plan when he gave you the fork."

"That makes a lot of sense, Ben," Ralph said. "Maybe you should get rid of it."

"Nuh-uh," Ben said. "No way. Even if that's true, it's mine. This's the baseball bat that gets me in the big leagues. Besides, the Devil's a pretty smart guy. If he wanted me to have it, maybe he knows we'll need it."

Valerie snorted. "Or, he's a jerk and just wants to fuck with us."

"I guess we'll see, huh?" Ben said.

They crossed the border into Arizona.

3

 HE FOLLOWING EVENING, the trio pulled up to the intercom at Damon Ripley's gate.

"I'll talk to him," Valerie said.

"Like hell you will," Ralph said. "The guy thinks you're dead. Ben too. Let me get us in there, and then we can confront him."

"And if he's really the guy behind the Ocularist and everything else?" Ben asked.

"Then I'll punch him so hard he'll go back to the future," Valerie said.

"That's heavy," Ben said.

"Shut up, you nitwits." Ralph leaned out the window and pushed the button.

"Hello?" crackled Damon's voice over the intercom.

"Damon? It's Ralph. I know you aren't expecting me—"

"Ralph? Come on in, buddy. I'll open the gate."

Motors groaned and chains pulled the gate open. Ralph shifted the Scarab into first and rolled up the driveway.

"I still don't think it's him," Ben said. "Damon can be an asshole sometimes, sure, but he's always been one of the good guys.

Since before we were born. Long after we're dead too, depending on time travel and your point of view."

"When God and the Devil both give you advice, you listen," Valerie said. "Who else could they be talking about?"

Ralph parked in front of the mansion and shut off the engine. "Be cool, you guys."

Damon opened the front door as they approached. His typical jovial expression transformed into shock as he looked past Ralph and saw Valerie and Ben.

Rushing forward, he hugged the two of them in an outlandish dual bear hug until Valerie shoved him back. "Not so fast, buddy. You've got some explaining to do."

"Me?" he asked, laughing. "I'm not the one back from the dead!"

"Can we come inside?" Ben asked. "We need to talk to you."

"Of course!" Damon waved a hand. "Get on in here!"

Bartlett was cleaning the bar. His eyes widened when he saw Valerie and Ben, but he went on about his business.

"You guys want a sandwich or something?" Damon asked. "Does coming back from the dead leave you with an appetite? I've never been resurrected, but it's on my bucket list. Or is that a paradox? I just restocked the bar. We could have piña coladas."

"Damon, are you the Ocularist?" Valerie asked.

Damon dropped the bottle of rum, which shattered against the floor. Bartlett froze. With a nod from Damon, he took his leave.

"No, I'm not the Ocularist," Damon said once the four of them were alone. "Where is this coming from? I've fought him a dozen times. We fought him together in Atlantis. Valerie, you and Ralph saw him die. That's all over."

"That Ocularist we fought in *your* museum was an innocent guy with a helmet controlling him," Ralph said. "Might have been the same thing in Atlantis. Someone told us we had to find out who was behind it all."

"Really?" Damon asked. "Who told you that?"

"God." Ben's fork popped into existence. "The Devil too."

Damon did a double take. "Nice gear. Guess you guys were really dead."

"I was," Ben said. "Valerie only kinda."

"Shoot-a-monkey," Damon said. "And you think I was behind it? Why would I smash up my own museum? That stuff was irreplaceable. It's not like you can buy giant novelty typewriters at the corner market."

"It's supposed to be someone we forgot about," Ralph said. "Stiff is trying to shut us down, but we didn't overlook him. Sandra is locked up, and I don't think she could be behind something like this."

Valerie said, "You have access to advanced technology. Maybe you made the eyeball helmets."

"What can I do to convince you I'm on your side?" Damon asked.

"You tell us," Valerie said.

Damon shifted his feet into a fighter's stance. "I don't know how to do that, Val. Except for maybe reminding you that I've been a friend and a confidant to you for *years*."

A door flew open and Bartlett stepped through, hefting a weapon covered with exposed circuit boards and flailing wires. He heaved the device at Damon, who plucked it out of the air like a football and leveled it at the other three. "Ralph, Val, I'm not in your league, muscle-wise. And I'm guessing you didn't bring ol' Ben in on your intervention road trip because of his exceptional skill at license plate bingo. But you're forgetting super science is still a valid Anom power. This here contraption can send you hundreds of miles straight up into space, giving me and Bartlett time to escape via rocket pack. Would that kill you, Ben? I'm trying to go non-lethal here."

Ben gripped his fork tighter. "I don't know."

The weapon hummed in Damon's hands. "Guys, I haven't been in a good-guy-on-good-guy-fight-over-a-misunderstanding since the fifties, when Darius the Diabolist changed his costume without giving anyone a heads-up. Do we really need to smash up my house to settle this?"

"We need some proof," Ben said. "It's hard to take something like this on faith."

"Oh, come on," Damon said. "Ben, who's been your buddy? Valerie, we've almost been more than friends, and we even came all the way back around to being friends again." He turned to Ralph. "Look, man, I know you don't remember. But we've faced the end of the world together. Stared into the abyss. *Abysses.* You've always had my back, and I've been there for you. Do you guys really think I could be behind this?"

Ralph stared into Damon's eyes, searching for answers.

I still don't know anything, Ralph thought. *The Ralph Rogers who lived this life might know if he could trust Damon, but my memories of him only go back a few months, and everything since then has been madness. But ...*

"Aw, geez," Ralph said. "I don't think it was Damon."

Valerie sighed. "Fine. I guess it probably isn't him."

"Told you." Ben banished his weapon.

"Then what do we do now?" Ralph asked. "We still have no idea who it could be."

Damon tossed the gun back to Bartlett. The butler flipped a switch and the humming sound stopped.

"I'll get us some coffee." Damon clapped Ralph on the shoulder. "We'll start from the beginning and figure this out. A *Who's Who* of Meta Man's life."

"And the life of plain old Ralph Rogers," Ralph said.

"Then we'll definitely need that coffee," Damon said. "Unless Valerie and Ben are zombies now. Should I send Bartlett out for some brains?"

"Trust us, Damon," Valerie said, "if we're hungry for brains, you're perfectly safe."

The four of them laughed as they walked upstairs to Damon's office.

4

BEN SAT AT THE MAMMOTH DESK, his crossed legs resting on top. He held a yellow legal pad covered with the names of Anom villains. Bride-Groom. Joisey Devil. Pygmalion. Hotsy-Totsy. Pandamonium. Every name had a line drawn through it. Damon and Ralph sat on a leather couch as Valerie filled another cup of coffee.

"That's all of Ralph's—I mean, Meta Man's enemies," Ben said. "Every single one is either officially dead or frozen in the Panopticon down in Atlantis."

"Which makes sense," Damon said. "The you who you are now never fought any of them. You didn't forget them, they were just irrelevant to you. We need to focus on people who *you* overlooked. I think we should take another look at Mr. Stiff."

"But we didn't forget Stiff," Valerie said. "He just wrecked Ralph's living room. We didn't forget any of the heroes, did we? Baron, Rika, even poor Wyvern. None of them make sense."

Damon poured another cup of coffee. "What are we even doing here? God told you it was someone you overlooked? Did he give anything to help you narrow it down?"

"No," Ralph said. "It was vague. He said, 'Trace it back. You forgot about someone, and you need to figure out who it is.' The person we're looking for, the one responsible for the shift, it could be anybody."

"What about your parents?" Ben asked Ralph.

"Seems pretty unlikely," Ralph said. "We get along pretty well. I don't see them trying to murder me—at least not since I was a teenager."

Valerie dropped two sugar cubes into her coffee. "Didn't you tell me your dad wanted to be a magician when he was a kid? When your world changed, could that have turned into real magic?"

"But I didn't forget my parents," Ralph said. "That's a stretch anyway; you might as well suggest Mrs. Jones and Mr. Gardener."

"Who the hell are they?" Damon asked.

"The teachers who caught us photocopying Meta Boy in junior high," Valerie said, grinning at Ralph as she returned to her seat next to him. "I don't know. Jones always seemed pretty shifty to me."

"Fine," Ralph said. "Add Jones to the list. Put a star next to her name."

"Don't you guys know how to brainstorm?" Ben asked. "No wrong answers. Just throw out some names. We'll vet them after."

"How about your skeezy agent?" Damon asked. "He sounded like a real prick to me. What was his name?"

"Franklin Reese," Valerie said. "He did seem pretty skeezy."

"Come on," Ralph said. "My agent isn't that bad."

Valerie and Ben stared at him.

"Okay," Ralph said, holding up his hands in defeat. "He is skeezy. And I haven't given him much thought since this started. Good name for the list."

Damon tilted his head back and released an exaggerated sigh. "Let's brainstorm the people you've spent time with. *All* of them, from just before the reality shift until now."

"Couldn't hurt," Ben said. "There were those other dealers at the comic con."

Ralph snapped his fingers. "Right. Anna May, and what was the other one's name?"

"Johnny," Ben said.

"Those are your friends?" Valerie asked. "That guy's a creep. Put him on the list."

Ben blushed. "They're more like business associates. Fine, they're listed."

"There were Cal and Martin," Ralph said, "The ones who messed up my sketch. But this seems a teeny bit beyond them. What about Damon's butler guy, Bartlett?"

"Hey, lay off Bartlett," Damon said. "I've know that guy since he was a kid."

The others gave him odd looks.

Damon shrugged. "I'm a time traveler. Give me a break. Fine, go ahead. List him. But I guarantee he's aboveboard."

"Who else?" Ben asked. "Come on, come on. Keep 'em coming."

"Scott from the sushi place," Ralph said.

"Oh, come on," Ben said. "You need to be more social if we're already listing Scott from the sushi place."

Valerie scolded him. "You're the one who said no wrong answers."

"How about Doug and Myra?" Ben asked. "Those folks we met in Heaven."

"We'd just met them," Ralph said. "How could either be someone I'd forgotten?"

"You talked to anyone recently from your days at Against the Grain?" Valerie asked Ralph.

Ralph shook his head. "Not since I was a kid."

"List them, then," Damon said. "How about the people at Pithos Comics? What about Alan Lang, the guy who hired you?"

"I never met Lang," Ralph said. "That was the other Ralph. But you could add Caulder, my editor. It's reaching, but you could also put down his assistant, Jenny."

Damon groaned. "If the mastermind ends up being your editor's assistant, I'm going to be wildly displeased."

"Is there absolutely zero chance that Sandra was behind it?" Valerie asked. "Maybe she just set it all in motion before we blued her in the Panopticon."

"Jeez, you hold a grudge," Damon said, laughing. "So the girl sends you to Hell. How long are you going to keep bringing it up?"

"Damon," Valerie warned, "I swear to God—"

"While you're talking to him," Damon said, "ask him to give better hints."

"Cool it, you nincompoops," Ben said, rapping the desk with his knuckle. "Ralph, this all started with those comics, right? Walk us through how you found them."

Damon and Valerie had heard it once already, but this was the first time Ben had heard the full story. While he told the story of finding the dead body and taking the comics, Ralph stared at the comic books in question, slabbed in hard plastic and expensively framed, hung on the wall of the office in a place of honor.

"Looting a dead man's comic books," Ben said. "That's cold, man. Damn cold."

"Not to mention selling them to me," Damon said. "You sure you didn't kill that poor bastard?"

"Like ninety, ninety-five percent sure," Ralph said. The other three looked at him in shock. "What? I was pretty obsessed. But I'm pretty sure he was already dead when I got there. Heck, I don't even own a gun."

"Did you ever find out if it was a murder or suicide?" Valerie asked.

While they spoke, Damon pulled out his cell phone and typed on a floating holographic interface that would have shocked Ralph six months earlier.

"I thought it was suicide at first, but I didn't see a gun. I guess he could have fallen on the gun. Been laying on it."

"A quick web search doesn't say anything about a death at that time in any Greenvale. What state was that in?"

"It was in ..." Ralph began. "That's weird. I have no idea."

"But you've been there twice," Valerie said. "Other heroes even met you there. How'd you get there?"

"I dunno," Ralph said. "The first time, I got in my car, and the GPS took me there. When I went back, my brain went on autopilot."

"What'd you type into the GPS?" Valerie asked.

"I—I don't know."

Damon asked, "What was the guy's name again?"

"Jordan Chill," Ralph said. "No, that's not right. It was Elliot. Elliot Chill."

Damon typed it into his phone. "Nothing's coming up."

Ben put down the yellow legal pad and took his feet off the desk. Leaning forward, he asked, "Ralph, would you say—and I'm not trying to suggest anything here—would you say you *forgot about* Elliot Chill?"

"I think that's exactly what he's saying," Damon said. "Valerie?"

Valerie smiled. "It's quite possible Elliot Chill had completely slipped his mind. Would you agree with that, Ralph?"

Ralph rubbed his face with his hands. "So what do we do next? Go to Greenvale?"

"If you've found it twice before," Valerie said, "you should be able to take us there."

"If we take the Scarab, we'll get there faster," Damon said.

"That old thing barely got us this far," Ben said. "No offense."

"None taken," Ralph said. "It's true."

Damon's jaw dropped, and he stared at Ralph with wide eyes. "You don't remember who gave you that Scarab, do you?"

Ben's eyes lit up. "You've got to be kidding."

"That's *the* Scarab," Damon said. "The one Danny Drastic used in the forties. The son of a bitch flies, and it's cloaked with thirtieth-century tech. Totally undetectable by Stiff's satellites. I lost it to Ralph in a bet."

"But how do we find Greenvale?" Ralph asked.

"Easy," Damon said. "You're going to fly us there."

Ralph gulped.

5

"**F**OR CHRIST'S SAKE, MAN, PULL UP!**"** Damon yelled.

Ralph pulled back on the Stout Scarab's steering wheel. The van's glowing wheels, which had turned their hubcaps toward the ground when they lifted off, now shifted so Ralph and his friends were no longer aiming for the ground.

"I think you're getting the hang of it, Goose," Ben said.

"Shut up, Maverick," Ralph said.

"This is a good demonstration of why everyone isn't driving flying cars," Valerie said. "I know you were hung up on that."

"So help me, I will crash this flying van and kill everyone in it," Ralph said.

"You sound just like my dad," Ben said. "But I guess that's kind of dark, considering he murdered me while under the control of aliens."

"Should we suit up for this thing?" Damon asked. "I keep my gear in a pocket dimension, so I've got it. But I don't want to dress up if you guys aren't dressing up."

"I'm powered up under this lovely sweatshirt," Valerie said.

"Don't worry about me," Ben said. "I'm going to be one of those street clothes heroes. No costume for this guy. Maybe a cool leather jacket or something down the line, but I'm good for now."

"I couldn't get mine out from under my studio," Ralph said. "Stiff turned off the electric door."

"Oh, sweetie, I got yours," Valerie said. "I punched through the floor when you were in the shower."

"Wow, thank you," Ralph said. "That was so thoughtful."

"Guys, after this is all over, I have an idea," Ben said. "Let's take this van on a real road trip. Non-flying, I mean. We'll solve crimes like on *Scooby-Doo*."

"I don't like *Scooby-Doo*," Valerie said.

"Oh, give me a break," Damon said. "Everybody loves *Scooby-Doo*. I grew up a thousand years in the future, and they're *still* showing reruns of that show."

"Has anyone ever tried to pull off a Scooby-Doo scheme in real life?" Ben asked. "Dress up like a monster or a ghost to scare people away from somewhere?"

"I've never heard of that actually happening, no," Damon said.

"Me, neither," said Valerie.

"Thank god some things are still sacred." Ralph pointed to lights down below. "There's Greenvale."

"Are you sure?" Ben asked. "So, do you know which state it's in now?"

"Don't ask things like that," Valerie said. "I dealt with this kind of weirdness all the time. Thinking about it just makes it worse."

Damon peered out the window. "I don't see anyone moving down there."

They landed the van in the middle of town, in the parking lot of the diner where Ralph had eaten. The lights were on in the twenty-four-hour restaurant, but no one was inside. It was just after dark, but no cars drove on the road.

"Eerie," Valerie said.

"Let's try Chill's house first," Ralph said.

As they rolled up to the house on a silent street, Ralph said, "There's a family living here now. Let's try not to freak them out too much."

They walked up to the door and Ralph knocked. No answer. Overwhelmed by déjà vu, Ralph tried the doorknob, which turned freely. With a shrug to the others, he walked inside with the others following behind.

The house was empty of furniture or signs of life. A familiar red stain dominated the living room carpet. Valerie crossed her arms, rubbing her elbows with her hands. "This quaint little town of yours is giving me the heebie-jeebies."

Ben walked into the living room. "Bedrooms are empty. I don't think anyone has lived here for months."

"I saw a family in the yard," Ralph said. "Later they were eating dinner."

"You saw what someone wanted you to see, buddy," Damon said. "Someone had us fooled this whole time. Looks like even the Ocularist and the Haberdashers were just a smokescreen."

"Smokescreen for what?" Ben asked.

"Something worse than an army with super weapons taking over the world," Valerie said.

"What about that secret room where you found the comics?" Ben asked.

"It's around that corner," Ralph said.

As Ben rounded the corner, Damon yelled, "Ben, stop—"

The house exploded.

6

URNED WOOD, SHEETROCK, AND BRICKS lit-
tered the ground. Scattered fires burned, searching for
more fuel.

A dark cloud fizzled and disappeared, revealing Damon, Valerie, Ben, and Ralph; all had been shielded from the blast. Ben,
shaking, held the Devil's trident at arm's length.

"Everyone all right?" Ralph asked.

Damon coughed. "All in one piece. Ben, next time—"

"I know, I know," Ben said, lowering the fork. "Sorry. I
stopped as soon as I heard you shout and threw up the shield."

Ralph dusted himself off. "How'd you know to do that, anyway?"

"The fork started talking to me, telling me how to use it. Basic
stuff. Flight. Barriers."

"Sentient satanic weapons aside," Valerie said, "we have another problem. You activated your power, which means we just
blipped on the Cadre's radar. Let's load up the van and vamoose."

"Too late," Damon said. "Feel that static in the air? We've
got incoming."

The group shielded their eyes against a violent flash of light. Mr. Stiff and Songweaver stood in front of them.

Damon and Ben readied their weapons. Valerie and Ralph raised their fists.

"Stand down," Mr. Stiff said.

"Forgive us if we don't," Valerie said, flying like a bullet toward Mr. Stiff. He twisted out of the path of the attack. Reaching out, he grabbed Titania by her loose sweatshirt and spun her off in another direction.

"You done goofed," Ben said, catching Stiff in a ring of black smoke. The skeleton-suited man squirmed. With a backflip, he escaped the trap. Stiff pulled something from his belt and prepared to throw it.

Grabbing Stiff's raised arm, Songweaver screamed, "Stop this nonsense! We're all on the same side here!"

"What's going on here, Song?" Damon asked.

She released Stiff's arm. "Rika and Jack contacted us right after I sent Ralph to Pennsylvania. Several experimental government spacecraft were stolen and launched. We put a pin in our disagreement, in order to figure out what happened."

Valerie landed beside Ralph, her sweatshirt and jeans abandoned to reveal her in full costume. "So, what happened?"

Songweaver nudged Stiff, who sighed and tapped his wrist. A floating two-dimensional image appeared, in which a security video played on a loop. In the video, a guard tried to stop a group of people, each of them wearing a dark suit and a blue-eyed Ocularist helmet. One of the intruders pointed his eye at the guard and blasted him into dust. At the end of the walkway, they opened a hatch and climbed inside.

"Over a dozen vehicles with the ability to leave Earth's atmosphere have been retrofitted with Shawyer Drives and launched by the Ocularists," Stiff said. "You can see why we're concerned. I'm sorry, Meta Man. For what it's worth, I should have listened to you."

"Damn right," Ralph said. "Why are they stealing the ships?"

Songweaver said, "All the ships have landed near the same location on the moon."

"The moon?" Damon asked. "We've all been there before, except for Ben and—depending on how you look at it—Ralph. It's a chunk of rock. There's nothing up there."

"You're forgetting about the Shackleton Crater," Stiff said.

"The Crater of Eternal Darkness," Songweaver said.

"Right. There's a stable, Earth-like atmosphere in the crater, left behind by the winged creatures who used to live there. The goons are building something there. It's safe to assume it's some kind of weapon."

"Then rally the troops and let's go get 'em," Ben said.

"It's not that simple," Stiff said. "The heroes are disconnected from the grid. Many of them are currently not useful."

"What does that mean?" Valerie said.

"It means, most of them are brainwashed into thinking they're civilians," Songweaver said.

"Brainwashed!" Damon said. "What the hell, Stiff?"

"More like hypnotized," Stiff said. "Completely reversible. These are people who have dedicated their lives to helping people. Did you think they'd sit on the sidelines because we asked politely? This was our plan, Damon. We all agreed. I implemented it as best I could."

"You're talking about our allies," Valerie said. "Our *friends*. And you neutered them."

Stiff shook his head. "I told you, it's reversible. Just not before the Ocularists finish constructing the weapon. There's no time to build a new ship, either, and they made off with everything we could have used to reach the moon."

"Can the Scarab get there?" Ralph asked Damon.

Damon shook his head. "The shields haven't worked since the fifties. Some of us can survive in the vacuum, but I don't know if any of us could handle the three or four days it would take to reach the moon."

"Songweaver, what about you?" Ralph asked. "Could you teleport us there?"

"I can only carry one or two people when I travel," she said. "And I've never tried to go somewhere that far away. I think I could figure out a winding path through different reality planes but—"

"But not before they finish the weapon. Maybe I can help." Valerie untied the fairy flag from around her neck. "Will you hold this up for me, Songweaver? It has to be a woman."

"Sure." Songweaver held the flag high, like a protestor holding a sign. "I'm picking up what you're putting down."

"Queen Titania," Valerie said, "I require an audience."

The silk shimmered, and the face of the fairy queen appeared. "It is good to hear from you, my child. We have been following your ordeal quite closely, although we have honored your request of non-interference."

Valerie nodded. "In Hell, I had many conversations with the ruler of that realm. He let it slip that my mother isn't dead."

Queen Titania's expression revealed nothing. "That aligns with my own suspicions."

"There are two reasons for my contacting you. I wish to apologize for any accusations I've made."

"You were hurt, my child, and your statements understandable. Consider it forgotten. As for your other reason for unfurling the flag, we have already discerned it." A shimmering portal opened behind Songweaver.

"Thank you, my queen."

"Thank you, child. Despite our differences, I have always been proud of you, and your mother would be proud of what you've accomplished with her legacy. You have long since escaped from her shadow."

The queen's face disappeared. Songweaver handed the cape back to Valerie.

Ralph took Valerie's hand. "You didn't say you talked to the Devil about your mom."

"Still processing." She gave his hand a squeeze. "We'll figure it out after we clean up this mess. But let's hurry. The full moon should help, but it might be a bumpy ride."

"What, that's it?" Ralph asked. "We drive the van to the moon? We don't have a plan, nothing?"

"I've got a plan now," Mr. Stiff said, smiling.

The six of them climbed into the Scarab, parked across the street from the wreckage.

"No offense, Ralph," Damon said, "but I'll drive this time."

"Shotgun!" Ben said, climbing into the front passenger seat.

"You sure there's an atmosphere?" Ben asked Mr. Stiff as they climbed into the back of the vehicle.

Stiff grinned. "We'll know soon enough, won't we?"

The Scarab lifted off the asphalt and into the sky. The hole in reality drifted in front of them like a drop of gasoline in water.

Ralph patted Ben on the shoulder and said, "Try not to throw up."

Damon plunged the Scarab into the rippling rainbow portal.

7

FOLLOWING A JARRING JUMP CUT, the Scarab emerged a few feet over the surface of the moon. Damon landed the van, sending up puffs of moon dust. Songweaver opened the door, and Ralph and the others climbed out.

"I can't believe this," Ben said. "Space. Is. Awesome."

The six of them stood near the lip of the dark crater. The others crouched down low and Ralph followed their example. In the area below were space shuttles, a retro-futurist rocket out of Buck Rogers, a giant bubble with a control panel, and a Nazi UFO covered in swastikas. Ralph could see slaves controlled by the Ocularist helmets hard at work on the weapon.

"Looks like we didn't alert the eyeballs," Stiff said. "Stay close. Don't want anyone accidentally leaving the atmosphere bubble."

Ralph stared at the alien surroundings in awe. Valerie laughed and bumped him with her arm.

"How many times has the real Meta Man been to the moon?" Ralph asked her.

"At least a few times. Other planets too. But Ralph, that other Meta Man never went to Hell and back for anyone. You're every bit the hero he was." She gave Ralph's hand a squeeze.

"Have you been here before?"

She shrugged. "Sure, but it was a different kind of trip. Like I said, the moon is important to Faerie, so the moon I usually go to is a bit more symbolic. But if you want a really good story, ask Damon about the time in the thirties they shot him up here in a space bullet."

"Here's the plan," Mr. Stiff said. "Cut a path through the ships to the weapon. With the equipment they stole, they can build something that puts the entire world in danger. We have to disable that thing before it's operational. Remember that these are innocent people, but they *will* kill you given the chance. Try to disable the helmets if you can. I'll be here, configuring this." He held up a disc about the size of a vinyl record. Circuitry and tiny dip switches covered it.

"What is that thing?" Ben asked before Ralph could open his mouth.

"Teleportation beacon," Stiff said. "This is how the cavalry will arrive."

Ralph said, "I thought you said everyone else was sidelined."

"I said *most* of them were useless," Stiff said. "Not—"

A beam hit the ground beside Stiff. Dust exploded into the air.

"Go!" Damon yelled.

He led the charge, Atomic Disintegrator in hand, rocket pack flaring behind him. Ralph looked back to see Mr. Stiff dodging blasts and setting up the beacon.

Running felt strange in the moon's weaker gravity. Ralph took to the air, staying as low as he could to remain inside the breathable atmosphere. He saw Valerie skimming the ground, while Ben leaped about like a madman, deflecting the Ocularists' blasts with the black energy of his fork.

Valerie and Ralph reached the advancing eyeball slaves first. Ralph barrel-rolled out of the way of oncoming blasts, just as he had practiced with Valerie. He reached down and plucked the helmet off an Ocularist. A black woman looked up at him with gratitude for an instant before collapsing to the ground, unconscious. Ralph threw the helmet, knocking down a group of three eyeball soldiers like so many bowling pins. Ben leapt onto the fallen and stabbed each one in the head with his fork. The helmets fell apart in pieces, leaving the person inside unharmed.

Songweaver strummed her harp, and the Ocularists nearest to her dropped to the ground. Darting back and forth from the ground to the air, Damon landed headshot after headshot, turning helmets to dust.

"This is too easy!" Ralph yelled. "The original Ocularist took on the whole Cadre!"

Valerie pulled off another helmet as she said, "Whoever is controlling them is spread too thin!"

A high-pitched squeal forced Ralph and the others to cover their ears. The dozens of remaining Ocularists dropped to their knees, screaming and clawing at the helmets. The white part of their eyeball helmets took on an intense red and their suits bulged and tore as muscles grew and skeletons took on an inhuman shape.

"You assholes just had to say something!" Ben yelled. He stabbed at the helmet of a crouched Ocularist but missed.

The monsters stood up. The transformed victims' backbones arched behind them, with spiked ridges stabbing up through their clothes. Their long, misshapen limbs moved with deliberate precision. The one Ben had just tried to save swiped at him with foot-long finger claws.

Ralph glanced back to see two upgraded Ocularists circling Stiff. Damon, Songweaver, Ben, and Valerie were occupied with their own fights. Pushing his speed as much as he could, Ralph arrived just in time to see a blast hit Stiff in the back.

Ducking below a beam, Ralph smashed one of the Ocularists in the iris. On the third punch, the helmet fell away to reveal a distorted, ruined human face. Ralph turned to see Stiff take down the other monster with a punch to the throat. When the monster hit the ground, Stiff reached inside the helmet and pulled free a handful of components.

"At least their nerve clusters are in the same place." Stiff looked in bad shape from the wound on his back. The smell of burnt flesh twisted Ralph's stomach. Stiff dropped to one knee. "Didn't see that one coming, which is a rare one for me."

Ralph helped him get back to the teleportation beacon. Wires and circuits now snaked into the ground, as if the disc had taken root. Mr. Stiff typed a few more commands into a hologram display floating above the center of the disc.

"You'll want to back up a bit," Stiff said. "You don't want to get knocked over when our friends arrive."

Ralph asked, "But what about you?"

Stiff smiled. "Just get back in the game."

Ralph nodded and flew out. The air around the beacon wavered, and a familiar outline appeared. The silhouette filled with a frail man attached to an IV pole. He pulled the needle from his arm. A transformation similar to those of the Ocularists took place, and the man's body grew to a monstrous size. His skin split into rocky scales, glowing with fluorescent blue-green energy. A flaming aura shimmered around him. The features of his face became sinister and wild.

The giant thing bellowed a battle cry as more heroes snapped into focus around him.

"Hope you saved some for us!" yelled Luke the Nuke.

8

ND THEY APPEARED—every hero who could not pass for human and those who did not care to try. Every Anom who'd been waiting out the reversion plan in Atlantis joined the fight.

Buscadera and her Outliers, vindicated and freed from stasis, took down wave after wave of monsters in eyeball helmets. The Lost Arcader wielded a pixelated buster sword and Hylian shield. Helena Ignatius fired a shoulder cannon of steel and steam, knocking down monsters with force-field bubbles. Ironworks lifted an Ocularist out of the atmosphere pocket and threw it violently back to the ground. Zambo, the zombie soldier, jumped onto the back of a monster and smashed its helmet with the butt of his machine gun. A man wearing Amish clothing with springs in place of his arms and legs bounded across the battlefield. There were many others Ralph didn't recognize, like a gray-furred werewolf and a woman with a wooden body covered in chipped paint. A man with a zoetrope for a head. A striped half-woman, half-cat and her anthropomorphic teammates. A man with transparent skin, his muscles and organs visible. A statuesque woman made of ivory.

Their allies from the Cloud Club also appeared. Jack Spratt flung himself past on his stretched limbs, and Rika lumbered by in her newly repaired mecha. The smell of oil and hydraulic fluid surrounded her as she traded blows with the enemy.

Hatches opened in the ground surrounding the weapon. Lunar dust poured into them as more of the Ocularist monsters climbed out to join the fight.

Ralph found that if he could keep clear of the claws, the monsters had a glass jaw. He knocked out one of them, but was nearly taken out by another when a booming voice distracted him.

The weapon array opened and a hologram appeared above it. A face none of them had ever seen appeared, but Ralph recognized the salt-and-pepper hair. The man had high cheekbones, and dark eyebrows. There was no evidence of the fist-sized hole Ralph had seen in his head back in Greenvale.

"Welcome, heroes. As I believe you've guessed by now, I am Elliot Chill. Few among you have any real idea what has happened to your world, and only one has experienced the shift for himself. Hello, Ralph. You'll excuse me if I don't call you Mr. Rogers, as it sounds ridiculous."

"Howdy, Chill." Ralph dodged a leaping Ocularist monster. "Thanks for not skimping on the welcoming committee."

"Oh, Ralph, I needed a reason for all of you to be here. The last of humanity's heroes, all gathered together in this crater of eternal darkness. I know it just means the sun never shines here, but doesn't it sound dramatic?"

"I don't know why, but I was sure he'd be bald." Jack entangled another Ocularist in a cloud of black smoke.

"I'm just glad it didn't turn out to be Jenny the receptionist," Damon called as he jumped onto the back of a passing monster.

Jack Spratt swung one monster into another with his rubber arms. "Am I the only one pissed that a guy named 'Chill' doesn't have ice powers?"

Chill laughed. "I'm glad you're all having such a good time. I wanted the chance to inform you that Ralph has told you the truth; up until a few months ago the world was a boring place. No magic, no super science, no Atlantis, no Anoms. You were nothing but a bunch of slaves to your gray little lives."

"Get over yourself!" Titania yelled.

"Let him do his spiel," Ben said. "This is one of my favorite parts."

"Thank you, Ben," Elliot Chill said. "What you couldn't know is that I came from a different world, a world that wasn't precisely real. The Ocularist was but a villain in a funny book from a failing publisher in the 1930s. But they wrote me a bit too clever, and I became self-aware. I realized that even if we were only ideas, with ink instead of blood, we could be as real as our counterparts in the real world. So I trapped the heroes of my four-color world, and I laid waste to it."

"Are you telling me you aren't even a real person?" Ralph yelled.

"Who are you to say who's real?" Chill said. "You weigh what? 150 pounds? In the reality you come from, Superman, a so-called fictional character, existed on ton after ton of printed paper, plastic, metal, you name it. The old Ralph Rogers was known by maybe a few thousand people, and none of them gave a shit about him. Superman was recognized and loved by *billions*. How conceited is it for you to claim to be real? Just because you're made of flesh and blood, while he's made of ink and hope?"

"Let me guess," Damon said. "You're composed of cheap newsprint and vanity?"

The Lost Arcader manifested a Donkey Kong cage, trapping the last of the Ocularist monsters. Songweaver played a note on her guitar and frowned.

"Sorry," Chill said. "No one's going anywhere. Consider yourselves on lockdown while this plays out. Now, ask me how I trapped the heroes."

"This is torture," Ralph said.

"No way, this is just getting good." Ben yelled to the hologram, "Hey, floaty ass face! How'd you trap the heroes?"

"The way you'd ensnare any idea. I trapped them in my head. But my reality was shallow and doomed. Without the heroes and their stories to sustain it, I knew it would soon fade away. I escaped to your world, but the rules were different here. I took the name Elliot Chill and, once it became apparent that I wasn't aging, I became Elliot Chill, Jr. I would have been content to go on like that forever, without dying or fading.

"But then Ralph had to go digging into the comic books that gave me life. They had all but faded from existence when I destroyed the world they contained. I kept the last remaining copies, because I didn't know how their destruction would affect me. It was Ralph's obsession that gave them substance again and awakened the ideas trapped in my head. When he tracked me down, they grew so strong they escaped."

"The hole in his head," Damon said. "It wasn't a gunshot wound."

"No shit," growled Luke the Nuke. "Try and keep up, future boy."

"Those ideas fought to be real, and molded this reality into one that could sustain them," Chill said. "They revolved around Ralph at first because he was at ground zero, but grew exponentially. The impossible turned plausible and then became fact.

"After my head put itself back together, I once again found myself in a world where a supervillain could win. So I pulled on the old skull-stomping boots and went to work. If this world survives me conquering it, maybe I'll turn it into a paradise. But if it doesn't make it, there are always other worlds. Thanks to our friend Ralph, I have the power to reach them."

"You distracted us with the Haberdashers and the Ocularist, while you solidified your power base," the Gentleman said. "Then we did your work for you and put the majority of this world's Anoms out of commission."

"But you're stuck with us," Damon said. "You know we'll stop you."

"I very much doubt that. I'll trap you the same way I trapped the last batch of heroes who limited my personal growth."

The hologram disappeared, and Elliot Chill rose up out of the dummy weapons array. He stood on a metal platform, wearing a leather uniform of black and red.

The Gentleman opened fire with his mystic automatics, but the bullets mushroomed harmlessly against Chill's chest. Luke and Titania led the charge.

Chill calmly closed his eyes, put his hand to his temples, and inhaled.

The bodies of the heroes stretched and swirled into a vortex. Their screaming faces and a costume kaleidoscope disappeared into Chill's mouth, nostrils, and ears.

The surface of the moon was now empty, save for unconscious Ocularists, a smiling Elliot Chill, and a horrified Ralph Rogers.

9

"YOU SON OF A BITCH," Ralph said.

Elliot Chill lifted his hands. "Relax, kid. This doesn't have to go the usual way, what with a knock-down, drag-out fight. Let's talk it through."

Ralph advanced toward him. "There's nothing you have to say I want to hear. Let them go."

"Not happening," Chill said. "I'll be keeping them safe and sound up here." He tapped his forehead.

"Then I'm going to hit you until they pop back out."

"I'm as strong as you are, Meta Boy," Chill said. "Maybe stronger. And I won't keep them trapped forever. Once I find out how to strip them of their power, I'll let them go. It won't take me long. While I'm at it, I'll scoop up all of Stiff's brainwashed buddies and the POWs down in Atlantis. Then it's just the stragglers."

"I'm not going to let that happen."

"I wouldn't be so sure, kid. I'll admit you caught me unaware last time. After decades of nothing, your little quest was all it took to bust open my melon. But that won't be enough this time."

Ralph's jaw dropped as understanding set in. "That's the whole reason we're here on the moon, isn't it? So we're far enough away from people's belief in the heroes."

"Exactly. Maybe being in the eye of the storm makes you immune to getting sucked in for now, but I'll figure it out. We created this world, Rogers, from your passion and my power. We're the gods."

"I met God recently, creep," Ralph said. "I'm pretty sure we're not him."

"We're close enough. It will be business as usual, only with me running things from behind the scenes. I'll let you keep your powers. You can play hero or do whatever you want. Hell, I'll even throw in the girl, if you're so fond of her. No powers for her, though. That magic fairy stuff is too much of a wild card."

Think about it, said a voice in Ralph's head. *Get back the normal world but stay special. Almost the way it ought to be. I could make sure he releases them. A safer world.* He looked from Chill to the Earth, floating just out of his reach. *No. The lesser evil is obvious. This time, at least, chaos is preferable to total oppression.*

"No deals," Ralph said. "How about I just take you apart?"

"I'm every bit a match for you," Chill said.

"Then why didn't you just kill me at the start?"

Chill laughed. "There's no handbook for this, no way to tell what would happen if I killed you. I can make the math say whatever I want. My people will hold on to you for now."

On Chill's cue, the Ocularist monsters started to stir, crawling out from under rubble and pulling apart their bonds.

"Even with all your friends, you were barely a match for my creations. If you won't join me, I'll put you on ice until you change your mind. Maybe just until I can take your power for myself. But together we could have it all. Isn't this everything you wanted, Ralph? A return to the regular world, but you get to keep the power and the girl?"

"I don't remember requesting a world run by an evil overlord," Ralph said.

The Ocularists became alert and started walking toward Ralph.

"Give it up," Chill said. "You're not really a hero."

Preparing for one last fight, Ralph looked up at Chill and around at the monsters closing in on him.

He's right, Ralph thought. *This is me pretending. I'm not a hero. I'm just a—*

Ralph smiled. He pulled a rebreather from his belt and plugged it into his nostrils.

Chill laughed. "That thing will give out long before you reach Earth. Do you really want to suffocate in the vacuum of space?"

Without a word, Ralph shot out of the crater in the direction of the earth's northern hemisphere. A few miles up, he turned to take in the full view of the moon, a bright silver dollar against the black backdrop. He plunged toward the gray surface, his fists swinging.

I N T H E E V E N I N G T W I L I G H T, three children played on their cul-de-sac in a quiet neighborhood of Flatland, Texas. In reality, they were Randy, Beth, and Beth's little brother Cory. In their minds, this was a climactic battle between Ambergris, Olympus, and Vainglorious.

"You're going down, Vainglorious, you big bozo!" Beth's bright orange windbreaker represented Ambergris's armor of light.

"Don't think so!" said Randy as Vainglorious. "Not when I have a missile launcher!" He pretended to lift a huge weapon onto his shoulder.

"A missile launcher can't stop Olympus!" Cory said. He ran up and faked a punch to Randy's mouth.

Randy rolled backwards in the green grass. "It can if it's a *super* missile launcher!" He mimed firing the invisible weapon. "*Kaboooom!*"

"Aargh!" Cory yelled, hitting the ground. "Help me, Ambergris!"

Beth knew it was only pretend, but seeing her baby brother blown up by a super missile launcher made her angry. "That's it,

Vainglorious! I'm taking you out for good!" She pointed her fist at Randy and said, "Amber spikes! Pyew! Pyew!"

Randy rolled to the side, shooting his missile launcher again. "Missed me! Boom! Kapow!"

"I didn't miss you, Randy, you big cheater!" Beth yelled.

"Did so!" Randy said. "Missed me by a mile!"

"Don't fight, you guys!" Cory said. "Randy, maybe only one of the spikes hit you."

The streetlights blinked on, signaling it was time for them to go inside.

"Crud," Beth said. "Keep going. We'll say we didn't notice."

Across the street, a front door opened. A woman's voice said, "Beth! Cory! Time to come in!"

"Aw, c'mon, Mom!" Beth said. "It's not even dark! Look how bright the moon is!"

Beth looked up and gasped.

"Mom!" Cory looked up too. "Something's wrong with the moon!"

11

CROSS THE WESTERN HEMISPHERE, people walked out of their houses and apartments. Employees and customers exited stores and restaurants and stared up into the night sky. Amateur and professional astronomers alike looked into their telescopes and felt their hearts beating faster. For the people around the globe that couldn't see it for themselves, there was live coverage on the television and internet.

One line at a time, an image formed on the moon. Not a trick of the light, or of the mind like the man on the moon, but a distinct picture. The simple shapes at the bottom of the moon's visible surface formed a long triangle. As more lines branched off, families in their front yards and friends standing on city streets argued what it could mean.

"It's gotta be aliens. They're building canals, like the ones on Mars."

"It's a picture of a snake. It's the end of the world."

"No, it's a letter. See? It's the start of a capital A."

But as the lines grew and the middle of the picture filled in, there was no doubt who was appearing. It was the body of a woman, with her arms stretched out at her sides, her cape and hair billowing behind her. On her chest was the letter T, terminating in an oval at her navel. Within minutes, the figure was finished.

"Titania," said the human race.

12

RALPH LEAPT INTO THE AIR AND CRASHED AGAIN, creating another iris and finishing his work. It was hardly his usual method, but time was a limiting factor. He launched himself off the side of the trench like a swimmer racing in a pool. The force of his push landed him back in the artificial atmosphere of the Shackleton crater.

The dust settled, revealing Chill. "Get it out of your system, hero?"

"You and I both know I'm not a real hero," Ralph said. "I'm only an artist, so I did what any artist would do. I drew a picture."

Chill laughed. "It's a nice thing, to be true to oneself. But I'm not impressed."

"I didn't make it for you." Ralph pointed a thumb at the earth. "I'm just testing a theory."

Chill looked angrily from Ralph's face to the Earth. Realization dawned on his face just as his head began to stretch and distort his face. A gloved fist shot out of the top of his skull.

Elliot Chill's body exploded.

As the red moon dust dispersed, Titania stood in front of the crowd of freed heroes. Damon and Ben stood on either side of her. She rushed toward Ralph, hugging him. Without Chill to control them, the Ocularist monsters looked around, confused. The other Anoms, seeing the battle was won, cheered.

"I missed the big finish, didn't I?" asked Ben. "How'd you beat him, Ralph? Knuckle sandwich? Gun duct-taped to your back? Care Bear stare. I bet it was the Care Bear stare."

Ralph stopped kissing Valerie long enough to say, "I gave him the old Tinkerbell bit."

"'I do believe in fairies?'" Ben shook his head in disgust. "That's the worst one!"

"Quit your bellyaching, Black Trident," Damon said, laughing. "Let's round up some monsters and go home."

13

T HE CLOUD CLUB had not seen such a party since 1945.

Every Anom that Ralph had ever heard of—and more than a few he hadn't—were laughing, yelling, and carrying on, all in full uniform. A band with members from the Millennials team played loud piano rock on a stage generated by the Lost Arcader. Bartlett served drinks with the assistance of Jack Spratt. Rubbery arms shot overhead, dipping down to hand people cocktails.

The elevator dinged, and Ralph and Valerie walked out, their arms around each other.

The full moon, now featuring Titania's portrait, was visible out the large, recently-replaced window.

Valerie blushed. "You made my boobs too big, you dirty perv."

"What can I say, I was working from memory." Ralph gave her hip a squeeze.

The two scanned the room until Ben waved them over to the booth where he sat with Damon.

"One hell of a crowd scene!" Valerie said over the music as she and Ralph sat down. "This has to be a fire-code violation. Like the Grudge doesn't already want us all in stasis."

"Don't worry," Damon said. "I had the whole building reinforced when I bought it. You never know when the Living Planetoid is going to come knocking. How are the Ocularist monsters?"

"Recovering nicely. What's the word on Chill?" Ralph asked.

"Ironworks and his crew gathered up what was left after the atmosphere wore off," Damon said. "If Chill could survive a hole in the head, we're not taking any chances. Even if he can reconstitute himself, we're storing whatever's left in separate locations."

Valerie asked, "Did you find Mr. Stiff?"

"His body wasn't in the crater," Ben said. "We're hoping he's still alive, but there's no way to tell. No one has any idea how he could get back to Earth. With that atmosphere gone, I'm not getting my hopes up."

"You don't know Stiff like I do," Damon said. "If anyone could make it, he could. My guess is, he's gone to ground to sulk about being tricked by Chill. I bet we'll see his bony ass again. But until he gets back, the Freedom Cadre is going to be even more shorthanded. Whaddya say?" He put his hand on Ben's shoulder.

"You couldn't keep me away, you hack!" Ben said.

"But we'll have to get you a proper costume," Valerie said.

Ben waved his hands and shook his head. "Let me get to the gym before you put spandex on me. So what's the plan on finding your mom, Val?"

"The queen's renewed the search, and Songweaver is following up some leads of her own. Right now, it's enough to know she's alive. But how about you? How's your dad doing?"

Ben sucked air in through his teeth. "Dad's good, but I haven't talked to him yet. He reopened the store when the Grudge released him. You guys will have to help me figure out how to tell him I'm back from the dead."

"As soon as I figure it out myself," Valerie laughed.

"We're taking bets on whether or not his body is in his coffin." Damon pulled out a roll of green bills.

"Doesn't matter if my body is in there or not," Ben said. "I'm going to start *living*. You guys know Baron?"

"From the Outliers?" Ralph asked.

Ben nodded and pulled a paper napkin from his pocket. Laying it on the table, he revealed a phone number. The other three cheered for him.

"I assumed he had a thing going with Buscadera," Ralph said.

Ben shrugged. "Buddy, you know what happens when you assume."

"Val, you still got that job at 78 RPM?" Damon asked. "Still doing that charity auction?"

"It took a while to convince them I wasn't dead, but yeah. The auction is on for next month."

"Then I want to donate my comic collection," Damon said. "The whole damned thing. Even the books Ralph found for me. And I'll emcee for you."

"That would be historic," Valerie said. "Why the change of heart?"

"Oh, I dunno. I can start all over again. Finding them is more fun than having them, anyway."

"I might know a comic shop owner who could help you with that." Ben laughed. "Ralph, something's been bothering me. Chill said he came out of a comic book. So, was he the first Anom? Or was there something about the comics that triggered everything? Or was it you?"

Ralph rubbed his temples. "I'm going to need another drink before I think about that."

"Hey, take your time," Ben said. "Damon, think they'll get your *Danny Drastic* movie back on track? I know how much you like to phone it in."

Ralph stared out at the crowd as the others joked with each other. Cartoon characters, monsters, and demigods laughed and took shots. He smiled as a young woman in a red cape did a keg stand on stage with the band.

Valerie gave his shoulders a squeeze and whispered in his ear, "Worried you made the wrong choice?"

Ralph smiled at her. "There's enough power in this room to destroy the world several times over. But even in my boring old version of the world, people had the ability to do that. Maybe with this much power we can save the world instead."

Valerie gave him a kiss on the cheek.

"Hey, you two, enough with the dramatics," Damon said. "We're going up to the roof, to see if Ben can fly with that stupid fork of his."

"Whose idea was that?" Ralph said.

"Rika's!" Damon yelled as he and Ben disappeared up the stairs.

Ralph and Valerie laughed until Ralph remembered how Rika taught him to fly.

"Oh, shit!" He grabbed Valerie and rushed for the stairs. ◢◣

AFTERWORD

I FINISHED THE FIRST DRAFT of *Four Color Bleed* the day my son turned fantastic four. We've just celebrated his seventh birthday, and the book is finally ready for publishing. The whole process has been crazy, but it's happening. And it's happening thanks to many of you.

My love affair with comics reaches way back into the murky mists of childhood. My mom used to buy boxes of Archie comics at garage sales, saving them for me as a special summer treat, and I still have a few of my dad's old funny books. My passion for reading and writing began with my parents' encouragement and comic book word balloons.

As I grew up, I found myself thinking more and more about the fictional multiverses of Marvel and DC comics, and the way they've grown organically and chaotically over nearly a century. At first, those worlds were small, barely reaching past the borders of a panel. But they grew with the demand for more stories, more heroes, more villains. All those masked and caped characters had to come from somewhere, and their adventures and backstories filled up so many worlds they overflowed into second and third Earths. They just keep going and going, with thousands of creators working together on the craziest quilt in creation.

I've always wondered, could I create a superhero world like that, not over the course of decades, but all at once, like God sticking newly-minted dinosaur fossils under a shopping mall?

Other creators have chased the same brass ring. Kurt Busiek's *Astro City* is the reigning king, and his "The Nearness of You" is a direct inspiration for the novel you now hold in your hands. Grant Morrison's metafiction has inspired me for years, and his *Zenith* series rattled around at the back of my brain during my writing binges. And any story about retroactive continuity owes a debt to Alan Moore and James Robinson, the comic writers who've done retcons the best.

The primary inspiration for this book's reality bleed is Philip K. Dick's *Ubik*, which I first read in the hospital while waiting for my son to arrive. If I could stop reading PKD, I'd probably stop writing books. William Gibson's short story "The Gernsback Continuum" also played a role, capturing that hauntological feeling I've been trying to put into words for most of my life.

You might not believe it, but this book was based on a true story. Yes, really. In 2006, an author and actor published a superhero board game based on his own self-published comic book. The game had an indie Silver Age vibe, and I had to have it. After years of begging, lying, and conniving, I finally got my hands on a copy. I decided to track down the comics that served as the game's source material.

This comic series was quoted on Wikipedia, had mentions in old online forums, even had a catalog number in WorldCat. I emailed every comic shop in its state of origin, but no one had ever heard of it. I tried contacting the author, the one man who could clear it up beyond a shadow of a doubt, but received no response.

As far as I'm concerned, those comics don't exist. They never existed. It was all a huge joke—and, as far as I can tell, I'm the only one who fell for it. I chased that unicorn everywhere, but no dice. I keep trying to prove a negative to myself: Those comics aren't real.

Unless they pop into existence tonight and pretend they've been here all along.

Before our time together ends, there are people I need to thank. Most of all, thank you to my beautiful wife for her support and endless encouragement, and thanks to my son and daughter for making every aspect of my life an adventure. Thanks to my parents for instilling in me a love of books, illustrated or not, and thanks to my in-laws, for always making a weirdo feel welcome.

As much as I'd love to hog the credit, many people had a hand in creating this book. Rian Gonzales, Weshoyot Alvitre, Ben Zmith, Morgan Perry (aka Geauxta), Ben Cohen, Kevin Kelly, Adam Prosser, and Chris "Chance!" Brown answered my crazy email and all delivered extraordinary illustrations. Phillip Gessert is doing the layout for the whole thing, and he understands my love for drop caps. Rory Harnden once again created a cover that grabs people by the imagination, and Jonathan Baker proved indispensable as an editor. Baker is also in my critique group, which worked tirelessly—or at least without complaining—to improve this book. Thanks, Mike Akins, Andrea Huskey, Monica Pinion, and Travis Erwin. I'm lucky to know so many talented people.

Let's hear it for the generous people who supported this work on Kickstarter. Your support and patience mean the world to me. This book only exists in this form because you believed in me, and I'll never forget that. For a complete list, please see the following page. Thank you, folks, I love you all.

Last but far from least, thank *you*. Yes, you, the monster at the end of this book. You read every word, or at least the important ones. I'd give you superpowers if I could, but I hope you'll settle for me writing another book.

I'm thinking something with robots.

Be seeing you.

~Ryan McSwain

May 30, 2017

Freedom Cadre Reserve Members

Th**ank you** to everyone who supported this project.

Mike and Jennifer Akins
Deanah Alexander
Hossain Ashraf
Jonathan Baker
Sara Simpson Biggs
Jessica Boling
Craig Boyd
Jesse Tannehill and Phoenix Bright
BrGaribaldi
Brienc
Marcus Briscoe
Stephanie Bryant
Gedimin A Bulat
Sherri Chandler
Christopher Ryan Clark
Jody Collins
Colin Cummings
Kirk Demarais
Jessica Eppen
Travis Erwin
Scott Everts
C Jordan Farmer
Kevin James Frear

Joseph and Olya Goodrick
Thomas Gore
Michael and Brian Goubeaux
Neal Ferguson
Lee Francis IV
James Harris
Tony Hill
Brandon Hubbard
Anthony Impenna
Eric and Cindy Ingram
Coby Jackson
Josh T Jordan
Karin
Avri Klemer
Jim Kosmicki
Angela Goff Latta
Brant and Ashley Latta
Ariel and Jared Lee
William and Elizabeth Lee
Dr. Victoria Lehman
Amanda Long
Long Wooden Spoon
Longbox Graveyard

Austin Martin
Michael May
My Hero: Ryan McCracken
George McGowan, iC3Ventures.com
Evan and Melissa McSwain
Kate McSwain
Vance and Pam McSwain
Christopher and
Chaundra McWhorter
The Millers
Tim & Jenna Mitchell Family
mizkat
Andrew Monroe
Trent Moore
Chris and Lizzy Moorehead
Lukas Myhan
Jojo O'Leary
Elbert Or
Leanna Pearson
Ryan Pennington
Monica Pinion
Matt Randolph

Wes Reeves
Suzana Sandoval
Jon and Kristen Sisco
Cynthia Shirley
Kevin Slackie
Darius Smith
Michael Che Snead
M.A. Solko
Matt Springer
Karlton Stephens
PK Sullivan
Dustin Taylor
Chris Thorne
Carol L. Tilley
Blake Tucker
Steve and LaDonna Tunnell
Chris Vaillancourt
Justin Velo
Bradley Walker
Rob Waybright
Seth Wieck

RYAN MCSWAIN lives in Amarillo, Texas, with his wife and their two children. Ryan spends his days playing with his kids, writing, and wallowing in nostalgia. If you'd like to change reality, please check with him first—he's currently living his best possible timeline.

You can reach Ryan using the red telephone in Commissioner Gordon's office or by visiting www.ryanmcswain.com.

51370130R00243

Made in the USA
San Bernardino, CA
20 July 2017